GROUP PORTRAIT WITH LADY

BOOKS BY HEINRICH BÖLL

Acquainted with the Night
Adam, Where Art Thou?
The Train Was on Time
Tomorrow and Yesterday
Billiards at Half-past Nine
The Clown
Absent Without Leave
18 Stories
Irish Journal
End of a Mission
Children Are Civilians Too
Adam and The Train
Group Portrait with Lady

GROUP PORTRAIT WITH LADY

c.1

by

Heinrich Böll

Translated from the German
by Leila Vennewitz

McGraw-Hill Book Company
New York St. Louis San Francisco
Düsseldorf Mexico Toronto

This book was set in Vladimir by University Graphics, Inc.

123456789BPBP79876543

Library of Congress Cataloging in Publication Data

Böll, Heinrich, 1917–
Group portrait with lady.

Translation of Gruppenbild mit Dame.
I. Title.
PZ4.B6713Gr [PT2603.0394] 833′.9′14 72-8835
ISBN 0-07-006423-7

Originally published in German under the title of
Gruppenbild mit Dame by Kiepenheuer & Witsch, Cologne,
Germany.

For Leni, Lev, and Boris

List of Characters

THE LADY

Leni Pfeiffer, née Gruyten

THE GROUP

THE FAMILIES

The Gruytens
Hubert, Leni's father
Helene, Leni's mother
Heinrich, Leni's brother
Lev, Leni's son

The Pfeiffers
Wilhelm, Leni's father-in-law
Marianne, Leni's mother-in-law
Alois, Leni's husband
Heinrich, Leni's brother-in-law
Hetti, his wife
Wilhelm } their sons
Karl }
Fernande, Alois's aunt

The Hoysers
Otto (Hoyser, Sr., Hubert Gruyten's head bookkeeper)
Mrs. Hoyser, his wife
Wilhelm, their son
Lotte, Wilhelm's wife
Werner } Lotte and Wilhelm's sons
Kurt }

The Schweigerts
Mrs. Schweigert, Helene Gruyten's sister and Leni's aunt
Erhart, her son and Leni's cousin and lover

The Pelzers

Walter ("Sonny Boy"), Leni's boss
Eva, his wife
Walter } their children
Eva }
Heinz } "Sonny Boy's" father and mother
Adelheid }

THE NUNS

Sister Cecilia
Sister Columbanus
Sister Klementina ("K")
Prudentia
Rahel ("Haruspica")
Sapientia

THE JESUITS

"J. I" and "J. II"

LENI'S FELLOW WORKERS

Grundtsch, head gardener
Helga Heuter
Liana Holthohne
Ilse Kremer
Heribert Kremp ("Dirty Bertie")
The Schelf woman
Marga Wanft
Frieda Zeven

OTHER INFORMANTS

Margret Schlömer, Leni's best friend
Hans and Grete Helzen
An (anonymous) exalted personage
Mimi, his wife
B.H.T., a book antiquarian
Bogakov, a Soviet prisoner of war
Marja van Doorn, the Gruytens' housekeeper
Alfred Scheukens, convent gardener
Dr. Schirtenstein, music critic
Dr. Scholsdorff } experts in Slavonic studies
Dr. Henges }
"Fritz," news vendor

OTHER CHARACTERS

Boris Lvovich, Leni's lover and father of Lev
Mehmet Şahin, Leni's lover
Belenko, Kitkin, and Genrikhovich, Soviet prisoners of war
Boldig and Kolb, camp guards

—and—
The Au.

1

GROUP PORTRAIT WITH LADY

The female protagonist in the first section is a woman of forty-eight, German: she is five foot six inches tall, weighs 133 pounds (in indoor clothing), i.e., only twelve to fourteen ounces below standard weight; her eyes are iridescent dark blue and black, her slightly graying hair, very thick and blond, hangs loosely to her shoulders, sheathing her head like a helmet.

The woman's name is Leni Pfeiffer, née Gruyten; for twenty-three years (with interruptions, of course) she has been subjected to the processes of that strange phenomenon known as the labor process: five years as an unskilled employee in her father's office, twenty-seven years as an unskilled worker in a nursery garden. As a result of having casually given away, during the inflation, a considerable fortune in real estate, a substantial apartment house in the new part of town that today would easily fetch four hundred thousand marks, she is now pretty much without resources, having, for no good reason and without being sufficiently sick or old, given up her job. Because she was at one time, in 1941, married for three days to a noncommissioned officer in the regular German Army, she draws a war-widow's pension which has not yet been supplemented by a social security pension. It can fairly be said that at the present time Leni is finding things pretty tough—and not only financially—especially now that her beloved son is in jail.

If Leni were to cut her hair shorter, dye it a little grayer, she would look like a well-preserved woman of forty; the way she wears her hair now, the discrepancy between her youthful hair style and her no longer quite so youthful face is too great, and one would judge her to be in her late forties. That is her true age; yet she is forfeiting a chance which she should not pass up, she gives the (quite unwarranted) impression of a faded blonde who leads or pursues a loose way of life. Leni is one of the very rare women of her age who could afford to wear a miniskirt: her legs and thighs show no sign of either veins or flabbiness. But Leni keeps to a skirt length that was fashionable around the year 1942, mainly because she still wears her old skirts, preferring jackets and blouses because, with her bosom, sweaters seem to her (with some justification) too ostentatious. As for her coats and shoes, she is still living off the high-quality and carefully preserved supplies that she had been able to acquire in her youth at a time when her parents had been temporarily well off. Sturdy tweeds, gray and pink, green and blue, black and white, sky-blue (solid color), and on the occasions when she considers a head covering appropriate she uses a head scarf; her shoes are of the kind that —provided one was sufficiently in funds—could be bought in the years 1935–39 as "made to last a lifetime."

Since Leni is now alone in the world without constant male protection or advice, she is the victim, as far as her hair style is concerned, of a permanent illusion; for this her mirror is to blame, an old mirror dating from 1894 which, to Leni's misfortune, has survived two world wars. Leni never goes into a beauty parlor, never enters a well-mirrored supermarket, she does her shopping at a small general store that is about to succumb to the economic trend. She is therefore wholly dependent on this mirror, of which her grandmother Gerta Barkel, née Holm, used long ago to say that it was a dreadful flatterer; Leni uses the mirror a great deal. Leni's hair style is one of the causes of Leni's troubles, and Leni does not suspect the connection. What is being forcibly brought home to her is the steadily mounting disapproval of her environment, in the building and in the neighborhood. In recent months Leni has had many male visitors: agents from credit institutions, bearers—since she had not reacted to letters—of final, definitely final notices; bailiffs; attorneys' messengers; and, ultimately, the bailiffs' men to take away seizable goods. Since, moreover, Leni rents out three furnished rooms that periodically change tenants, it was only natural that more youthful males in search of rooms should also have come to see her. Some of these male visitors made advances—without success, needless to say; we all know that the makers of unsuccessful advances are the very ones to boast of their successes, so it is easy to guess how quickly Leni's reputation was ruined.

The Author is far from having insight into all aspects of Leni's body-, soul-, and love-life, yet everything—everything—has been done to obtain the kind of information on Leni that is known to be factual (the informants will even be mentioned by name at the appropriate junctures), and the following report may be termed accurate with a probability bordering on certainty. Leni is taciturn and reticent—and since two character traits have now been named, let us add two more: Leni is not bitter, and she is without remorse, she does not even feel remorse at not having mourned the death of her first husband. Leni's lack of remorse is so absolute that any degree of "more" or "less," in terms of her capacity for remorse, would be beside the point; she probably does not even know the meaning of remorse; in this—as in other respects—her religious education must have failed or be deemed to have failed, probably to Leni's advantage.

What emerges unmistakably from the statements of the informants is that Leni no longer understands the world, in fact doubts whether she has ever understood it. She cannot understand the hostility of her environment, cannot understand why people are so angry at her and with her; she has done nothing wrong, not even to them. Lately, when obliged to leave her apartment to buy a few essential items, she has been openly laughed at, expressions such as "dirty bitch" or "worn-out mattress" being among the more harmless. Even insults rooted in events of thirty years back are to be heard again: "Communist whore," "Russian sweetie." Leni does not react to the abuse. To hear the word "slut" muttered as she passes is for her an everyday experience. She is considered insensitive, or even entirely devoid of feeling; neither is true for, according to the statements of reliable witnesses (witness: Marja van Doorn), she spends hours sitting in her apartment crying, her conjunctiva and her tear ducts in a state of considerable activity. Even the neighborhood children, with whom until now she has always been on friendly terms, are being set against her, and they call out after her using expressions that neither they nor Leni properly understand. And yet, to judge by copious and detailed evidence that exhausts even the ultimate, the very ultimate source on Leni, it is possible to establish here and now that up to this point in her life Leni has probably, with a probability bordering on certainty, had sexual intercourse a total of two dozen times: twice with the man to whom she was later married, Alois Pfeiffer (once before, once during, the marriage, which lasted a total of three days), and on the other occasions with a second man whom she would have married if circumstances had permitted it. Within a few minutes of Leni's being allowed to enter directly into the action (this will not be for a while yet), she will for the first time have made what might be called a wrong move: she will have yielded to a Turkish worker who, on his knees and in a language unintelligible to her, is going to ask for her favors, and she will yield—this as advance information—because she cannot bear to see anyone kneel to her (the fact that she herself is incapable of kneeling is one of her known character traits). It should perhaps be added that both Leni's parents are dead, that she has a few embarrassing relatives by marriage, others, less embarrassing, not by marriage, but blood relations, in the country, and a son of twenty-five who bears her maiden name and is at present in jail. One physical characteristic may be of significance, among other things, in assessing male advances. Leni has the well-nigh imperishable bosom of a woman who has been loved with tenderness and to whose bosom poems have been dedicated. What the people in Leni's environment really want is for her to be either eliminated or removed; the cry is even heard as she passes: "Get lost!" or "Get out of here!," and there is evidence that from time to time someone demands that she be gassed; this wish has been verified, although whether such a possibility exists is not known to the Au.; all he can add is that the wish is expressed with vehemence.

A few additional details must be supplied concerning Leni's daily habits. She enjoys eating, but in moderation; her main meal is breakfast, for which she positively must have two crisp fresh rolls, a fresh, soft-boiled egg, a little butter, one or two tablespoons of jam (more precisely: the plum purée known elsewhere as *Powidl*), strong coffee that she mixes with hot milk, very little sugar; midday dinner scarcely interests her: soup and a modest dessert are all she wants; then in the evening she has a cold meal, some bread, two or three slices, salad, sausage and cold meat when she can afford them. What Leni cares about most is the fresh rolls; rather than have them delivered she picks them out herself, not by fingering them, merely by inspecting their color; there is nothing—in the way of food, at least—that she hates as much as limp rolls. For the sake of the rolls and because breakfast is her daily feast, she ventures out in the morning among people, accepting insults, spiteful gossip, and abuse as part of the bargain.

As regards smoking: Leni has been smoking since she was seventeen, normally eight cigarettes a day, never more, usually less; during the war she gave it up for a time in order to let someone she loved (not her husband!) have her cigarettes. Leni is one of those who enjoy a glass of wine now and again, never drink more than half a bottle, and allow themselves, depending on the weather, a schnapps or, depending on mood and financial situation, a sherry. Other information: Leni has had a driver's license since 1939 (issued by special authority, details to follow), but since 1943 she has had no car at her disposal. She loved driving, almost with a passion.

Leni still lives in the house where she was born. By a series of unaccountable coincidences, her part of the city was spared the bombings, at least *relatively* spared; only thirty-five percent of it was destroyed: in other words, it was favored by Fortune. Not long ago something happened to Leni that has made her quite talkative, and she could hardly wait to tell it to her best friend, her chief confidante, who is also the Au.'s star witness: that morning, as she was crossing the street to pick up her rolls, her right foot recognized a slight unevenness in the pavement which it—the right foot—had last felt forty years before when Leni was playing hopscotch with some other girls; the spot in question is a tiny chip in a basalt paving stone which, at the time the street was laid out, around 1894, must have been knocked off by the paver. Leni's foot instantly passed on the message to her brainstem, the latter transmitted this impression to all her sensory organs and emotional centers and, since Leni is an enormously sensual person who immediately transforms everything—everything—into terms of eroticism, her delight, nostalgia, recollection, and state of total stimulation caused her to experience that process which in theological reference works—although with a somewhat different meaning—might be termed "absolute self-fulfillment"; which, when embarrassingly reduced, is termed, by clumsy erotologists and sexotheological dogmaticians, an "orgasm."

Before the impression arises that Leni has been deserted, we must list all those who are her friends, most of whom have stood by her through thin, two through thick and thin. Leni's solitary existence is due solely to her taciturnity and reticence; one might even call her laconic; the fact is that it is very rare for her to "come out of her shell," not even with her oldest friends Margret Schlömer, née Zeist, and Lotte Hoyser, née Berntgen, who stood by Leni when things were at their thickest. Margret is Leni's age, a widow like Leni, although this term may be misleading. Margret has carried on a good deal with men, for reasons to be given later: never from expediency, although sometimes—when she was really down and out—for a fee; yet the best way to describe Margret would be to say that the only erotic relationship she ever had that was based on expediency was the one with her husband, whom she married when she was eighteen; it was then, too, that she made the only verifiable whorelike comment, when she said to Leni (it was in 1940): "I've hooked myself a rich guy who insists on going to the altar with me."

Margret is at present in hospital, in an isolation ward, she is gravely and probably incurably ill with venereal disease; she describes herself as being "a complete goner"—her entire endocrine system is out of order; the only way one may talk to her is through a glass panel, and she is grateful for every package of cigarettes, every drop of schnapps, one takes along, no matter if it is the smallest pocket flask filled with the cheapest liquor. Margret's endocrine system is so disorganized that she "wouldn't be surprised if urine suddenly started coming out of my eyes instead of tears." She is grateful for any kind of narcotic, would even accept opium, morphine, hashish. The hospital is outside the city, in pleasant surroundings, laid out in bungalow style. In order to gain access to Margret, the Au. had to resort to a variety of reprehensible methods: bribery, the multiple felony of fraud combined with false claims to office (pretending to be a professor of the sociopsychology of prostitution!).

By way of advance information on Margret it must be stated here that "strictly speaking" she is a far less sensual person than Leni; Margret's undoing was not her own desire for the pleasures of love, it was the fact that so many pleasures were desired of her which she was endowed by Nature to bestow; it will be necessary to report on this later. Be that as it may: Leni is suffering, Margret is suffering.

"Strictly speaking" not suffering, only suffering because Leni (to whom she is really very devoted) is suffering, is a female person already mentioned whose name is Marja van Doorn, aged seventy, formerly a housekeeper employed by Leni's parents, the Gruytens. She now lives in retirement in the country, where an old-age pension, a vegetable patch, a few fruit trees, a dozen hens, and a half-interest in a pig and a calf in whose fattening she shares, ensure her a reasonably pleasant old age. Marja has stood by Leni only through thin, she had no reservations until things "really went too far," none—it must be specifically stated—on moral grounds (surprisingly enough), but some on the basis of nationality. Marja is a woman who fifteen or twenty years ago probably had "her heart in the right place"; meanwhile this overrated organ has slipped, assuming it to be still there at all; certainly not down "into her boots," for she has never been a coward. She is horrified at the way people are treating her Leni, whom she really knows very well, certainly better than the man whose name Leni bears ever knew her. After all, Marja van Doorn did live from 1920 to 1960 in the Gruyten home, she was present at Leni's birth, shared in all her adventures, in all that befell her; she has almost decided to move back to live with Leni, but before doing so she is exerting her entire (and quite considerable) energy in a plan to get Leni to come out to the country and live with her. She is horrified at the things that are happening to Leni and the threats being made to her, and is even prepared to believe certain historical atrocities which hitherto she has not exactly regarded as impossible but of whose extent she was skeptical.

A special position among the informants is that occupied by Dr. Herweg Schirtenstein, the music critic. For forty years he has been living in the rear portion of an apartment that forty years ago might have been regarded as baronial but which after World War I declined in prestige and was subdivided. He occupies an apartment on the ground floor of a building which, since the rooms facing the courtyard adjoin the rooms in Leni's apartment facing the courtyard, has enabled him for decades carefully to follow Leni's practicing and progress and eventual partial mastery of the piano without ever discovering that the player was Leni. True, he knows Leni by sight, having for forty years been running into her from time to time on the street (it is quite likely that he even watched Leni in the days when she was still playing hopscotch, for he is passionately interested in children's games and the subject of his Ph.D. thesis was "Music in Children's

Games"); and, since he is not insensitive to feminine charms, we can be sure that over the years he has followed Leni's general appearance attentively, that he has now and again given an appreciative nod, possibly even harbored covetous thoughts. Nevertheless, it must be said that, if one compares Leni to all the women with whom Schirtenstein has hitherto been intimate, he would have considered her "a shade too vulgar" to merit serious consideration. Were he to suspect that it is Leni who, after many years of rather ineffectual practice, has learned to play two, although only two, pieces by Schubert with consummate mastery, and in such a way that even decades of repetition have not bored Schirtenstein, perhaps he would change his mind about Leni—he, the critic who inspired even a Monique Haas not only with dread but with respect. It will be necessary to return later to Schirtenstein, who subsequently and inadvertently entered upon an erotic relationship with Leni that was not so much telepathic as telesensual. In all fairness it must be said that Schirtenstein would have stuck with Leni through thick and thin, but: he never had an opportunity.

Much about Leni's parents, little about Leni's inner life, almost everything about Leni's external life, was imparted by an informant eighty-five years of age: Otto Hoyser, head bookkeeper, who has been drawing a pension for the last twenty years and lives in a comfortable retirement home that combines the advantages of a luxury hotel with those of a luxury sanatorium. At more or less regular intervals, he either visits Leni or is visited by her.

A witness with a fund of information is his daughter-in-law, Lotte Hoyser, née Bertgen; less reliable are her sons Werner and Kurt, aged respectively thirty-five and thirty. Lotte is as full of information as she is bitter, although her bitterness has never been directed at Leni; Lotte is fifty-seven, a war widow like Leni, and works in an office.

Lotte Hoyser, sharp-tongued, describes her father-in-law

Otto (see above) and her youngest son Kurt, without the slightest qualification or regard for blood kinship, as gangsters on whom she places almost the entire blame for Leni's present near-destitution; it is only recently that she has "found out certain things that I haven't the heart to tell Leni because in my own heart I haven't yet been able to accept them entirely. It's simply beyond belief." Lotte lives in a two-room-kitchen-and-bath apartment in the center of town for which she pays about a third of her income in rent. She is considering moving back into Leni's apartment, out of fellow feeling but also, as she (for as yet mysterious reasons) ominously adds, "to see whether they would actually evict me too. I am afraid they would." Lotte works for a union "without conviction" (as she gratuitously added), "merely because, naturally enough, I like to eat and stay alive."

Further informants, not necessarily the least important, are: Dr. Scholsdorff, the specialist in Slavic languages and literature who turned up in Leni's career as the result of a complicated involvement or entanglement; the entanglement, no matter how complicated, will be explained. Because of a chain of circumstances, which will also be explained when the time comes, Scholsdorff now finds himself in the upper hierarchy of the income-tax department; he intends to terminate this career shortly by way of early retirement.

A further Slavic specialist, Dr. Henges, plays a subsidiary role; in any case, as an informant he lacks credibility, although he is aware of this lack and even stresses it, indeed almost enjoys it. He describes himself as "a total wreck," a description that the Au. prefers not to adopt precisely because it comes from Henges. Unasked, Henges has admitted that, while in the Soviet Union "recruiting" workers for the German armaments industry (he was at the time in the service of a recently murdered diplomat of aristocratic descent), he "betrayed my Russian language, my glorious Russian language." Henges is living "in not uncomfortable financial circumstances" (H. about H.) near Bonn, in the country, employed as a translator for a variety of journals and offices dealing with Eastern European politics.

It would be going too far to enumerate all the informants in detail at this early stage. They will be introduced at the proper time and portrayed in their own context. Mention should be made, however, of one more informant, an informant not on Leni herself, but merely on an important figure in Leni's life, a Catholic nun: a former book antiquarian who feels that he is sufficiently authenticated by the initials B.H.T.

A weak, but still living, informant, who need only be rejected as prejudiced when he is personally involved, is Leni's brother-in-law Heinrich Pfeiffer, aged forty-four, married to one Hetti, née Irms, two sons, eighteen and fourteen, Wilhelm and Karl.

Still to be introduced at the proper time, and in such detail as befits their importance, are: three highly placed personages of the male sex, one a local politician, another from the realm of big business, the third a top-ranking official in the Ordnance Department, two pensioned female workers, two or three Soviet individuals, the proprietress of a chain of flowershops, an old nursery gardener, a not quite so old former nursery-garden owner who (his own statement!) "now devotes himself entirely to the administration of his estates," and a number of others. *Important* informants will be introduced with exact data as to height and weight.

The furnishings of Leni's apartment—or such of them as remain to her after numerous seizures—are a blend of the styles of 1885 and 1920–25: inherited by her parents in 1920 and 1922, a few art-nouveau pieces, a chest of drawers, a bookcase, two chairs, are now in Leni's apartment, their antiquarian value having so far eluded the bailiffs; they were described as "junk," unfit for seizure. Seized and removed from the apartment by the bailiffs were eighteen original paintings by contemporary local artists from the years 1918 to 1935, almost all of them dealing with religious subjects; their value, because they were originals, was overestimated by the bailiff, and their loss caused Leni no pain whatsoever.

Leni's wall decorations consist of detailed color photographs depicting the organs of the human body; her brother-in-law Heinrich Pfeiffer obtains them for her. He works at the Department of Health, part of his duties being the administration of teaching aids, and "although I can't quite square it with my conscience" (H. Pfeiffer), he brings Leni the worn-out and discarded wall posters; in order to follow correct bookkeeping procedures, Pfeiffer acquires the discarded posters in exchange for a small fee. Since he is also "in charge" of the acquisition of replacements for the posters, now and again Leni manages to acquire through him a new poster which she obtains direct from the supplier, paying for it, of course, out of her own thinly lined purse. She restores the worn-out posters with her own hands, carefully cleaning them with soap and water or benzine, retracing the lines with a black graphite pencil and coloring the posters with the aid of a box of cheap water colors, a relic of her son's childhood days at home.

Her favorite poster is the scientifically accurate enlargement of a human eye that hangs over her piano (in order to redeem the frequently attached piano, to save it from being carried off by bailiffs' agents, Leni has demeaned herself by begging from old acquaintances of her deceased parents, by obtaining rent in advance from her subtenants, by borrowing from her brother-in-law Heinrich, but mostly by visits to old Hoyser, whose ostensibly avuncular caresses Leni does not altogether trust; according to the three most reliable witnesses—Margret, Marja, Lotte—she has even stated that for the sake of the piano she would be prepared "to walk the streets"—an unusually daring statement for Leni). Less frequently observed organs, such as human intestines, also adorn Leni's walls, nor are the human sexual organs, with an accurate description of all their functions, absent as enlarged tabulated wall decorations, and they were hanging in Leni's apartment long before porno-theology made them popular. At one time there used to be fierce arguments between Leni and Marja about these posters, which were described by Marja as immoral, but Leni has remained adamant.

Since it will sooner or later be necessary to broach the subject of Leni's attitude toward metaphysics, let it be said at the outset: metaphysics present no problem whatever for Leni. She is on intimate terms with the Virgin Mary, receiving her almost daily on the television screen, and she is invariably surprised to find that the Virgin Mary is also a blonde, by no means as young as one would like her to be; these encounters take place in silence, usually late at night when all the neighbors are asleep and the TV stations—including the one in the Netherlands—have signed off and switched on their test patterns. All Leni and the Virgin Mary do is exchange smiles. No more, no less. Leni would not be in the least surprised, let alone alarmed, if one day the Virgin Mary's Son were to be introduced to her on the TV screen after sign-off time. Whether indeed she is waiting for this is not known to this reporter. It would certainly come as no surprise to him after all that he has meanwhile found out. Leni knows two prayers that she murmurs from time to time: the Lord's Prayer and the Ave Maria. Also a few scraps of the Rosary. She does not own a prayer book, does not go to church, believes that the universe contains "creatures with souls" (Leni).

Before proceeding to a more or less piecemeal account of Leni's educational background, let us glance at her bookcase, the bulk of whose contents, inconspicuously gathering dust, consists of a library once bought by her father as a job lot. It is on a par with the original oil paintings and has so far escaped the clutches of the bailiff; it contains among other things some complete sets of an old Catholic church-oriented monthly which Leni occasionally leafs through; this periodical—an antiquarian rarity—owes its survival solely to the ignorance of the bailiff, who has been taken in by its unprepossessing appearance. What has unfortunately not escaped the bailiff's notice is the complete sets for 1916–40 of the periodical *Hochland,* together with the poems of William Butler Yeats that had once belonged to Leni's mother. More attentive observers such as Marja van Doorn, who for many years was obliged to handle them in the course of her dusting, or Lotte Hoyser, who during the war was for a long time Leni's second-most intimate confidante, do, however, discover in this art-nouveau bookcase seven or eight surprising titles: poems by Brecht, Hölderlin, and Trakl, two prose volumes of Kafka and Kleist, two volumes of Tolstoi (*Resurrection* and *Anna Karenina*)—and all of these seven or eight volumes are so honorably dog-eared, in a manner most flattering to the authors, that they have been patched up over and over again, not very expertly, with every conceivable kind of gum and gummed tape, some of them being merely held together loosely by a rubber band. Offers to be presented with new editions of the works of these authors (Christmas, birthday, name day, etc.) are rejected by Leni with a firmness that is almost rude. At this point the Au. takes the liberty of making a remark that goes beyond his scope: he is firmly convinced that Leni would have some of the prose volumes of Beckett there too if, at the time when Leni's literary adviser still had an influence over her, they had already been published or known to him.

Among Leni's intense pleasures are not only the eight daily cigarettes, a keen appetite (although kept within bounds), the playing of two piano pieces by Schubert, the rapt contemplation of illustrations of human organs—intestines included; not only the tender thoughts she devotes to her son Lev, now in jail. She also enjoys dancing, has always been a passionately keen dancer (a fact that was *once* her undoing in that it led her into the everlasting possession of the, to her, distasteful name of Pfeiffer). Now where is a single woman of forty-eight, whom the neighbors would be quite happy to see gassed, to go dancing? Is she to frequent the haunts of youthful devotees of the dance, where she would undoubtedly be mistaken for, if not mishandled as, a sex-granny? She is also barred from joining in church activities where there is dancing, having taken no part in church life since her fourteenth year. Were she to dig up friends of her youth other than Margret—who is probably barred from dancing to the end of her days—she would probably end up in various kinds of strip or swap parties, without a partner of her own, and for the fourth time in her life would blush. To date Leni has blushed three times in her life. So what does Leni do? She dances alone, sometimes lightly clad in her bed-sitting room, sometimes even naked in her bathroom and in front of that flattering mirror. From time to time she is observed, surprised even, at this activity —and this does nothing to enhance her reputation.

On one occasion she danced with one of the boarders, a minor official of the judiciary, the prematurely bald Erich Köppler; Leni would *almost* have blushed had not the gentleman's palpable advances been altogether too clumsy; in any event she had to give him notice because—he was not without intelligence and certainly not without intuition—he had recognized Leni's enormous sensuality and, ever since the "impromptu little dance" (Leni) that had resulted so spontaneously from his coming to pay the rent and catching Leni while she was listening to dance music, had stood every evening whimpering outside the door of her room. Leni would not yield because she did not like him, and ever since then Köppler, who found himself a room in the neighborhood, has been one of her most malicious denouncers, from time to time, during his confidential chats with the proprietress of the small general store that is about to succumb to the economic trend, enlarging on the intimate details of his imaginary love affair with Leni. These details arouse the proprietress—a person of ice-cold prettiness whose husband is absent during the daytime (he works in an automobile factory)—to such a state of excitement that she drags the bald-headed judiciary official (who has meanwhile been promoted) into the back room, where she commits repeated assaults on him. This person, Käte Perscht by name, aged twenty-eight, is Leni's most vicious vilifier, she makes libelous moral accusations against her although she herself, through the good offices of her husband, hires herself out to a night club at times when an overwhelming majority of male trade-fair visitors flood the city. Here she does a "Trade Fair Strip" for which she is well paid and, before her appearance, she lets it be known through the medium of an unctuous announcer that she is prepared to follow through and satisfy any and all states of excitation brought on by her performances.

Recently Leni has had the odd opportunity to dance again. As a result of certain experiences, she now only rents rooms to married couples or foreign workers, and so has rented two rooms to a nice young couple whom for simplicity's sake we will call Hans and Grete, at a reduced rent—and this despite her financial position! And it is this Hans and Grete who, while they were listening to dance music with Leni, correctly interpreted both her external and internal twitchings, so now and again Leni goes to them for an "innocent little dance." Hans and Grete sometimes even cautiously try to analyze Leni's situation for her, advise her to update her clothes, change her hair style, advise her to look for a lover. "Just spruce yourself up a bit, Leni, a snappy pink dress, some snappy nylons on those fabulous legs of yours—and you'd soon find out how attractive you still are." But Leni shakes her head, she has been too badly hurt, she no longer goes to the store to buy groceries, lets Grete do her shopping for her, and Hans has relieved her of her morning walk to the bakery by quickly, before he goes to work (he is a technician with the highways department, Grete works in a beauty parlor and has offered Leni her services free of charge, so far without success), picking up her vitally essential fresh crisp rolls which she refuses to forgo and which are more important to Leni than any sacrament could ever be to anyone else.

Needless to say, Leni's wall decoration does not consist solely of biological posters, she also has family photographs on the walls; photos of deceased persons: her mother, who died in 1943 at the age of forty-one and was photographed shortly before her death, a woman bearing the marks of suffering, with thin gray hair and large eyes, wrapped in a blanket and seated on a bench by the Rhine near Hersel, close to a landing stage on which that place-name is legible; in the background, monastery walls; Leni's mother, it is plain to see, is shivering; one is struck by the lack-luster expression in her eyes, the surprising firmness of her mouth in a face that hardly gives an impression of great vitality; it is clear that she has lost the will to live; were one asked to guess her age, one would be embarrassed, not knowing whether to say that this is a woman of about thirty who has been prematurely aged by hidden suffering, or a fine-boned sixty-year-old who has retained a certain youthfulness. Leni's mother is smiling in this photo, not exactly with difficulty, but with effort.

Leni's father, likewise photographed with a simple box camera shortly before his death in 1949 at the age of forty-nine, is also smiling, with not even a trace of effort; he is to be seen in the frequently and painstakingly mended overalls of a mason, standing in front of a ruined building, in his left hand a crowbar of the kind known to the initiated as a "claw," in his right a hammer of the kind known to the initiated as a "mallet"; in front of him, left and right beside him, behind him, lie iron girders of various sizes, and possibly it is these that make him smile, as a fisherman smiles at his day's catch. As a matter of fact they do—as will subsequently be explained in detail—represent his day's catch, for at the time he was working for the above-mentioned former nursery-garden owner who was quick to sense the coming "scrap boom" (statement by Lotte H.). Leni's father is shown bareheaded, his hair is very thick, only just turning gray, and it is very hard to apply any relevant social epithet to this tall, spare man whose tools lie so naturally in his hands. Does he look like a proletarian? Or like a gentleman? Does he look like someone doing an unaccustomed job, or is this obviously strenuous work familiar to him? The Au. tends to think that both apply, and both in both cases. Lotte H.'s comment on this photo confirms this, she describes him in this photo as "Mr. Prole." There is not the slightest suggestion in the appearance of Leni's father that he has lost his zest for life. He looks neither younger nor older than his age, is in every way the "well-preserved man in his late forties" who could undertake in a marriage advertisement "to bring happiness to a cheerful life companion, if possible not over forty."

The four remaining photos show four youths, all about twenty, three of them dead, one (Leni's son) still alive. The pictures of two of these young men display certain blemishes applicable only to their clothing: although these are head portraits only, in both cases enough of the chest is visible to give a clear view of the uniform of the German Army, and attached to this uniform is the German eagle and the swastika, that symbolic composite known to the initiated as the "ruptured vulture." The two youths are Leni's brother Heinrich Gruyten and her cousin Erhard Schweigert, who—like the third dead youth—must be numbered among the victims of World War II. Heinrich and Erhard both look "somehow German" (Au.), "somehow" (Au.) they both resemble all the pictures one has ever seen of cultured German youths; perhaps it will make for clarity if at this point we quote Lotte H., for whom both boys resemble the ideal German youth embodied in that Medieval Statue, the Bamberg Rider, a description, as will later become apparent, by no means entirely flattering. The facts are: that E. is blond, H. brown-haired; that both are smiling, E. "to himself, warmly and quite spontaneously" (Au.), an endearing smile, really nice. H.'s smile is not quite so warm, the corners of his mouth already showing a trace of that nihilism that is commonly mistaken for cynicism, and that for the year 1939, the year in which both pictures were taken, can be interpreted as somewhat premature, in fact almost progressive.

The third photo of a deceased subject shows a Soviet individual by the name of Boris Lvovich Koltovsky; he is not smiling; the photo is an enlargement, almost graphic it seems, of a passport picture taken by an amateur in Moscow in 1941. It shows B. as a solemn, pale person whose noticeably high hairline might lead one at first glance to assume premature baldness but which, his hair being thick, fair, and curly, is a personal characteristic of Boris K. His eyes are dark and rather large, reflected in his spectacles in a way that might be mistaken for some graphic gimmick. It is immediately apparent that this person, although solemn and thin and with a surprisingly high forehead, was young when the picture was taken. He is dressed in civilian clothes, an open shirt with a wide collar, no jacket, a sign of summer temperatures at the time the picture was taken.

The sixth photo is of a living person, Leni's son. Although at the time the picture was taken he was the same age as E., H., and B., he nevertheless appears to be the youngest; this may be due to the fact that photographic materials had improved since 1939 and 1941. Unfortunately there is no denying it: young Lev is not only smiling, he is laughing in this photo taken in 1965; no one would hesitate to describe him as a "jolly-looking boy"; the resemblance between him, Leni's father, and his father Boris is unmistakable. He has the "Gruyten hair" and the "Barkel eyes" (Leni's mother's maiden name was Barkel. Au.), a fact that gives him an added resemblance to Erhard. His laugh, his eyes, permit the unhesitating conclusion that there are two of his mother's traits which he most certainly does not possess: he is neither taciturn nor reticent.

Finally we must mention an article of clothing to which Leni is attached as otherwise only to the photographs, the illustrations of human organs, the piano, and the fresh rolls: her bathrobe, which she persists, erroneously, in calling her housecoat. It is made of "terrycloth of prewar quality" (Lotte H.), formerly, as can still be seen from the back and the pocket edges, wine-red, by this time faded to the color of diluted raspberry syrup. In a number of places it has been darned—expertly, we must admit—with orange thread. Leni is rarely parted from this garment, which nowadays she hardly ever takes off; she is said to have stated that she would like, "when the time comes, to be buried in it" (Hans and Grete Helzen, informants on all details of Leni's domestic surroundings).

Brief mention should perhaps be made of the present state of occupancy of Leni's apartment: she has rented two rooms to Hans and Grete Helzen; two to a Portuguese couple with three children, the Pinto family, consisting of the parents, Joaquim and Ana-Maria, and their children Etelvina, Manuela, and Jose; and one room to three Turkish workers, Kaya Tunç, Ali Kiliç, and Mehmet Sahin, who are no longer all that young.

2 Now Leni, of course, has not always been forty-eight years old, and we must turn our eyes toward the past. From photos taken in her youth, no one would hesitate to describe Leni as a pretty, wholesome-looking girl: even in the uniform of a Nazi girls' organization—at the ages of thirteen, fourteen, and fifteen—Leni looks nice. In passing judgment on her physical charms, no male observer would have gone lower than "not bad, I tell you." The human copulative urge ranges, as we know, from love at first sight to the spontaneous desire to, quite simply, with no thought of a permanent relationship, have intercourse with a person of the other or one's own sex, a desire going all the way to the deepest, most convulsing passion that leaves neither body nor soul in peace, and every single one of its variants, whether unorthodox or uncodified, from the most superficial to the most profound, could have been aroused by Leni, and has been. At seventeen she made the crucial leap from pretty to beautiful that comes more easily to dark-eyed blondes than to light-eyed ones. At this stage in her life, no man would have gone lower in his opinion than "striking."

A few additional comments are required in regard to Leni's educational background. At sixteen she went to work in her father's office. He had duly noted the leap from a pretty girl to a beauty and, mainly because of her effect on men (the year is now 1938), used to see that she was present at important business discussions, in which Leni, pad and pencil on her knee, would participate, from time to time jotting down a few key words. She did not know shorthand, nor would she ever have learned it. It was not that abstract thinking and abstractions were entirely without interest for her, but "chopped-up writing," her name for shorthand, was something she had no wish to learn. Her education had consisted, among other things, of suffering, more suffering on the teacher's part than on her own. After having twice, if not exactly failed to be promoted, "voluntarily repeated a year," she left primary school after Grade 4 with a passable, much interpolated report card. One of the still surviving witnesses from the school's teaching staff, the sixty-five-year-old retired principal Mr. Schlocks, who was traced to his rural retreat, could state that there had been times when some consideration had been given to shifting Leni to a "special school," but that two factors had saved her from this: first, her father's affluence, which—Schlocks is careful to stress—had no direct bearing, only an indirect one, on the matter, and second, the fact that for two successive years, at the ages of eleven and twelve, she won the title of "the most German girl in the school" that was awarded by a roving commission of racial experts who went from school to school. On one occasion Leni was even among those selected for "the most German girl in the city," but she was relegated to second place by a Protestant minister's daughter whose eyes were lighter than Leni's, which at that time were no longer quite as light a blue. Was there any way that "the most German girl in the school" could be sent to a school for slow learners? At twelve Leni entered a high school run by nuns, but by the time she was fourteen it was already necessary to withdraw her as having failed. Within two years she had once fallen hopelessly short of promotion, once been promoted upon her parents' giving a solemn promise never to take advantage of the promotion. The promise was kept.

Before any misunderstanding can arise, let us now present, as factual information, an explanation for the dubious educational circumstances to which Leni was obliged to submit, or to which she was subjected. In this context there is no question of *blame,* there were not even—either at the primary school or the high school attended by Leni—any serious disagreements, at most there were misunderstandings. Leni was thoroughly capable of being educated, in fact she hungered and thirsted after education, and all those involved did their best to satisfy that hunger and thirst. The trouble was that the meat and drink offered her did not match her intelligence, or her disposition, or her powers of comprehension. In most—one can almost say all—cases, the material offered lacked that sensual dimension without which Leni was incapable of comprehension. Writing, for example, never posed the slightest problem for her although, considering the highly abstract nature of this process, the reverse might have been expected; but for Leni writing was associated with optical, tactile, even olfactory perceptions (one has only to think of the smells of various kinds of ink, pencils, types of paper), hence she was able to master even complicated writing exercises and grammatical nuances: her handwriting, of which she unfortunately makes little use, was and still is firm, attractive and, as the retired school principal Mr. Schlocks (our informant on all *essential* pedagogic details) convincingly assured us, nothing short of ideally suited for the evocation of erotic and/or sexual excitement.

Leni had particularly bad luck with two closely related subjects: religion and arithmetic (or mathematics). Had even one of her teachers thought of explaining to the little six-year-old Leni that it is possible to approach the starry sky, which Leni loved so much, in terms of both mathematics and physics, she would not have resisted learning the multiplication tables, by which she was repelled as other people are by spiders. The pictures of nuts, apples, cows, and peas with which an effort was made to try, in primitive terms, to achieve mathematical realism, meant nothing to her; in Leni there was no latent mathematician, but there was most certainly a gift for the natural sciences, and had she been offered, in addition to the Mendelian blossoms that were forever cropping up in textbooks and on blackboards in red, white, and pink, somewhat more complex genetic processes, she would—as the saying goes—have "thrown herself into" such material with burning enthusiasm. Because the biology instruction was so meager she was denied many joys that she has had to wait until middle age to find, as she goes over the outlines of complex organic processes with the aid of a box of cheap water colors. As has been convincingly assured by Miss van Doorn, there is one detail dating from Leni's preschool existence that she will never forget and to this day makes her as "uncomfortable" as Leni's genitalia wall posters. Even as a child, Leni was fascinated by the excremental processes to which she was subject and on which —unfortunately in vain!—she used to demand information by asking: "Come on now, tell me! What's all this stuff coming out of me?" Neither her mother nor Marja van Doorn would give her this information!

It remained for the second of the two men with whom she had until then cohabited, a foreigner at that and a Soviet individual to boot, to discover that Leni was capable of astounding feats of sensibility and intelligence. And it was to him that she recounted the incident which she later described to Margret (between late 1943 and mid-1945 she was much less taciturn than she is today): that she experienced her first and complete "self-fulfillment" when, at the age of sixteen, just removed from boarding school, out for a bicycle ride one June evening, she achieved—as she lay on her back in the heather, "spread-eagled and in total surrender" (Leni to Margret), her gaze on the stars that were just beginning to sparkle in the afterglow of sunset—that state of bliss which these days is far too often striven for; on that summer evening in 1938 as she lay spread-eagled and "opened up" on the warm heather, Leni—so she told Boris and as she has told Margret—had an overwhelming impression of being "taken" and of having "given," and—as she later went on to tell Margret—she would not have been in the least surprised if she had become pregnant. Consequently, of course, she has no trouble at all understanding the Virgin Birth.

Leni left school with an embarrassing report card on which she was given a D in religion and mathematics. She then went for two and a half years to a boarding school where she was taught home economics, German, religion, a little history (as far as the Reformation), and music (piano).

At this point, before proceeding to memorialize a deceased nun —a person as crucial to Leni's education as the Soviet individual (about whom there will be much to say later)—we must mention as witnesses three nuns, still living, who, although their associations with Leni go back thirty-four and thirty-two years, still vividly remember her, and all three of whom, when visited by the Au. with pencil and pad in three different places, exclaimed at the mention of Leni's name: "Ah yes, the Gruyten girl!" To the Au., this identical exclamation seems significant, a proof of the deep impression Leni must have made.

Since not only the exclamation "Ah yes, the Gruyten girl!" but also certain physical traits are common to all three nuns, a number of details may be synchronized for space-saving purposes. All three have what is called a parchment skin: delicately stretched over thin cheekbones, yellowish, slightly wrinkled; all three offered the reporter tea (or had it offered). It is not ingratitude, merely devotion to facts, that obliges him to say that the tea offered by all three nuns was on the weak side. All three offered dry cake (or had it offered); all three began coughing when the Au. started to smoke (discourteously omitting to ask permission because he did not want to risk a No). All three received him in almost identical visitors' rooms that were adorned with religious prints, a crucifix, a portrait of the reigning pope and one of the regional cardinal. All three tables in the three different visitors' rooms were covered with plush tablecloths, all the chairs were uncomfortable. All three nuns are between seventy and seventy-two years of age.

The first, Sister Columbanus, had been the principal of the girls' high school attended by Leni for two years with so little success. An ethereal person with lusterless, very shrewd eyes, who sat shaking her head throughout almost the entire interview, shaking her head in self-reproach for not having brought out all there was in Leni. Over and over again she would say: "There was something in her, something strong in fact, but we never brought it out." Sister Columbanus—a graduate mathematician who still reads technical literature (with a magnifying glass!)—was a typical product of the early emancipation years of the feminine urge for education, an urge that, in a nun's habit, unfortunately brought little recognition and even less appreciation. When politely asked for details of her career she told him she had been going around in sackcloth ever since 1918 and had been more laughed at, despised, and scorned than many of today's hippies. On hearing details of Leni's life from the Au., her lackluster eyes brightened a little, and she said with a sigh, yet with a hint of enthusiasm: "Extreme, that's it, extreme—her life was bound to turn out that way." A remark that aroused the Au.'s suspicions. On taking his leave he looked sheepishly at the four cigarette butts embedded with such provocative vulgarity in their ashes in a ceramic ashtray shaped like a vine leaf, that was probably seldom used and in which the only object ever to grow cold may be the occasional prelate's cigar.

The second nun, Sister Prudentia, had been Leni's German teacher; she was a shade less ladylike than Sister Columbanus, a shade redder in the cheeks, which is not to say that she was red-cheeked: merely that the former redness of her cheeks still glowed through, while the skin of Sister Columbanus's face unmistakably radiated a permanent pallor that had been hers from the days of her youth. Sister Prudentia (for exclamation on hearing Leni's name, see above) contributed a few unexpected details. "I really did my best," she said, "to keep her in school, but it was no use, although I gave her, and was justified in giving her, a B in German; she wrote a really splendid essay, you know, on *The Marquise of O___*, a book that was banned, that was thoroughly disapproved of in fact, the subject matter being, shall we say, extremely delicate, but I thought, and I still think, that girls of fourteen should feel free to read it and make up their own minds about it—and the Gruyten girl wrote something really splendid: what she wrote was an ardent defense of Count

F., an insight into—well, let's say, male sexuality—that surprised me—splendid, and it was almost worth an A, but there was that D, actually an E plus, in religion, because no one, as you can imagine, wanted to give the girl an E in religion, and that big fat D in mathematics, no doubt thoroughly justified from an objective point of view, that Sister Columbanus was obliged to give her, although she wept as she did so, because she had to be fair—and that was the end of the Gruyten girl . . . she left, she had to leave."

Of the nuns and teachers at the boarding school where, from her fourteenth to almost her seventeenth year, Leni continued her education, it was possible to trace only one, the third of the nuns presented here, Sister Cecilia. It was she who for two and a half years had given Leni private piano lessons; immediately aware that Leni was musical, but horrified, desperate in fact, at her inability to read music, let alone recognize the sound expressed by the written musical note, she spent the first six months playing phonograph records to Leni and letting her simply play what she had heard, a dubious but successful experiment that—according to Sister Cecilia—proved, moreover, "that Leni was capable of recognizing not only tunes and rhythms but also structures." But how—countless sighs from the nun!—how to teach the required ability to read music? It occurred to her—an idea almost amounting to inspiration—to try resorting to geography. True, the geography instruction was somewhat meager—consisting chiefly of repeating, pointing to, and reciting over and over again all the tributaries of the Rhine together with the low mountain ranges or other parts of the country bordered by these rivers—and yet: map reading was something Leni had learned: that black line twisting and turning between the hills of the Hunsrück and the Eifel, the Moselle River, was recognized by Leni not as a twisting black line but as a symbol for an actually existing river. All right then. The experiment worked: Leni learned to read music, laboriously, resisting it, often in tears of rage, but she learned it—and since Sister Cecilia was receiving from Leni's father a substantial special fee that flowed into the coffers of the Order, she felt she "really must teach Leni something." She succeeded, and: "The thing I admired about her was: she grasped at once that Schubert was her limit—attempts to go beyond that failed so miserably that even I advised her to keep within her limitations, in spite of her father's insistence that she learn to play Mozart, Beethoven, and all those."

Apropos Sister Cecilia's skin, one further comment: it still showed a few milky places, soft and white, not quite so dry; the Au. freely admits that he was aware within himself of the possibly frivolous wish to see more of the skin of this gracious celibate old lady, despite the fact that this wish may lay him open to the suspicion of gerontophilia. Unfortunately, when asked about a sister-nun who was important to Leni, Sister Cecilia became decidedly icy, virtually rebuffing him.

At this stage we can do no more than indicate something which in the course of this account may eventually be proved: that Leni has an unrecognized genius for sensuality. Unfortunately she spent many years in a category of sufficient convenience to be in popular use: silly goose. Old Hoyser actually admitted that to this day he continues to place Leni in this category.

Now it might be supposed that Leni, all her life a splendid eater, had been an excellent cookery pupil and that home economics must have been her favorite subject. Not at all: the cooking classes, although held at the stove and the kitchen table, using materials that could be smelled, handled, tasted, seen, seemed to her (if the Au. has correctly interpreted certain of Sister Cecilia's remarks) more abstract than mathematics, as asensual as religious instruction. It is hard to determine whether in Leni the world has lost an excellent cook, still harder to determine whether the downright metaphysical fear that nuns have of spices caused the food prepared during cooking classes to seem "bland" to Leni. That she is *not* a good cook is unfortunately indisputable; soups are the only dishes in which she is now and again successful, also desserts; moreover—something not to be taken for granted—she makes good coffee and was also a dedicated baby-food cook (as attested to by M.v.D.), but the achievement of a proper menu would be beyond her. Just as the fate of a sauce may depend on the swift hand movement, as unorthodox as it is uncodified, with which a particular ingredient is added, so Leni's religious education was a complete washout (or rather: fortunately failed to succeed). When the subject was bread or wine, or embraces or laying-on-of-hands, when terrestrial matters were involved, she had no problem. To this day she has not the slightest difficulty in believing that a person can be cured by the application of saliva. But then who would apply saliva to a person? Not only did she heal the Soviet individual and her son with saliva: by a mere laying-on-of-hands she could induce a state of bliss in the Soviet individual and soothe her son (Lotte and Margret). But then who would lay their hands on a person? What kind of bread was it they gave her at her First Holy Communion (the last religious activity in which she participated), and where, where for God's sake, was the wine? Why didn't they give it to her? Fallen women and so forth, those rather numerous women with whom the Virgin's Son associated, all that pleased her enormously and could have induced the same ecstasy in her as the sight of a sky full of stars.

One can well imagine that Leni, who throughout her life so dearly loved her fresh rolls in the morning and for the sake of them would even expose herself to the scorn of the neighborhood, looked forward fervently to the celebration of her First Communion. Now in high school Leni had been excluded from receiving the First Communion because on several occasions during the preparatory instruction she had lost patience and positively attacked the religious instructor, a white-haired, very ascetic person, elderly even in those days, who has unfortunately been dead for twenty years, and after the lesson she kept asking, with childish insistence: "Please, please give me this Bread of Life! Why must I wait so long?" This teacher of religion, of whom the name, Erich Brings, and a number of publications have survived, found Leni's spontaneous expression of sensuality "criminal." He was appalled at this manifestation of will which for him came under the heading of "sensual craving." Needless to say, he brusquely rejected Leni's unreasonable demand, putting her back two years on account of "proven immaturity and the inability to comprehend the Sacraments." For this incident there are two witnesses: old Hoyser, who remembers it well and is still able to report that "at the time a scandal was narrowly avoided," and that it was solely because of the politically precarious situation of the nuns (1934!), of which Leni had no idea, that it was decided "not to spread it about." The second witness was the old gentleman himself, whose hobby was the doctrine of Particles, which involved devoting months, years if need be, to considering all the casuistically conceivable circumstances of what may or might happen, or might have or ought to have happened, to the Particles of the Eucharist. This gentleman, then, who as an expert on Particles still enjoys a certain reputation, later published a series of "Sketches from My Life" in a theological literary journal, revealing among other things this experience with Leni, whom he shamelessly and unimaginatively abbreviates to "a certain L.G., at that time aged twelve." He describes Leni's "flaming eyes," her "sensuous mouth," patronizingly notes her dialect-tinged pronunciation, describes her parents' home as "typically nouveau riche, vulgar," and concludes with the sentence: "A craving for the most holy of objects, expressed in such proletarian and materialistic terms, naturally obliged me to refuse to administer the same." Since Leni's parents, while neither overwhelmingly religious nor particularly church-minded, were nevertheless so conditioned by the part of the country and the milieu in which they lived that they regarded as a blemish, indeed a disgrace, the fact that "Leni had not yet joined the others," they saw to it that Leni, at the age of fourteen and a half, when she was already in boarding school, "joined the others," as the saying goes; and since Leni had already—according to convincing statements by Marja van Doorn—entered upon womanhood, the church ceremony was a total failure, the secular one also. So passionately had Leni longed for this piece of bread that her entire sensory apparatus had been ready to fall into ecstasy—"And then" (as she described it to the shocked Marja van Doorn) "that pale, fragile, dry, tasteless thing was placed on my tongue—I almost spat it out again!" Marja crossed herself a number of times and found it surprising that the tangible sensuousness offered: candles, incense, organ- and choir-music, had not been able to help Leni over this disappointment. Not even the customary banquet of ham, asparagus, and vanilla ice cream with whipped cream could help Leni over this disappointment. That Leni herself is a "Particlist" is something she proves daily by gathering up all the bread crumbs from her plate and putting them into her mouth (Hans and Grete).

Although obscenities will be avoided wherever possible in this account, for the sake of completeness it may be in order to describe the sexual enlightenment offered to the girls before they left boarding school—the youngest at sixteen, the oldest at twenty-one—by the school's religious instructor (who admitted Leni to her First Communion solely at the principal's insistence), a youngish, similarly ascetic type by the name of Horn. In a soft voice, availing himself almost exclusively of culinary symbolism and with not so much as a hint of accurate biological details, he compared the result of sexual intercourse, which he called a "necessary reproductive process," with "strawberries and whipped cream," rambling on in improvised analogies intended to describe permissible and prohibited kisses, analogies in which "snails" played a (to the girls) unaccountable role. The fact is that Leni, while the soft voice held forth in indescribable, purely culinary symbolism on indescribable details of kissing and sexual intercourse, for the first time in her life blushed (Margret); and, being herself incapable of remorse—a fact that made confession easy for her, reducing it to a routine act in which she could reel off a string of words—this attempt at enlightenment must obviously have had an impact on certain of her as yet undiscovered emotional centers. If we are to try and present Leni's direct, proletarian, almost inspired sensuality with reasonable credibility, the following must be added: she was not immodest, hence her first blush must be recorded as a sensation. In any event, sensational, agonizing, and painful was how this process of violent blushing, occurring beyond her control, seemed to Leni. There is no need to reiterate that an immense erotic and sexual anticipation slumbered in Leni, or that for a religious instructor to give such an explanation for something that was held up to her, along with Holy Communion, as a sacrament, intensified her indignation and confusion to the point of provoking her first blush. Stammering with rage, crimson-cheeked, she simply left the classroom, thus earning herself another D, this time in religion, on her final report card.

Also repeatedly drummed into her during religious instruction without arousing any enthusiasm in her: the three mountains of the Western world—Golgotha, the Acropolis, and the Capitol, although she did not dislike Golgotha, a mountain known to her from Bible instruction to be merely a hill and not in the Western world at all. Bearing in mind that, despite all this, Leni still remembers the Lord's Prayer and the Ave Maria, in fact still makes use of these prayers; that she can still recite a few fragments of the Rosary; that her association with the Virgin Mary seems perfectly natural to her—this might be the appropriate place to remark that Leni's religious gifts have remained as unrecognized as her sensuality—that in her, of her, a great mystic might have been discovered and fashioned.

We must now finally get down to the task of at least sketching the design for a memorial to a female person who unfortunately can no longer be either visited or summoned or cited as a witness; she died at the end of 1942 in still unexplained circumstances, as a result not of direct violence but of the threat of direct violence and the neglect that those around her allowed her to suffer. B.H.T. and Leni were probably the only people whom this person loved; her name in private life did not yield even to painstaking research, nor did her place of origin or her background; the only name she was known by—and for this there are witnesses enough, Leni, Margret, Marja, and that selfsame former book antiquarian's apprentice who considers himself adequately authenticated by the initials B.H.T.—was her convent name: Sister Rahel. Also her nickname: Haruspica.

Her age, at the time when she first met Leni and simultaneously this B.H.T. (1937–38), may be estimated at around forty-five. She was short, wiry (not even Leni, only B.H.T., did she tell that she had once been German Junior champion in the 80-meter women's hurdles!); probably [in 1937–38 she had every reason to keep details of her origin and education to herself] she was what in those days used to be called a "highly educated person," which by no means precludes the possibility of her having a master's degree and perhaps (under another name, of course) even a Ph.D. Her height can only be guessed at from the recollections of witnesses: about five foot one; her weight around, say, 98 pounds; color of hair: black streaked with gray; eyes: light blue; possibility of Celtic, also Jewish, origin, not to be discounted. This B.H.T., now working as a librarian (nongraduate) in a medium-sized public library where he studies the old-books catalogue and exerts a certain influence on the new-acquisitions policy, a (for his age) relatively burned-out person, kind, although rather lacking in initiative and temperament, must, despite a difference in age of at least twenty years, have been in love with this nun. His managing to evade military service until 1944, thus representing a kind of "missing link" between Leni and Sister Rahel (when he was called up in the fifth year of the war he was almost twenty-six and in perfect health, so he maintains), bespeaks a dogged and systematically functioning intelligence.

In any event, he brightened up, became almost enthusiastic, when addressed on the subject of Sister Rahel. He is a nonsmoker, a bachelor, and—to judge by the odors in his two-room apartment—an excellent cook. For him the only books are old books: for new publications he has nothing but contempt: "A new book is not a book at all" (B.H.T.). Prematurely bald, existing on a presumably good but one-sided diet, his organism inclines toward the formation of fatty deposits: a large-pored nose, as well as a tendency toward small growths behind the ears, observed over the course of numerous visits, point to this. By nature not very talkative, he positively bubbles over with information when the subject is Rahel-Haruspica; and for Leni, known to him from the nun's tales merely as that "uniquely lovely blond girl for whom many wonderful and many painful things are in store," he harbors an infatuation, both idealistic and youthful, which might tempt the Au. (supposing he were inclined to such things and were not himself in love with Leni), at this late stage, some thirty-four years later, to pair off the two. Whatever peculiar traits, covert and overt, this B.H.T.-fellow may have, of one thing there is no doubt: he is faithful. Possibly even to himself.

Much could be said about this fellow but it would be irrelevant since he has almost nothing to do with Leni directly and can only render certain services as a medium.

It would be a mistake to suppose that Leni had suffered at this boarding school; no, something wonderful happened to her there: she fared as all favorites of Fortune are wont to fare: she fell into the right hands. What she learned in the classroom was more or less uninteresting; her private lessons from the quiet and kindly Sister Cecilia were important and bore fruit. The crucial figure in Leni's life, at least as crucial as the Soviet individual who cropped up later, was Sister Rahel, who (in 1936!) was forbidden to teach, the only duties she performed being those held in very low esteem: the duties of what the girls called a "floor sister," and her social status was roughly that of a not very superior cleaning woman.

Her duties were to waken the girls on time, supervise their morning ablutions, and explain—something the biology sister steadfastly refused to do—what was happening to them and in them when they were suddenly confronted with the evidence that they had entered upon womanhood; and she had a further duty that was regarded by all the other nuns as disgusting, as being beyond the call of duty, but that was carried out by Sister Rahel with nothing short of enthusiasm, with devoted attention to detail: the inspection of the products of youthful digestion in solid and liquid form. The girls were required not to flush away these products into the invisible regions before Rahel had inspected them. She did this for the fourteen-year-old girls in her charge with a quiet diagnostic composure that astounded the girls. Need it be pointed out that Leni, whose interest in her digestive process had hitherto remained unsatisfied, became a truly enthusiastic adept at the hands of Rahel? In most cases a glance was enough for Rahel, enabling her to state with accuracy the physical and mental condition of the girl in question, and, since she could predict even scholastic achievement on the basis of excrements, she used to be positively beleaguered before the writing of term papers, and from one year to the next (starting in 1933) she inherited the nickname Haruspica, as she was dubbed by one of her former pupils who later tried her hand at journalism. It was assumed (an assumption confirmed by Leni, who later became Rahel's confidante), that she kept carefully detailed records. She accepted her nickname as an endearment to which she was entitled. Taking two hundred and forty school days as an annual average, times twelve girls and five years of floor-service (as a kind of monastic duty sergeant), it is no trick to calculate that Sister Rahel kept statistical records and condensed analyses of some twenty-eight thousand eight hundred digestive processes: an astounding compendium that would probably fetch any price as a scatalogical and urinological document. Presumably it has been destroyed as trash! The Au.'s analyses, the conduct and expressions relating to Rahel that appear from the direct reports of B.H.T., from the indirect (filtered through Marja) reports of Leni, the in turn direct reports of Margret, permit the assumption that Rahel's training had been in three scientific areas: medicine, biology, philosophy—all suffused by a theological admixture of wholly mystical origin.

Rahel also took a hand in areas for which she was not actually responsible: beauty culture; and hair, skin, eyes, ears, hairdos, footwear, lingerie. When it is remembered that she advised the black-haired Margret to wear bottle green, and the fair-haired Leni to wear a subdued fiery red and, on the occasion of a house dance with the inmates of a Catholic students' hostel, cinnamon-red shoes; that for the care of Leni's complexion she recommended almond bran, regarded ice water as not unconditionally, merely conditionally, wholesome, her overall tendency may be summed up in negative terms: she was not the old-fashioned soap-and-water type. If we go on to add that she not only did not *dis*courage but actually *en*couraged the use of lipstick (in moderation and good taste, according to type), it is clear that she was far in advance of her time and most certainly of her environment. She was downright strict in her insistence on care of the hair, on vigorous, prolonged brushing, especially at bedtime.

Her position in the convent was ambiguous. By most of her sister-nuns she was regarded as an existence halfway between toilet attendant and cleaning woman, an attitude which, even if that is what she had been, was shameful enough. A number of them respected her, a few were afraid of her. With the mother superior she was on a footing of "permanently strained respect" (B.H.T.). The mother superior, an austere and intelligent ash-blond beauty who, a year after Leni left school, shed her habit and offered her services to a Nazi women's organization, did not even decry Rahel's advice on the subject of cosmetics, although it was contrary to the spirit of the convent. In view of the fact that the mother superior bore the nickname "Tigress," that her chief subject was mathematics, her secondary subjects French and geography, one can understand that she found Haruspica's conduct as an "excremental mystic" merely ludicrous and not dangerous. She considered it beneath the dignity of a lady to vouchsafe so much as a glance at her own excrement (B.H.T.) and regarded the whole thing as more or less "heathenish," although (B.H.T. again) it is said to have been precisely the heathenish element that drove her into that Nazi organization for women. In all fairness one thing must be said (all this according to B.H.T.): even after leaving the convent she never betrayed Rahel. She is described by Leni, Margret, and B.H.T. as a "proud person." Although, judging by all available statements, she was a very beautiful and most certainly "erotically susceptible" person (Margret), she remained, even after her resignation from the convent, unmarried, probably out of pride; because she wished to show no weaknesses, to avoid exposing herself in any way. At the end of the war, scarcely fifty years old, she disappeared between Lvov and Cernauti, where, with the rank of a senior civil servant, she had been implementing a high-level "cultural policy." Most regrettable. The Au. would have so much liked to "interrogate" her.

Seriously speaking, Rahel had no functions to perform at the school on either the educational or medical level, yet she performed on both levels; all she was required to do was report obvious cases of diarrhea and suspected threats of infection, also noticeable lack of cleanliness in terms of the digestive process as well as breaches of accepted standards of morality. This latter she never did. She considered it highly important to give the girls a little talk, on their very first day, on cleansing methods to follow every type of bowel movement. Pointing out the importance of maintaining all muscles, especially the abdominal ones, in a constant state of flexibility and efficiency, for which she advocated field athletics and calisthenics, she would proceed to her favorite topic: that for a healthy and—she would stress—intelligent person it was possible to perform this bodily function without so much as a scrap of paper. However, since this ideal state was never, or rarely, achieved, she would explain in detail how, should paper be necessary, it was to be used.

She had read—and here B.H.T. is an invaluable source—a great deal about such things, almost the entire bagnio and prison literature, and had conducted intensive research into all the memoirs of prisoners (criminal or political). Silliness and giggling from the girls during this talk was something for which she was fully prepared.

It must be stated here, since it has been verified by Margret and Leni, that when Sister Rahel looked at the first of Leni's bowel movements which she was called upon to inspect she went into a kind of ecstasy. Turning to Leni, who was not used to a confrontation of this kind, she said: "My girl, you're one of Fortune's favorites—like me."

So when, a few days later, Leni achieved "paperless" status, simply because that "muscle business" amused her (Leni to Marja—confirmed by Margret), an unbreakable bond of fellow feeling was created that provided Leni with some advance consolation for all the educational reverses that were in store for her.

Now it would be a mistake to allow the impression that Sister Rahel displayed her genius in the excremental sphere only. After a lengthy and involved training, she had become first a biologist, then a physician, later a philosopher, had converted to Catholicism, and entered the convent to "instruct the young" in a blend of biology, medicine, philosophy, and theology; but during the very first year of her teaching activity her teaching permit had been revoked by the General Council in Rome because she was suspected of biologism and mystical materialism. The punishment of being demoted to floor duties had actually been designed to make convent life unacceptable to her, and one had been prepared to accord her an "honorable" secularization (all this Rahel to B.H.T., verbally); but not only had she accepted the demotion as a promotion: she had also felt and regarded and seen her floor duties as offering far better opportunities for applying her doctrines than did the classroom. Since the year in which her difficulties with the Order happened to occur was 1933, one had refrained from actually expelling her, hence she still had five more years as a "toilet attendant" (Rahel on Rahel to B.H.T.).

The obtaining of cleaning materials, toilet paper, antiseptics, and even bed linen, etc., was reason enough for her to go by bicycle from time to time to the neighboring medium-sized university town, where she spent many hours in the university library, later many days in that well-stocked antiquarian bookstore where she struck up a platonic but passionate friendship with this B.H.T. He allowed her to browse to her heart's content among his boss's stock, even placing at her disposal—contrary to regulations—a hand catalogue for internal use only; he allowed her to read in numerous corners, even letting her have some of the coffee from his Thermos flask, indeed now and again, when her absorption seemed unduly prolonged, even giving her one of his sandwiches. Her main interest was pharmacological, mystical, and biological literature, also herbal lore, and in the space of two years she had developed into a specialist in a delicate area: that of scatological aberrations, insofar as these could be explored in the mystical literature so plentifully represented in the antiquarian bookstore.

Although everything—everything—has been done to clarify Sister Rahel's background and origin: beyond the statements made by B.H.T., Leni, and Margret there was no more to be learned; a second and third visit to Sister Cecilia brought to light no further information on their former sister-nun; all that the Au.'s persistence accomplished was that Sister Cecilia blushed—it is freely admitted that the blushing of an old lady of over seventy with milky tones in her skin is not an unpleasant sight. A fourth attempt—the Au. is persistent, as can be seen—was thwarted at the convent entrance: he was no longer admitted. Whether he will succeed in finding out more in the Order's archives and personnel files in Rome depends on whether he can afford the time and expense of the trip and—most important of all—whether he will be granted access to the Order's secrets. There remains the duty to recall the situation as it was in 1937-38: an eager little nun, with a mania for mysticism and a mania for biology, suspected of scatology, accused of biologism and materialistic mysticism, sitting in the dark corner of the antiquarian bookstore, is offered coffee and sandwiches by a young man, a (then) not even remotely bald or greasy young man. This genre picture, worthy of perpetuation by a Dutch master of the stature of a Vermeer, would require, in order to do justice to the political situation at home and abroad, a scarlet background, blood-flecked clouds, if it is borne in mind that somewhere the Storm Troopers were always on the march and that the threat of war was greater in 1938 than in the following year when it actually did break out; and even if this passion of Rahel's for digestive matters is found to be excessively mystical, her preoccupation with internal secretion (to the point where she yearned to discover the precise composition of that substance known as sperm) bizarre—*one* thing must be said for her: it was she who, on the basis of her private (forbidden) experiments with urine, gave the young book-antiquarian the advice which enabled him to evade service in the German Army, by explaining to him in detail, while he drank his coffee (with which she occasionally spattered priceless antiquarian rarities—her respect for the outward appearance of any book was slight), what he must drink, eat, and swallow in the way of tinctures and pills in order to achieve a not only superficial but permanent classification as "unfit" when his urinc was examined at recruiting time; when all is said and done, her knowledge and the results of her reading enabled her to submit his urine to a "progressive plan" (verbatim quotation from Rahel, verified by B.H.T.) that continued to guarantee sufficient albumen throughout the most varied tests even during a stay in army hospital of one, two, or three days. This information merely as consolation for all those who feel the lack of a political angle here. Unfortunately, B.H.T. lacked the nerve to pass on this "progressive plan" in all its details to potential young army recruits. "As a civic employee" he was afraid of running into trouble with his superiors.

It would probably have been a source of enormous pleasure to Rahel (Au.'s hypothesis) had she been permitted at least once to spend a week in a boarding school for boys, performing similar duties and obtaining similar insights to those she had been accustomed to perform and obtain among girls. Since the literature on the digestive differences between men and women was in those days meager, she had to rely solely on assumptions that gradually consolidated into a prejudice: she regarded almost all men as "hard stoolers." Had her desire become known in Rome or elsewhere, she would naturally have been instantly excommunicated and expelled.

With the same passion with which she inspected the john bowls, she would look each morning into the eyes of the girls in her charge and order eye-bathings, for which she kept a small selection of eyecups and a jug of spring water in readiness; she would immediately discover any sign, even the slightest, of inflammation or trachoma, and invariably—to a far greater degree than when describing digestive processes—went into ecstasy as she explained to the girls that the retina was approximately as thick or as thin as a cigarette paper but consisted in addition of three layers of cells, the sensory cells, the dipolar cells, and the ganglion cells, and that in the first layer alone (approximately one third as thick or as thin as a cigarette paper) there were some six million cones and one hundred million tiny rods distributed, not regularly but irregularly, over the surface of the retina. Their eyes, she would preach to the girls, were an immense, irreplaceable treasure; the retina was only one of the eye's fourteen layers, with a total of seven or eight layers each of which was in turn separated from the next. So when she then got going on ganglia, papillae, villi, and cilia, her second nickname would sometimes be murmured: Silly Billy Sister, or Sister Silly Billy.

One must remember that Rahel's opportunities for explaining anything to the girls were occasional and limited; the girls' timetable was fixed, and most of them really did regard her as being responsible for not much more than the toilet paper. Needless to say, she also spoke of sweat, pus, menstrual blood, and—somewhat at length—of saliva; it is almost superfluous to state that she was strongly opposed to excessive tooth-brushing; in any event she would tolerate vigorous tooth-brushing first thing in the morning only against her convictions, and even then only after vehement protests on the part of parents. As well as the girls' eyes, she also inspected their skin—unfortunately, as it turned out, because on a few occasions she was accused by parents of immodest physical contact—not breast or abdomen, merely arms above and below the elbow. Later she proceeded to explain to the girls that, when one had acquired some personal experience, a glance at the excrements ought really only to confirm what one was aware of anyway on rising: the degree of well-being; and that it was almost superfluous—after sufficient experience—to look at them, unless one was not certain of one's condition and needed a glance at them for further confirmation (Margret and B.H.T.).

When Leni feigned illness, which happened more and more often as time went by, she was sometimes allowed even to smoke a cigarette in Sister Rahel's little room; Rahel explained that at Leni's age, and for a woman, more than three to five cigarettes was not good. When she grew up she should never smoke more than seven or eight cigarettes, certainly remain below ten. Who would dare contradict the value of education when it can be stated that at forty-eight Leni still adheres to this rule, and that she has now begun, using a sheet of wrapping paper measuring five feet by five (in the present state of her finances, white paper of this size is more than she can afford), to realize a dream for which she has hitherto lacked the time: to paint a faithful picture of a cross section of *one* layer of the retina; she is actually determined to reproduce six million cones and one hundred million tiny rods, and all this with the child's paint box that was left behind by her son and for which she occasionally buys additional little cakes of cheap paint. When we consider that her daily output is at most five hundred rodlets or conelets, her annual output roughly two hundred thousand, we can see that for the next five years she will be fully occupied, and perhaps we shall understand why she has given up her job as a florist's assistant for the sake of her rod- and cone-painting. She calls her picture "Part of the Retina of the Left Eye of the Virgin Mary alias Rahel."

Is anyone surprised to learn that Leni likes to sing as she paints? Texts to which she randomly adds Schubert and folk-song elements and what she hears on the program "Around the Home" (Hans), mixed with rhythms and tunes that draw from a Schirtenstein "not only emotion but attentiveness and respect" (Schirtenstein). Her song repertoire is obviously more extensive than her repertoire on the piano: the Au. is in possession of a tape made for him by Grete Helzen to which he can scarcely listen without the tears streaming down his cheeks (Au.). Leni sings rather softly, in a dry, firm voice that only sounds soft because of her shyness. She sings like someone singing from a dungeon. What is she singing?

> Silvery is she in the mirror
> A stranger's portrait in the twilight
> Fading duskly in the mirror
> And she shivers at its purity
>
> My vows are to be unchaste and poor
> Oft has unchastity sweetened my innocence
> What we do under God's heaven is sure
> To bring us on God's earth to penitence. . . .

The voice it was of the noblest of rivers, of the free-born Rhine—but where is he who was born, like the Rhine, to remain free all his life and to fulfill his heart's desire—from propitious heights and that sacred womb, like the Rhine?

When no peace came in the war's first year
With spring's returning breath
The soldier saw his duty clear
And died a hero's death

Yet I knew thee better
Than I ever knew mankind
I understood the silence of the spheres
Words of mankind I never understood. . . .
And I learned to love among the flowers. . . .

The last verse is sung fairly often and is heard in four different variations on the tape, once even in Beat rhythm.

As we see, Leni treats otherwise hallowed texts with a good deal of freedom; depending on her mood, she combines elements of both music and text:

The voice of the free-born Rhine—kyrieleis
And I learned to love among the flowers—kyrieleis
Break ye the tyrants' yoke—kyrieleis
My vows are to be unchaste and poor—kyrieleis
As a girl I had an affair with the sky—kyrieleis
Superb, violet, he loves me with man-love—kyrieleis
Ancestral marble turned to gray—kyrieleis
Till it is expressed the way I mean it, the secret of my soul—kyrieleis

So we see that Leni, beyond being merely occupied, is productively occupied.

Without lapsing into any misplaced symbolism, Rahel gave Leni, who was invariably alarmed when confronted with the evidence of womanhood, a detailed explanation of the process of sexual intercourse, without the slightest necessity for Leni or her to blush: such explanations, of course, had to remain secret, for Rahel was clearly exceeding her authority. Perhaps this explains why Leni blushed so violently and angrily when a year and a half later during her official sex-education course she was fobbed off with "strawberries and whipped cream." Nor did Rahel hesitate to apply the term "classical architecture" to the various shapes of bowel movements (B.H.T.).

It was also during her very first month at boarding school that Leni found another friend for life, that Margret Zeist whose reputation as a "hussy" had preceded her; the well-nigh unmanageable daughter of extremely pious parents who were no more able "to cope with her" than any of her former teachers had been. Margret was always cheerful, was considered "full of fun," a dark-haired little person who, compared with Leni, seemed downright garrulous. It was Rahel who, while inspecting Margret's skin (shoulders and upper arms), discovered after two weeks that the girl was carrying on with men. Since Margret is the sole witness to these events, a certain caution may be advisable here; personally, however, the Au. gained an impression of absolute credibility on Margret's part.

In Margret's opinion, Rahel found this out not only with her "almost infallible chemical instinct" but also by assessing the physical condition of her skin, of which Rahel later maintained, in a private conversation with Margret, that it "had radiated a tenderness both received and given," whereupon—to Margret's credit—Margret blushed, not for the first and far from the last time in her life. Moreover, she admitted that at night she used to let herself out of the convent by a method she could not divulge and meet the village boys, not the men. Men turned her off, she said, because they stank, she knew this from her experience with a man, in fact with the very teacher who had claimed to be unable to cope with her. "Oh," she added in her dry, Rhenish intonation, "he managed to cope with me all right." Boys, she said, of her own age, that was what she liked, men stank—and—she candidly added—it was so wonderful the way the boys enjoyed themselves, some of them shouted for joy—so she would too, besides it wasn't good for the boys to "do it alone"; the point was, it gave her, Margret, pleasure to give them pleasure—and it must be noted here that for the first time we see Rahel bursting into tears: "It was just terrible, the way she cried, and I got scared, and now, lying here, forty-eight years old and with syphilis and God knows what else, now at last I know why she cried so terribly" (Margret in the hospital). Rahel, after her tears had dried up—which, according to Margret, must have taken quite a while—looked at her thoughtfully, without any hostility, and said: "Yes, you're a *fille de joie* all right." "An allusion which at the time, of course, I didn't understand" (Margret). She had to promise—and solemnly at that—not to lead Leni onto similar paths, nor to divulge to her how she let herself out of the school; although Leni was among those marked out for the bestowal of much joy, she was not a *fille de joie.* And Margret swore she would not, kept her word too, and "anyway Leni was never in any danger of that, she knew what she wanted." And besides, Rahel was right, it was a skin that was loved with such tenderness and desired so intensely, especially the skin of her breast, and it had been quite incredible, all the things the boys had done with it. Asked by Rahel whether she had carried on with one or many, Margret blushed for the second time in twenty minutes and said—again in her flat, dry, Rhenish intonation: "Only with one at a time." And once again Rahel had wept, murmuring that it wasn't good, what Margret was doing, not good at all and could only end in disaster.

After that, Margret's stay in boarding school did not last long; it all came out, what she was doing with the boys in the village (most of them altar boys), there was trouble with the boys' parents, with the priest, with the girls' parents, there was an investigation of the case at which Margret and all the boys refused to testify—Margret had to leave school at the end of her first year. For Leni there remained: a friend for life who later was often to prove her worth in situations that were dicey if not extremely dangerous.

One year later, not in the least embittered but with a still unsatisfied curiosity, Leni joined the labor force: as an apprentice (official designation: junior clerk) in the office of her father, at whose urgent request she became a member of that Nazi organization for girls in the uniform of which she even (may God forgive her) managed to look nice. Leni—it must be said—attended the "den evenings" without enthusiasm—and it must also be added, before misunderstandings arise, that Leni had no conception whatever, not the slightest, of the political dimensions of Nazism; she did not like the brown uniforms at all—the Storm Troopers' uniform was particularly distasteful to her, and those who feel able to some degree to put themselves in her place in terms of her scatalogical interests and of her scatalogical training at the hands of Sister Rahel will know, or at least suspect, why she found this brown so exceedingly unpleasant. Her halfhearted attendance at the "den evenings," which she finally dropped because from September 1939 on she was working in her father's business as a "war-essential" employee, had other reasons: she found the whole atmosphere there too redolent of convent piety, for the group to which she was assigned had been "commandeered" by a strong-minded young Catholic woman whose intention it was to infiltrate "this business," and who, after making sure—without due thoroughness, unfortunately—that the twelve girls in her charge were trustworthy—restructured whole evenings by devoting them to the singing of songs to the Virgin Mary, meditations on the Rosary, etc. Now Leni, as can be imagined, had nothing against songs to the Virgin Mary, nothing against the Rosary, etc., the only thing was—at this point in time she was barely seventeen—that after two and a half years of painfully endured convent-school piety she was not all that interested, and she found it boring. Needless to say, the infiltration attempts on the part of the young lady—one Gretel Mareike—did not pass unnoticed, she was denounced by a girl—one Paula Schmitz—Leni was even called as a witness, remained (duly coached by Gretel Mareike's father) steadfast, denied without batting an eyelid (as did ten of the twelve girls, incidentally) that they had sung songs to the Virgin Mary, with the result that Gretel

Mareike was spared considerable suffering; what she was not spared was two months' Gestapo arrest and interrogation, which was "more than enough for her"—and that was all she ever said about it (condensed from several conversations with Marja van Doorn).

By now it is the summer of 1939. Leni enters upon the most talkative period of her life, one that will last for a year and three quarters. She is known as a beauty, obtains her driver's license by special authority, enjoys driving, plays tennis, accompanies her father to conventions and on business trips. Leni is waiting for a man "whom she means to love, to whom she can give herself unreservedly," for whom she is already "dreaming up daring caresses—he is to find joy in me and I in him" (Margret). Leni never misses an opportunity to go dancing, this summer she likes to sit on terraces, drink iced coffee, and play a little at being the "society woman." There are some startling photos of her from this period: she could still apply for the title of "most German girl in the city," in the district, in fact—perhaps even in the province, or that political-historical-geographical entity that has become known as the German Reich. She could have appeared as a saint (also as Mary Magdalene) in a miracle play, modeled for an advertisement for face cream, perhaps could even have acted in movies; her eyes are now quite dark, almost black, she wears her thick blond hair as described on page 1, and not even the brief Gestapo interrogation and the fact that Gretel Mareike has spent two months in detention have substantially impaired her self-confidence.

Because she feels that not even Rahel has told her enough about the biological differences between men and women, she does some intensive research on the subject. She thumbs through encyclopedias, with not much result, ransacks—with just as little result—her father's and mother's libraries; sometimes she goes to see Rahel on Sunday afternoons, taking long walks with her through the convent grounds and entreating her for information. After some hesitation Rahel relents and explains, once again without the slightest necessity for either of them to blush, further details that she had withheld two years earlier: the instrument of male sexuality, its stimulation and stimulability, with all the attendant consequences and pleasures; and since Leni asks for illustrated material on the subject and Rahel refuses to give it to her, saying it is not good to look at pictures of it, Leni telephones a book dealer for advice, speaking (quite unnecessarily) in a disguised voice, and is directed to the "Civic Health Museum," where under "Sex Life" the main displays consist of venereal diseases: starting with ordinary clap and proceeding by way of soft chancre to "Spanish collar" and covering every phase of syphilis, all naturalistically displayed by true-to-life colored plaster models, Leni learns of the existence of this unwholesome world—and is infuriated; not that she was prudish, what made her so angry was the fact that in this museum sex and venereal disease appeared to be regarded as identical; this pessimistic naturalism enraged her no less than the symbolism of her religious instructor. The Health Museum seemed to her a variation of the "strawberries and whipped cream" (witness Margret, who—blushing again—refused to contribute personally to Leni's enlightenment).

Now the impression may have been given that Leni's interests were confined to a wholesome and healthy world. Not at all: her materialistically sensual concretism went so far that she began to be less brusque in declining the numerous advances to which she was exposed, and she finally yielded to the ardent entreaties of a young architect from her father's office whom she found agreeable, and consented to a rendezvous. Weekend, summertime, a luxury hotel on the Rhine, dancing on the terrace in the evening, she blond, he blond, she seventeen, he twenty-three, both healthy—surely there will be a happy ending or at least a happy night—but nothing came of it; after the second dance Leni left the hotel, paid for the unused single room where she had hastily unpacked her housecoat (= bathrobe) and toilet articles, and went to see Margret, whom she told that during the very first dance she had felt that "the fellow" did not have "tender hands," and that a certain fleeting sense of being in love had instantly evaporated.

At this point there is a distinct feeling that the reader, thus far fairly patient, is becoming impatient and wondering to himself: For God's sake, is this Leni girl supposed to be perfect? Answer: almost. Other readers—depending on their ideological point of departure—will put the question differently: For God's sake, what kind of dirty-minded hussy is this Leni? Answer: She isn't one at all. She is merely waiting for "the right man," who fails to appear; she continues to be pestered, invited for dates and weekend trips, never feels shocked, merely pestered; even the most embarrassing propositions—often phrased with considerable coarseness—that are sometimes whispered in her ear arouse no indignation, she merely shakes her head. She loves wearing pretty clothes, swims, rows, plays tennis, even her sleep is not restless, and "it was a real treat to watch her enjoy her breakfast—I tell you, it was just a treat the way she ate her two fresh rolls, two slices of black bread, her soft-boiled egg, a bit of honey, and sometimes a slice of ham—and the coffee, really hot, with hot milk and sugar—I tell you, you really should've seen it because it was a treat—a daily treat, to watch that girl enjoy her food" (Marja van Doorn).

She also likes going to movies, "so she could have a little cry in the dark in peace" (quotation via Marja van Doorn). A movie such as *Unshackled Hands,* for instance, makes two of her handkerchiefs so damp that Marja mistakenly assumed Leni had caught cold at the movie. A movie such as *Rasputin, Demon Lover,* leaves her completely cold, as does *The Battle Hymn of Leuthen* or *Hot Blood.* "After movies like that" (Marja van Doorn), "not only were her hankies not damp, they looked as if they had just been ironed, that's how dry they were." *The Girl from Fanö,* on the other hand, drew tears from her, but not quite as much as *Unshackled Hands.*

She gets to know her brother, whom so far she has rarely seen; he is two years older than she, was only eight when he went to the boarding school where he remained for eleven years. Most of his school vacations have been utilized to further his education: trips to Italy, France, England, Austria, Spain, because his parents were so keen on turning him into what in fact he was turned into: "a truly well-educated young man." Again according to M.v.D., young Heinrich Gruyten's mother regarded "her own background as too low-class," and since she herself, brought up and educated in France by nuns, retained a certain "nervous and at times excessive sensitivity" throughout her life, we may assume her to have wanted something similar for her son. On the basis of available information she seems to have succeeded.

We must devote a short time to this Heinrich Gruyten, who for twelve years, like a disembodied spirit, like a god almost, a blend of the young Goethe and the young Winckelmann with a touch of Novalis, lived a life apart from his family, occasionally—some four times in eleven years—making an appearance at home, and of whom all Leni knew thus far was that he "is so sweet, so terribly sweet and nice." True, this is not much and does sound rather like her First Communion; and since not even M.v.D. has much more than Leni to say about him ("Very well educated, beautiful manners, but never proud, never"), and since Margret saw him only twice officially in 1939, when she was invited to the Gruytens' for coffee, and once more—unofficially—in 1940, one rather chilly April night, the night before Heinrich was sent off as a tank gunner to conquer Denmark for the aforesaid German Reich, Margret, in view of Leni's reticence and M.v.D.'s lack of knowledge, remains the sole nonclerical witness.

This reporter feels awkward about describing the circumstances under which he obtained information on Heinrich from a woman of barely fifty who is suffering from venereal disease. All Margret's remarks have been typed verbatim from a tape, they have not been doctored. Well, let us begin: Margret became quite ecstatic, her face (already considerably disfigured) taking on a look of childlike fervor as she started right off by saying: "Yes, I loved that man. I really did love him." Asked whether he had loved her too, she shook her head, not as if to say No, rather as if to express doubt, certainly not—as is attested here under oath—in any affectation of martyrdom. "Dark hair, you know, and light eyes, and—oh, I don't know—noble-looking, yes that's it, noble. He had no idea of the extent of his charm, and for him I'd have literally walked the streets, literally, so he could read books, or whatever else it was he learned besides how to read books and judge churches, study chorales, listen to music—Latin, Greek—and all about architecture; well, he was like Leni—a dark version of her, and I loved him. Twice I was there in the afternoon for coffee and saw him—in August '39; and on April 7, 1940, he phoned me—I was already married to that rich guy I'd hooked—he phoned me, and I went to him at once, to Flensburg, and when I got there I found the men had been confined to barracks, and it was cold outside; so I must have got there on the eighth. They were quartered in a school, everything packed so they could leave that night, whether they flew or went by ship—I don't know. Confined to barracks. No one knew, and no one ever found out, that I was with him, neither Leni nor her parents nor anyone else. He got out of the building in spite of the orders to remain inside. Over the wall of the girls' john into the school playground. No hotel room, not even one in a rooming house. The only place open was a bar, in we went, and a girl let us have her room in exchange for all the money I had on me, two hundred marks, and my ruby ring, and all his money, a hundred and twenty, and a gold cigarette case. He loved me, I loved him—and it made no difference that the room and all that was so tarty. Makes no difference, makes no difference at all. Yes" (the tape was carefully monitored twice to see if Margret had actually used the present tense: makes no difference, makes no difference at all. Objective conclusion: she did). "Well, and soon after that he was dead. What a crazy, crazy waste." When asked how the surprising word "waste" had occurred to her in this context, Margret replies (typed verbatim from the tape): "Well you see, all that education, all those good looks, all that masculine vigor—and twenty years old, how many times, how many times might we—could we—have made love, and not only in tarts' rooms like that one, but out of doors, once it got warmer —and it was all so pointless—waste, that's what I call it."

Since Margret, Leni, and M.v.D. all persist in what amounted to an iconolatrous attitude toward Heinrich G., some rather more objective information was sought here too: it was obtainable only from two parchment-skinned Jesuit fathers, both over seventy, both seated in studies that were impregnated with pipe smoke, editing manuscripts which, although for two different periodicals, dealt with similar subjects (Opening to the Left or to the Right?), one a Frenchman, the other a German (possibly a Swiss), the first with graying fair hair, the second with graying black hair; both wise, benign, shrewd, humane, both exclaiming as soon as they were asked: "Ah yes, Heinrich, the Gruyten boy!" (identical wording, including grammatical and syntactical details, even punctuation, since the Frenchman also spoke in German), both put down their pipes, leaned back in their chairs, pushed aside the manuscripts, shook their heads, then, pregnant with memories, nodded their heads, sighed deeply, and began to speak: at this point total identity ends and a merely partial one begins. Since one of them had to be consulted in Rome, the other near Freiburg, preparatory telephone calls over lengthy distances in order to arrange appointments had been unavoidable, and the result was considerable expense which, it must be said, did not eventually pay off, aside from the "human value" of such encounters, a value that might be gained at much less expense. For these two fathers did no more than contribute to an enhanced idolization of the deceased Heinrich G.: one of them, the Frenchman, said: "He was so German, so German and so noble." The other one said: "He was so noble, so noble and so German." In order to simplify our report, the two men, for as long as we require them, will be called J.[esuit]I and J.II. J.I: "We haven't had another such intelligent and gifted student in the past twenty-five years." J.II: "For the past twenty-eight years we've not had another such gifted and intelligent pupil." J.I: "There was a potential Kleist in that boy." J.II: "In that boy there was a potential

Hölderlin." J.I: "We never tried to win him for the priesthood." J.II: "No attempts were made to win him for the Order." J.I: "It would have been a waste anyway." J.II: "Even those of the brothers who thought only of the Order refused to try such a thing." Asked about scholastic achievements, J.I said: "Oh well, he simply got an A in everything, even in phys. ed., but there was nothing boring about it, and every one of his teachers —every single one—dreaded the moment when a choice of career would have to be faced." J.II: "Well, needless to say his marks were very good all the way through. Later on we created a special category for him: Excellent. But what career could he have taken up? That was what frightened us all!" J.I: "He might have become a diplomat, a cabinet minister, an architect, or a jurist—in any case, a poet." J.II: "A great teacher, a great artist, and—inevitably and always, a poet." J.I: "There was only one thing he was not fitted for, one thing he was too good for: any kind of army." J.II: "Only not a soldier, not that." J.I: "And that's what he became." J.II: "And that's what they turned him into."

We know for a fact that between April and late August of 1939 this Heinrich, equipped with the proof of education called a matriculation certificate, made little use—possibly did not want to make use—of his education. He and a cousin joined an institution bearing the modest name "Reich Labor Service," and starting in May 1939 Heinrich had periodic leave from 1 P.M. Saturday to 10 P.M. Sunday. Of the thirty-five hours granted him, he spent eight on trains, used the remaining twenty-seven to go dancing with his sister and cousin, play a little tennis, take a few meals with the family, sleep approximately four to five, spend two or three arguing with his father, who wanted to do everything—everything—for him, and would have if he could have managed to get Heinrich exempted from the impending ordeal known in Germany as military service—but Heinrich would have none of it. Witnesses have testified to violent arguments that took place behind the locked living-room door, with Mrs. Gruyten whimpering softly to herself, Leni excluded, the only verifiable words being an outburst of Heinrich's, clearly heard by M.v.D.: "Dirt, dirt, dirt—that's what I want to be too, just dirt." Since Margret is certain about having had coffee with Heinrich on two Sunday afternoons in August, and since it is also known (through Leni, for once) that his first leave did not occur until the end of May, it may be safely calculated that Heinrich was at home a total of seven times, i.e., spent a total of some one hundred and eighty-nine hours—approximately twenty-four of these asleep—at home, fourteen of these quarreling with his father. It must be left to the reader to decide whether H. is to be numbered among Fortune's favorites. True: coffee with Margret twice. And a few months later a night of love with her. What a pity that, apart from "Dirt, dirt, dirt—that's what I want to be too, just dirt," there are no verifiable verbatim quotations of his. Did this person, who was equally outstanding in Latin and Greek, in rhetoric and history of art, never write any letters? He did. M.v.D., coaxed and cajoled, bribed with countless cups of coffee and a few packages of nonfilter Virginia cigarettes (she took up smoking at the age of sixty-eight and finds "these things marvelous"), went to Leni's inherited chest of drawers, which Leni seldom opens, and temporarily abstracted three letters that could be speedily photocopied.

The first letter, dated October 10, 1939, two days after the end of the war in Poland, has neither salutation nor conclusion and is composed in a clearly legible, unusually agreeable and intelligent handwriting that would be worthy of a better topic. The letter reads:

"The ruling principle is that no more suffering is to be inflicted on the enemy than is required for the attainment of the military objective.

"The following are *prohibited:*

"1. Use of poison and poisoned weapons.

"2. Assassination.

"3. Killing and wounding of prisoners.

"4. Refusal of pardon.

"5. Bullets or weapons that cause unnecessary suffering, e.g., dumdum bullets.

"6. Misuse of the truce flag (also of the national flag), military insignia, enemy uniform, Red Cross emblem (but watch out for military ruses!).

"7. Willful destruction or removal of enemy property.

"8. Coercion of enemy nationals to fight against their own country (e.g., Germans in the French Foreign Legion)."

Letter 2: dated December 13, 1939. "The good soldier behaves toward his superior in an unaffected, willing, helpful, and attentive manner. *Unaffected* behavior is shown by naturalness, alertness, and cheerful performance of duty. For the attainment of *willing, helpful,* and *attentive* behavior, note the following examples: Should his superior enter the room and ask for a man who is temporarily absent, the soldier should not confine his answer to the negative but should go in search of the man in question. Should his superior drop an object, the subordinate should pick it up for him (however, when on parade, only on demand). Should the subordinate notice that his superior wishes to light a cigar, he should hand him a lighted match. Should his superior leave the room, the subordinate should open the door for him and close it quietly behind him. The helpful and attentive soldier should assist his superior in putting on his topcoat and belt, entering or leaving an automobile, and mounting or dismounting from a horse. *Exaggerated helpfulness* and exaggerated attentiveness are unsoldierly ('eye service'); a soldier should avoid giving any such impression. Nor should he entertain such irregular ideas as offering gifts or issuing invitations to his superior."

Letter 3: dated January 14, 1940: "To perform *ablutions* the body is stripped to the waist. The soldier washes himself with cold water. The use of soap is a measure of cleanliness. To be washed daily: hands (several times!), face, neck, ears, chest, and armpits. Fingernails are to be cleaned with a nail cleaner (not

a knife). Hair is to be worn as short as possible. It is to be combed to one side and parted. Poodle-cuts are unsoldierly (see illustration)." (The illustration was not attached to the letter. Au.'s note.) "If necessary, the soldier is to shave daily. He must appear freshly shaven: for sentry duty, for inspections, when reporting to superior officers, and on special occasions.

"After each washing the body is to be dried *forthwith* (the skin to be rubbed until red), otherwise the soldier will catch cold, and in cold air the skin will become chapped. Face towels and hand towels are to be kept separate."

Leni seldom talks about her brother; she knew him so little, has and had not much more to say about him than that she used to be "scared of him because he was so terribly well educated" and "then was surprised to find him so terribly, terribly nice" (confirmed by M.v.D.).

M.v.D. herself admits to having been shy of him, although he was "terribly nice" to her too. He would even help her bring up coal and potatoes from the cellar, did not mind helping her with the dishes, etc., "and yet—there was something about him, you know—something about him—well, it was just something, maybe—well, something very noble—and in this he was even like Leni." That "even" is really worthy of a detailed commentary, from which the Au. will abstain.

"Noble," "German," "awfully, awfully nice," "terribly nice"—does this amount to much? The answer has to be: No. We are left with a miniature, not a portrait. And were it not for that night with Margret in the upstairs room of a Flensburg bar and the only guaranteed direct quotation (Dirt, etc.), and were it not for the letters and finally the end: found guilty, at barely twenty-one, with his cousin, of desertion and treason (contacts with Danes) and "attempted disposal of military equipment" (an antitank cannon)—there would be little left but the recollections of two pipe-smoking, parchment-skinned, all but yellowed Jesuits, "a flower, a flower still blooming in Margret's heart," and that terrible year of mourning, 1940–41. So Margret may be allowed to have the definitive word on him (tape): "I told him he should just go off, simply go off with me, we would've managed all right, even if I'd had to walk the streets—but he didn't want to desert his cousin, he said his cousin would be done for without him, and where could we go anyway. And all that tarty stuff around us, those ghastly pink lamps and plush and pink junk and dirty pictures and so on, it *was* disgusting, I must say. He didn't cry either—and what happened? O God, that flower's still blooming inside me—and even if he'd lived to be seventy, or eighty, I'd still have loved him with all my heart, and what did they feed him: the Western world. With the whole Western world in his stomach, that's how he died—Golgotha, the Acropolis, the Capitol [hysterical laughter]—and the Bamberg Rider thrown in for good measure. It was for that kind of crap that a wonderful boy like that lived. For that kind of crap."

Leni, asked about her brother when someone notices the photo on the wall, always turns cool, almost ladylike, uttering no more than the unexpected remark: "He has been resting for thirty years in Danish soil."

Needless to say, Margret's secret has been kept: neither the Jesuits nor Leni nor M.v.D. were ever told about it; the Au. is merely wondering whether to persuade Margret to tell Leni about it herself some day: it might be a small consolation to Leni to know that before his death her brother had spent the night with the eighteen-year-old Margret. Leni would probably smile, and a smile would do her good. The Au. has no evidence of H.'s poetic gifts other than the above-quoted texts, which may perhaps be allowed to pass as early examples of concrete poetry.

3 In order that we may finally get to the background, we must now approach a personality on whom the Au. is reluctant to focus—reluctant because, although there are plenty of photos of this person extant, and numerous witnesses (more than for Leni), the fact remains that, because or in spite of these numerous witnesses, an indistinct picture emerges: Leni's father, Hubert Gruyten, who died in 1949 at the age of forty-nine. Apart from those directly associated with him—e.g., M.v.D., Hoyser, Lotte Hoyser, Leni, Leni's parents-in-law, her brother-in-law—it was possible to trace twenty-two persons who had known him in the most varied situations and of whom the majority had worked with him: one as his superior, most of them under him. Eighteen persons from the building trade, four civil servants: architects and lawyers, a retired prison official. Since all save one of the persons worked under him, technicians, draftsmen, statisticians, planners, with ages ranging today from forty-five to eighty, perhaps it would be best to listen to them first after supplying the reader with the bare idea concerning Gruyten himself.

Hubert Gruyten, born 1899, a mason by trade, served for one year in World War I ("as a private, and without enthusiasm," testimony of Hoyser, Sr.), advanced briefly after the war to the position of foreman, in 1919 married ("above his station") Leni's mother, the daughter of an architect in a fairly senior government position (superintendent of construction); part of Helene Barkel's dowry was a pile of now worthless shares in the Turkish Railways, but the principal item was a solidly built apartment house with a good address, the very one, in fact, in which Leni was later born. Moreover, it was she who discovered "what he had in him" (Hoyser, Sr.), persuaded him to study for a degree in structural engineering, three years which old Gruyten greatly disliked hearing described as his "student years"; his wife loved to speak of life during "those student days" as "hard but beautiful," which embarrassed Gruyten; it was clear that he did not see himself as a student. From 1924 to 1929, after completing his studies, he was much in demand as a construction manager, even for major projects (not without the aid of his father-in-law); in 1929 he founded a contracting business, until 1933 sailed pretty close to bankruptcy, in 1933 began to operate on a large scale, reached the pinnacle of his success early in 1943, then spent two years, until the end of the war, in jail or doing forced labor, returned home in 1945, rid of all ambition, and was content to get together a small team of plasterers with which, until his death in 1949, he "managed quite well to keep his head above water" (Leni). He also worked as a "wrecker" (Leni).

When witnesses outside the family are asked about the probable motivation behind his business ambition, it is this very ambition that some dispute and other describe as "one of his basic traits"; twelve dispute the ambition, ten argue the case for "basic trait." They *all* dispute what even a man of Hoyser's age disputes: that he had had even the slightest talent as an architect; he is not even credited by anyone with having any talent as a "building man" in general terms. What he does seem to have been, and this nobody disputes, is: a good organizer and coordinator who, even when he employed nearly ten thousand workers, "always knew exactly what was going on and where" (Hoyser). It is worth noting that, of the twenty-two nonfamily witnesses, five (two from the "no ambition" party, three from the "basic trait" party) defined him, independently of one another, as a "brooder." When asked what prompted them to this surprising definition, three said simply: "Oh well, a brooder, you know—a brooder's a brooder, that's all." Only two, on being asked what he might have brooded on, deigned to give additional information. Mr. Heinken, a retired chief superintendent of construction now living in the country where he raises flowers and bees (and curiously enough expressed, unasked, his hatred of chickens—into every other sentence he wove the remark "I hate chickens"), declared Gruyten's brooding to be "a clear case of brooding on existence—if you ask me: an existential brooder, forever in conflict with some moral problem that cut clear across his path." The second one, Kern the statistician, aged about fifty and still very active in his profession, now in the service of the Federal Government, put it this way: "Well, we all regarded him as being a very vital sort of man, and undoubtedly that's what he was, and since I myself am not even the least bit vital" (an admission that, although not requested, was apposite. Au.), "I naturally respected and admired him, above all—he came from a very simple background, you know—for the way he negotiated with, you might even say, bossed around, the most prominent people, and how he always knew the ropes, but often, very often, when I had to go to his office—and I had to go there very often—he would be sitting at his desk, staring into space, brooding, if you ask me, just plain brooding, and he wasn't brooding over business; it was because of him that I started thinking how unjust we unvital people are toward vital people."

Finally, old Hoyser, when queried about the "brooder," looked up in surprise and said: "The idea would never have occurred to me, but now that you mention it I must say: not only is there some truth to it, it's the very word. I was Hubert's godfather, after all, he was my cousin, you know; in the years after the war" (meaning World War I. Au.) "I helped him a bit, and later he helped me in the most generous way. When he founded his business he took me in at once, although I was well on in my thirties; I became his head bookkeeper, his manager, later on his partner—well, he didn't laugh very often, that's true, and there was more than a touch of the gambler about him, there was a lot. And when disaster struck I didn't know why he had done it, maybe the word 'brooder' is one explanation for it. Only" (spiteful laughter) "what he did later with our Lotte, there wasn't much brooding about that."

Not a single one of the twenty-two surviving former co-workers disputed that G. was generous, "easy to get along with, matter-of-fact, but easy."

One sentence, uttered by G. in 1932 when he was close to bankruptcy, may be regarded as authentic since it has been confirmed by two independently questioned witnesses. It must have been a few weeks after the fall of the Brüning government. M.v.D. quotes the sentence as follows: "I can smell concrete, my lads, billions of tons of cement, I can smell fortifications and barracks," while Hoyser only quotes the sentence in the following form: "I can smell fortifications and barracks, my lads, barracks for at least two million soldiers. If we can hold out for another six months, we'll have it made."

In view of the copious information available on Gruyten, Sr., it is impossible to name each individual informant here. It may be taken for granted that no effort has been spared to obtain reasonably objective information on a subsidiary character who is important in terms of background only.

In dealing with Marja van Doorn, a certain caution is advisable where G. Sr. is concerned; since she was (is) approximately his age and came from the same village, it is not impossible that she was in love with him, or at least had cast an eye in his direction and is prejudiced. In any event, at the age of nineteen she came as household help to the home of the young bridegroom Gruyten, who six months previously had aroused the passions of Helene Barkel, just turned seventeen, at an architects' ball to which Helene's father had invited G.; whether his passion for her was equally aroused cannot be established with certainty; whether it was right for such a newly married couple to take in a nineteen-year-old country girl whom everyone credited with a vitality that was as unbroken as it was unbreakable may be doubtful. What is not doubtful is that almost all of Marja's statements about Leni's mother tend to be negative, while she sees Leni's father in an unfailingly iconolatrous light, something like the light of a little everlasting oil lamp, a wax or electric candle or a neon tube, in front of a picture of the Sacred Heart or Saint Joseph. From a few statements made by Miss van Doorn one is free to assume that under certain circumstances she would even have been prepared to enter into an adulterous relationship with Hubert Gruyten. Her remark, for example, that from 1927 on the marriage had "begun to fall apart," but that she had been prepared to give him everything that his wife no longer could or would give him, must surely be taken as a fairly clear hint, and when such a hint is reinforced by the additional remark—made, admittedly, almost under her breath—"in those days I was still a young woman, mind you," the clarity leaves nothing to be desired. When asked point-blank whether such a hint was meant to imply that the intimacy regarded as the focal point of conjugal relations had come to an end, Miss van Doorn said in her disconcertingly direct way, "yes, that's what I mean," and what was then expressed in her still expressive brown eyes—mutely, needless to say—prompts the Au. to assume that she had acquired this knowledge not merely as an observer of family life but also as keeper of the bed linen. On being then asked whether she believed that Gruyten had "sought consolation elsewhere," she responded with an emphatic and conclusive No, adding—the Au. is almost sure he heard a suppressed sob in her voice—"He lived like a monk, like a monk, but without being one."

If we look at the photos of the deceased Hubert Gruyten—baby pictures will be ignored here, the first photo to be seriously consulted will be the school graduation picture—we see him in 1913 as a tall, slim youth, blond, long-nosed, somehow "determined," dark-eyed, not quite as stiff as his schoolmates in the picture, who look like recruits, and we believe instantly in the assumption that has been passed on, merely by word of mouth, in almost mythical form as having been identically uttered by teacher, priest, and family: "That boy will amount to something one day." To what? The next photo shows him when he had just completed his apprenticeship, aged eighteen, in 1917: for the term "brooder" that was later applied to him, this photo provides some psychological nourishment. G. is a serious youth, that much is obvious at a glance, his evident good nature being in only apparent contradiction to his manifest determination and will power; since he was always photographed straight on—right up to the last pictures of him taken in 1949 with a wretched little box camera belonging to Leni's brother-in-law, the aforesaid Heinrich Pfeiffer—the proportion of length of nose to the rest of the face is never visible or demonstrable, and since not even the famous portrait painter who painted a naturalistic portrait of him in 1941 (oils on canvas, not bad at all, although lacking in depth—it was possible to unearth and briefly view it in a private collection in highly disagreeable surroundings) took the opportunity of painting Gruyten from at least a three-quarter view, it can only be assumed that, stripped of his modern trappings, he must have looked as if he had stepped out of a painting by Hieronymus Bosch.

While Marja only hinted at laundry secrets, she spoke openly of kitchen secrets. "She didn't like strong flavors, while he liked everything highly flavored. That meant problems right from the start because I usually had to flavor everything twice: bland for her, strong for him. It finally ended up by his adding salt and pepper to his own food at table; even when he was a boy everyone in the village knew you could please him better with a pickle than with a piece of cake."

The next photo worthy of mention is a picture taken on the honeymoon, during which the couple visited Lucerne. There is no doubt about it: Mrs. Helene Gruyten, née Barkel, looks charming: affecting and affectionate, gracious and ladylike; one can tell from looking at her what all the initiated, even Marja, agree on: that she has learned to play her Schumann and her Chopin, speaks French fairly fluently, can crochet, embroider, etc., and—it must be said—one can tell that in her the world may have lost an intellectual, perhaps even a potentially Leftist intellectual.

Needless to say, she never "touched" Zola—as she had been taught not to, and one can imagine her horror when eight years later her daughter Leni asked about her (Leni's) *bowel movements.* For her, Zola and excrement were probably almost identical concepts. There was probably no latent physician in her, but she would undoubtedly have had no difficulty obtaining a degree in history of art. One must be fair: were one to invent a few conditions for her that did not exist—an education geared less to the elegiac than to the analytical, less soulfulness and more soul (if at all), and had she been spared all the prudishness that went with her boarding-school life, she might have become a good doctor after all. One thing is certain—had such frivolous books come within her reach, even if only as potential reading, she would have been more likely to become a reader of Proust than of Joyce; as it was, she did at least read Enrica von Handel-Mazzetti, Marie von Ebner-Eschenbach, and copiously in that Catholic illustrated weekly which has by now acquired antiquarian value and *in those days* was the most ultramodern of the ultramodern in its category, the 1914–1920 counterpart to the *Publik* of the 1970's, and when it is also known that on her sixteenth birthday her parents gave her a subscription to *Hochland,* we can see that she was equipped with not only progressive but the most progressive reading matter. It was probably through her reading of *Hochland* that she was so well informed on the past and present of Ireland, names such as Pearse, Connolly, even such names as Larkin and Chesterton, were not unfamiliar to her; and there is evidence, by way of her sister Irene Schweigert, née Barkel, who is still alive and at the age of seventy-five is living in a ladies' rest home in the company of fondly warbling budgerigars, "calmly waiting for death" (her own words), that as a young girl Leni's mother was "among the first, if not the very first, feminine readers of the German translations of William Butler Yeats, and certainly—as I personally know because I gave it to her—of Yeats's prose that appeared in 1912, and of course Chesterton."

Now there can be no question of using a person's literary background or lack of it either for or against him, its only use is to throw light on a scene that around 1927 was already casting tragic shadows. Of one thing there is no doubt when one studies the honeymoon picture taken in 1919: whatever else of her and in her may have been frustrated—Leni's mother was most certainly not a frustrated courtesan. She appears to be not very sensual and far from bursting with hormones, whereas he obviously is bursting with hormones. It is quite possible that both of them—whose mutual love we have no right to doubt—were, erotically speaking, totally inexperienced when they embarked on the adventure of marriage, and it may very well be that during the first few nights Gruyten proceeded, if not exactly roughly, perhaps a little impatiently.

As far as *his* acquaintance with books is concerned, the Au. is far from inclined to rely on the opinion of a surviving business competitor who, described as a "giant in the construction field," expressed himself in these words: "That fellow and books—his ledger maybe, that might have been a book that interested him." Indeed, we have reason to believe that Hubert Gruyten did in fact read very few books: the technical literature he was obliged to read during his engineering studies, and otherwise, as can be verified, a popular biography of Napoleon, and apart from that, according to the identical testimonies of Marja and Hoyser, "all he wanted was the newspaper and later on the radio."

After old Mrs. Schweigert had finally been tracked down, an explanation presented itself for a phrase of Marja's that had thus far been unexplainable and unexplained, a phrase that had remained so long in the Au.'s notebook without being checked off that it very nearly fell victim to impatience: for Marja accused Mrs. Gruyten of having been "just crazy about her Finns." Since not a single one of the available statements could be found to contain even the remotest reference to Finland, this expression must have been meant to denote the "Fenians," Mrs. Gruyten's partiality for Ireland having subsequently taken a romantic and to some degree even sentimental turn. In any event, Yeats had always been her favorite poet.

There being a complete absence of any exchange of correspondence between Gruyten and his wife, and nothing beyond the statements of Miss van Doorn (which in this case must be regarded as highly dubious), we are left with the superficial analysis of the photograph of the honeymoon taken on the lakeside promenade at Lucerne, and expressed in negative terms: erotic, let alone sexual, harmony does not appear to exist between these two. Emphatically not. Moreover, even this early photo clearly indicates something that is confirmed by many later ones: Leni takes more after her father, Heinrich took more after his mother, although, apropos spices and even rolls, Leni takes more after her mother, and there is even evidence that in her poetic and musical sensibility she also takes more after her mother. The hypothetical question as to what kind of children would have resulted from a possible marriage between Marja and Gruyten can be answered more easily in the negative than in the positive: most certainly not the kind whom parchment-skinned nuns and Jesuit fathers would have remembered, even decades later, at the very mention of their names.

Whatever went wrong or whatever misunderstandings arose between the two spouses, it has been testified by the persons with the most intimate knowledge of the Gruytens' family life, even by the jealous van Doorn woman, that: never at any time did he show lack of courtesy, chivalry, or even affection toward her, and that she always "idolized" him seems to be a matter of record.

Mrs. Schweigert, née Barkel, an old lady who has nothing whatever of Yeats or Chesterton about her, frankly admitted that she had "not been particularly keen" to associate with her brother-in-law or even her sister after their marriage: she would have much preferred to see her sister married to a poet, painter, sculptor, or at least an architect; she did not say outright that she had found Gruyten too low-class, she expressed it negatively: "not refined enough"; when asked about Leni she would utter no more than two little words: "Oh well," and on being urged to say more about Leni she stuck to her "Oh well," whereas she made no bones about claiming Heinrich for the Barkels; not even the fact that her son Erhard was "to all intents and purposes on Heinrich's conscience, he would never have done such a thing on his own," could lessen her liking for Heinrich; she declared him to have been "extreme, very extreme, but gifted, almost a genius," and the Au. gained the ambiguous impression that she did not particularly bemoan her son's premature death, tending rather to resort to such phrases as "hour of Destiny," especially since she went so far as to make a statement which, applied to her son and even to Heinrich, was exceedingly odd and would require much checking and historical correction. "They both looked"—these were her very words—"as if they had fallen at the Battle of Langemarck." When we consider the ambiguities surrounding not only Langemarck but the very myth of Langemarck, the discrepancy between 1914 and 1940, and finally roughly four dozen complicated misunderstandings (which do not all have to be gone into here), we are hardly surprised that the Au. took leave of Mrs. Schweigert courteously but coolly, although not finally: and since he later learned from the witness Hoyser that Mrs. Schweigert's husband, a hitherto shadowy figure, had been severely wounded at Langemarck, had spent three years in an army hospital—"he was simply shot to pieces" (Hoyser)—and in 1919 had married Irene Barkel, his volunteer nurse; that this marriage had produced the son Erhard but that Mr. Schweigert—"so morphine-addicted and emaciated that he could hardly find another spot to stick a needle in" (Hoyser)—had died in 1923 at the age of twenty-seven, official occupation student, it may occur to some that this uncommonly ladylike Mrs. Schweigert might have secretly harbored the wish that her husband had fallen at Langemarck. She had earned her living as a real-estate agent.

From 1933 on, the Gruyten business began to take an upward turn, at first steadily, from 1933 steeply, from 1937 vertically; according to statements made by his former staff members and a number of experts, he made money "hand over fist" with the "Siegfried Line," but according to Hoyser he had spent large sums as early as 1935 to buy up "the best available experts on fortifications and concrete dugouts," long before he could actually "put them to work." "We constantly worked with loans so big that it still makes me dizzy to think of them." Gruyten was quite simply betting on what he called the "Maginot complex" of all statesmen; "years after the Maginot myth has been destroyed, it will" (Gruyten's words quoted by Hoyser) "persist and continue to persist. The Russians are the only ones who don't have this complex; their frontier is too long for them to be able to afford it, but whether this will spell their salvation or their doom remains to be seen. Hitler at any rate has it, however much he may propagate and practice a war of mobility, *he personally* has the dugout and fortifications complex, you wait and see" (early 1940, statement made before the conquest of France and Denmark).

Be that as it may: by 1938 the Gruyten firm was six times as large as it had been in 1936, when it had been six times as large as in 1932; in 1940 it was twice as large as in 1938, and (Hoyser) "by 1943 you couldn't have established any ratio at all."

One characteristic of Gruyten, Sr., is confirmed by everyone, although in two different terms: some call him "courageous," others "fearless," a certain minority of perhaps two or three call him "a megalomaniac." Experts testify to this day that without any doubt Gruyten, at a very early stage, hired or lured away the best fortifications experts on the market, later ruthlessly employing even French engineers and technicians who had been involved in the building of the Maginot Line, and that he had "known perfectly well" (a high-ranking official of the Ordnance Department who also would prefer to remain anonymous) that: "to economize on wages and salaries during a time of inflation is nonsense." Gruyten paid well. At the time in question he is forty-one years of age. Custom-made suits of "expensive, but not ostentatiously expensive material" (Lotte Hoyser) have turned a "fine figure of a man" into a "fine figure of a gentleman"; he was not even ashamed of being nouveau riche, expressing himself as follows to one of his colleagues (Werner von Hoffgau, an architect from an old-established family), "all wealth was at one time new, even yours, at the time when your family was becoming wealthy but hadn't yet attained wealth." Gruyten refused to build himself a villa (to the end of his days he referred to a house as a "home") in that part of town which was then mandatory for those well on the way to prosperity.

It would be irresponsible to regard Gruyten as a naive, crude self-made man; among his abilities is one that cannot be learned and cannot be inherited: he understands human nature, and all his staff—architects, technicians, businessmen—admire him, and most of them respect him. The education and upbringing of his son are carefully planned and closely watched by him, he keeps an eye on them; he visits the boy frequently, seldom bringing him home because—surprising statement, verified by Hoyser—he does not want the boy to soil his hands with business. "What he had in mind for the boy was a scholarly career, not just any old professor, more like the one we built that villa for." (Hoyser; according to H.'s statement this referred to a fairly well-known specialist in Romance languages, whose library, cosmopolitanism, and "straightforward cordial manner with people" must have impressed Gruyten.) With some impatience he finds that at fifteen his son "doesn't speak Spanish as well as I had expected."

One thing he never did: regard Leni as a "silly goose." Her rage over the administering of the First Communion did not annoy him in the least, he laughed aloud over it (something he was known to have done very rarely during his lifetime), and his comment was: "That girl knows exactly what she wants" (Lotte H.).

While his wife becomes paler and paler, a bit tearful and even a bit pietistic, he is entering on "his prime." One thing he has never had and never will have as long as he lives: feelings of inferiority. He may have had dreams—for his son certainly and, as to his hopes for his son's knowledge of Spanish, most certainly. Thirteen years after conjugal relations between him and his wife have ceased (according to Marja van Doorn) to exist, he still does not deceive his wife, at least not with other women. He has a surprising aversion to dirty stories, an aversion he shows openly on the occasions when he is obliged to attend "stag dinners" and inevitably, toward two or three in the morning, a certain stage is reached at which one of the men demands a "hot-blooded Circassian maiden." Gruyten's coolness toward dirty stories and "Circassian maidens" earns him a certain amount of ridicule, which he accepts without protest (Werner von Hoffgau, who for the space of a year sometimes accompanied him to stag dinners).

What kind of fellow is this, the reader must be wondering with increasing impatience, what kind of fellow is this who lives a life of chastity, so to speak, makes money out of preparations for war, out of war itself, whose turnover (according to Hoyser) rose from approximately one million a year in 1935 to one million a month in 1943, and who in 1939, when his turnover presumably amounted to one million every quarter, did everything he could to exclude his son from a business at which he himself was making a fortune?

During 1939 and 1940 a certain tension, amounting even to bitterness, arises between father and son. Heinrich is now back home, having come down from the three mountains of the Western world and, at a distance of four hours by train, is occupied somewhere draining marshes, capable though he has meanwhile become—at the insistence of his father, who has paid a Spanish Jesuit tutor a fat fee for the purpose—of reading Cervantes in the original. Between June and September the son visits the family some seven times, between the end of September 1939 and the beginning of 1940 some five times, and has refused to make use of the frankly proffered "pull" of his father, for whom it "would have been no trick" (all quotations from Hoyser, Sr., and

Lotte) to have him "transferred to a more suitable job" or to effect his discharge once and for all as a war-essential employee. What kind of son is this who, when asked at the breakfast table about his health and what life in the army is like, draws from his pocket a book entitled: Reibert, *Handbook of Army Regulations, Edition for Tank Gunners,* revised by a Major Allmendiger, and proceeds to read a section from it that he has not yet committed to a letter: a dissertation covering nearly five pages headed "Military Salutes" and describing in detail every type of salute to be performed while walking, lying, standing, on horseback, and in an automobile, and who salutes whom and how? It must be borne in mind that this father is not one who spends all his time sitting around the house waiting for his son's visits; this is a father who now has a government aircraft at his disposal (Leni enjoys flying enormously!) and, as a man occupied with matters of great, sometimes extreme, sometimes supreme, importance, must get out of commitments as occasion arises, cancel important engagements, cancel appointments with cabinet ministers (!), often by using threadbare excuses (dentist, etc.), so as not to miss seeing his beloved son—and who then has to listen to a passage on regulation saluting by some fellow called Reibert, revised by a certain Major Allmendiger, being read aloud to him by a beloved son whom he really wanted to see as director of the History of Art (or at least Archeological) Institute in Rome or Florence?

Is any further comment required on the fact that these "coffee gatherings," these breakfasts and midday dinners, became "for all concerned not merely uncomfortable but increasingly agonizing, nerve-racking, and finally ghastly" (Lotte Hoyser)? Lotte Hoyser, née Berntgen, then aged twenty-six, daughter-in-law of the much-quoted manager and head bookkeeper Otto Hoyser, worked as a secretary for Gruyten, who also for a time took on her husband Wilhelm Hoyser as a draftsman. Since Lotte was already in Gruyten's employ during the crucial months of 1939 and was sometimes present at the coffee gatherings with the son who was on leave, her assessment of Gruyten himself, whom she described as "simply fascinating but in those days, when you got right down to it, a crook," ought perhaps to be mentioned only marginally. Old Hoyser loves to hint at the "erotic but of course platonic relationship" between his daughter-in-law and Gruyten, Sr., "in whose erotic sphere of interest she naturally belonged, since they were barely fourteen years apart in age." Theories have even been voiced (strangely enough by Leni, although not directly, only indirectly, confirmed by the unreliable Heinrich Pfeiffer) that "even in those days Lotte probably represented a genuine temptation for Father, by which I don't mean she was a *temptress.*" In any event, Lotte describes the family coffee parties, for which Gruyten, Sr., sometimes flew in from Berlin or Munich, even from Warsaw, it is said, as "simply ghastly," "downright unbearable." M.v.D. describes them—the meals—as "horrible, simply horrible," while Leni's only comment is "awful, awful, awful."

The evidence is, even from so prejudiced a witness as M.v.D., that these leave-periods "simply destroyed" Mrs. Gruyten; "what went on there was just too much for her." Lotte Hoyser speaks unequivocally of an "intellectual variation of patricide" and maintains that the politically destructive motive for quoting from the aforesaid Reibert had "hit Gruyten hard because he was in the thick of politics, was often hearing of, had often heard of, top political secrets such as the construction of barracks in the Rhineland long before it was occupied and the planned construction of giant air-raid shelters—and this was precisely why he didn't want to hear about politics at home."

Leni experienced these bitter nine months not quite so overwhelmingly, possibly not quite so attentively, as did other observers. She had meanwhile—approximately in July 1939—yielded to a man, no, she would have yielded to him had he asked her; true, she did not know whether this was really the right man, the one whom she was so ardently awaiting, but she did know that she would not find out until he had asked her. It was her cousin, Erhard Schweigert, son of the Langemarck victim and the lady who maintained that he had looked as if he had fallen at the Battle of Langemarck. Erhard, "because of a hypersensitive nervous disposition" (his mother), had failed to scale as rugged an educational barrier as matriculation; furthermore, he had been temporarily sent home from as remorseless an institution as the Reich Labor Service and was now aiming for what he regarded as the "repulsive" (his own word, according to M.v.D.) profession of grade-school teacher, having taken the first step by starting to study at home for an aptitude test. But then in the end he was drafted into that rugged institution where he met his cousin Heinrich, who took him under his wing and, while they were both on leave, tried quite openly to pair him off with his sister Leni. He bought them movie tickets with which he "sent them off" (M.v.D.), he arranged to meet them after the show "but then didn't turn up" (see above). Since this meant that Erhard spent not only the greater part of his leave but his entire leave with the Gruytens, paying only brief sporadic visits to his mother, the latter is still bitter about it; with outright indignation she rejected the possibility that a love affair "with serious intentions" might have existed between her son and Leni. "No, no, and again no—that Oh-well girl—no!" Now, if one thing is certain it is the indisputable fact that right from the first leave—in about May 1939—Erhard absolutely adored Leni; there are tried-and-true witnesses to this: in particular Lotte Hoyser, who frankly admits that "Erhard would certainly have been better than what came later, anyway than what came in 1941. Maybe not better than what came in 1943." On her own admission she repeatedly tried to entice Leni and Erhard into her apartment, to leave them alone there "so that—damn it all—it would finally happen. For God's sake, the boy was twenty-two, healthy, unusually thoughtful and kind. Leni was seventeen and a bit, and she was —I tell you straight—she was ripe for love, she was a woman, a marvelous woman even in those days, but the shyness of that Erhard was something you wouldn't believe."

At this point, in order to avoid misunderstandings again, or yet again, it is necessary to describe Lotte Hoyser. Born 1913, height five feet four and a half inches, weight 122 pounds, graying brown hair; powder-dry, dialectically inclined if not trained, she may be called a person of remarkable candor, even more candid than Margret. Since she lived with Gruyten on fairly intimate terms during the Erhard period, she would seem to be a far more reliable witness than Miss van Doorn, who, in everything concerning Leni, inclines to iconolatry. Lotte, when queried about her controversial relationship with Gruyten, Sr., spoke candidly about that too: "Well, something might have developed between us two even in those days, I admit, he might have developed into what he became in '45; I disapproved of almost everything he did, but could understand it, if you know what I mean. His wife was too timid, besides she was scared by all that armaments stuff, it filled her with panic, paralyzed her; if she'd been an active woman and less of a daydreamer she would've hidden her son somewhere in Spain in some monastery or maybe in that land of the Fenians where she could've made a trip to see everything for herself, and in the same way, of course, it would've been possible to put my husband and Erhard beyond the reach of German history. Don't get me wrong: Helene Gruyten was not only nice, she was kind and clever, but history was too much for her, if you know what I mean, too much—whether it was politics or the business or the appalling self-destruction that boy was deliberately heading for. It's true, of course, what others have told you" (Margret's name was not betrayed. Au.). "He had devoured the whole Western world—and what was he left with? A little pile of shit, if you ask me, and he was confronted with that indescribable crap. Too much Bamberg Rider and too little Peasants' War. Even when I was a kid of fourteen in night school, back in 1927, I had a course in the sociopolitical background to the Peasants' War and took all kinds of notes—and I know, of course, that the Bamberg Rider has nothing to do with the Peasants' War—but I ask you, cut off his curls and give him a shave—and what've you got? A pretty cheap and sentimental Saint Joseph. In other words: too much Bamberg Rider in the boy and too much Rosa Alchemica—she once gave me that to read, it was really beautiful, she was a marvelous woman all right, and probably all she needed was a few hormone injections; and the boy, Heinrich: that was a boy to fall in love with, that's for sure, and I don't suppose there was a woman for miles around who didn't give a strange little smile when she saw him; it's only a few smart homosexuals and women, you know, who can smell a poet. Of course it was sheer suicide the way he was carrying on, no question, and sometimes I wonder why he dragged Erhard into it—but maybe Erhard wanted to be dragged into it. One can't tell, two Bamberg Riders who wanted to die together, and God knows they did: they put them up against a wall, and you know what Heinrich shouted before they shot him? 'Shit on Germany.' And that was the end of an education and an upbringing that must have been unique, and since he was in that shit army maybe it was the best thing: God knows there were enough chances of dying between April 1940 and May 1945. The old man had plenty of pull and got hold of the file, some old general or other wangled it, but he never opened it, he just asked me to tell him the gist of it: what had happened was that those two boys simply offered to sell a whole antiaircraft cannon to the Danes, or rather, they wanted its fictitious scrap value, something in the neighborhood of five marks, and d'you know what that quiet, shy Erhard said during the trial? 'We are dying for an honorable profession, for the arms trade.'"

The Au. felt the necessity of paying another visit to Mr. Werner von Hoffgau, aged fifty-five, who, "after being temporarily employed by the Federal Army, at whose disposal I had placed my experiences in an official capacity as a construction expert," was now living in a wing of the little moated castle that had belonged to his ancestors and in which he maintained a small architect's office "that serves peaceful purposes only, i.e., designing housing estates." One must picture von H. (who did not voluntarily describe himself as unvital, but might have) as a gentle, gray-haired person, a bachelor, for whom, in the Au.'s modest opinion, the "architect's office" is only an excuse to spend hours watching the swans in the moat and the activities inside and outside the leased estate, to go for walks through the meadows (more precisely: sugar-beet fields), to glower at the sky whenever another of those Starfighters flies overhead; who avoids associating with his brother (who lives in the castle) "on account of certain transactions he wangled, using my name but without my knowledge, in the department I then headed." Von H.'s plumpish, sensitive features reveal bitterness, not of a personal kind, rather an abstract moral bitterness which, so it seemed to the Au., he deadens with a drink that, when consumed in quantity, is among the most dangerous: old sherry. In any event, the Au. discovered a surprisingly large number of empty sherry bottles on the garbage heap and a surprisingly large number of full ones in von H.'s "draftsman's cabinet." It required numerous visits to the village inn to obtain, at least in colportage form, the information that was refused by von H. with the words "my lips are sealed."

The following is the synopsis of conversations conducted by the Au. with approximately ten Hoffgausen villagers during three visits to the inn; the sympathy of the villagers was clearly on the side of the unvital Werner, their esteem, their respect, expressed in almost trembling voices, on the side of the apparently very vital brother Arnold. Apparently—according to the villagers—Arnold, with the aid of Christian-Democrat deputies, bankers, and lobbyists representing various groups in the defense committee, and by exerting sufficient pressure on the Minister of Defense himself, had managed to persuade the planning board for the construction of military airfields, of which his brother was head, to choose the "famous and ancient Hoffgau Forest," plus the requisite large number of adjacent fields, as the site for a NATO airfield. That—according to statements made by the villagers—had been a "fifty-, forty-, at the very least thirty-million-mark deal," and all this took place (villager Bernhard Hecker, farmer) "*in* his department *against* his wishes *with* the approval of the defense committee."

Hoffgau, "forever indebted to Gruyten because he saved me as a young man from that German Army by making me his personal adviser, although, when the going got really tough for him later on, I could at least do him a favor in return," hesitated a while before giving any information on the mysterious Heinrich-Erhard affair. "Since it seems to mean so much to you I'll let you in on what happened. Mrs. Hoyser never knew about the whole dossier, or about the whole problem. All she got to see was the transcript of the trial, and an incomplete one at that, and the report of the lieutenant in command of the firing squad. As a matter of fact, the affair was so complicated that I'm going to have a hard time reconstructing it just the way it was. Let's see now, Gruyten's son refused his father's protection, but Gruyten protected him against his will and saw to it—an easy matter for him—that first of all he and his cousin were transferred to a paymaster's office in Lübeck, a couple of days after the occupation of Denmark. Now he—Mr. Gruyten senior, that is—hadn't reckoned with the obstinacy of his son who, it's true, went to Lübeck with his cousin but when he got there saw what he had landed up in and returned at once to Denmark, with no marching orders, no transfer—that, leniently interpreted, was going Absent Without Leave, strictly interpreted, was desertion. That could have been fixed up; what couldn't be fixed up was that the two boys tried to sell an antitank cannon to a Dane, and although the Dane didn't take up the offer—it would have been suicide, of course, and utterly futile—that was a crime, and no amount of protection could help, nothing could help them now, and the inevitable happened. I'll be frank with you and admit that, even as Gruyten's personal adviser, and although we had large projects under way in Denmark at the time and knew almost all the generals personally, I had trouble getting at the dossier, and when I'd read it I passed it on—well, let's say, in an expurgated or, if you like, edited version to Mrs. Hoyser, who was Gruyten's secretary, for it contained a good many references to 'crooked deals'—and I wanted to spare him that."

Lotte H., who has to heave a sigh whenever she thinks of giving up her attractive little apartment with its roof garden in the center of town, had to sigh and light cigarette after cigarette, keep passing her hand swiftly over her smooth, cropped gray hair, and sip repeatedly at her coffee when she spoke "about that affair." "Yes. Yes. They're dead all right, no doubt about that, whether because of desertion or because they tried to flog that cannon—they're dead, and I don't know whether that was what they really wanted. I always felt there was a good deal of romancing about the whole thing, and I could imagine that they were quite surprised and shocked as they stood there against the wall and heard the order 'Ready—Aim!' When all's said and done, Erhard had Leni, and Heinrich, well—he could have had any girl. It seems pretty German to me, what those two boys did, and right there too, in Denmark, where our really big projects were getting under way at the time. Oh well. Let's call it 'symbolllism,' if you like, with three l's, please. But it wasn't that with my husband, who was sent to his death near Amiens a few days later; he'd have liked to live, and not just symbolically either; and he wouldn't have liked to die symbolically either, he was scared, that's all, there was a lot of good in him but they destroyed that in the seminary he went to till he was sixteen to study for the priesthood, till he finally realized that that's all a lot of crap, only it was too late. And he never lost that wretched complex of not having finished high school—they'd drilled that into him too; then we met in the Free Youth, with 'Brothers, toward sunlight, toward freedom' and so on, and we even knew the last verse—'Brothers, take hold of your rifles, On to the last final fight, To Communism all honor, To it be all power and might'—the only thing was, of course, that no one had taught us that the Communism of 1897 was a different matter from the Communism of '27–'28—and my Wilhelm, he wasn't the kind to have ever taken hold of a rifle, never, and it was for those idiots that he had to do it, and they allowed him the privilege of being killed for that crap—there were even people in the firm who claimed that his own father, with Gruyten's approval, took Wilhelm's name off the list of war-essential employees, and there were even mutterings about Uriah's wife, but I couldn't and never could have—you can't deceive a loyal person like Wilhelm, I couldn't do it even right after he was dead. And now about Gruyten. Yes, something might have developed between us, even in those days.

The thing that fascinated me about him was how that tall bony country boy with the plebeian features turned into a tall bony man, a distinguished-looking gentleman, not a contractor, not an architect—a strategist, if you ask me. And that was the thing about him, apart from his tall thin boniness, that fascinated me: that talent for strategy. He might just as easily have become a banker, without 'understanding' the first thing about money, if you know what I mean. He had a map of Europe hanging on the wall of his office, used to stick pins in it and sometimes a little flag, and a glance was enough for him—he never bothered with details. And of course he had one very effective trick he'd simply pinched from Napoleon—I believe the only book he ever read was a pretty stupid biography of Napoleon—the trick was so simple, maybe it wasn't even a trick, maybe there was even a bit of genuine sentiment in it. He had started in '29, a bit on the grand side, with forty workers, foremen, and so on—and he managed, in spite of the Depression, to hang on to them all, not to fire a single one of them, and he knew every bank trick in the book, he had no scruples about stringing along his creditors, even borrowed at exorbitant rates—and so by 1933 he had about forty men who simply thought the world of him, even the Communists among them, and he thought the world of them and helped them out in all their troubles, even their political ones, and you can imagine that over the next few years they all worked their way up into pretty good jobs, just like Napoleon's sergeants; he'd hand over whole projects to them, and he knew every one of them by name, every last one of them, even the names of their wives and kids, he'd ask after them every time he saw them, with all the details—he knew, for instance, when one of the kids had to repeat a year in school, and so on. And when he got to a construction site and saw a bottleneck he'd grab a shovel or a pick, he even drove a truck in an emergency—and he always pitched right in where help was really needed. The rest you can imagine for yourself. And another secret: money meant nothing to him. He needed it, of course, for props: clothes, cars, getting about, now and again a big party, but as soon as it came in, the big money, it was immediately reinvested, and debts were incurred over and above that. 'Owe money, owe money, Lotte,' he said to me once, 'that's the only way.' And now for his wife: yes, she was the one who saw 'what he had in him'—right, but *what* he had in him and what came of it simply sent her into a panic; she wanted to make a big man of him, to run a big house, and so on, but she didn't want to be married to the chief of a general staff. If you'll let me put it in a funny way I think maybe you'll understand: *he* was the abstract one and she was the realist, though it may've seemed the other way round. My God, I thought it was criminal, what he was doing: building fortifications and airfields and headquarters for that bunch, and whenever I go to Holland or Denmark I see the fortifications still standing there along the beach, the ones we built, and I feel sick—and yet you know: it was a time of power, an era for power, and he was a man of power to whom power itself meant nothing, no more than money did. For him the appeal lay in the game, he was a gambler all right—but he was too vulnerable: they had the boy, and that boy didn't want to be kept out of the dirt."

An attempt to bring Lotte back to the second topic of the interview, Leni's relationship with Erhard, failed at first. Another cigarette and an impatient gesture. "I'm coming to that, let me finish. Just to make this clear: we two, we suited each other, even in those days, and there were even a few little expressions of affection, or whatever you want to call it, that for a man of forty with a woman of twenty-seven are rather touching. Flowers of course, and twice a kiss on the forearm and then something really sensational: he once danced half the night with me at a hotel in Hamburg; that wasn't like him at all. Haven't you ever noticed that 'great men' are always poor dancers? Now I'm a pretty standoffish person with men other than my own husband, and I've got one miserable habit that I couldn't get rid of for the longest time: I'm faithful. It's like a curse. No merit to it, it's more of a disgrace—how do you think I used to lie there, alone in my bed at night, when the kids were asleep, after they'd let my Wilhelm, my husband, give his life near Amiens for that crap? And I wouldn't let a soul, not a soul, touch me till '45—and all against my convictions, for I'm no believer in chastity and all that, and by

'45 five years had passed, five years, and we two, he and I, moved in together. Now about Leni and Erhard, if you like: I must've told you already that the shyness of that boy Erhard was something you simply wouldn't believe—nor Leni's shyness either, for that matter. He adored her from the very first moment, she must've seemed to him like some kind of mysterious resurrected Florentine blond beauty or something, and not even Leni's extremely dry Rhenish manner of speech, not even her ultradry way of expressing herself, could bring him down to earth. And he didn't give a damn that she turned out to be totally uneducated in his sense of the word, and that bit of secretion-mysticism she had, and still has, in her head, wouldn't have particularly impressed him either, I imagine, if she'd ever trotted it out. Well, what didn't we all do, we three—Heinrich, Margret, and I, I mean —to bring it off between them. There wasn't much time, mind you: between May '39 and April '40 he was there maybe eight times in all. Naturally nothing was said in words between Heinrich and me, just with our eyes, after all we could see how much in love they were. It really was sweet, yes I repeat, it was sweet to see them together, and maybe the fact they didn't go to bed together isn't so tragic after all. I got movie tickets for them, for crappy movies like *Comrades on the High Seas* or trash like *Beware, the Enemy Is Listening,* and I even sent them to that *Bismarck* movie because I thought: What the hell, it's a three-hour program, and it's as dark and warm in there as in the womb, and they're bound to hold hands, and maybe it'll eventually occur to them" (very bitter laughter! Au.'s remark) "to try a kiss or two, and when they get that far surely it'll go farther—but nothing doing, it seemed. He took her to the museum and explained how you tell a painting that's only attributed to Bosch from a genuine Bosch. He tried to get her away from her Schubert tinklings onto Mozart, he gave her poems to read, Rilke most likely, I've forgotten just what, and then he did something that struck a spark: he wrote poems to her and sent them to her. Well, that Leni was such an enchanting creature—she still is, if you ask me—that I was a bit in love with her myself: if you could've seen, for instance, how she danced with Erhard when we all went out together, my husband and I, Heinrich, Margret, and those two—it made you just long for a great fourposter bed for the two of them, all ready and waiting for them to enjoy one another—so then he wrote poems to her, and the most amazing part about it is: she showed them to me, though I must say they were pretty daring; he didn't exactly mince matters in singing the praises of her breast, which he called 'the great white flower of your silence' and from which he claimed he would 'strip the petals one by one,' and he wrote one really good poem on jealousy that might even have been fit for publication: 'I am jealous of the coffee you drink, of the butter you spread on your bread, Jealous of your toothbrush, and of the bed in which you sleep.' I mean to say, those were all pretty unmistakable things, all right, but paper, paper. . . ."

Asked whether there was no possibility of intimacies having occurred between Leni and Erhard of which she, Heinrich, and the others had no knowledge, Lotte blushed, surprisingly enough (the Au. admits that, in the course of what was often laborious research, a blushing Lotte gave him pleasure) and said: "No, I can be pretty sure of that—you see, a little over a year later she ran off with that Alois Pfeiffer, whom she was then stupid enough to marry, and Pfeiffer boasted later on, in fairly unmistakable terms, to his brother Heinrich, who naively passed it on to me, that he had 'found Leni untouched.'" Lotte's blushing persisted. When she was asked whether there were any chance that this Alois Pfeiffer might have been boasting to his brother Heinrich of a trophy, so to speak, which he was not entitled to claim, she became uncertain for the first time, saying: "He was a show-off all right, one can hardly deny that—and what you've just said makes me wonder. No," she said after a brief shake of the head, "no, I think that's quite out of the question, though they had plenty of opportunity," and, to the Au.'s astonishment, blushed again as she said: "Leni didn't behave like a widow after his death, if you can see what I mean, she behaved, if you really do see, like a platonic widow." To the Au. this statement was sufficiently clear, he admired her directness but was still not entirely convinced, although he regretted having taken so long to discover Lotte Hoyser, née Berntgen, in her full capacity as a witness. What amazed him was that Leni had been so communicative, one might almost say talkative, during that period of her life. An explanation for this was offered by Lotte Hoyser, now more pensive, quieter, no longer quite so voluble, from time to time giving the Au. an almost brooding look:

"It was obvious that she loved Erhard, that she loved him *expectantly,* if that conveys anything to you, and sometimes I had the feeling that *she* was on the brink of taking the initiative. Now, I'd like to tell you about something, something I've never told anybody: I once saw Leni clearing out a plugged-up john, and I simply couldn't get over the girl. One Sunday evening in 1940, we were all sitting around in Margret's apartment, having a few drinks and dancing a bit—my husband Wilhelm was there too—and suddenly someone says the john's plugged up; horrible business, I can tell you. Someone had tossed something in—a good-sized apple that was going bad, as it turned out—that was blocking the waste pipe, so the men set to work to remedy this embarrassing mishap; first Heinrich—no luck, he poked around in there with an iron bar, then Erhard, he tried, and not so stupidly at that, with a rubber hose he got from the laundry room, and tried using mechanical pressure by blowing like crazy into the hose which he stuck, with no squeamishness whatever, into that sickening mess—and then, because Wilhelm, who had after all been a pipefitter, later a technician, and finally a draftsman, turned out to be surprisingly squeamish, and because I and Margret were almost throwing up, do you know who solved the problem: Leni. She simply plunged her hand down, her right hand, and I can still see her lovely white arm covered with yellow muck to above the elbow, then she grabbed the apple and threw it into the garbage pail—and all that horrible mess instantly gurgled away out of sight, and then Leni washed herself—thoroughly, mind you, and over and over again, wiping eau de cologne all over her arms and hands, and she made a remark—now it comes back to me—a remark that I found quite electrifying: 'Our poets never flinched from cleaning out a john.' So now, when I say she could tackle any job that had to be done, what I mean is, maybe she ended up by simply tackling that Erhard: I'm sure he wouldn't have objected. Which reminds me, by the way: not one of us ever got to see that husband of Margret's."

Since Lotte Hoyser's statements did not quite tally with Margret's, it was necessary to interrogate the latter once again. Was it true that she had danced with the people named by Lotte on some occasions in her apartment, was it possible that she had already had a more intimate relationship with Heinrich long before that event which we will call the "Flensburg incident"? "As for the last thing," said Margret, in whom a potent slug of whiskey had induced a gentle euphoria tinged with melancholy, "I can flatly deny that, I should know after all, and I'd have no reason to disclaim it. I did make one mistake, I introduced my husband to Heinrich. Schlömer was hardly ever home, I never really found out whether he was in armaments, or an informer, or what, he always had plenty of money whatever it was, and all he asked of me was to 'be there for him' whenever he sent me a telegram. Older than I was. In his mid-thirties in those days. He wasn't at all bad-looking, dressed smartly and all that, a man of the world, you might say, and the two of them got along quite well together. And Heinrich, he was a terrific lover but not exactly an adulterer—in those days he wasn't *that* yet; I'd always been an adulteress, but he hadn't reached that stage yet, and it was probably because he was shy after meeting my husband that he hadn't got around to it yet. But as for the other thing—it must've been Lotte who told you that, that I saw him more than twice, and I danced with him, and in the apartment with the others—it's true, but we certainly didn't see each other more than four times all told."

Asked about Erhard and Leni, Margret smiled and said: "I don't really want to know about it, and at the time I didn't really want to know about it either. What had it got to do with me? The details certainly didn't concern me. Do I or did I want to know if they kissed, if at least their hands took pleasure in each other, if they went to bed together, in my apartment I mean, or in

Lotte's, or in the Gruyten home? I just found it wonderful the way those two behaved together, and the poems he wrote to her and sent her, Leni couldn't keep it to herself, and it was during those few months that for the first time she came out of her shell, after that she shut herself away again completely. Does it matter so much whether Erhard or that stupid Alois was the first, what difference does it make? Why bother? She loved him, tenderly and passionately, and if nothing happened by then it would have happened during his next leave, I guarantee, and you know, of course, how it all ended, in Denmark against a cemetery wall. Gone. Why don't you ask Leni?"

Ask Leni! That's easier said than done. She won't let one ask her, and when one does ask her she doesn't answer. Old Hoyser called the Erhard incident "a touching but purely romantic affair, although with a tragic ending. That's all." Rahel is dead, and that B.H.T. naturally knows nothing about Erhard's affairs. Since it is known that Leni made frequent visits to the convent, Rahel would certainly have known something. The Pfeiffers did not enter her life until later, and she most certainly told *them* nothing of what was "precious" to her. "Precious" is how M.v.D., to whom the Au. resorted with a sigh, described the Erhard affair.

The Au. was obliged to correct some hasty judgments of her that he had made after her remarks about Mrs. Gruyten. When the subject is not Mrs. Gruyten and her husband, Miss van Doorn shows herself capable of giving quite subtle information, fine-grained, you might say. "Now please," she said, when traced to her rural place of retirement, surrounded by asters, geraniums, and begonias, scattering feed for the pigeons, stroking her dog, an elderly mongrel-poodle, "don't meddle with that precious thing in Leni's life. It was like a fairy tale, you see, those two, just like a fairy tale. They were so openly in love, so at ease with each other, I saw them a few times sitting there in the living room —the room that Leni's now rented to the Portuguese—the best china from the cabinet, and tea, drinking tea—though Leni's never liked tea, but with him she drank it, and while he didn't exactly complain about the army, he showed his disgust and dislike so openly that she put her hand on his arm, to comfort him, and you could tell just by looking at him that that touch was enough to cause a real revolution of his senses, or his sensibility, if you like. There were plenty of moments, believe me, when he had the chance to conquer her completely, she was, she stood—and if you'll pardon my putting it rather crudely—she *lay* there ready, ready for him, and since I'm talking about it anyway, it was just that Leni was getting a bit impatient, that's all, impatient—biologically impatient too; not annoyed, no, not angry with him—and if he'd ever been there for at least two or three days in a row, well, things would've turned out differently, I'm sure. I'm an old maid and I've never had any direct experience with men, but I've observed them pretty closely, you know, and I ask you, what must it be like when a man turns up with his return ticket in his pocket and is always thinking of the timetable and the barracks gate he has to go through before a certain hour, or the remustering depot? I tell you—and I say this as an old maid who realized this in the first war as a girl and in the second as an observant woman: leave is a terrible thing for a husband and wife. Everyone knows, when the husband comes home on leave, what the two have in mind—and every time it's almost like a public wedding night—and people, the ones in the villages hereabouts anyway, and in the towns too, aren't that sensitive and keep making hints—Lotte's husband Wilhelm, for instance, he always went scarlet, he was a very sensitive person, you see, and do you think I didn't know what was supposed to happen when my father came home on leave during the war—and Erhard, it's just that he'd have needed a bit more time to conquer Leni—how could he when he was always on the point of leaving, and he just wasn't the man to take the bull by the horns. Those poems of his, they were explicit enough surely, almost too explicit. 'You are the earth I shall one day become'—can anybody be more explicit than that? No, what he lacked was *time,* he didn't have enough time. You must remember that he had altogether maybe twenty hours alone with Leni—and it so happened that he wasn't a go-getter. Leni didn't take offense at this, only she was sad, for she was *ready.* Even her mother knew that, and she *wanted* it, I tell you. I used to see how she took care that Leni wore her prettiest dress, the saffron-yellow one with the low round neck, and the jewelry to go with it: she made her wear coral earrings, they looked like freshly picked cherries, and she bought her some smart little shoes and some perfume—she dressed her up like a *bride;* even she knew it and wanted it—but there wasn't enough time, that's all it was—just one more day and she'd have been his and not—oh well. It was awful for Leni."

There was no getting around it, Mrs. Schweigert had to be called on once more; asked over the telephone by the concierge, she consented to see him, she consented not all that ungraciously but with obvious impatience, over a cup of tea yet without offering any, "to answer a few more questions"; yes, her son had once presented that "Oh well" girl to her, she stressed the distinction between being *introduced* and *presented;* besides, there had been no need for an introduction, she had known the girl for quite a while and had gained some insight into her educational background and career; there had, of course, been "some talk of a love affair," but again she rejected any idea of a permanent relationship, marriage in other words, as being out of the question, a relationship such as the permanent one between her sister and the girl's father; she volunteered the information that the girl had also visited her once alone, she had—in all fairness—behaved very properly as she drank her tea, the sole topic of conversation had been—yes, it sounded extraordinary but it was true—heather; the girl had asked her when and where the heath was in bloom—was it just then, for instance? "It was toward the end of March, you must realize, and I felt as if I were talking to an idiot"; imagine asking whether the heath was in bloom at the end of March—and in 1940, during wartime, at that—in Schleswig-Holstein; the girl had been totally ignorant of the difference between Atlantic and rock heather, also of their differing soil requirements; in the end, said Mrs. Schweigert, everything had turned out for the best—she evidently found her son's death at the hands of a German Army firing squad preferable to his possible marriage to Leni.

It must be conceded that, in her brutally succinct way, Mrs. Schweigert did throw light on much of the background. She explained the obscure business of the "Fenians," or at least contributed to the explanation—and when we bear in mind that at the end of March 1940 Leni actually took the trouble to go and see Erhard's mother and talk to her about heather in Schleswig-Holstein, furthermore that, according to Miss van Doorn's statement, she was *prepared*—even in Lotte Hoyser's opinion prepared—to take the initiative, and if we think back to her experience in the heather under that starry summer sky—we are justified in concluding, even objectively, that she was toying with the idea of visiting Erhard up north and finding fulfillment with him in the heather; and even if we objectivize the botanical and climatological conditions and come to the conclusion that any such plan was doomed on account of damp and cold, the fact remains that in March, according to the Au.'s experience at least, certain parts of the heath in Schleswig-Holstein are actually, if only for a short time, warm and dry.

Finally, after repeated urgings, Margret was induced to admit that Leni had asked her for advice as to how one went about getting together with a man; and when Margret referred her to her parents' spacious and often undisturbed seven-room apartment, which caused Margret, not Leni, to blush, Leni shook her head; when she was finally referred to her own room in that apartment, a room she could lock and to which she need admit no one, Leni again shook her head; and when Margret, becoming impatient, then pointed out with considerable bluntness that there were after all such things as hotels, Leni reminded her of her misadventure (still quite recent) with the young architect and expressed a notion that Margret was reluctant to pass on, "as Leni's most intimate communication to date," the notion that "it" must and should not happen "in bed" but out of doors. "In the open, in the open. This whole business of going to bed together is not what I'm looking for." Leni conceded that, when two people happened to be married, the bed would at times be unavoidable. Only: with Erhard, she didn't want to go to bed the very first time. She was all set to go to Flensburg but changed her mind and decided to wait until May—so her rendezvous with Erhard remained a Utopia thwarted by military history. Or did it? No one knows for sure.

Judging by the statements of all family and nonfamily witnesses, the year from April 1940 to June 1941 merits but one description: grim. Leni lost not only her good spirits but her talkativeness, even her appetite. Her pleasure in driving vanishes for a time, her delight in flying—she flew with her father and Lotte Hoyser three times to Berlin—vanishes. Once a week only does she get into her car and drive the few miles to Sister Rahel. Sometimes she stayed there quite some time; nothing is known of her conversations with Rahel, not even via B.H.T., who after May 1941 sees no more of Rahel in the antiquarian bookstore and—presumably from lethargy or lack of imagination—never thinks of going to see her. A huge convent orchard in summer, in fall, in the winter of 1940–41, a girl, eighteen and a half, who now wears nothing but black, whose sole product of external secretion is a complex one: tears. Because of the arrival only a few weeks later of the news of the death of Wilhelm Hoyser, Lotte's husband, the circle of weepers is widened by old Hoyser, his wife (then still living), by Lotte and her five-year-old son Werner; whether the youngest son, Kurt, then still in his mother's womb, cries too, no one ever knew.

Since the Au. neither is in a position to meditate on tears nor considers himself suited to do so, information on the origin of tears, their chemical and physical composition, can best be obtained from a handy reference work. The seven-volume encyclopedia put out by a controversial publisher, 1966 edition, gives the following information on tears:

"Tears, Lat. lacrimae, the fluid secreted by the T.-glands that moistens the conjunctiva, protects the eye from desiccation, and continuously washes small foreign bodies out of the eye; it" (probably the fluid. Au.'s note.) "flows into the inner corner of the eye and thence out through the nasolacrimal duct. Irritation (inflammation, foreign bodies) or emotional stimulus increases the flow of T. (weeping)." Under *Weeping* we read in the same reference work: "Weeping—like⟶Laughter, form of expression in time of crisis, i.e., of grief, emotion, anger, or happiness; *psychologically*" (italics are not the Au.'s), "an attempt at mental or emotional release. Accompanied by the secretion of tears, by sobbing or convulsive heavings, is related to the sympathetic nervous system and the brainstem. Takes the form of compulsive W. and uncontrollable W.-spasms in general depression, manic-depressive illness, multiple sclerosis."

Since potentially interested readers of these simple facts may break out into that which is indicated by⟶and might like to have this reflex explained, we shall now, in order to obviate the necessity of acquiring an encyclopedia, or even of consulting one, quote the paragraph in question:

"Laughter, *anthropologically*" (*none* of the italics, including those to follow, are the Au.'s), "a physically resonant expression of emotional reaction to situations of crisis⟶Weeping. *Philosophically,* L. of the sage, smile of the Buddha, the Mona Lisa, from a sense of confidence in Being. *Psychologically,* mimic expressive movement indicating joy, mirth, amusement. In the form of childlike, blasé, ironical, emotional, relieving, despairing, spiteful, coquettish L., reflects values of attitude and character. *Pathologically,* in diseases of the nervous system and in psychoses, compulsive L. in the form of laughing fits, sardonic L. accompanied by facial distortion, and hysterical L. in the form of laughing spasms. *Socially,* L. is infectious (ideomotor activity prompted by imagination)."

Now that we are obliged to enter upon a more or less emotional and, inevitably, tragic phase, it is no doubt advisable to complete our definition of concepts: there is no explanation for the concept of Happiness in this encyclopedia: between Happenstance and Happy Warrior all we could find was Happy Hunting Ground, but *Bliss* was there, defined as the "quintessence of perfect and lasting fulfillment of life; sought instinctively by every human being, depending on whatever it is in which he seeks this ultimate fulfillment, on the choice that determines the entire content of his life; according to Christian doctrine, true B. is to be found only in eternal—>Beatitude."

"*Beatitude,* the state, free of all pain or guilt, of everlasting and perfectly fulfilled happiness, anticipated by all religions as the purpose and object of human history. In the *Cath.* doctrine, primarily the B. of God in the infin. possession by Himself of His perfect Being; secondly, the B. of Man (& Angel) in communion with God through charismatically granted participation in His beatifying life, a participation that begins in temporal life as intimacy with Christ (Divine bliss) and is perfected in eternal B. with—>Resurrection and eschatolog. transformation of all reality. According to *Prot.* belief, perfect union with God's Will, the true destiny of Man, his salvation and his redemption."

Now that T. and W., L. and B., have been sufficiently defined, and we know where to look up the definition whenever we need these tools, it is not necessary for this report to concern itself for long with the description of emotional states, it being enough to point to their definition in the encyclopedia as occasion arises and to refer to them merely by the suitable abbreviation of each. Since T., L., and W. are to be expected in crisis situations only, it might be appropriate at this point to congratulate all those who proceed through life crisis-less, crisis-free, or merely crisis-resistant, who have never shed a T., have been spared W., have never wept for someone else, and have refrained from L. where it was against regulations. A toast to all those whose conjunctiva have never been summoned into action, who have survived all vicissitudes dry-eyed, and who have never used their T.-ducts. A toast, too, to those who have their brainstems firmly under control and, in a state of perpetual confidence in Being, have never had to laugh or smile from any sense of Being other than that of wisdom. Three cheers for Buddha and the Mona Lisa, who were so utterly confident in their Being.

Since *Pain* is also due to occur, the pertinent paragraph, instead of being quoted here in toto, will be edited so as to allow only one crucial sentence to appear here: "The degree of sensitivity to P. varies with the individual, chiefly because to physical P. is later associated the experience of mental or spiritual P. Both together result in subjective P."

Because Leni and all those affected not only felt P. but *suffered,* let us, in order to complete our set of referents, quickly quote the operative sentence in the encyclopedia that deals with *Suffering.* It (S.) "is felt by a person with a severity proportionate to his quality of life and to the sensitivity of his nature."

One thing is certain: in the case of all those associated with the Gruyten and Hoyser families, including Marja van Doorn, who was linked equally with both families, rather important aspects of the quality of life must have been seriously affected. In Leni's case, alarming signs appeared: she lost weight, acquired among outsiders the reputation of being a crybaby; her magnificent hair, while it did not exactly fall out, lost its luster, and not even Marja's fabulous inventiveness with soups, in the production of which even her eyes were constantly T.-filled—she paraded her whole rich gamut of soups before Leni and procured the very freshest of fresh rolls—nothing could remedy Leni's lack of appetite. Photos from that time, taken secretly by one of her father's employees and later found in Marja's possession, show Leni looking downright peaked, pale from P. and S., totally debilitated by W. and T., without even a suggestion of the rudiments of L. Was it possible that Lotte Hoyser had not been quite so right after all in disputing Leni's widowhood, and that at some deeper level, hidden from Lotte, Leni had indeed been a widow and not only platonically? Be that as it may, Leni's subjective P. must have been quite considerable. Nor was it any less in the case of the others. Now her father did not merely lapse into brooding, melancholy set in, and (according to the information of those who had dealings with him) he "lost interest." Since old Hoyser was equally broken, and even Lotte (according to her own information) "hadn't been herself for ages," and Mrs. Gruyten, now gradually fading away, kept to her bedroom anyway, "now and again swallowing a few spoonfuls of soup and half a slice of toast" (M.v.D.), an explanation for the fact that the business not only continued to flourish but actually expanded is the one offered by old Hoyser, which sounds more or less plausible: "It had such a sound basis and was so well organized, and the auditors, the architectural and construction experts, who had been engaged by Hubert, were so loyal, that it simply continued to run of its own momentum, at least for the year when Hubert was a complete washout, and myself too. But the main thing was: the hour of the old-timers had struck—there were a few hundred of them by that time, and they took charge of the business!"

The subject now becomes too delicate for us to choose Lotte Hoyser as witness for an unexplained period in the life of Gruyten, Sr.: we must reluctantly forgo her wonderfully dry, pregnant manner of speaking.

For, to use a rather fashionable expression, during the ensuing year (which must be calculated from April 1940 to roughly June 1941) she was his "constant companion." He may also have been her constant companion, for both were in need of the consolation that in the end it seems they did not find.

They traveled around, the pregnant widow with the melancholy man who did not read the file on the misfortune that had befallen his son and his nephew but merely had Lotte and Hoffgau give him the gist of it; a man who from time to time would mutter to himself "Shit on Germany," ostensibly traveling from construction site to construction site, from hotel to hotel, in reality not casting so much as a single glance anywhere at the drawings, accounts, files, or construction sites. He travels by train and by car, or by plane, pathetically pampering the five-year-old Werner Hoyser who today, at thirty-five, lives in a smart self-owned apartment full of modern furniture, is enthusiastic about Andy Warhol, and could "kick himself in the arse" for not having bought soon enough; hc is a pop fan, a sex fan, and the owner of a betting office; he clearly remembers long walks by the beaches of Scheveningen, Mers les Bains, Boulogne, and that "Grandpa Gruyten's" hands used to shake and Lotte used to cry; he remembers construction sites, T-beams, workmen in "funny clothes" (probably prisoners. Au.). From time to time Gruyten, who no longer lets Lotte out of his sight, stays home for a few weeks, sits at his wife's bedside, relieving Leni and trying desperately to do what Leni is trying to do: read something Irish to his wife, fairy tales, legends, ballads—but with no more success that Leni; Mrs. Gruyten wearily shakes her head, smiles. Old Hoyser, who seems to have got over his P. more quickly and by September has already stopped shedding T., is "going to the office again," at intervals hearing himself asked the astonishing question: "Hasn't the business gone to the dogs yet?" No. It is even continuing to improve: his old-timers stand firm, their ranks are unbroken.

Is this man Gruyten already worn out at forty-one? Can't he come to terms with the death of his son, while all around him the sons of others are dying en masse without those others being broken? Is he beginning to read books? Yes. One. He digs out a prayer book from the year 1913 that was given to him at his First Communion and "seeks consolation in religion" ("which he never had," Hoyser, Sr.). The only result of this reading is that he starts giving money away, "scads of it," as Hoyser and his daughter-in-law Lotte both testify, and the van Doorn woman too, who instead of "scads" says "wads" ("He gave me wads of it too, so I bought back my parents' little farm and a bit of land")—he goes to churches but can never stand being in there longer than "a minute or two" (Lotte). He "looked seventy while his wife, who had just turned thirty-nine, looked sixty" (van Doorn). He kisses his wife, sometimes kisses Leni, never Lotte.

Is decline setting in? His former family doctor, a Dr. Windlen, aged eighty, who has long since risen above the myth of professional secrecy, sitting in his old-fashioned apartment where remnants of his practice—white cabinets, white chairs—are still to be seen, wholly engrossed in unmasking as idolatry the fashionable craze for medication, maintains that Gruyten had been "as fit as a fiddle; all the tests, every single one, were negative—liver, heart, kidneys, blood, urine—besides, the fellow hardly smoked at all, maybe a cigar a day, and drank maybe a bottle of wine a week. Gruyten a sick man? Not on your life—I tell you, he knew what was what, he knew what he was doing. The fact that people say he sometimes looked seventy proves nothing—psychically and morally, mind you, he had been terribly injured, but organically: no. The only thing he remembered from the Bible was: 'Make to yourselves friends of the mammon of unrighteousness,' and that affects a person's disposition."

Is Leni devoting as much attention as ever to the products of her digestion? Probably not. She visits Rahel more often, even talks about it. "Strange goings-on," as Margret testifies. "I didn't believe a word of it, and then one day I went along and saw it was true. Haruspica no longer had any specific job, she wasn't even a 'toilet attendant.' And was only allowed in the church when the choir wasn't singing or a service wasn't going on. She didn't even have her wee little room any more, she was cooped up in the attic in a tiny closet where they used to keep brooms and brushes, cleaning materials and dusters, and you know what she asked us both for? Cigarettes! I didn't smoke in those days, but Leni gave her a few, and she lighted one right away and inhaled deeply; then she nipped off the end—I've often seen people nip the end off a cigarette, but the way she could do it! It was perfect, the work of an expert, like people do in the clink or in hospital in the john, she took her scissors and very carefully snipped off the burning end and poked around in it to see if there wasn't a shred of tobacco in there—and all into an empty matchbox. And all the time she kept murmuring: 'The Lord is nigh, the Lord is nigh, He is at hand.' It didn't sound crazy, or ironical, the way she said it, it sounded serious—she certainly wasn't nuts, just a bit scruffy, as if she weren't being given quite enough soap. I didn't go again: to tell the truth, I was scared—my nerves were all shot anyway, what with the boy being dead and his cousin too; when Schlömer was away I used to hang around the soldiers' bars and then go off with one or another; I was finished, though I was only nineteen—and that business with the nun, I just couldn't bear to see it, she was caged like a mouse left to die, you could tell; she was more wizened than ever, she took a big bite out of the bread Lotte had taken her and kept saying to me: 'Margret, stop it now, stop it.' 'Stop what?' I asked. 'What you're doing.' I didn't have the guts any more, I couldn't take it, my nerves were shot—Leni, of course, went on visiting her for years. She used to say funny things like: 'Why don't they just finish me off instead of hiding me?' And to Leni she kept saying: 'For God's sake, you've got to live—live, I tell you, do you hear?'—and Leni would cry. She was very fond of her. Well, later on it all came out ["What?"] that she was Jewish and that the Order hadn't even registered her, simply acted as if she'd disappeared during a transfer, they hid her, but they didn't give her much to eat. Because, you see, she didn't have any ration cards, yet they had that orchard, and the pigs they fattened. No, my nerves couldn't take it. Like a little shriveled-up old mouse she was, cooped up in there—and the only reason they let Leni see her was that she was so determined, and because they knew how naive she was. She just thought the nun was being disciplined. Right to the end, Leni never bothered to distinguish between Jews and non-Jews anyway. And even if she had known, and had known how dangerous it was, she would've said: 'So what?' and would have gone on visiting her, I swear it. Leni had courage—she still has. It was terrible to hear the nun say: 'The Lord is nigh, the Lord is nigh,' and to see her look toward the door as if He were just coming in, that very instant—that scared me, but not Leni—she would look toward the door, expectantly—as if it wouldn't surprise her to see the Lord come walking in. But by that time it was early 1941, I already had a job at the military hospital, and she looked at me then and said: 'It's not only what you're doing that's not good, what you're taking is worse, how long have you been taking it?' And I said:

'Two weeks.' And she said: 'Then there's still time.' And I said: 'No, I'll never give it up now.' Morphine, of course—didn't you know, or didn't you at least suspect?"

The only person who never seems to have been in need of consolation is Mrs. Schweigert, who about this time often turns up at the Gruyten house to visit her dying sister, trying to make her understand that "Fate cannot break a person, it can only make him strong"; that her husband, Gruyten, is displaying his poor breeding by being so "broken." She even has the nerve to expostulate with this sister who has one foot in the grave: "Think of the proud Fenians." She talks about Langemarck, is hurt, hurt to the quick, when, after inquiring about the cause of Leni's manifest grief, she learns from Miss van Doorn, who is our informant for all these utterances, that Leni is probably grieving for Mrs. Schweigert's son Erhard. She is indignant that this "heather girl" (a variation, at least, of the "Oh well girl." Au.) should have the effrontery to grieve for her son while she is not even grieving for him herself. After this "shocking piece of information" she makes no further visits and leaves the house with the remark: "That's really too much, I must say—heather indeed!"

Needless to say, movies are being shown this year too, and every now and then Leni goes to the movies. She sees *Comrades on the High Seas, Dancing Through the Night,* and *Bismarck* again.

The Au. doubts whether even a single one of these movies brought her anything like consolation or even distraction.

Did the hit tunes of the day, "Brave Little Soldier's Wife," "We'll Storm the Coasts of England," console her? It is doubtful.

At times all three Gruytens, father, mother, daughter, lie in bed, in darkened rooms, not leaving their rooms even for air-raid warnings, and "staring for days, weeks, at the ceiling" (van Doorn).

Meanwhile all the Hoysers have moved in with the Gruytens,

Otto, his wife, Lotte, her son Werner—and an event takes place which, although it could be foreseen, in fact precisely calculated, is nevertheless regarded as a miracle and even contributes to the general recovery: Lotte's child is born, in the night of December 21 to 22, 1940, during an air raid; it is a boy, weighing seven pounds two ounces, and since he arrives a little earlier than expected and the midwife is not prepared, "busy elsewhere" (with the birth of a girl, as it turns out), and the determined Lotte proves, surprisingly enough, to be as weak and helpless as the van Doorn woman, a further miracle occurs: Mrs. Gruyten leaves her bed and gives her instructions to Leni in a precise, firm, yet pleasant voice; while the final labor pains assail Lotte, water is heated, scissors are sterilized, diapers and blankets are warmed, coffee is ground, brandy set out; it is an icy, dark (the darkest) night of the year, and the emaciated Mrs. Gruyten, "now hardly more than a disembodied spirit" (van Doorn), has her finest hour, in her sky-blue bathrobe, continually checking the necessary instruments laid out on the chest of drawers, dabbing eau de cologne on Lotte's forehead, holding her hands, spreading Lotte's legs apart without any embarrassment, then helping her into the prescribed squatting position; quite unafraid she receives the baby as it is born, washes the mother down with vinegar and water, cuts the umbilical cord, and sees to it that the baby is kept "warm, warm, warm" as it is placed in a laundry basket that has been well padded by Leni. She is not in the least bothered by the bombs exploding not very far away, and the air-raid warden, a certain Mr. Hoster, who keeps demanding that the lights be put out and everyone go down to the cellar, is dismissed by her so summarily that all the witnesses to this event (Lotte, Marja van Doorn, old Hoyser) unanimously state, independently of one another, that she acted "like a real sergeant major."

Did the world lose a doctor in her after all? In any event, she "cleans up the maternal parts" (Mrs. Gruyten according to Hoyser, Sr.), checks the expulsion of the afterbirth, has coffee and brandy with Leni and Lotte; to everyone's surprise the vigorous van Doorn woman "proved to be a broken reed" (Lotte) and found flimsy excuses for spending most of her time in the kitchen serving coffee to Gruyten and Hoyser and, by speaking constantly of "we" ("We'll see to that, we'll manage all right, we won't let it upset us, we etc."—with a very subtle dig at Mrs. Gruyten: "I hope her nerves can stand it! Let's hope it's not too much for her!"), she keeps her distance from where the action is, Lotte's bedroom, only appearing on the scene when the worst is over. When Mrs. Gruyten looks around, as if doubting her own capacity for tackling the job, she comes into the bedroom with little Werner and whispers to him: "Now let's have a look at our baby brother, shall we?" As if someone had doubted it, Mr. Gruyten said to old Hoyser: "I've always known and always said that she's a wonderful woman."

A certain tension sets in some days later when Lotte positively insists on having Mrs. Gruyten as godmother but refuses to have the boy, whom she would like to call Kurt ("That's what Willi wanted if it was a boy—a girl would have been called Helene") christened. She inveighs against the churches, "especially that one" (an expression that could never be properly explained; with a probability bordering on certainty we may assume her to have meant the Roman Catholic Church, she hardly knew any others. Au.). Mrs. Gruyten is not angry about it, only "very, very sad," consents to be godmother, and attaches great importance to giving the boy something really good, tangible, and lasting. She makes him a gift of a vacant building lot on the outskirts of the city that she had inherited at the death of her parents; she does all this very correctly, through an attorney, and Gruyten, Sr., makes a promise that he certainly would have kept but will not be able to keep: "And I'll put up a building for him on it."

The period of deepest melancholy seems to be over. Mr. Gruyten's hitherto passive-apathetic melancholy becomes active: "triumphantly, gleefully you might even say" (Hoyser, Sr.) he accepts the information that early on the morning of February 16, 1941, his office building has been hit by two bombs. Since these were not followed by incendiary bombs and the explosion did not start any fires, his hope "that the whole bloody place will burn to the ground" remains unfulfilled; after a week of salvaging operations, in which Leni takes part with no particular enthusiasm, it turns out that scarcely a file has been lost, and after a further four weeks the building has been restored.

Gruyten never enters it again, to the amazement of all those around him he becomes something he has never yet been, "not even in his young days, really—he turned sociable" (Lotte Hoyser). Lotte Hoyser goes on: "He got really nice, it surprised us all. Every day he insisted we all get together for coffee between four and five, in the apartment, Leni had to be there, my mother-in-law, the kids, everyone. After five he stayed behind with my father, who brought him up-to-date on all the details of the business, the bank position, receivables, future plans, construction sites—he had a balance sheet prepared and spent hours with attorneys, as well as other legal experts, to figure out a way of turning the firm—which was in his name only—into a company. An 'old-timers' list' was drawn up. He was smart enough to know that at forty-two—and in perfect health at that—he was still liable to be called up, and he wanted to ensure a position for himself as consultant on the board. On the advice of his customers—pretty big brass, a sprinkling of generals among them too, who all wanted the best for him, it seems—he changed his title to 'head of planning'; I was made personnel manager, my father became treasurer—but with Leni, then just eighteen and a half, there was nothing doing: she refused to be made a director. He thought of everything—there was only one thing he forgot: to make Leni financially secure. Later, at the time of the scandal, we all knew, of course, why he had fixed things the way he had, but Leni and his wife were left high and dry. Well, anyway, he was nice—and another thing, even more amazing: he started talking about his son; for nearly a year the name had never been mentioned, wasn't allowed to be mentioned. Now he talked about him; he wasn't so stupid as to talk about Destiny or any such nonsense, but he did say he thought it was a good thing Heinrich had died 'actively' rather than 'passively.' I didn't know quite what he meant because after more than a year that whole Danish business was beginning to have a sour taste in my mouth, I found it pretty stupid, or, let's say, I would have found it stupid if those two hadn't died for it—today I feel that 'to die for something' doesn't make that something any better, greater, or less stupid; to me it just leaves a sour taste, that's all I can say. Finally Gruyten had completed his 'reorganization' of the firm, and in June, the twelfth anniversary of the founding of the firm, he gave this party where he planned to announce the whole thing. It was on the fifteenth, right between two air raids—as if he'd had a premonition. The rest of us suspected nothing. Not a thing."

Leni resumed her attempts at the piano, with concentration and an "expression that had suddenly become very determined" (Hoyser, Sr.), and Schirtenstein, who has already been mentioned, and who (all this according to his own statement) had listened to her, "not entirely without interest but by and large rather bored" as he stood meditating at the window, "suddenly pricked up my ears and then one evening in June I heard the most astonishing interpretation I have ever heard. All of a sudden there was a discipline in the playing, an almost icy discipline, such as I had never heard before. If you'll allow me—an old man who has torn many a performer to shreds—a comment that may surprise you: I was hearing Schubert as if for the first time, and whoever was playing—I couldn't have told you whether it was a man or a woman—hadn't merely learned something but had understood something—and it's very rare for a nonprofessional to achieve that kind of understanding. That wasn't someone playing the piano—that was *music happening,* and again and again I found myself standing by the window and waiting, usually in the evening between six and eight. Soon after that I was called up and was gone for a long time, a very long time—and when I got back the apartment was occupied by the military, 1952—yes, I was gone eleven years, a prisoner of war—in Russia, where I strummed away far, far below my level—didn't have too bad a time of it—dance music, hit tunes—terrible stuff; do you know what it means for an 'intimidating music critic' to play 'Lili

Marleen' about six times a day?—and four years after I returned, it must have been in '56, I finally got back my old apartment—I happen to love these trees in the courtyard, and the high ceilings—and what do I hear and recognize after fifteen years—the moderato from the Sonata in A minor and the allegretto from the Sonata in G, with greater clarity, discipline, and depth than I had ever heard them, even in 1941 when I suddenly began paying attention. It was playing of the very highest caliber."

4

What follows now might well be headed: Leni does something foolish, Leni strays from the path of virtue—or: What's got into Leni?

On the occasion of the firm's anniversary party, scheduled for mid-June 1941, Gruyten had included in his invitation "all staff members who happened to be on home leave at the time." What no one could suspect, "what was, in fact, not conveyed by the invitation" (Hoyser, Sr.), "was that it could occur to anyone that *former* staff members might consider themselves invited, and even the term 'former staff member' would have been somewhat of an exaggeration for *him,* in 1936 he had once worked for us as a trainee for six weeks—no, he didn't want to be called an apprentice, that was too 'primitive' a word for him, he had to be a 'trainee' right off, but he had no intention of learning anything, all he wanted was to teach us how to build—we got rid of him fast, and then pretty soon he went into the army, he wasn't really such a bad sort, that boy, just a romancer, not a good romancer like young Erhard, say—a bad romancer with a tendency toward megalomania which didn't suit us at all. His idea was to get away from concrete and 'rediscover' the 'majesty' of stone—well, fair enough, maybe there was something in it, but we simply had no use for him, mainly because he didn't want to handle stone and didn't know how to. Damn it all, I've been in the building game for nearly sixty years now, even in those days I'd been in it for almost forty, and I had a pretty good idea of the 'majesty of stone'; I've watched hundreds of masons and mason's apprentices handling the stuff—you ought to have a look one day at how a real mason handles stone! Fair enough—but that fellow, he simply didn't have the right hands or the right feeling for stone: he just liked to talk big. He didn't mean any harm by it, oh no—he was just full of highfalutin ideas, and we knew where they came from."

A further unforeseen, unfortunate aspect of the party: Leni was dead set against going. She had lost all interest in dancing, she was 'a very serious, very quiet girl these days, got along well with her mother, studied French with her and a bit of English and was head over heels in love with her piano" (van Doorn). Besides, she knew "all the local staff quite well enough, there wasn't a single one of them capable of reviving her interest in dancing" (Lotte H.). It was only from a sense of duty and at the urgings of her parents that she went to the party.

The point has now been reached where, although he plays only a minor role, it is unfortunately necessary to say a few words about this Alois Pfeiffer who has been so witheringly described by Hoyser, and about his clan, his background.

A.'s father, Wilhelm Pfeiffer, had been a "school chum and wartime buddy" of Gruyten, Sr.; they came from the same village, and until Gruyten's marriage they had carried on a casual friendship that ceased when Wilhelm P. began "to get on Gruyten's nerves to the point where Gruyten couldn't stand it any more" (H.). The two men had fought together in a battle of the Great War (near the Lys, as it turned out), and after they came home from the war Pfeiffer, at that time twenty, "suddenly began" (H., including all of the following) "to drag his right leg as if it were crippled. Now I don't mind, of course, if someone manages to wangle a pension, but he overdid it, he talked of nothing else but a 'shell splinter the size of a pinhead' that had hit him at a 'critical spot'; and he certainly had stamina, for three years he dragged his leg from doctor to doctor, from pension board to pension board, till they finally gave him a pension and, what's more, financed his teacher-training course. Fair enough. Fair enough. Nobody wants to be unjust to a fellow creature, and maybe he was—I mean, is— really crippled, but no one ever found that splinter—and that needn't be the fault of the splinter, and I'm not saying the splinter doesn't exist, fair enough—and of course he got his pension and became a teacher and so on, but it was a funny thing: it irritated Hubert to distraction to see Pfeiffer coming along dragging his leg; it got worse and worse, at times he would even speak of amputation, and later on his leg did, as a matter of fact, appear to be stiff—but no one ever saw or found any evidence of that 'splinter the size of a pinhead' even on the most sensitive X-ray screen, never. And because no one had ever seen it Hubert said to Pfeiffer one day: 'Tell me, how d'you know the splinter is the size of a pinhead, if no one's ever seen it?' I must say, it was a staggering argument —and there's no doubt that from then on Pfeiffer's feelings were hurt beyond repair. But then he turned the whole thing into a kind of pinhead-*Weltanschauung,* and over and over and over again the kids in school out at Lyssemich were told about the splinter and about the 'Lys,' and this went on for ten, twenty years, and again Hubert said something very much to the point—we were always hearing things about him, you know, from the village where we all come from and have so many relatives—Hubert said: 'Even if he has a splinter in it, that's the phoniest leg I ever heard of, and there he goes dragging it around; and all that talk about a battle is nonsense, I was there, wasn't I?—we were in the third or fourth wave, and never even got into the battle—of course there were some shells and so on, but—well, we all know war makes no sense, but it wasn't anything like as bad as he makes out, and that's a fact, and for us two it only lasted a day and a half—surely that's not enough to live on for the rest of your life.' Well" (a sigh from H.), "so then Wilhelm's son, Alois, turned up at the ball."

A few visits to the village of Lyssemich, to obtain some factual information on Alois, could not be avoided. Two innkeepers, about the same age as A., were interviewed, together with their wives, who still remember him. A visit to the parsonage proved fruitless: the only thing the priest knew about the Pfeiffers was that the parish register "showed them to have been living in Lyssemich since 1756," and as Wilhelm Pfeiffer eventually moved away (although not until 1940), "not so much because of his political activities, which were rather embarrassing, but because we just couldn't stand him any more" (Zimmermann, innkeeper in Lyssemich, aged fifty-four, a solid citizen and plausible informant), traces of the Pfeiffer family have all but disappeared; the only witnesses are unfortunately all—one way or another—prejudiced: Marja van Doorn, all the Hoysers, Leni (Margret knows nothing about the Pfeiffers); the particulars supplied by both partisan groups do not contradict one another in data, merely in their interpretation.

All the witnesses of the anti-Alois party state that, at fourteen, Alois—in this respect his career has some resemblance to Leni's—had had to give up all idea of high school, while the Pfeiffers maintain he had been "the victim of certain intrigues." What no one disputes, although this characteristic too is mentioned in the most varied ironical refractions, is: that he was "handsome." Leni has no photo of him on the wall, the Pfeiffers have about ten, and it must be said: if the term "handsome" has ever had any meaning, it fits Alois. He had light blue eyes, dark, almost blue-black hair. In the context of extremely vulgar race theories, much has been said about A.'s blue-black hair; his father was fair, as were his mother and all his ancestors (the following information all comes from the Pfeiffer parents), inasmuch as anything is known or has been handed down regarding the color of their hair. Since all the known ancestors of the Pfeiffers and the Tolzems (Mrs. Pfeiffer's maiden name) first saw the light of day in the geographical triangle of Lyssemich–Werpen–Tolzem (a triangle with a total periphery of 16.2 miles), extended travel was not required. Two of Alois's sisters, Berta and Käthe, who died young, were—like his still surviving brother Heinrich—fair-if not golden-haired. There must have been fantastic black-hair/fair-hair mutterings among the Pfeiffers, whose No. 1 breakfast-table topic this must have been. There was even a willingness to resort to the repulsive measure of casting suspicion on the Pfeiffer ancestors as an explanation for A.'s hair; within the geographical triangle mentioned (although in view of its dimensions no great expenditure of effort could have been required), some snooping around went on in church and municipal records (the district registry was located at Werpen), in the hope of digging up female ancestors who could be suspected of introducing—by way of amorous adventures—the dark hair into the family; "I remember," says Heinrich Pfeiffer in talking about his family, quite without irony by the way, "that in 1936 they finally dug up a woman in the Tolzem church records whose legacy might have included my brother's surprising dark hair: it was a certain Maria, of whom only the first name was entered although her parents are registered as 'vagabundi.'"

Heinrich P. lives with his wife Hetti, née Irms, in a single-family house in a settlement of company houses with a denominational background. He has two sons, Wilhelm and Karl, and is on the point of buying a small car. H.P. is an amputee (having lost one leg below the knee), not disobliging but a bit edgy, for which his explanation is "worrying about new acquisitions."

Now in this geographical triangle dark hair is by no means rare; as far as can be visually ascertained and superficially assessed, it is on an average the most common, as the Au. was able with his own eyes to convince himself. But there was a family legend, a family pride, that was hawked around as the phrase "the famous Pfeiffer hair"; a woman with "Pfeiffer hair" was somehow considered favored, blessed, at any rate beautiful. Since, according to Heinrich P.'s information, the investigations within the Tolzem–Werpen–Lyssemich triangle uncovered numerous cross-connections with the Gruytens and their ancestors (not with the Barkels, they had been city-dwellers for generations), it is not impossible, in the Au.'s view, for Leni to have acquired this Pfeiffer hair by way of some such cross-connections. Now we want to be fair: seen objectively—from a barber's point of view, as it were—A.'s hair was undeniably handsome: thick, dark, naturally wavy. The fact that it was wavy was in turn cause for numerous speculations, because Pfeiffer hair—like Leni's!—was smooth and straight, etc., etc.

We may take it as objectively proved that from the very day of his birth too much fuss was made over this Alois. Quite in accord with Pfeiffer practice, a virtue was swiftly made of necessity, and he was regarded as "our gypsy," but only until 1933, from then on he counted as "classic Mediterranean"; the Au. considers it important to note that A. was in no sense a Celtic type, it being easy to take this mistaken view since Celts often have light eyes and dark hair. A. simply lacked—as we shall see later—Celtic sensibility and imagination; if he really must be placed in a racial category, the only description he merits is: substandard Teuton. He was shown around, held up, and for months—probably years—described as "cute"; even before he could speak with reasonable articulation fantastic careers were being dreamed up for him, artistic ones mostly, he was weighed down with high expectations: sculptor, painter, architect (writing did not enter the family's field of speculation until later. Au.). Everything he did was added to his credit a few sizes too large. Since, naturally, he was also a "cute altar boy" (we imagine that his first name makes any mention of denomination unnecessary), aunts, cousins, etc., already saw him as a "painter-monk"; perhaps even as a "painting abbot." There is evidence (by way of the Lyssemich innkeeper's wife, Mrs. Commer, now aged sixty-two, as well as her mother-in-law, Grandma Commer, now eighty-one, whose good memory is extolled throughout the village) that church attendance rose steadily as long as A. was altar boy in Lyssemich, i.e., during the years 1926 to 1933. "Would you believe it, sometimes we went to Crystalation on weekdays as well as Sundays, it was just too cute to see that dear little boy" (Grandma Commer; what religious exercise was meant by "Crystalation" is something we have not yet been able to ascertain. Au.).

A number of interviews had to be conducted with Mr. Pfeiffer and his wife Marianne, née Tolzem. Suffice it to say that the P.s' milieu was "one degree above" that of their son H.: a slightly larger row house and the car already in the garage. P., Sr., now retired, still drags his leg. Since the P.s are eager to supply information there was no difficulty at all in gathering material on A. from his parents; everything he ever produced is kept, like relics, in a glass showcase. Among the fourteen drawings on display, perhaps two or three were not too bad: colored pencil drawings of the countryside around Lyssemich, the extreme flatness of which—variations in level of twenty to thirty feet (such as depressions caused by streams), unavoidable even on plains, are quite a sensation—seems to have provided a constant motivation for A. to draw. Because the sky in these parts always comes down to the earth, a fertile earth, A.—whether consciously or unconsciously could not, of course, be ascertained—looked for the secret of light to be found in Dutch painting, a secret that on two or three of the sheets he had approached, taking (with some originality) as a source of light the Tolzem sugar factory, shifting it closer to Lyssemich and hiding the sun in its white steam. The P.s' claims that there had been hundreds of these drawings could not be verified, merely noted with skepticism. A few elementary woodworking jobs done by A.: a cactus bench, a jewelry box, a pipe stand for his father, and an enormous lamp (fretwork), left—to put it mildly—an embarrassing impression. Other objects on display were: some half-dozen respectable sports diplomas—track and field, swimming—a citation from the Lyssemich Football Club. A mason's apprenticeship begun by A. in Werpen and discontinued after six weeks was described by Mrs. P. as his "practical training" that "came to naught because of the intolerable rudeness of the foreman, who failed to understand his suggested innovations." In a nutshell: quite obviously A. was considered by others and by himself to be destined for "higher things."

Also displayed in a showcase at the P.s' were a few dozen poems by A. which the Au. prefers to pass over in silence: there was not one, not one line, which even began to approach the expressive power that Erhard Schweigert had been known to possess. After quitting his apprenticeship, "Alois threw himself heart and soul" (P., Sr.) into a career that for one of his character, which was weak at the best of times, turned out to be disastrous: he wanted to become an actor. A few successful appearances on the amateur stage in which he played the leading role in *The Lion of Flanders* have left behind in the P. showcase three newspaper clippings in which he received "unqualified praise"; the fact that it was one and the same critic writing for three different local papers under differing initials has to this day escaped the P.s' notice. The reviews all have the same wording—except for a few minute variations ("unqualified" is once replaced by "unalloyed," another time by "undisputed"). The initials are B.H.B., B.B.H., H.B.B. Needless to say, the acting also came to naught, because of people's failure to understand A.'s "intuition"; also because of their envy of his "wonderful good looks" (Mrs. P.).

Among the P. family's proudest relics are a few specimens of *printed* prose which, slightly faded, gilt-framed, adorn the top shelf of the glass case and were show to the Au. by Mrs. P. with the remark: "Just look, *in print,* that's true talent, you know, and think of the money he might have made with it." (This mixture of loftiest idealism and blatant materialism is typical of the P.s. Au.).

Forward March!

I.

Eight months have passed since the war began, and still we have not fired a single shot. The long cold winter was utilized for rigorous training. Now spring is here, and we have been waiting many weeks for orders from the Führer.

In Poland there were battles while we had to keep the Watch on the Rhine; Norway and Denmark were occupied without us being allowed to be there; some have already claimed that we will spend the whole war in our native land.

We are in a small village in the Eifel hills. On May 9 at 16:30 hours comes the order to march to the West. Alert! Messengers run, horses are harnessed, everywhere packs are being readied, a farewell word of thanks to the people with whom we have been quartered, the girlies have red-rimmed eyes—Germany is marching to the West, toward the setting sun, be on your guard, France!

The battalion gets under way that evening. In front of us are troops, close behind us others follow, and on the left-hand side of the road an endless stream of motorized columns overtakes us. We march through the night.

Dawn is but a glimmer and already the air is quivering with the thunder of German aircraft as they roar away overhead to bid good morning to the Western neighbor. And still the motorized troops overtake us. "German troops crossed into Holland, Belgium, and Luxembourg at dawn and are now continuing their westward advance"—for the benefit of the marching column, someone has called out this special bulletin as he drives by. There is a burst of enthusiasm, we wave to our brave comrades of the Luftwaffe as they continue to fly past overhead.

II. The River Meuse 1940

The Meuse is not a river. It is a single stream of fire. The heights along both banks are hills spewing fire.

Every bit of natural cover is made use of in this countryside that is so ideally suited for defense. Where Nature has proved inadequate, technology has stepped in. Everywhere machine-gun nests, at the foot of the cliffs, between crevices in the cliffs, deep in the cliffs. Tiny chambers, bored into the cliffs, hollowed out of the rock, lined with concrete, and towering above them a one-hundred-and-fifty-foot roof, hundreds of feet high, of centuries-old massive rock.

III. The River Aisne 1940

A hundred and twenty Stuka engines roar their song of iron! A hundred and twenty Stukas thunder across the Aisne!

But not one finds its target.

Nature has spread a protective blanket of thick ground-fog over the Weygand Line.

It's your turn, unknown foot-soldier, today it is up to you to prove the superiority of your rigorous training. Your victory drive must break the toughest resistance.

When you descend from the heights of the Chemin des Dames, remember the blood that has flowed here.

Remember the thousands who passed this way before you. It is up to you—soldier of 1940—to complete their task. Have you not read on the memorial stone: "Here stood Ailette, destoyed by the barbarians"? What criminal mentality deludes your foes, in whose eyes you—a human being fighting for his right to live—are once again a barbarian?

In the early morning of June 9 our division stands ready for the assault. Comrades of a sister regiment have the task of attacking in our sector. We have been posted as divisional reserve.

Alert! Get going!

It is four in the morning. Dazed with sleep, one man after another crawls out of the tent. A lively bustle ensues.

IV. A Hero

The story of this hero is an example of fearless courage and the uncompromising willingness of German officers to risk their own lives. It has been said that an officer must have the courage to show his men how to die. But every soldier, the moment he enters the battle arena and grasps the enemy by the throat, concludes a pact with Death. He casts out fear from his heart, tenses all his resources like a bowstring, his senses suddenly become unnaturally acute, he throws himself into the arms of capricious Fortune, and he feels, without realizing it, that Fortune favors only the brave. The fainthearted are carried away by the example of the brave, and the model of a single man who *sets an example of fearless courage* kindles the torches of dauntless courage in the hearts of the men around him. Such a one was Colonel Günther!

V.

The enemy fights grimly, with cunning and, when trapped, to the last man. He almost never surrenders. We are fighting blacks from Senegal, in their element here, masters of bush warfare. Marvelously camouflaged behind tree roots, behind artificial or natural screens of leaves, dug in wherever a path or a more open part of the forest lures on the attacker. The shooting is at close range, almost every shot finds its mark and almost always fatally. The tree-snipers are almost invisible too. Often they allow the attacker to pass by in order to finish him off from behind. It is impossible to eradicate them, they plague the reserves, dispatch riders, headquarters, artillerymen. Long since cut off, half starved, they continue for many days to shoot down single soldiers. They lie, stand, or sit huddled against a tree trunk, often still wrapped in a camouflage net, lying in wait for their prey. Whenever it is possible actually to detect one of them, the savage is usually already aware of this, and he merely drops like a sack from above to vanish like lightning into the undergrowth.

VI.

Onward, we must not dally here, not here of all places. The battalion is marching without cover through the valley. Who knows whether the enemy is ensconced on the slopes to right or left—ever onward! It is like a miracle, no one impedes our advance. The villages have been looted and destroyed by the wave of retreating French.

"Over there you can see the Chemin des Dames," a comrade next to me says in a low voice—his father had been killed in the Great War. "That must be the Ailette hollow, that's where he was wounded as a ration runner."

A broad highway leads across the Ailette hollow to the broad dominating heights above the Chemin des Dames. To the right and left of the highway there is hardly a single spot of ground that was not repeatedly torn up by shells during the Great War. Nowhere is there a tree of any size with a proper trunk. In 1917 there were no more trees here at all, everything had been blown to pieces. In the intervening years the roots have sprouted again, and every tree stump has become a bush.

VII.

Every few moments we look at the time. A last check, a last sighting. Final directions—and a shot rends the silence. Attack! From the edges of the forest and from behind lines of bushes, the German cannons blaze forth. Slowly the rolling gunfire rumbles up the slope of the opposite bank of the Aisne. The entire valley of the Aisne is shrouded in a cloud of smoke so that at times we can observe very little. When the firing is at its peak, the sappers bring up the rubber rafts and convey the infantry across. Heavy fighting begins for the crossing of the

> Aisne and the canal. Toward noon the heights on the far side have been reached, despite the enemy's desperate resistance. Observation is now no longer possible from our post. The advance observer and the two radio operators have already gone on ahead this morning with the infantry. In the afternoon the observation post and the firing position also receive orders to take up new positions. The hot sun beats down. After a short time we reach the Aisne. The new observation post is to be set up on Height 163.

The Au., all too self-conscious when it comes to the production of prose, must refrain from comment.

If we add up all the *factual* particulars on A. and reduce all the *nonfactual* ones to a kernel that would correspond to the factual ones, he may well have had the makings of quite a good Phys.-ed. teacher who could have taught drawing on the side. Where he did in fact end up after a few abortive careers is long since known to the reader: in the army.

Now it is well known that in the army, as anywhere else, one never gets something for nothing, most certainly not when one is obliged to pursue the career of noncommissioned officer, the only one open to A., who "had to quit school at fourteen" (H., Sr.). And at this point it is only fair to say that the seventeen-year-old A., who volunteered first for the Labor Service, then for the genuine article, is beginning to see the light. In letters to his parents (all in the showcase for everyone to inspect) he writes as follows: "This time I really do want to stick it out, come what may, and no matter how difficult other people may make things for me I don't want to be always putting all the blame on them, so please, Mum and Dad, when I've started a career don't go right away looking at its summit." That is not badly expressed and is an allusion to a remark of Mrs. P.'s who, the first time Alois came home on leave in uniform, already saw him as "military attaché in Italy, or something."

If, finally, we apply the always desirable pinch of compassion, as well as a minimum of what might be called fairness, and take into account A.'s deplorable upbringing, we see that he was not so bad after all, and the farther he got away from his family the better he became, since among strangers there was no one to see him as a future cardin- or admiral. When all is said and done, he managed after a year and a half in the army to get as far as corporal; and even taking into account that the imminent war was favorable to careers, there is not much to be ashamed of in that. When France was invaded he was made a sergeant, and it was in that capacity, the "bloom" still on him, that in June '41 he attended the Gruyten anniversary party.

Reliable details about Leni's rekindled pleasure in dancing that evening are not available, only rumors, whispers, both of a mixed nature: benevolent, spiteful, jealous, old-maidish; assuming that between eight in the evening and four in the morning dance music was played some twenty-four to thirty times, and Leni left the ballroom with A. after midnight, it is likely—if we average out the rumors and whispers—that Leni took part in twelve dances; however, of these assumed twelve dances she did not dance most or *almost* all with Alois, she danced them all with him. Not even with her father would she consent to a token dance once around the floor, not even with old Hoyser—no, she danced only with him.

Photos on display in the P. showcase, in addition to a medal and a combat pin, reveal the A. of those days to have been one of those shining-eyed fellows who were eminently suited in wartime not only to adorn the covers of illustrated weeklies but also to publish in such weeklies prose of the type quoted, in fact even in peacetime. According to all that Lotte, Margret, and Marja knew of him (both directly as well as filtered through Leni's meager information), and according to the Hoyser statements, we must picture him as one of those lads who, still shining-eyed after a twenty-mile march, machine rifle (loaded, safety catch released) at the chest, unbuttoned tunic from which the first medal dangles, enters a French village at the head of his platoon in the firm conviction of having captured it; who, after convincing himself with the aid of his platoon that there are neither partisans nor courtesans hidden in the village, has a thorough wash, changes his underwear and socks, and then voluntarily marches eight more miles through the night (not sufficiently intelligent first to make an intensive search in the village for a bicycle that might have been abandoned—perhaps he was just intimidated by the deceptive signs saying LOOTERS WILL BE SHOT); alone, undaunted—off he marches, merely because he claims to have heard that in the little town seven miles away there are some women; a few whores, no longer young, as it turns out on closer inspection, victims of the first German sex-wave of 1940; drunk, exhausted in the wake of considerable professional activity; after the medical orderly on duty has disclosed a few statistical details to our subsidiary hero and allowed him to have "a quick look, no obligation" at the pitifully old-looking women, he marches the eight miles back again, mission uncompleted (and only *now* does it occur to him that even the tiresome search for a concealed bicycle would have been worthwhile), ruefully calls to mind his first name with its attendant obligations and, after a march of altogether thirty-four miles, sinks instantly into a deep, short sleep, before waking, possibly "doing a bit of writing" in the gray dawn, and marching off again to capture more French villages.

It is with him, then, that Leni has danced an estimated twelve times ("You've got to hand it to him: he was a fantastic dancer!" Lotte H.), before letting herself be carried off, shortly before one in the morning, to a nearby castle moat that had been turned into a park.

Needless to say, this event has given rise to much speculation, theorizing, polemicizing, and analysis. It was a scandal, almost a sensation, that Leni, who had the reputation of being "unapproachable," should slip off "with *him*" of all people (Lotte H.). If we average out, as it were, the opinions and feelings expressed over this event, as we did in order to determine the frequency of dances, we arrive at the following result in our opinion poll: more than 80 percent of the observers, participants, and those in the know attributed material motives to A.'s seduction of Leni. In fact, by far the majority believes in some connection with A.'s aspirations toward an officer's career; his idea had been—so they say—to catch Leni for the sake of the financial security it would give him (Lotte). The entire Pfeiffer clan (including a few aunts, but *not* Heinrich) were of the opinion that Leni had seduced Alois. Most likely neither assumption is true. Whatever A. may otherwise have been, he was not calculating in a materialistic sense, and in this he was refreshingly different from his family. It is to be supposed that he fell head over heels in love with Leni in the radiance of her second blooming; that he was sick of his tiring and somewhat squalid adventures in French bordellos, that Leni's "freshness" (Au.) sent him into a kind of ecstasy.

As for Leni, let us make allowances for her and say that she simply "forgot herself" (Au.) and accepted the invitation to go for a walk along what used to be the castle moat, it was a summer night after all; and assuming that A. undoubtedly became affectionate, possibly even insistent, the worst conclusion one can reach is that Leni's mistake was less of a moral than of an existential nature.

Since the castle moat, still a park, is still in existence and an on-site inspection presented no difficulty, this was undertaken: a kind of botanical garden has been made out of it, and one section, about sixty square yards in extent, is planted with heather (Atlantic variety). The park administration, however, claimed to be "unable to trace the planting layout for 1941."

Leni's sole recorded comment apropos the next three days was: "too embarrassing for words"; this phrase, spoken identically to Margret, Lotte, and Marja, was her only contribution. Other available information allows us to conclude that A. was not a very sensitive lover and certainly not an imaginative one. Early next morning he dragged Leni off to an obscure aunt, Fernande

Pfeiffer, whose first name derives from her father's francophile and Separatist (in equal proportions) inclinations which, of course, were disavowed by the family. She was living in a one-room apartment in an old-fashioned building dating from 1895, not only without bath but also without water—i.e., the latter was not laid on in the apartment but was outside in the corridor. This Fernande Pfeiffer, who still, or, more accurately, again—for at one time she had been well off—lives in one room in an old-fashioned building (this time 1902), remembers "exactly, of course, when those two turned up, and—believe me—they didn't seem one bit like turtledoves, with those hangdog faces. I mean, surely the least he could have done for her was take her to some nice hotel, once they were through with that nature-children bit—some nice hotel where they could have had a wash, changed, and fixed themselves up. That silly boy really had no idea how to live."

Mrs. (or Miss) Fernande Pfeiffer herself impressed the Au. most emphatically as having known "how to live." *She* has the much-vaunted Pfeiffer hair and, although no longer young—somewhere in her mid-fifties—and living in reduced circumstances, she too had a bottle of the finest dry sherry close at hand. The fact that Fernande is disowned by the P.s, including Heinrich, "because she tried several times—and unsuccessfully at that—to operate a bar," renders her in no way less plausible to the Au. Her concluding remark was: "And I ask you, what sort of position was that for a nice girl—cooped up in my one-room apartment? Was I supposed to go out so the two of them could, well—let's say—carry on with their fun or their sinning, or was I supposed to stay in the room with them? It was worse for her than in the sleaziest hotel room, where at least you have a wash-basin and towel and can lock the door."

Finally, toward evening, Alois announced his decision to "face their parents, hand in hand, firm of countenance and without regard for corrupt bourgeois morality" (F. Pfeiffer), a phrase which Leni, to judge not by her words but by her "disdainful expression," did not seem to like. It is hard to determine objectively whether A. was just faking a bit and spouting a few phrases from his *Lion of Flanders* days, or whether a genuinely idealistic streak was showing itself in him as a result of the "pure experience" (the way he described the whole affair to his aunt, embarrassingly enough, in Leni's presence). It was obvious that he was an inveterate bandier or inventer of phrases, and it is not hard to imagine how this kind of talk brought a frown to the brows of our earthly-materialistic, human-divine Leni. Whether the shady aunt is to be believed or not, the fact remains that, according to her, Leni appeared to have little interest in spending another night with A. either in bed or on the heather, and that, when A. went out to visit the toilet on the half-landing, Leni had taken his leave pass from his pocket and, dismayed at the length of his leave, wrinkled her little nose. One item in this report is certainly not correct: Leni does not have a little nose, she has a well-developed, impeccably shaped nose.

With Alois showing no signs of wanting to elope or anything of the sort, there remained nothing else to do late that evening, after "we had sat there like graven images and drunk up all my coffee," than to confront the respective families. The first and most embarrassing encounter was with the Pfeiffers, who had been living in a remote suburb ever since old P. had been "transferred back into town." P., scarcely managing to conceal his triumph, croaked out a reproach: "How could you do such a thing to the daughter of my old friend," Mrs. P. restricted herself to an insipid "that wasn't a very nice thing to do." Heinrich Pfeiffer, then fifteen, maintains he clearly remembers the night being spent over coffee and brandy (Mrs. P.'s comment: "We don't care what it costs") and concocting detailed marriage plans, on which Leni made no comment, especially since she was not consulted. Eventually she fell asleep while further plans were being concocted. Even the size and furnishing of the apartment, down to the last detail, were discussed ("He can't settle his daughter in anything less than five rooms—that's the least he can do for her," and "mahogany, nothing less will do." "Perhaps he'll finally get around to building himself a house, or at least one for his daughter.")

Toward morning (all according to Heinrich P.) Leni made an "obviously provocative attempt to behave like a tart. She smoked two cigarettes, one after the other, inhaled, blew the smoke out through her nostrils, and smeared on a thick layer of lipstick." Someone went out to telephone for a taxi (this time Mr. P.: "We don't care what it costs") ("What?" Au.), and they all drove off to the Gruyten apartment, where—from now on we are dependent on the witness van Doorn, since Leni persists in silence—they "arrived embarrassingly early, that's to say around seven thirty in the morning." Mrs. Gruyten, who had not had much sleep (air-raid alarm and her godchild Kurt's first cold), was still in bed and having breakfast ("coffee, toast, and marmalade, have you any idea how hard it was to get hold of marmalade in 1941? —but of course he'd have done anything for her").

"So there she was, Leni—'risen on the third day,' that's how she seemed to me—ran at once to her mother and put her arms around her, then went to her room, asking me to bring her some breakfast, and—would you believe it?—she sat down at the piano. Mrs. Gruyten, I must grant her this, 'rose'—if you know what I mean—calmly got dressed, placed her mantilla—a wonderful piece of old lace that was always handed down to the youngest daughter of the Barkel family—around her shoulders, went to the living room, where the Pfeiffers were waiting, and asked pleasantly: 'Yes? What can I do for you?' Right off there was an argument about her formal manner: 'But Helene, why so formal all of a sudden?' and Mrs. Gruyten, 'I cannot remember ever having addressed you informally,' whereupon old Mrs. Pfeiffer said: 'We've come to ask for your daughter's hand for our son.' Thereupon Mrs. Gruyten, 'Hm.' That was all, then she goes to the phone, calls the office, would they please locate her husband and send him home as soon as he had been found."

Now clearly what went on for the next hour and a half was the enactment of that embarrassing blend of comedy and tragedy that is customary in middle-class marriage negotiations. The word "honor" was uttered some five dozen times (Miss van Doorn claims she can prove this, having made a mark on the doorpost for each one). "Now if it hadn't been Leni that all the fuss was about I'd have found it funny, for the second they saw how unimportant it was for Mrs. Gruyten to restore her daughter's honor by way of marriage to this A., they backtracked and switched to the honor of their son—making him out to be some kind of seduced virgin, besides, they said, their son's honor as a future officer—which he wasn't and never would be—could only be restored by marriage. In fact, it was more than funny when they began singing the praises of his physical qualities too: his lovely hair, his six foot two, his muscles."

Fortunately, it was not long before the dreaded appearance of Gruyten, Sr., who ("although he was known to rage like a madman") turned out to be "immensely gentle, quiet, almost friendly, to the great relief of the Pfeiffers who, needless to say, were scared to death of him." Words like "honor" ("We have our honor too, you know," old P. and his wife in the same words and at the same time) he abruptly dismissed; he gave A. a long long look, smilingly kissed his wife's forehead, and asked A. to tell him what was his division, his regiment, "became more and more thoughtful," then went to get Leni from her room, "didn't reproach her one bit" and asked her dryly: "What do you say, my girl, marriage or not?" Thereupon Leni (probably for the first time) looked at A. properly, thoughtfully, and as if once again she had some inkling (Has Leni already had some inkling? Au.). with pity too, for after all she had run off with him, and of her own free will, and she said 'marriage.'"

"With a certain gentleness in his voice" (van Doorn), Gruyten then looked at A. and said, "all right then," adding: "Your division is no longer near Amiens, it's at Schneidemühl."

He even offered to help A. obtain permission to marry, there being "some urgency." It is easy, of course, to say with hindsight that G., Sr., had known since the end of 1940 about substantial troop movements, and that during the night before the marriage was decided upon had heard, in a conversation with old friends, that the attack on the Soviet Union was imminent; "in his new post of 'head of planning' he heard a lot of things" (Hoyser, Sr.). Every objection to the marriage put forward during the day by Lotte and Otto Hoyser he waved away with a "Don't, please . . . don't. . . ."

The fact remains that, when A. received the wire granting him permission to marry, he was at the same time ordered to "terminate his leave forthwith and report to his division at Schneidemühl on June 19, 1941."

Civil ceremony, church ceremony; must they be described? It may be significant that Leni refused to wear white; that it was only in a state of extreme nervous tension that A. managed to get through the wedding banquet; that Leni did not seem at all depressed over the cancellation of the official wedding night, in any event she accompanied him to the station and allowed him to kiss her. As Leni later—during a particularly heavy air raid in 1944—confided to Margret in the latter's air-raid cellar, A. had forced Leni, only an hour before his departure, to have intercourse with him in what was then the ironing room of the G.s' apartment, "honorably and legitimately," with specific reference to her conjugal duties, and as a result A. "as far as I was concerned was dead before he was killed" (Leni according to Margret).

By the evening of June 24, 1941, the news was already received that A. had become a "fatal casualty" during the capture of Grodno.

The only significant aspect of all this is that Leni refused to wear mourning or show mourning; dutifully she tacked up a photo of A. beside the photos of Erhard and Heinrich, but at the end of 1942 she took A.'s photo down from the wall again.

There follow two and a half tranquil years in which Leni reaches nineteen, twenty, and finally twenty-one. She never goes dancing any more, although every now and then Margret and Lotte offer her the chance to do so. She sometimes goes to the movies, sees (acc. to Lotte H., who still gets her movie tickets for her) the films *Boys, Riding for Germany,* and *More Than Anything in the World.* She sees *Ohm Kruger* and *Sky Dogs*—and not a single one of these films draws as much as a single tear from her. She plays the piano, takes loving care of her mother (now failing again), and drives around a good deal in her car. Her visits to Rahel become more frequent, she takes along a Thermos flask of coffee, a lunch box of sandwiches, cigarettes. Since the war economy is becoming increasingly strict and Leni's job with the firm increasingly fictitious, she is threatened early in '42, after a searching scrutiny of the firm's activities, with losing her car, and those in the know are aware that for the first and only time in her life Leni asks for something; she asks her father to let her "keep the thing" (meaning her car, an Adler), and when he explains that this is no longer entirely within his power, she begs and implores him until he finally "throws all the switches and wangles her a six-months' reprieve" (Lotte H.).

Here the Au. indulges in considerable interference by taking the liberty of constructing a kind of hypothesis of fate, of wondering what Leni might have, would have, should have become if . . .

First of all, if Alois, as the only one of the three men thus far important to Leni, had survived the war.

It is more than likely that, since a military career appeared to be his true vocation, A. would have forged ahead not merely as far as Moscow but beyond it, become a lieutenant, a captain, possibly—we will spare him a hypothetical capture by the Soviets—a major by the end of the war, would have survived, chest covered with medals, a POW camp, would have been forced at some point to lose his partial naiveté or would have been—possibly forcibly—deprived of it; would have worked as a returning veteran for two years, as a "delayed" returning veteran for one year—as an unskilled laborer, perhaps for Gruyten, Sr., to whom a humbled A. would certainly have been preferable to a triumphant one; would undoubtedly have soon returned to the army, now the Bundeswehr, undoubtedly have become—by now fifty-two—a general. Would he ever again have been Leni's partner in conjugal nights, let alone passionate nights? The Au. maintains: No. The fact that Leni is so little suited to hypotheses renders this speculation difficult, of course. Had Leni not experienced an intense love (yet to be described), if . . . The Au. maintains: she would have experienced it, even if . . .

There is no doubt that A., who even at fifty-two would certainly still have been handsome, and preserved from baldness by the Pfeiffer hair, would have been able, had there been a shortage, to volunteer as an altar server in Bonn Minster or Cologne Cathedral; and what can one do with handsome generals who are expert at passing missals with the right flourish, at humbly proffering jugs of water for liturgical cleansing, and little carafes of wine? What indeed? Let us assume that Leni would have "stayed with him" even if not faithful to him and would have now and again fulfilled her conjugal duties. Would she then, with three or four "cute" youngsters, with A. as a general-*cum*-server, have attended that first (and not last) Bundeswehr service on October 10, 1956, conducted by Cardinal Frings at the Church of St. Gereon in Cologne? The Au. maintains: No. He cannot *see* Leni there, he sees A. there, even the "cute" youngsters, but not Leni. Another place where he sees A.: on the covers of illustrated weeklies or with the handsome Messrs. Nannen and Weidemann at some Eastern bloc reception. He—the Au.—sees A. as military attaché in Washington, in Madrid even—but nowhere can he see Leni, and certainly not in the company of the handsome Messrs. Nannen and Weidemann. Perhaps it is the Au.'s visual deficiencies that make him see A. everywhere but not Leni—even her children he sees there, but Leni he does not see. No doubt his visual powers are minimal, but then why does he see A. so clearly and nowhere Leni? Since somewhere in the universe there must be an as yet undiscovered flying body in which a giant computer (probably the size of Bavaria) has been installed and is spewing out hypothetical life stories, we will presumably have to wait until the object is eventually discovered. One thing is certain: Leni, had she been forced by herself or someone else to continue her life at A.'s side, would have become stout with unhappiness, and her weight today would be not twelve to fourteen ounces below standard weight but twenty pounds above it, and then there would have to be another giant computer (the size of North Rhineland-Westphalia) specializing in the study of secretions and capable of discovering which internal and external processes might have caused a creature such as Leni to become stout. Can we see Leni as an attaché's wife dancing and playing tennis in Saigon, Washington, or Madrid? A fat Leni perhaps, but the one we know, never.

What a pity the celestial instruments that calculate unshed T., all P., all B., each W., L., and S., in terms of over- or underweight, have not yet been discovered. It is so inexpressibly difficult to imagine Leni in any hypothetical situation, but since these computers do exist why does science let us down (which the encyclopedias do not)?

So if the Au. sees A.'s hypothetical career with almost crystal clarity, he sees Leni nowhere, he does not—quite frankly—even see her fulfilling any conjugal duties.

Too bad, too bad, that we have as yet no access to the heavenly instruments that would answer the Biblical question: Tell me how much too much or too little thou weighest, and I will tell thee whether too much or too little T., W., L., B., P., or S. in thy stomach, thy bowels, in brainstem, liver, kidney, pancreas, is converting thy wrongdoing and wrong-feeling into that too much or too little. Who is going to answer the question of how much Leni would weigh if

secondly: only Erhard had survived the war.
thirdly: Erhard *and* Heinrich
fourthly: Erhard, Heinrich *and* A.
fifthly: Erhard and A.
sixthly: Heinrich and A.

All we know for sure is that, had Erhard survived, that as yet undiscovered celestial instrument would have rejoiced over Leni's weight (computers rejoice too), at the fantastic balance of Leni's secretion. And—the most important question of all: In cases 1 to 6, would Leni have landed up in Pelzner's nursery garden and, had conflicts of loyalty arisen, how would she have overcome them?

There is at least reason to view with skepticism Leni's hypothetical life with A., whereas the meeting in the heather of Schleswig-Holstein that had obviously been planned by Leni would most certainly have turned out well. We may also be sure that the fact of being married would not have bothered Leni in the least if the "right man" had come along. To judge by what we know of Erhard, it is quite easy to see her as the wife of a high-school teacher (his subject: German), as the wife (or life-companion) of a producer of "think" programs, as the wife of the editor of an avant-garde journal (and, it must be stated here, Erhard would also have acquainted her with that German-language poet whom she later came to know through someone else: Georg Trakl). We may be sure of one thing: Erhard would have always loved her, whether she would have always loved him—no twenty-year warranty of this can be given, but we may be just as sure that Erhard would not have insisted on rights of any kind, and this would have guaranteed him one thing for the rest of his life: if not the certainty of Leni's permanent devotion, nevertheless her affection. Something else that the Au. (surprisingly for him) cannot *see* is Heinrich; he simply cannot see him anywhere in any hypothetical occupational situation—no more than could all the Jesuits combined.

At this point—in connection with certain encyclopedic data—the question must be asked: What, then, do we mean by "quality of life"? Who tells us whose values are superior, and whose inferior? There are awkward gaps in the encyclopedias, even in the good ones. We know there are people for whom two marks fifty represent more value than any human life other than their own; and there are even those who, for the sake of a piece of salami that they may or may not get, will recklessly gamble away the values of their wives and children, which may be: a happy family life and the sight of a father who is for once all smiles. And how about that value extolled to us as B.? Damn it, one man is pretty close to B. when he has finally collected the three or four cigarette butts that are all he needs to roll a fresh cigarette, or when he has a chance to gulp down the remains of vermouth in a discarded bottle; another man needs—according to the Western practice of instant lovemaking, at any rate—roughly ten minutes to be happy or, more precisely: in order to have quick sex with the person desired by him at the time, he requires a private jet in which he can make a fast flight, without attracting the attention of the person whom church and state have provided as his lawful source of B., between breakfast and afternoon coffee to Rome or Stockholm or (for this he would need until the next breakfast) Acapulco—so as to have man-to-man, woman-to-woman, or simply man-to-woman sex with the object of his desire.

So there is no getting away from the fact that many UFO's with many computers are still to be discovered.

Where, for instance, is the mental experience of P. registered, and where the physical; where is the activity of our conjunctiva expressed as graphically as in a cardiogram; who counts our T. when we secretly give way at night to W.? And who takes note of our L. and S.? Damn it, are Au.'s supposed to solve all these problems? What good to us is science when they send off those expensive objects to collect moon dust or bring back dreary rocks, while no one is in a position to as much as locate the UFO that might give us some data on the quality of life? Why for example, are some women paid two villas, six cars, and a million and a half in cash for the right to have quick sex with them, while—as statistics prove—in an ancient and holy city with a considerable tradition of prostitution, around the time when our Leni was seven or eight years old, girls have, for a cup of coffee worth eighteen pfennigs (with a tip of twenty or, more precisely, 19.8 pfennigs—but what mint would ever conceive coining 0.1- or 0.2-pfennig pieces of which ten—or five as the case might be—would yield but one solitary pfennig?) and a cigarette worth two and a half pfennigs, i.e., for a total of 22.5 pfennigs, given themselves and even satisfied desires for additional caresses?

We must assume the indicators of the "quality of life" computer to be in a constant state of extreme agitation since they have to register such substantial differences—ranging from 22.5 pfennigs to roughly two million marks—as the price for identically the same service.

What degree of sensitivity registers, say, the quality of life of a match, not of a whole one, not of half a one, but of a quarter of a match with which a prison inmate lights his cigarette in the evening, while others—nonsmokers at that!—have butane table-lighters as big as two clenched fists standing uselessly and futilely around on their desks?

What kind of world is this? What has happened to justice?

Well, our intention is merely to indicate that many questions remain unanswered.

Not much is known about Leni's visits to Rahel, the nuns residing in the convent being none too keen to publicize Leni's intimacy with Rahel because of plans at which Margret has already hinted but which have still to be revealed. In this case, too, care had to be taken over a witness who exposed himself to the Au. to some considerable extent and has had to pay dearly for it: we refer to the gardener Alfred Scheukens, who as an amputee (one leg, one arm) of less than twenty-five had been assigned to the nuns in 1941 as gardener and assistant gatekeeper and must have been fairly accurately informed on Leni's visits. He could be interrogated only twice, after the second interview he was transferred to a convent on the Lower Rhine; and when an attempt was made to locate him there it was found that he had already been retransferred, and the Au. was given to understand, in no uncertain terms, by a forty-five-year-old, very determined nun called Sapientia, that no obligation was felt to give information on the Order's personnel policy. Since the disappearance of Scheukens coincided closely with Sister Cecilia's refusal to grant the Au. a fourth interview, this time exclusively about Rahel, the Au. infers manipulation, intrigues, and by now he also knows why: the Order is trying to get a Rahel-cult under way, if not actually to make the first moves toward beatification or sanctification—hence "informers" (that is what he was called) are, and Leni most certainly is, unwelcome. As long as Scheukens talked and was still allowed to talk because no one suspected what he was talking about, he could at least testify that until the middle of 1942 he had secretly let Leni in to see Rahel twice, indeed sometimes three times, a week, into the cloister grounds by way of his gatekeeper's cottage, and "once in the grounds, of course, she knew her way around pretty well." Lotte, who has never "thought much of this mystical and mysterious nun," has no information to give, and Margret seems to have heard from Leni only about Rahel's death. "She wasted away there," she told me, "starved to death, although toward the end I always took her some food, and then when she was dead they buried her in the garden, just in shallow earth, with no gravestone or anything; as soon as I got there I sensed that she had gone, and Scheukens said to me: 'No use now, Miss, no use—unless you want to scratch open the ground?' So then I went to the mother superior and asked very determinedly for Rahel, and they told me she had gone away, and when I asked where to, the mother superior got nervous and said: 'But child, have your wits deserted you?' Well," Margret went on, "I'm glad I didn't go there any more and that I managed to persuade Leni not to make a denunciation; it might have turned out badly—for Leni, the convent, and everyone. That 'the Lord is nigh,' that was enough for me—and when I think what it would've been like if He'd really come through the door—— " (here even Margret made the sign of the cross).

"I always wondered, of course" (Scheukens during my last visit, when he was still eager to talk), "who that woman was, always snappily dressed and with that snappy car; the wife or girl friend of some Party boss, is what I thought—after all, who could still drive their own car even in those days—only Party or big business.

"No one was supposed to know, of course, and I used to let

her in secretly through the garden, through my cottage here and out again through here too; but it got out because they found cigarette butts up there in the nun's room and because it smelled of cigarette smoke, and once we had a row with the air-raid warden, he insisted he'd seen light in one of the windows—it must've been the matches when those two sat up there smoking, you can see that for miles in the blackout. There was a big fuss, and the old girl was moved down into the cellar." ("The old girl?") "That's right, the little old nun who I only got to see once, when she switched rooms—she had a prie-dieu and a bed, she didn't want to take along the crucifix; No, she said: 'That's not Him, that's not Him.' It was weird all right. But that snappy blonde kept on coming, she meant business, I tell you, she tried to talk me into helping her abduct the little nun. She wanted to carry her off, just like that. Well, I did a stupid thing, I let her bribe me—with cigarettes, butter, coffee—and went on letting her in, even into the cellar. At least there you couldn't see when they smoked, the window's lower than the level of the chapel, see? Well, one day she was dead, and we buried her in the little cemetery in the garden." ("With coffin and cross and priest?") "Coffin yes, no priest, no cross. I just caught Mother Superior saying: 'Now at least she can't pester us any more about her tiresome cigarette rations.'"

So much for Scheukens. He did not make too good an impression, but his volubility had aroused hopes that in the end were not fulfilled; items of information from gossips have a qualified value in their sum total, when one has discovered at what point they become "revealing," and Scheukens was indeed beginning to reveal himself—but just then he was forcibly separated from the Au., and even that gracious Sister Cecilia, from whom the Au. had gained the impression that the attraction was mutual, dried up as a source.

We can be quite sure, however, that toward the end of '41 and early in '42 Leni reached the acme of her taciturnity and reticence. Toward the Pfeiffers she shows open contempt by simply leaving the room as soon as they appear. Their visits, and a cloying solicitude for Leni, were such that it took a down-to-earth person like Miss van Doorn six weeks to suspect the object of their attentiveness: it was not merely to check up on Leni's behavior as a widow—the real reason was their hopes for an heir. Within six weeks of A.'s death, at a time when old Pfeiffer's "proud grief had reached a point at which his pride and grief were about to make him start dragging the other leg just as phonily—whether the left or the right was the sound one I couldn't tell you, but he had to have one good leg, didn't he, so as to be able to drag the other, right? Well, they were forever turning up with their revolting soggy homemade cakes, and because no one paid any attention to them, neither Mrs. Gruyten nor Leni nor the old man, and least of all Lotte, who couldn't stand the sight of the whole bunch of them, they would settle down in my kitchen, and I must confess that, whenever they asked if there was any 'change' in Leni I always thought they were talking about her being a widow, whether she had a lover or something; I didn't get it till it finally dawned on me that they were almost prepared to have a peek at Leni's laundry. So that's what they wanted to know, and when I tumbled to what they were after I led them a bit of a dance, I told them Leni had changed quite a bit, and when they fell on me like ducks with their beaks and asked *how* she had changed I told them without batting an eyelid that she had changed inwardly, and they backed off again. After two months there came a point where that Tolzem woman—Mrs. P., I mean, you must remember that to me she's always the Tolzem woman, since we all come from the same village—was on the verge of challenging Leni direct, I mean head on, so I got fed up and said: 'No, I know for a fact that it's no use your hoping she's in the family way.' Just what they'd've liked, of course, to smuggle a little Pfeiffer into the nest—only the funny thing was that Hubert was showing the same kind of curiosity, just that he wasn't quite so blatant about it, more wistful, I'd say, he'd have liked a grandson, I expect, even if it'd been from *that* fellow. Well, he got his grandson in the end, of course—and one who bore his name at that."

Here the Au. is completely stymied because he would have liked to consult the encyclopedia about a quality that he thinks Leni possesses and that is generally known as innocence. There is a good deal in the encyclopedia about "innocent converter," "innocent conveyance," while "innocent party" and "innocent passage" are also fully defined. Furthermore, "nocence" and "nocent" are given as archaic terms for guilt and guilty. All in all, the information on these terms exceeds the total information on T., W., L., B., P., and S. combined. Not a word about innocence, no mention of it whatever. What kind of world is this? Do people find archaic guilt more important than laughter and weeping, pain and suffering and bliss combined? The omission of innocence is highly annoying, for without an encyclopedia it is very difficult to apply this term correctly. Does science let us down after all? Is it perhaps enough to say that everything Leni did she did in all innocence, and simply omit the quotation marks? Leni, of whom the Au. is extremely fond, cannot be understood without this term. On the other hand, the fact that she was not deprived of the chance to attain consciousness is something that will soon—in about a year—come to light, when she is almost exactly twenty-one.

What kind of young woman is this who, in wartime, drives about the countryside, a "snappy blonde" in a snappy car, bribing voluble gardeners (who probably press their attentions on her in the dark convent garden) in order to take coffee, bread, and cigarettes to a despised nun who appears condemned to waste away, a young woman who shows no alarm whatever when the nun says, staring at the door: "The Lord is nigh, the Lord is nigh"—and, looking at the crucifix: "That's not Him"? She goes dancing while everyone else is dying a hero's death, she goes to the movies while bombs are falling, allows herself to be seduced, married, by a—to put it mildly—not overwhelmingly impressive fellow, goes to the office, plays the piano, refuses to be appointed a director, and while more and more people are being killed she continues to go to the movies and sees such films as *The Great King* and *Sky Dogs.* One or two verbatim utterances of hers are known to date from those two war years. One hears things from others, of course, but are they reliable? One learns that she is sometimes found in her room shaking her head as she stares at her identity card, with photograph, on which she is stated to be Helene Maria Pfeiffer, née Gruyten, born August 17, 1922. Marja also remarks that Leni's hair is once again in its full glory; that Leni hates (among other things, needless to say) the war and, before the war, Sundays, when no fresh rolls are to be had.

Doesn't she notice the strange cheerfulness of her father who, now "at the peak of his elegance" (Lotte H.), spends the greater part of the day in his town office, where he is "in conference," quite the "head of planning," no longer owner, no longer even a shareholder, dependent merely on a fairly high "salary plus expenses"?

It is with outright contempt, manifested merely by facial expression and movements of the eyebrows, that Leni receives the news that her father-in-law intends to award himself a medal for his participation in a battle that took place twenty-three years ago, not only the Combatant's Cross of Honor but also the Iron Cross Second Class, and that he was "pestering" his friend Gruyten, who naturally had occasion to deal with generals at his office, to assist him in acquiring this coveted decoration. And still no doctor had discovered the shell splinter "the size of a pinhead" that had caused the permanent dragging of the "lost leg." Doesn't she notice that the Pfeiffers are trying to trick her by taking it upon themselves to register Leni for a widow's pension—doesn't she notice that she signs the application, and that, starting July 1, 1941 (with the arrears duly paid up), sixty-six marks are credited monthly to her bank account? Have the Pfeiffers done this just so as to take malicious revenge for roughly thirty years by having their otherwise quite agreeable son Heinrich—who far from dragging a leg has manifestly lost one—calculate in Leni's presence that she has earned at least forty thousand marks, probably fifty thousand, from the name of Pfeiffer by having "collected" over a period of nearly thirty years the occasionally increased and, because of her employment, constantly fluctuating widow's pension—and, annoyed with himself for having gone that far, and probably (Au.'s opinion, not confirmed by any witness) out of jealousy because he has been secretly mad about Leni from the very first day, he goes even farther and shouts at her, in the presence of witnesses (Hans and Grete Helzen): "And what did you do for those fifty thousand marks? Lie once with him in the bushes, and the other time—well, we all know about that—he had to beg you, that poor fellow who a week later was dead and left you a spotless name, while you—while you—while, while you——" one look from Leni shut him up.

Does Leni feel like a whore after having the accusation "hurled at her" that in return for having twice allowed intercourse she has collected some fifty thousand marks—while she—while she—while she . . .

Leni not only avoids the office, she hardly ever goes into it, she confesses to Lotte H. that the "sight of those stacks of freshly printed money" make her sick to her stomach. She defends her car against a further threat of confiscation, she only uses it now for "driving around," to "drive around town," although these days taking her mother more and more often with her, "and they spend hours sitting in nice cafés and restaurants that are as close as possible to the Rhine, exchanging smiles, looking at the boats, smoking cigarettes." What distinguishes all the Gruytens at this time is that "indefinable cheerfulness that in the long run could drive a person crazy" (Lotte H.). Mrs. G.'s disease has finally been diagnosed with little hope of improvement: multiple sclerosis, now approaching its final stage with ever-increasing speed. She is carried by Leni into the car, out of the car; she no longer reads, not even Yeats, from time to time "she passes her rosary through her fingers" (van Doorn) but does not ask for "the consolations of the Church."

This period in the lives of the Gruytens—between early '42 and '43—is described unequivocally by all concerned as the "most luxurious." "It was irresponsible, really irresponsible—and when I say that maybe you'll understand better why, if I'm not exactly hard on Leni today, I'm not soft either—the way they enjoyed everything that was to be had on the European black market—and then that terrible business was exposed, and to this day I don't know why Hubert did it. He didn't need the money, after all—truly he didn't" (M.v.D.).

The only way "that business" was exposed was through an absurd and purely literary coincidence. Gruyten later called it "merely a notebook enterprise," which meant that he constantly carried all the data around with him in his briefcase and a notebook; his postal address for it was his office in town, he let no one in on it, dragged no one into it, not even his friend and head bookkeeper Hoyser. It was a risky affair, a gamble for high stakes, in which, as we now know, Gruyten was interested less in the stakes than in the gamble, and to this very day Leni is probably the only one who "understood" him as his wife "understood" him, and—although with certain limitations—Lotte H., who as a matter of fact understood almost everything, only not the "damn suicidal part about it, it was suicide, you know, nothing but suicide—and what did he do with the money? Those were the stacks, the heaps, the bundles he gave away! It was so senseless, so nihilistic—so abstract, crazy."

For the purposes of this "business," G. had founded a firm he called "Schlemm & Son" in a small town about forty miles away. He had obtained false identification papers, forged orders with forged signatures ("He could get hold of the forms any time, and he never thought signature that important, during the Depression years from '29 to '33 he would sometimes even forge his wife's signature on promissory notes, saying: 'She'll understand all right—why worry her about it now?'" Hoyser, Sr.).

Well, the gamble, the business, lasted a good eight or nine months and is known throughout the entire construction world as the "Dead Souls scandal." This mammoth scandal consisted of an "abstract notebook game" (Lotte H.) that featured vast quantities of cement that were paid for, even taken delivery of, but diverted via the black market from their proper purpose, plus a whole company of paid but nonexistent "foreign workers," a game in which architects, building superintendents, foremen, even cafeterias, cooks, etc., existed solely in Gruyten's notebook; not even the inspection certificates were lacking, nor the proper signatures on these certificates; bank account, bank statements, it was all there, "everything in apple-pie order, or I should say, that's how it seemed" (Dr. Scholsdorff later in court).

Although only thirty-one at the time, this Scholsdorff had, without resorting to tricks ("although I wouldn't have minded using tricks, it was just that I didn't need them"), been designated unfit by all, even the strictest recruiting boards, although suffering from no organic disease, simply because he was so exceedingly delicate, sensitive, and high-strung that no one wanted to take a chance on him—and that means something when we consider that as late as 1965 members of recruiting boards, German doctors, were "tempted to prescribe a Stalingrad cure" for slightly overweight young Germans. "To be on the safe side," a friend from S.'s student days, who was "ensconced" in an influential position, had S. officially transferred to the tax department of that small town where, surprisingly, S. familiarized himself so quickly and thoroughly with the new material that after one year he was already "not only indispensable but positively irreplaceable" (Dr. Kreipf, Director of Taxes, Retired, S.'s superior, who is still around and could be tracked down in a spa for diseases of the prostate). Kreipf went on: "Although a philologist, he was not only a good mathematician but capable of grasping complex financial and accounting procedures, of recognizing the doubtfulness of certain transactions—all of which had nothing to do with his actual talent." This "actual talent" was the study of Slavic languages and literature, to this day still S.'s overriding passion, his special field being: nineteenth-century Russian literature, and "although I received some attractive offers for the job of interpreter, I preferred this one in the tax department—did they think I was going to translate the German of sergeants or even generals into Russian? Was I supposed to debase this, to me, sacred object and turn it into a vocabulary suitable for interrogations? Never!"

During a harmless routine check, Scholsdorff came across the records of the firm "Schlemm & Son," found nothing, nothing whatever, to object to in them, it was only by chance that he began to study the payroll lists, and he became "leary, no, it was more than that: I was indignant, not only did I come across names that seemed familiar but there were names there that I was still living with." Now we must in all fairness add that it is just possible for a few notions of revenge to have been dormant in S., not against G. but against the construction trade; he had begun as a payroll accountant in a construction company to which he had been recommended by his influential friend, but as soon as his genius for numbers and figures was discovered he was always shifted and promoted with high praise, because no construction company was really all that keen on having its accounts scrutinized with a thoroughness that would not have been expected from a philologist. For in his almost indescribable naiveté S. had believed that these firms were genuinely interested in having the very thing that in fact they had to avoid: a thorough insight and overview into and over their manipulations. An unworldly, half-crazy philologist had been taken on "out of pity and in the desire to see that he got enough to eat and to save him from the clutches of the army" (Mr. Flacks, of the construction firm of the same name, still a thriving business), and then "we were stuck with a fellow who was more meticulous than any tax auditor. We just couldn't risk that."

Scholsdorff, who could have told you exactly how many square feet Raskolnikov's student digs measured, how many stairs Raskolnikov had to go down to reach the courtyard, now suddenly came across a worker called Raskolnikov who, somewhere in Denmark, was mixing cement for Schlemm & Son and eating in their cafeteria. Not yet suspicious, but already "very upset," he found a Svidrigailov, a Razumikhin, and finally discovered a Chichikov and a Sobakevich—and then in about the twenty-third place came across a Gorbachov, turned pale, but trembled with indignation when further scrutiny revealed a Pushkin, a Gogol, and a Lermontov as underpaid war-slaves. Not even at the name of Tolstoi had they called a halt. Let there be no mistake: this Scholsdorff was not in the least interested in such things as the "spotless reputation of the German war economy," he could not have cared less about such things; his scrupulous exactitude as a tax auditor was merely (interpretation of the Au., who had frequent and lengthy conversations, and quite recently, with S., and will probably have many more in the future) a variation of the scrupulous exactitude with which he knew, loved, and interpreted the entire assembly of characters in nineteenth-century Russian literature. "I discovered, for instance, that in that list Chekhov and all his characters were missing, so was Turgenev, and I could have told you even then who had drawn up the list: it could only be my old university pal Henges, completely gone to seed now—but a devotee of Turgenev and an absolute worshipper of Chekhov, although to my mind these two writers have little in common, and although I am quite frankly willing to admit that in my student days I underestimated Chekhov, grossly underestimated him." Moreover, it is a fact that S. never, not even in this case, denounced anyone: "To my mind that was too drastic, although I loathe shady dealings and despise profiteers, I've never denounced anyone, I would have them come to my office, give them the works, tell them to amend their declarations and pay up their arrears—and because my department could show the largest number of paid-up arrears I was always in Kreipf's good books. That's all, but a denunciation—you see, I knew the kind of justice machinery I would have been throwing those people into, and I didn't want to do that even to profiteers and shady operators. When you imagine that people were sentenced to death for stealing a few sweaters, no. But this was more than I could take. I blew my top: Lermontov as a slave of the German construction industry in Denmark! Pushkin, Tolstoi, Razumikhin, and Chichikov—mixing cement and eating barley soup. Goncharov and his Oblomov each wielding a shovel!"

As a matter of fact, S., soon to be retired with the rank of a senior civil servant and still engrossed in Russian literature, even contemporary Russian literature, had a chance to apologize to Gruyten, Sr., and make generous amends by teaching Gruyten's grandson, Leni's son Lev, fantastically good Russian; and when Leni sometimes has flowers (which she still loves, although for almost twenty-seven years she handled them as other people handle peas) in her room, they are from Scholsdorff! Scholsdorff is at the moment completely absorbed in the poems of Akhmadullina. "So I need hardly tell you I didn't denounce the firm, I began by writing a letter which went roughly as follows: 'I must request your immediate attendance at my office. The urgency of the matter cannot be sufficiently emphasized.'" He sent reminders, once, twice, tried to trace Henges, without success—"and since I myself was also subject to routine checks, my own investigations were discovered, and an official inquiry into 'Schlemm & Son' was launched. And then—then the juggernaut got under way."

S. became the chief witness for the prosecution in a trial that lasted only two days, G. having pleaded guilty on all counts. He remained cool, becoming confused only when required to specify the "name supplier" ("Imagine that, 'name supplier'"—Scholsdorff), whom even S., although he knew precisely who it was, did not betray. Some three hours of the second day of the trial were spent in an educational test carried out by an expert in Slavic languages and literature summoned from Berlin, G. having claimed that he had obtained the names from books—it was proved that he had never read a single Russian book in his life, "or a German book, for that matter, not even *Mein Kampf*" (S.); then it was "Henges's turn." It was not Gruyten who betrayed him, Scholsdorff had meanwhile run him to earth. "He was in fact working for the Army with the rank of officer on special duty, trying to persuade Russian prisoners of war to betray military secrets. A man who, as a Chekhov specialist, could have acquired an international reputation."

Henges, who had actually volunteered to testify, appeared in court in his officer's uniform, which "somehow didn't look quite right on him, he'd only had it on for a month" (S.). Yes, he admitted to having supplied Gruyten with a list of Russian names when approached by him. What he failed to mention was that he had collected a fee of ten marks for each name. He had previously conferred with Gruyten's defense attorney on this point and explained to him: "I simply can't afford to do that now—do you understand?" Whereupon Gruyten and his attorney agreed to omit this embarrassing detail, one which, however, Henges admitted to Scholsdorff, with whom he continued his dispute in a bar near the courthouse. For in court an argument had arisen between Scholsdorff and Henges during which Scholsdorff shouted indignantly to Henges: "All of them, you betrayed all of them, except for your Turgenev and your Chekhov!" This "Russian farce" was broken off by the district attorney.

The moral of this interlude is self-explanatory: contractors who keep forged payroll lists should have a good literary background and—tax auditors with a good literary background can prove to be of undeniable usefulness and benefit to the state.

At this trial only one person was found guilty: G. He confessed to everything and made his situation more difficult by refusing to admit to greed as his motive; when asked about his motive, he refused to make any statement, asked whether he had had sabotage in mind, he denied it. Leni, later questioned several times on his motive, murmured something about "revenge" (revenge for what? Au.). G. narrowly escaped the death sentence, and only after the intensive intervention "of very, very influential friends who put forward his undisputed services to the German war construction industry" (according to H., Sr.); he was sentenced to life in the penitentiary, and his entire fortune was confiscated. Leni had to appear twice in court but was acquitted on account of proven innocence, as were Hoyser and Lotte and all friends and employees. The only object to escape confiscation was the apartment building in which Leni had been born, and for this she is indebted solely to the "otherwise very aggressive prosecutor," who put forward her "hard fate as a war widow; her proven innocence," and rattled on embarrassingly as he "rehashed" (Lotte H.) A.'s heroic exploits; even Leni's association with a Nazi girls' organization was placed by him on the side of her moral credit. "It would be unfitting, Your Honor, to rob this gravely ill mother" (meaning Mrs. G.), "who has lost a son and a son in law, and this courageous young German woman, whose immaculate life has been proven, of a financial asset which, incidentally, became part of the family fortune not through the defendant but through his wife."

Mrs. Gruyten did not survive this scandal. Since she was not fit to be moved she was interrogated a few times in bed; "that did it" (van Doorn), "and she wasn't all that sad either to leave this world—when all's said and done a fine decent brave woman. She would've dearly liked to say farewell to Hubert, but it was too late, and we buried her very quietly. Church ceremony, of course."

Leni has now reached the age of twenty-one; needless to say, she no longer has a car, she thinks it right to give up her position with the firm, her father has for the time being disappeared without trace. How does all this affect her—not at all or very much? What will become of the snappy blonde with the snappy car, who in the third year of the war appears to have had little else to do than play the piano a bit, read Irish legends to her sick mother, visit a dying nun; who has been widowed, so to speak, for the second time, with no sign of grief, and now loses her mother while her father disappears behind iron bars? Few direct utterances of hers have come down to us from that time. The impression she made on all those close to her is a surprising one. Lotte says that Leni had been "somehow relieved," van Doorn says, "she seemed to feel freer," whereas old Hoyser puts it this way—"she seemed somehow to breathe a sigh of relief"; the "somehow" in two of these statements does not, of course, help us much, but it does offer the imagination a crack in Leni's reserve. Margret expresses it as follows: "She didn't seem depressed, the impression I got was more that she was taking a new lease on life. What was much worse for her than the scandal with her father and her mother's death was the mysterious disappearance of Sister Rahel." Confining ourselves to the facts: Leni had to register for a job and landed up, as the result of the intervention of a well-wisher who, working quietly in the background, "could pull a few strings" and wishes to remain anonymous, but is known to the Au.—at a wreathmaker's.

5 A later generation may wonder how it was possible, in 1942–43, for wreaths to be considered war-essential. The answer is: so that funerals might continue to be conducted with as much dignity as possible. Wreaths may not have been in such great demand just then as cigarettes, but they were in short supply, no doubt about that, and they were in demand and important to the psychological conduct of the war. Government wreath requirements alone were vast: for air-raid victims, for soldiers dying in military hospitals, and since there would naturally be "the odd private death" too (Walter Pelzer, one-time nursery gardener, Leni's former boss, now living in retirement on the revenue from his properties), and "quite often important Party, business, and military people were given state funerals of various categories," every type of wreath, "from the simplest, modestly trimmed, to the rose-garlanded giant wheel" (Walter Pelzer), was considered war-essential. This is not the place for an appreciation of the state in its capacity as organizer of funerals; we may take it for granted, both historically and statistically, that there were a great many funerals, wreaths were in demand, both publicly and privately, and that Pelzer had managed to ensure for his wreath-making business the status of a war-essential enterprise. The farther the war progressed, in other words the longer it lasted (the connection between progress and duration is to be specifically noted), the scarcer, of course, did wreaths become.

Should the prejudice exist "somewhere" that the art of wreath-making is trivial, any such notion—if only for Leni's sake—must be firmly contradicted. When we consider that a wreath of blossoms represents the ultimate and basic design, that the unity of the total design must be unfailingly preserved; that there are different designs and techniques for forming a wreath frame, that in selecting the greenery it is important to select greenery suitable for the design that has been chosen; that there are nine principal types of greenery for the frame alone, twenty-four for the finished wreath, forty-two for bunching and wire-picking (overall category: stemming), and twenty-nine for "romanizing," we arrive at a total figure of one hundred and twelve types of tying greenery; and although some of these may overlap in the various categories of their use, we are still left with five different categories of use and a complicated system of twining; and although one or the other greenery may be used both for tying and for the finished wreath, for stemming (which again subdivides into bunching and wire-picking), and for "romanizing," we still find the basic principle applying here too: it is all a matter of know-how. Who, for instance, among those who look down on wreathmaking as an inferior occupation, knows when to use the green of the red spruce for the frame or the finished wreath, when he is to use arborvitae, Iceland moss, butcher's-broom, mahonia, or hemlock fir? Who knows that in each case the greenery must form a solid layer, that skill in tying is expected throughout? So it will be seen that Leni, who has so far done nothing but light and random office work, now found herself thrust into no easily negotiable terrain, no easily learned craft, but into what almost amounts to an art studio.

It is perhaps hardly necessary to state that for a time, while the Germanic motif was being vigorously promoted, the "romanized" or Roman wreath fell into disrepute, but that the controversy came to an abrupt end when the Axis was formed and Mussolini took somewhat vehement exception to the defamation of the Roman wreath; that the verb "to romanize" could then be freely used until mid-July 1943 when, however, in view of the Italian betrayal, it was once and for all stamped out (comment by a fairly high Nazi leader: "There will be no more romanizing in this country, not even in the making of wreaths or bouquets"). Every observant reader will understand at once that in extreme political situations not even the wreathmaking business is without its perils. Since, moreover, the Roman wreath had evolved as an imitation of the carved ornamental wreaths on Roman façades, the strict ban on it was reinforced by an ideological rationale: it was pronounced "dead," and all other wreath designs were pronounced "living."

Walter Pelzer, an important witness for that period of Leni's life, unsavory though his reputation may be, was able to prove with a fair amount of plausibility that at the end of 1943 and the beginning of 1944 he had been denounced to the craftsmen's guild "by envious people and competitors" and that the following "intensely dangerous" (Pelzer) comment had been entered in his dossier: "continues to romanize." "Good God, that could've cost me my neck in those days!" (P.). Needless to say, after 1945, when his unsavory past came under discussion, Pelzer tried to make out, "and not only on that basis," that he had been "a victim of political persecution," an attempt which—through Leni's assistance, we are sorry to say—met with success. "For those were the wreaths which she—Leni, I mean the Pfeiffer girl—actually invented herself: firm, smooth wreaths of heather that actually looked as if they'd been enameled, but I don't mind telling you—they really made a hit with the public. That had nothing whatever to do with romanizing or anything else—it was an invention of the Pfeiffer girl's. But it almost cost me my neck because it was taken to be a variation of the Roman wreath."

Pelzer, now seventy, living in retirement on the revenue from his properties, twenty-six years after the events, began to look genuinely nervous and had to put aside his cigar for a minute in apparent preparation for a coughing fit. "And anyway—the things I did for her, the things I covered up—that really was appallingly dangerous, worse than the suspicion of romanizing."

Of the ten persons with whom Leni worked for a long time in close daily contact, it was still possible to trace five, including Pelzer himself and his head gardener Grundtsch. If Pelzer and

Grundtsch are taken, quite correctly, to be Leni's superiors, of the eight with whom she worked more or less as an equal there still remain three.

Pelzer lives in an architectural structure which, although he personally calls it a bungalow, may without hesitation be described as a bombastic villa, a yellow-tiled building that had merely the appearance of a single story (the finished basement contains a sumptuous bar, a recreation room where Pelzer has installed a kind of wreath museum, a guest suite, and a well-stocked wine cellar); next to yellow (the tiles), the predominant color is black: wrought iron, doors, garage door, window trim—all black. The association with a mausoleum does not seem unfounded. Pelzer lives in this house with a rather sad-looking wife, Eva née Prumtel, who appears to be in her mid-sixties and mars her pretty face with bitterness.

Albert Grundtsch, now eighty, still lives, "withdrawn into his shell," virtually in the cemetery (G. about G.), in a large two-and-a-half-room stone (brick) shed from which he has easy access to his two greenhouses. Grundtsch has not, as Pelzer has done, profited from the cemetery expansion (nor does he wish to, let it be added) and grimly defends "the acre of greenhouses I was fool enough to give him at the time" (Pelzer). "You could almost say that the parks and cemetery administration will heave a sigh of relief when he kicks the—when he pegs—well, when he departs this life, let's put it that way."

In the heart of the cemetery, which has swallowed up not only the few hectares of Pelzer's nursery garden but also other nurseries and stonemasons' yards, Grundtsch leads an almost autarkical existence: the recipient of an old-age pension ("Because I kept up his contributions," P.), he lives rent-free, grows his own tobacco and vegetables and, since he is a vegetarian, has little trouble providing his own food; clothing problems are almost nil—he is still wearing a pair of old Gruyten's pants which the latter had made in 1937 and which Leni passed on to Grundtsch in 1944. He has switched entirely to the (his own words) "seasonal potted-plant business" (hydrangeas for Low Sunday, cyclamen and forget-me-not for Mother's Day; for Christmas, small potted firs trimmed with ribbons and candles to put on the graves—"the stuff they bring along to put on their graves—you wouldn't believe").

The Au. felt that the parks administration, if it really is speculating on G.'s death, will have a longish wait. For he is not at all the kind of person he is made out to be, "an indoor type, always shut away in his greenhouses" (municipal park employee); on the contrary, he uses the now immense cemetery "after business hours when the bell's rung, and that's usually pretty early, as a private park; I go for long walks, smoke my pipe on a bench some place, and when I feel like it sometimes go to work on a grave that's been neglected or forgotten and give it a decent foundation—moss or spruce green, sometimes I even lay a couple of flowers on it, and, believe it or not, apart from thieves looking for copper and such, I've yet to meet a soul; of course there's the occasional crazy person who refuses to believe a certain person's dead when that person is dead; they climb over the wall so that even at night they can cry and curse and pray and wait beside the grave—but in fifty years I've only run across two or three of those—and then of course I make myself scarce, and every ten years or so some couple turns up with no fear or prejudice, lovers who've grasped the fact that there's scarcely a place in the world where you can be so undisturbed—and then I've always made myself scarce too, of course, and these days naturally I've no way of knowing what goes on in the outlying parts of the cemetery—but believe me, even in winter it's beautiful, when it's snowing, and I go for a walk at night, all muffled up and wearing my felt boots and smoking my pipe—it's so quiet, and they're all so peaceful, so peaceful. As you can imagine, I've always had problems with girl friends, when I wanted to take them back to my place: nothing doing, I tell you—and the more tarty they were the less there was doing, even for money."

On being asked about Leni he became almost embarrassed. "Yes, of course, the Pfeiffer girl—do I remember her! As if I could forget her! Leni. Of course, all the men were after her, all of them it seemed, even Sonny Boy Walt" (referring to Pelzer, now seventy. Au.), "but no one really had the nerve. She was unapproachable, not in any prissy way, I must say, and because I was the oldest—I was already fifty-five or thereabouts—I never even thought I had a chance; of the others, I guess it was only Kremp who tried, the one we called 'Dirty Berty,' and in her cool offhand way she snubbed him so thoroughly that he gave up. How far Sonny Boy Walt tried it with her I don't know—but you can be sure he never got anywhere, and the others, of course, were just women, conscripted for war jobs naturally, and the women were divided pretty evenly for and against—not for or against her, but that Russian who later turned out to be the darling of her heart. Can you imagine that the whole business lasted for nearly a year and a half—and none of us, not one, noticed anything serious? They were smart and they were careful. Well, of course there was a good deal at stake: two necks, or one and a half for sure. My God, I still get ice-cold shivers running down my spine right into my arse when I think of it now, what the girl was risking. On the job? How she was on the job? Well, maybe I'm prejudiced because I was fond of her, really fond of her, the way you can be fond of a daughter you've never had or—I was thirty-three years older then her, remember—of a woman you love and never get. Well, she simply had a natural talent—that tells the whole story.

"We only had two trained gardeners, three if you count Walter, but all he ever thought of was his ledgers and his cash. Two, then: Mrs. Hölthohne, she was more of what you might call an intellectual gardener, Youth Movement and all that, she'd gone to university and then taken up gardening, a romantic sort of person—you know, the soil, and working with one's hands and all that—but she knew her job all right, and then there was me. The rest were untrained, of course, Helga Heuter, Kremp, Miss Schelf, Mrs. Kremer, Marga Wanft, and Miss Zeven—a bunch of women, and they weren't chicks either, at least there wasn't one youd've wanted to lay among the peat moss and the wire-picking material. Well, it only took me two days to realize there was one thing the Pfeiffer girl wasn't suited for, and that was making wreath frames, that's rough work and quite hard too, and the Heuter-Schelf-Kremp group took care of that, they were simply given a list and their pile of greens for tying, depending on supply—as time went on we couldn't get much but oak leaves, beech leaves, and pine—and then they were told the size—usually standard, but for big funerals we had a code of abbreviations, PB 1, PB 2, PB 3—meaning: Party Boss 1st, 2nd, and 3rd class; when it came out later that our private code also included H 1, H 2, and H 3 for Hero 1st, 2nd, and 3rd class, there was a row with that Dirty Berty Kremp who said it sounded insulting and took it as a personal insult because he was a Hero 2nd class: an amputee, one leg, and a few decorations and medals. So, Leni didn't fit into the wreath-frame group, I saw that right off and put her into the trimming group, where she worked alongside Kremer and Wanft—and believe me, she was a natural genius for trimming, or, if you like, a wire-picking whiz. You should've seen how she handled cherry-laurel and rhododendron leaves, you could trust that girl with the most expensive material, not a scrap was wasted or snapped off—and she caught on right away to something many people never grasp: the hub, the center of gravity, of the trim must be in the top left quarter of the wreath frame; that gives a cheerful, sort of optimistic upward sweep to the wreath; if you put the center of gravity on the right, you get the pessimistic feeling of a downward slant. And it would never've occurred to her to mix geometric trimming designs with vegetation ones—never, I tell you. She was an either/or type—and that's something you can see even from trimming a wreath. There was one habit I had to break her of, though, time and again and relentlessly: she had a weakness for pure geometric forms—rhomboids, triangles, and once as a matter of fact—it was a PB 1 wreath, too—she improvised a Star of David out of marguerites, just playing around with geometric designs, I'm sure it wasn't on purpose, it just took shape under her hands and I doubt if she knows to this day why it made me so nervous that I got really mad at her: just imagine if the wreath hadn't been checked and had got onto the hearse—and anyway, people liked the vague vegetation designs better, and Leni could make those up very nicely too: she would weave little baskets into the wreath, little birds even—well anyway, if it wasn't exactly vegetation it was at least organic—and when there was a PB 1 wreath that rated roses and Walt didn't stint with the roses he let her have, and especially when they were long-stemmed beauties in bud: Leni became a regular artist: whole scenes took shape under her fingers, too bad, in a way, because they lasted such a short time: a miniature park with a pond and swans on it; well, I tell you, if there'd been prizes she'd have won them all, and the most important thing—for Walt at least—was: with very little trimming material she achieved a far greater effect than many people did with a lot. She was economical in other ways, too. Then the finished wreath would go through the checking group, that was Mrs. Hölthohne and Miss Zeven—and no wreath left the place that hadn't eventually gone through my hands. It was Mrs. Hölthohne's job to check the wreath frame and the trim and improve them where necessary, and the Zeven woman was what we called the ribbon lady, she would put on the ribbons that were delivered to us from town—and of course she had to watch like a hawk to be sure there was never any mix-up. If someone who'd ordered a wreath with the inscription 'For Hans—a last farewell from Henriette' got a wreath with a ribbon saying 'From Emilie for my unforgettable Otto,' or vice versa—with that quantity of wreaths that might've had embarrassing consequences; and finally there was the delivery van, a rickety little three-wheeler that took the wreaths to the chapels, hospitals, army headquarters, to Party branch office or funeral homes, and Walt wouldn't let anyone else do that job because then he could goof off, pocket the money, and play hooky for a while."

Since Leni never complained about her work either to Miss van Doorn or Margret, or even to old Hoyser or Heinrich Pfeiffer, it must be assumed that in fact she enjoyed it. The only thing that seems to have worried her was that her fingers and hands took a real beating: after she had used up her mother's and father's supply of gloves, she asked around in the whole family for "cast-off gloves."

It may be that she used to think quietly about her dead mother, about her father, that many thoughts were devoted to Erhard and Heinrich, possibly even to the deceased Alois. She is described as "nice and friendly and very quiet," as far as that year was concerned.

Even Pelzer describes her as "silent, my God, she scarcely ever opened her mouth! But she was nice, friendly and nice and the most efficient help I had at that time, apart from Grundtsch, who was a real old pro, of course, and that Mrs. Hölthohne, but with her there was something so damned pedantic, so academic, about the way she sometimes corrected good ideas. Besides the Pfeiffer girl wasn't only good at designing, she also had a feeling for the botanical side, she knew by instinct that you can—in fact must—handle cyclamen blooms differently from a long-stemmed rose or a peony, and I don't mind telling you it was always a financial sacrifice for me when I had to let them have red roses for wreaths—there was a nice little black market, you see, for young blades who thought roses were the only possible gift from an admirer—you could've really cleaned up, specially in hotels where young officers went with their girl friends. How many times did I get phone calls from hotel porters, they'd offer me not only money but good merchandise for a bouquet of long-stemmed roses. Coffee, cigarettes, butter, even cloth—genuine worsted—was offered me once, somehow it seemed a shame, really, that almost everything went for the dead and hardly anything was left for the living."

In the meantime, while Pelzer was having his rose problems, Leni was on the verge of becoming a victim of housing control: the authorities regarded the occupation of a seven-room apartment with kitchen and bath by a total of seven persons (Mr. Hoyser, Sr., Mrs. Hoyser, Sr., Lotte with Kurt and Werner, Leni, Miss van Doorn) as insufficient. Up to this point the city had, after all, gone through more than five hundred and fifty air-raid alarms and a hundred and thirty air raids, and the entire Hoyser clan was allocated three—admittedly large—rooms, and Leni and Marja van Doorn, "after every possible string had been pulled, were allowed to keep one room each" (M.v.D.). It may be assumed that the high-placed local government official who would rather remain anonymous played a part in this, although he modestly denies "having been of assistance." Be that as it may, two rooms remained to be "controlled," "and those awful Pfeiffers, who had meanwhile been driven out of their rabbit hutch by a bomb explosion" (Lotte H.) "moved heaven and earth 'to live under the same roof as our dear daughter-in-law.' Old Pfeiffer enjoyed being an air-raid victim as much as he enjoyed his gammy leg, and he had the bad taste to say: 'Now I've also sacrificed my humble but honestly acquired possessions to the Fatherland." (Lotte H.) "Needless to say, we all got a scare, but then Margret found out through her friend at city hall" (??A.) "that old Pfeiffer was about to be transferred to the country with his class, so we gave in—and actually had them on our necks for three weeks, then in spite of his game leg he had to go off to the country, taking his mopey old missus with him, and we were left just with that nice Heinrich Pfeiffer, who had volunteered and was only waiting to be called up, and just after Stalingrad at that" (Lotte H.).

A number of difficulties arose in obtaining reliable information on Leni's chief adversary at the nursery; it did not occur to the Au. to solicit the services of the war-graves commission until he had thoroughly and unsuccessfully ransacked the citizens' registration lists, regimental records, etc. An inquiry at the war-graves commission yielded the information that one Heribert Kremp, aged twenty-five, had been killed in March near the Rhine and buried close to the Frankfurt-Cologne *Autobahn;* to progress from the address of Kremp's grave to the address of his parents was not difficult, although the conversation with them was disagreeable in the extreme; they confirmed that he had worked at Pelzer's nursery, that there, "like everywhere else that he lived and worked, he had dedicated himself to order and decency—and then there was no holding him when the Fatherland was so woefully threatened, he volunteered in mid-March '45 for the Home Guard, in spite of having lost a leg above the knee, and died the finest death he could ever have wished for." The Kremp parents seemed to regard their son's death as perfectly normal and expected something from the Au. that he could not offer: a few words of appreciation, and since he was unable to react very cordially, even when confronted by the photo they showed him, it seemed best—as with Mrs. Schweigert—to take a hasty departure; the photo showed a (to the Au.) rather unprepossessing person, with a wide mouth and low forehead, woolly fair hair, and button eyes.

In order to trace the three surviving female witnesses from Leni's wartime employment at the nursery, all that was needed was a straightforward request for information at the citizens' registration bureau, which, after payment of an appropriately modest fee, was duly complied with.

The first, Mrs. Liane Hölthohne, who had been in charge of the wreath-checking unit and is now seventy, is the owner of a chain of florists with four outlets. She lives in a remarkably pretty little bungalow, four rooms, kitchen, hall, two bathrooms, in a suburb that is still almost rural; the rooms are furnished in impeccable taste, color and contours harmonize, and since she is almost suffocating in books anyway she has been spared the problem of interior decoration. She was matter-of-fact but not curt, silver-haired and *soignée;* and from the photo of an office party taken in 1944 and shown by Pelzer, it is doubtful whether anyone would have recognized in that short, rather dumpy woman wearing a head scarf and a severe expression the fine-drawn venerable beauty who now presented herself to the Au. with dignity and reserve; earrings of fine silver filigree, shaped like tiny baskets with a loose coral bead trembling in each, made her head—her still strongly pigmented brown eyes being in continual movement—a point of focus that in its fourfold movement was very hard on the eyes: the earrings quivered, inside the earrings the corals quivered, her head quivered, and in her head the eyes quivered; her makeup, the slightly withered skin at neck and wrists, gave an impression of good grooming, but not at all as if Mrs. H. were trying to conceal her age. Tea, petits fours, cigarettes in a silver box (that had barely room for eight cigarettes), a lighted wax candle, matches in a hand-painted porcelain container showing the signs of the Zodiac but only eleven pictures, the center one depicting a stylized archer standing out in pink against the other signs, painted in blue, made it reasonable to assume that Mrs. H. was born under the sign of Sagittarius; curtains of old rose, furniture light brown, walnut, rugs white, on the walls—where the books had left any space—engravings with views of the Rhine, carefully hand-tinted, six or seven engravings (the Au. cannot guarantee perfect accuracy on this point) measuring at most two and a half by one and a half inches, exact and with a gemlike clarity: Bonn seen from Beuel, Cologne seen from Deutz, Zons from the right bank of the Rhine between Urdenbach and Baumberg, Oberwinter, Boppard, Rees; and since the Au. also remembers having seen Xanten, moved by the artist somewhat closer to the Rhine than geographical accuracy would have permitted, there must have been seven engravings after all.

"Yes indeed," said Mrs. Hölthohne, offering the silver box to the Au. and looking almost, it seemed to him, as if she were expecting him not to take a cigarette (he had to disappoint her and noticed a very, very faint clouding of her brow). "You see correctly, views of the left bank of the Rhine only" (thus in her perceptiveness swiftly outstripping the Au.'s speed of grasp, awareness, and interpretation!). "I used to be a Separatist, and still am, and not only theoretically; on the fifteenth of November, 1923, I was wounded near the Ägidienberg, not for the honorable side but for the dishonorable one which to me is still the honorable side. No one can talk me out of my belief that this part of Germany doesn't belong to Prussia and never has, nor in any kind of so-called Reich founded by Prussia. A Separatist to this day, not for a French Rhineland but for a German one. The Rhine as the border of the Rhineland, with Alsace and Lorraine forming part of it too, of course; for a neighbor, an unchauvinistic France, republican naturally. Well, in 1923 I fled to France, where I recovered, and even in those early days I needed a false name and false papers to return to Germany, that was in 1924. Then in '33 it was better to be called Hölthohne than Elli Marx, and I didn't want to leave again, emigrate again. Do you know why? I love this part of Germany and the people who live in it: it's just that they've ended up in the wrong history, and you can quote all the Hegel you want" (the Au. had no intention of quoting any Hegel!) "and tell me that no one can end up in the wrong history. I thought the best thing for me to do after 1933 was to forfeit my flourishing business as a landscape architect, I simply let it go bankrupt, that was the simplest and least obtrusive way, though it was hard because the office was doing well. Then came that business with the Aryan pass, tricky, risky, but of course I still had my friends in France and I had them look after it. You see, this Liane Hölthohne had died in a Paris bordello in 1924, and Elli Marx from Saarlouis was simply allowed to die in her stead. I had this nonsense with the Aryan papers done by a lawyer in Paris, who in turn knew someone at the embassy, but although it was done very discreetly a letter turned up one day from a village near Osnabrück, and in this letter a certain Erhard Hölthohne wrote to this Liane offering "to forgive her everything, please come back to your own country, I'll build a new life for you here." Well, we had to wait till all the papers for the Aryan pass had been assembled and then have this Liane Hölthohne die in Paris while in Germany she went on living as an employee at a nursery garden. Well it worked. I was fairly safe but not a hundred-percent safe, and that's why it seemed wisest to lie low at a Nazi's like Pelzer."

Excellent tea, three times as strong as at the nuns, delicious petits fours, but the Au. reached too often—this was already the third time—into the silver cigarette box, although the ashtray, scarcely the size of a nutshell, would hardly hold the ashes and remains of the third cigarette. No doubt about it: Mrs. Hölthohne was an intelligent and *moderate* woman, and since the Au. did not contradict her Separatist views, nor cared to do so, it seemed that, despite his immoderate smoking and tea-drinking (this was already his third cup!), her liking for him did not wane.

"You can imagine my apprehension, though in actual fact

there was little reason for it because the relatives of this Liane never showed up, but there might have been a thorough inspection of Pelzer's accounts and personnel, and then there was also that wretched Nazi Kremp, and the Wanft woman, and that Nationalist Frieda Zeven at whose table I worked. Pelzer, who is and always was a genius at sensing an atmosphere—he must have sensed that I didn't feel all that secure because when he began quite blatantly working his crooked deals with the flowers and the greenery I was afraid I'd find myself in serious trouble, not *because of* myself but *through* him, so I decided to give notice, and when I told him he gave me such a funny look and said: 'You give notice? Can you afford to?,' and I'm sure he didn't know anything but his sixth sense told him something—and I got cold feet and withdrew my notice, but of course he saw that now I was *really* nervous and had reason to be, and he was constantly emphasizing my name as if it were a false one, and of course he knew that the Kremer woman's husband had been murdered in a concentration camp as a Communist, and with the Pfeiffer girl, too, he sensed that something was going on, and there again with his sixth sense he was actually onto something more momentous than he or any of us suspected. That there was a bond of understanding between the young Pfeiffer girl and Boris Lvovich was fairly clear, and that in itself was risky enough, but *that*—I would never have credited her with the courage. By the way, Pelzer also proved his sixth sense when he knew right off in 1945 that what had always been 'Blumen' to him were now 'flowers,' only with wreaths he got it wrong, he called them 'circles,' and for a time the Americans thought he meant 'underground circles.'"

A break. Brief. A few questions by the Au., who during the break managed with some difficulty to accommodate the remains of his third cigarette in the silver nutshell and noted with approval that on the otherwise immaculate wall of books the volumes of Proust, Stendhal, Tolstoi, and Kafka seemed *very* well thumbed, not dirty, not soiled, merely well thumbed, well worn like a favorite garment that has been mended and washed over and over again.

"Yes indeed, I love to read, and I keep rereading books I've already read many many times, I first read Proust in the Benjamin translation back in 1929—and now about Leni: a splendid girl, of course, yes, I say 'girl' although she's in her late forties; only: you couldn't get really close to her, either during the war or after; not that she was cold, just quiet and so silent; friendly—but silent, and stubborn; I was the first one to be given the nickname of 'the lady,' then when Leni started work there we were known as 'the two ladies,' but in less than six months they'd stopped calling her 'the lady,' and again there was only one 'lady' there, me. Strange—it wasn't till later that I realized what made Leni so unusual, such an enigma—she was proletarian, yes, I mean it, her feeling for money, time, and so on—proletarian; she might have gone a long way, but she didn't want to; it wasn't that she lacked a sense of responsibility, or that she was incapable of assuming responsibility; and as for her ability to plan—well that, we might say, she proved to the full, for almost eighteen months she had this love affair with Boris Lvovich, and not one of us, not a single one, had thought such a thing possible, not once was she found out, or was he found out, and believe me, the Wanft and Schelf women and Dirty Berty watched over those two like lynxes, so that sometimes I got scared and thought, *if* there's something going on between those two, then God help them. The only danger was at the beginning, when—simply for practical reasons—there *couldn't* be anything between them, and I naturally sometimes doubted whether she—if she . . . knew what she was doing; she was rather naive, you know. And as I said: no feeling for money or for property. We all earned, depending on extras and overtime and so forth, between 25 and 40 marks a week, later on Pelzer paid us an additional 'list premium,' as he called it: 20 marks extra for every wreath that was 'recycled,' you'd call it now, so that meant a few extra marks a week, but Leni would use up at least two weeks' wages every week just on coffee, that was bound to lead to difficulties even though she also got the revenue from her building. Sometimes I used to think, and I still think: that girl is a phenomenon. You never quite knew whether she was very deep or very shallow—

and it may sound contradictory but I believe she is both, very deep and very shallow, only one thing she isn't and never was: a light woman. That she wasn't. No.

"I didn't get any restitution in 1945 because it was never clarified whether I had gone into hiding as a Separatist or as a Jewess. For Separatists in hiding there was no compensation, of course—and as a Jewess, well, you just try and prove you deliberately went broke to divert attention from yourself. What I did get, and that only through a friend in the French Army, was a permit for a nursery garden and florist's business, and right away at the end of 1945, when Leni was having rather a thin time of it with her child, I took her into the business, and she stayed with me twenty-four years, till 1970. Not ten or twenty times, no, more than thirty times I offered to make her manager of one of the branches, even a partnership, and she could have worn a nice dress and looked after customers out front, but she preferred to stand in her smock in the cold back room, making wreaths and bouquets. No ambition to get on or ahead, no ambition. Sometimes I think she's a dreamer. A bit crazy but very very lovable. And of course, and here again I see something proletarian, rather spoiled: do you know that, even as a worker earning at most fifty marks a week, she kept on her old maid right through the war—and do you know what that maid baked for her every day with her own hands? A few fresh rolls, crisp and fresh, and I tell you, sometimes it made my mouth water and —in spite of being quite 'the lady'—I was sometimes tempted to say: 'Let me have a bite, child, do let me have a bite.' And she would have, you can be sure of that—oh, if only I had asked her, and if only, if she's so badly off now, she wouldn't mind asking me for money; but you know what she is as well? Proud. As proud as only a princess in a fairy tale can be. And as for her wreathmaking abilities, there she was very much overrated; she had clever fingers, I grant you, and a gift, but for my taste her trimming had too much filigree about it, it was too dainty, like embroidery, not like that lovely knitting done on big needles; she would have made a very good gold- and silversmith, but with flowers—this may surprise you—you sometimes have to treat them roughly and boldly, she never did, there was courage in her trimming but no daring. Still, when you consider that she was completely untrained, it was remarkable, subjectively quite remarkable, how quickly she picked it up."

Since the teapot was no longer being lifted, the silver cigarette box no longer being opened and proffered, the Au. gained the impression that the interview was (for the time being justifiably, as it turned out) at an end. He felt that Mrs. Hölthohne had made a substantial contribution to the rounding out of the Leni-image. Mrs. H. permitted him a glance into her little studio, where she had recently resumed her work as a landscape architect. For cities of the future she is designing "hanging gardens," which she calls "Semiramis"—a term that, to the Au., seems relatively uninspired for such an avid Proust reader. In taking leave he was left with the impression that *this* visit was definitely at an end but that further ones were not out of the question, for a great deal of amiability, albeit fatigued, remained behind on the face of Mrs. H.

In the case of the ladies Marga Wanft and Ilse Kremer we can again resort to partial synchronization: both are old-age pensioners, one aged seventy, the other sixty-nine, both white-haired, both living in one-and-half-room public-housing apartments, stove heating, furniture dating from the early fifties, both giving an impression of "slender means" and frailty, but—here the differences begin—one (Wanft) with a grass-parrakeet, the other (Kremer) with a shell-parrakeet. Marga Wanft—here the differences become considerable—severe, almost unapproachable, tight-lipped, as if she were constantly spitting out cherry stones and, because of her small mouth, with difficulty at that, was not prepared "to say much about that hussy. I knew it all along, I sensed it, and I could still kick myself for not getting to the bottom of it. That's a girl I'd have liked to see with her head shaved, and a bit of running the gauntlet wouldn't have hurt her either. To take up with a Russian while our boys were at the front and her husband killed in action and her father a war profiteer of the first water—and after three months *she* was given the trimming group and it was taken away from me. No. A slut, that's all she was—no sense of honor, and that provocative body of hers—she drove all the men crazy; Grundtsch used to fawn over her like a tomcat, for Pelzer she was a sex nest-egg, and even Kremp, who was a good worker and always gave of his best, had his head turned by her so that he got quite unbearable. And always pretending to be a lady while actually she was nothing but a down-at-heel nouveau riche. No thanks. How well we all got along together before she came! After that there was always a kind of crackle in the air, tensions that were never resolved, a good beating would've been the best way to clear the air. Yes, and that sentimental amateurish dabbling in flowers, she fooled the lot of them with that. No, I was isolated, downright isolated, after she came, and she never fooled me with all that nonsense about offering coffee and so on, that's what we call 'sweet talk,' that's all she was, a trollop, a tart practically, and no better than she should be."

This did not emerge as rapidly from the Wanft lips as it is recorded: bit by bit, stone by stone, as if pressed out through her mouth, and she wanted to say no more yet did say more, described old Grundtsch as a "frustrated faun or Pan, take your choice," and Pelzer as the "worst scoundrel and opportunist I ever met, and to think that it was for him that I used my influence with the Party, that he was the one I vouched for. Being in a position of trust with the Party" (Gestapo? Au.), "I was always being asked, of course. After the war? When they cut off my pension because my husband hadn't been killed in the war but in street-fighting in 1932–33? Not a word from Mr. Walter Pelzer, although he'd been in the same Storm Trooper unit as my husband. Nothing. With the help of that little tart and that Jewish *lady* he managed to wiggle out of everything, while I was in it up to my neck and stayed that way. No, don't you talk to me about them. There's no gratitude in this world, and no justice either, and it so happens we're stuck with it."

Mrs. Kremer, who could be visited the same day, had little information to yield concerning Leni, merely calling her "the poor dear thing—the poor dear unsuspecting thing. And that Russian, well I must say I was very suspicious and still would be today. I wouldn't be surprised if he wasn't a Gestapo informer in disguise. The way he could speak German and was always so helpful, and why should he of all people be assigned to a nursery and not sent out on suicide missions like removing bombs or repairing railway tracks? A nice lad of course, but I never dared talk to him much, at any rate no more than was necessary for the job."

Mrs. Kremer must be pictured as a washed-out erstwhile blonde with eyes that must once have been blue and are now practically colorless. Soft face, the outlines dissolving in softness, not spiteful, only a little peevish, troubled, not in trouble, offering coffee but drinking none; she spoke slackly, letting the words flow lightly, a bit lukewarm, almost disregarding punctuation in the rhythm of her speech. What was not merely surprising but downright electrifying was the extraordinary precision with which she rolled her cigarettes: with moist honey-gold tobacco, immaculately, without need of scissors to cut off loose shreds.

"Yes, that's something I learned to do early in life, it may have been the first thing I ever learned, for my father in the clink in 1916, later for my husband in jail, then when I spent six months in jail myself; and during the Depression of course, and again during the war—I never got out of practice rolling cigarettes." At this point she lighted one, and all of a sudden, seeing the freshly rolled white cigarette between her lips, one could imagine she had once been young and very pretty; she offered one too, of course, casually, simply pushing a cigarette across the table and pointing to it.

"No, no, I've had enough. I'd had enough even in 1929; I never had much strength, now I've none at all, and during the war it was only my boy, my Erich, who kept me on my feet, I'd always hoped he wouldn't be old enough before the war was over, but he was, and they took him away even before he'd finished his mechanic's apprenticeship; a quiet, silent, solemn boy, never said much, and before he left I said something political for the last time in my life, taking a risk: 'Go over,' I said, 'the minute you can.' 'Go over?' he asked, frowning as usual, and I explained what 'go over' means. Then he gave me a funny look, I got scared he'd talk about it somewhere somehow, but even if he'd wanted to I dare say he didn't have time. In December '44 they took him off to the Belgian frontier to dig fortifications, and it wasn't till the end of '45 that I heard he was dead. Seventeen. Always looked so solemn and glum, that boy. Illegitimate, I ought to tell you, father a Communist, mother the same. He got to hear it often enough at school and in the street. His father dead since '42, his grandparents had nothing of course. Oh well. I met Pelzer back in 1923. Like to guess where? You'll never guess. In the Communist Party. It seems Pelzer had seen a Fascist propaganda film that was supposed to act as a deterrent; but on him it acted as an attraction. Walter took the revolution in the movie for a chance at looting and stealing, he'd got it all wrong, he was kicked out of the Red Front, joined the Liberation Corps, then the Storm Troopers, way back in 1929. For a while he was a pimp too. He could turn his hand to anything. He was a gardener too of course, and a black-market operator, you name it. A lady-killer. Think for a moment what the staff at the nursery consisted of: three rabid Fascists—Kremp, and the Wanft and Schelf women; two neutrals—Frieda Zeven and Helga Heuter; myself as a disabled Communist; the *lady* as a Republican and a Jewess; Leni, politically unclassified but nevertheless marked by the scandal over her father and a war widow, after all; then the Russian, whom he really did make rather a fuss over—what could possibly happen to him when the war was over? Nothing. And nothing did. Till 1933 he called me Ilse, when we met he'd say: 'Well, Ilse, who's going to come out on top, your lot or ours?' From '33 to '45 he called me Miss Kremer, and the Americans hadn't been there five days before he had a permit again, came to see me, started calling me Ilse again, and said he thought I ought to be on the city council now. No, no, no—I waited too long, I should've quit when the boy left. I'd had enough, more than enough. At the end of '44 Leni came to my place one day, sat and smoked a cigarette, smiling at me all the time a bit nervously as if she wanted to say something, and I knew more or less what she might've said but I didn't want to know about it. One should never know too much. I didn't want to know anything and because she sat there without a word and with that nervous smile I finally said: 'Well, it's obvious you're pregnant and I know what it means to have an illegitimate child.' Oh and then after the war all that fuss about resistance and pensions, restitution and a new Communist Party with people who I know had my Willi on their conscience. You know what I called them? Altar boys. No, no—and that unsuspecting Leni caught up in the middle, the poor dear thing, they actually talked her into being a kind of blond election-mascot by calling her the 'widow of a brave Red Army fighter.' And by calling her little boy Lev Borisovich Gruyten—well, I imagine her friends and relatives all tried to talk her out of it and she dropped it, but she had more to live down then than during the war. Years later people were still calling her 'the blonde Soviet whore'—the poor dear thing. No, she's never had an easy time of it, and she still hasn't."

6 We must wait no longer, if we are to avoid unfounded speculation and destroy false hopes in good time, before introducing the chief male protagonist of the first section. A number of people (not only Mrs. Ilse Kremer), and thus far almost all of them in vain, have been wondering how it was possible for this individual, a Soviet individual by the name of Boris Lvovich Koltovsky, to find himself in the favored situation of being permitted to work in a German wreathmaking business in 1943. Since Leni, even on the subject of Boris, does not become what one might call talkative but can at times turn relatively communicative, she was prepared—after the joint urgings of Lotte, Margret, and Marja over a period of three years—to name two persons who might give information on Boris Lvovich.

The first of these knew Boris only slightly but intervened powerfully in his destiny. This person made him a favorite of Fortune by taking a strong and persistent hand, even to the point of personal sacrifice, in his destiny. This man is a very exalted personage in the world of industry who in any circumstances, and no matter what the cost, must not be named. The Au. cannot afford the slightest indiscretion, the cost to himself would simply be too great, and since he has also firmly committed himself to it—discretion—toward Leni (verbally, of course), he prefers to remain a gentleman and stick by his commitment. Unfortunately it was a long time, too long, before this personage got onto Leni's track, not until 1952, it being only then that he discovered Boris to have been a dual favorite of Fortune: not only had he been permitted to work in Pelzer's wreath business, he was also the one for whom Leni appeared to have been waiting.

Boris has been the subject of almost every conceivable suspicion: he is said to have been an informer infiltrated by the Germans, his objective being Pelzer and Pelzer's mixed bag of employees; in addition, of course, he is said to have been a Soviet informer. With what objective: the secrets of German wartime wreathmaking, or to report on the mixed morale of German workers? All we can say is that he was simply one of Fortune's favorites. No more than that. At the end of 1943, when he appeared upon the scene, he was probably—here we have to rely on estimates—between five foot ten and five foot eleven in height, very thin, with fair hair, weighing (with a probability bordering on certainty) 120 pounds at most, and wearing army spectacles as issued by the Red Army. At the time when he entered Leni's life he was twenty-three, spoke German fluently but with a Baltic accent, Russian like a Russian. In 1941 his entry into Germany had been peaceful, and a year and a half later he returned as a Soviet prisoner of war to this strange (and to some people mysterious and sinister) country. He was the son of a Russian worker who had advanced to the post of member of the Soviet trade mission in Berlin; he had memorized several poems by Trakl, even some by Hölderlin (in German of course); and as a graduate highway engineer had been a lieutenant in an engineer unit.

At this point a number of prior advantages must be clarified for which the Au. is not to blame. Who can be expected to have a diplomat for a father and an exalted personage in the armaments industry for a benefactor? And how is it that the chief male protagonist is not a German? Not Erhard, or Heinrich, or Alois, not G., Sr., or old H., or young H., not even the remarkable Pelzer or the kindly Scholsdorff, who as long as he lives will be distressed that someone had to go to prison, nearly paid with his life even, simply because he, Scholsdorff, was such a fanatical authority on Slavic literature and could not bear to allow the name of a fictitious Lermontov employed in Denmark in fictitious bunker construction to remain on a list? Must—Scholsdorff wonders—someone, even if a single person, and as agreeable as G., Sr., at that, almost lose his life because a fictitious Raskolnikov totes fictitious sacks of cement and gulps fictitious barley soup in a fictitious cafeteria?

Well, Leni is to blame. She is the one who in this case did not want a German hero for a hero. This fact—like so many things about Leni—must simply be accepted. Moreover, this Boris was quite a decent fellow, he had even had an adequate education—even at school. He was a graduate highway engineer, after all, and even if he had never learned a word of Latin there were two Latin words he knew very well: "De profundis," because he knew his Trakl so well. And even if his schooling cannot be remotely compared to something as priceless as matriculation, it may still be said, objectively, that it might *almost* have been a kind of matriculation. If one accepts the well-attested fact that as a youth he had even read Hegel in German (he did not come through Hegel to Hölderlin but through Hölderlin to Hegel), perhaps even culturally demanding readers will be inclined to admit that he was not to be ranked too far below Leni and at least as a lover was worthy of her and—as will be seen—worth her.

Until the last moment even he was completely bewildered by the favor that had come his way, as we discovered from the plausible statements made by his former POW fellow camp inmate Pyotr Petrovich Bogakov.

Bogakov, now sixty-six, afflicted by arthritis, his fingers so badly twisted that he usually has to be fed and even his occasional cigarette has to be held for him and raised to his lips, chose not to return to the Soviet Union. He openly admits that he "must have regretted it a thousand times and must have regretted his regret a thousand times." Reports on the fate of returning prisoners of war that kept cropping up made him suspicious, so he hired himself out as a watchman for the Americans, became a victim of McCarthyism, and found refuge with the British, for whom he in turn worked as a watchman, dressed in a British Army uniform dyed blue. In spite of having applied several times for German citizenship, he was still stateless. His room in a home backed by a religious charity was shared with an immensely tall Ukrainian elementary-school teacher by the name of Belenko. This Belenko, bearded and moustached, lapsed after his wife's death into a state of permanent mourning punctuated at intervals by sobbing and now spends his time between church and cemetery and in constant search of a food item which, for as long as he has been living in Germany, i.e., twenty-six years, he has been hoping to find some day as "cheap popular nourishment, not a delicacy": pickled cucumbers.

Bogakov's other roommate is one Kitkin, from Leningrad, frail and, in his own words, "ill with homesickness": a thin taciturn fellow "who," again in his own words, "just can't fight his homesickness." From time to time old quarrels flare up among the three old men, Belenko saying to Bogakov "You godless fellow, you," Bogakov to Belenko "Fascist," Kitkin to both "windbags," and is himself called by Belenko an "Old Liberal," by Bogakov a "reactionary." Because Belenko has only been sharing the room with the other two since his wife's death, i.e., for six months, he is looked upon as "the newcomer."

Bogakov was not prepared to discuss Boris and his time in the POW camp in the presence of his two roommates, so it was necessary to wait for the moment when Belenko was at the cemetery, in church, or "out looking for pickles," and Kitkin had gone for a walk and, needless to say, "for cigarettes." Bogakov speaks fluent German which, apart from a questionable and frequent use of the word "salubrious," is perfectly intelligible. Since his hands, from "that damn standing around all those years at night, no matter how cold it was, and later even with a rifle over my shoulder," are really badly twisted, the Au. and B. first spent some time speculating on how to improve B.'s opportunities for smoking. "My having to depend on someone else to light it for me may still be salubrious for me, but for every puff, no—and after all I do like to smoke my five or six a day, or, when I have them, even ten." Finally the Au. (who, departing from custom, must here thrust himself forward) hit on the idea of asking the floor sister for one of those stands used to hang up bottles containing infusion fluids; with the aid of a piece of wire and three clothespins, and enlisting the cooperation of the (by the way charming) floor sister, a contraption was devised that the delighted Bogakov called a "salubrious smoking gallows"; two clothespins were used to loop the wire onto the gallows, the third clothespin was attached to the wire at the level of Bogakov's mouth and to this clothespin was fastened a cigarette mouthpiece on which Bogakov now has only to draw when the "Fascist pickle-eater or the homesick fellow with the GPU kisser" have lighted his cigarette and stuck it into the mouthpiece. There is no denying that, with the rigging up of the "salubrious smoking gallows," the Au. aroused a certain liking on the part of B. and thus encouraged him to talk, or that he helped B. stretch his modest allowance of 25 marks a month by gifts of cigarettes, not only—he swears—from selfish motives. Now to Bogakov's statement, interrupted as it was from time to time by asthmatic breathing-spaces and by smoking, but reproduced here for the record without pause and without a break.

"In absolute terms, of course, our situation was not salubrious! But relatively speaking it was. As far as Boris Lvovich is concerned, he was utterly, and I do mean utterly, at a loss, and to him it was an extraordinary stroke of good luck that he wound up in our camp at all. He must have guessed that someone was behind it all, but he didn't find out who till later, though he might have had some idea. While we were considered only just worthy, under the strictest guard, of demolishing or extinguishing burning buildings, repairing bomb damage in streets and along railway tracks—and anyone who risked pocketing so much as a nail—yes, just an ordinary nail, and for a prisoner a nail can be something precious—could, if he was caught—and he *was* caught—confidently regard his life as over—so that's what we were doing, and that unsuspecting lad was picked up every morning by a good-natured German sentry who took him to this highly salubrious nursery. There he spent his days, later half the night too, doing light work, and he even had—I was the only one to know about this and when I heard about it I trembled for that boy's salubrious head as if it were my own son's—a girl, a mistress! If it didn't make us suspicious it made us envious, and the two together, though not really salubrious, are common enough among POW's. In Vitebsk, where I went to school after the revolution, there was one kid who got driven to school every morning in a horse-drawn carriage, a regular taxi—and that's how Boris seemed to us. Later on, when he brought back bread, and even butter and sometimes newspapers, but always reports on the war situation—and even sensationally bourgeois garments such as can only have been worn by a capitalist—his situation improved somewhat, but it still wasn't salubrious because Viktor Genrikhovich, the self-appointed commissar of our camp, refused to believe that the many salubrious aspects of Boris's situation were due to what the bourgeois call coincidences, since these—according to Viktor Genrikhovich—ran counter to historical logic. The terrible part about it was that in the end he found he'd been right. How he discovered it Heaven only knows. In any event, after seven months he had the whole story: back in 1941, in Boris's father's apartment in Berlin, Boris had met this friend of his father's, a Mr." (here the name was pronounced that the Au. has undertaken not to publicize). "After the war broke out, Boris's father had been transferred to the intelligence service, he was a contact man for Soviet spies in Germany and used one of his numerous strings and contacts to inform that gentleman that his son had been taken prisoner and to ask for his help. In terms of the period in question: what he did was misuse his office to enter into a treasonable relationship with a leading German capitalist of the worst kind in order to wangle the most salubrious treatment possible for his son. Now don't ask me how Viktor Genrikhovich discovered that! Most likely they had their intelligence satellites even in those days, the bastards. What came out later and what Boris never knew was: that his father was picked up for this, taken away—and rat-a-tat. So was Viktor Genrikhovich right or not, in suspecting that there is only the logic of history and not the bourgeois coincidence that my pious friend and pickle-eater Belenko would, needless to say, call Providence?

"So for Boris's father the affair ended most insalubriously

but not for Boris, for now Viktor Genrikhovich was suspecting more to it than there really was: might those fantastic garments have come *directly* from the hand of that person who was known to be against the war with the Soviet Union and in favor of a strong, durable, unbreakable alliance between Hitler and the Soviet Union, and who could even afford to accompany Boris, his father and mother and sister Lydia to the station in Berlin, to embrace them all warmly and, as a parting gesture, suggest that he and Boris's father use first names? Was Boris in direct contact with this person when he went to that comical nursery to make wreaths and compose inscriptions for ribbons to go on Fascist wreaths? No, no, no, he had no contacts, except with the men and women working there, so—in order for those blasted salubrious conditions to yield at least some positive result—what was the mood among them, what was the mood among the German workers? Three were clearly in favor, two were noncommittal, and probably two, though they couldn't actually say so, were against! That, again, ran counter to Viktor Genrikhovich's information, according to which German workers in 1944 were on the verge of rebellion. Damn it, the lad was in a complicated situation, I tell you, and paid dearly for those salubrious conditions. His position was totally beyond the logic of history, and if it had got out that he actually had a girl, and that later on he even managed, and quite often at that, to pick all the flowers that delightfully pretty girl had to offer—for God's sake. So he stuck to his story that the gifts—which, as time went on, became quite substantial, clothing, coffee, tea, cigarettes, butter—were left for him by some unknown person hidden in a pile of peat moss, and as for the war news, he said, he got this in whispers from his boss, that florist and wreath supplier. Now Viktor Genrikhovich was incorrigible but not incorruptible: he accepted gifts of a genuine cashmere vest, cigarettes, and—this really was a sensational gift—a tiny map of Europe that had been torn out of a pocket calendar and skillfully folded into roughly the size of a flat candy—and that was a gift from Heaven; at last we knew exactly where we were and what we were up against. Viktor hid his cashmere vest under his tattered undershirt where, being gray, it looked like a dirty rag. That vest, you see, could've aroused the greed of the German sentry, he'd have found it most salubrious too. Now came the time when Boris kept us supplied with reliable news on the position of the front, the advance of Soviet and Allied troops—and he became highly salubrious to Viktor Genrikhovich, who was in urgent need of such news in order to boost our morale—and because he was so salubrious to Viktor he naturally lost the confidence of the others—that goes without saying once you know the POW dialectic."

In order to obtain all this information from Pyotr Petrovich Bogakov, five favorable opportunities were needed: the Au. had to buy an infusion-bottle gallows because the one that had been at their disposal was sometimes put to its original use; he even invested in movie tickets so that he could send Belenko and Kitkin off to color movies of *Anna Karenina, War and Peace,* and *Doctor Zhivago,* and concert tickets so that they would not have to miss Mstislav Rostropovich.

It was at this point that the Au. found it opportune to trouble that exalted personage; suffice it to add that the name is one before which every German in every historical period between 1900 and 1970, and every Russian and Soviet functionary during the same era, would stand to attention, before which all doors to the Kremlin—probably even the modest door to Mao's study (if it has not already done so), would to this day open wide. Leni has received the same promise that she also gave: never, never to divulge that name, not even under torture.

In order to induce a favorable mood in this person, and also to request, not with servility but with becoming modesty, the favor of possible future interviews, the Au. was obliged to travel some forty-five minutes by train in a—this much may be revealed—north-north-easterly direction, and to invest in flowers for the lady of the house and a leather-bound copy of *Eugene Onegin* for the husband; he drank several cups of quite good tea (better than the nuns', less good than Mrs. Hölthohne's), discussed the weather, literature, and mentioned Leni's precarious financial situation (from the wife's suspicious question: "Who's that?" and the husband's ungracious reply: "Oh, *you* know, the woman who was in touch with Boris Lvovich during the war," the Au. deduced that the lady suspected a liaison). Then came the moment when, inevitably, the weather, literature, and Leni ceased to form topics of conversation, and the husband, rather brusquely, one must say, and plainly enough, said: "Now Mimi, do you mind leaving us," whereupon Mimi, now firmly convinced that the Au. was the conveyor of a billet-doux, left the room, her feelings visibly hurt.

Is it necessary to describe this personage? Mid-sixties, white-haired, not lacking in warmth but grave, in a drawing room roughly half the size of a school auditorium (say, in a school for six hundred students), overlooking the parklike grounds, English lawns, German trees, the youngest of these some hundred and sixty years old, beds of tearoses—and over it all, including the person's face, even over the Picasso, the Chagall, the Warhol, and the Rauschenberg, over the Waldmüller, the Pechstein, the Purrmann—over it all, everything, a certain—the Au. takes the plunge!—poignancy. Here, too, T., W., S., and P.! No trace of L.?

"So you want to know whether this Bogakov—I'll see that something's done for him, by the way, don't forget to give my secretary his name and address—has given you an accurate report. Well: I can only say, on the whole Yes. How that commissar in Boris's camp found out about it, where he can have obtained his information" (shrug) "—but Bogakov's report *as such* is correct.

"I got to know Boris's father in Berlin between 1933 and 1941, and we became real friends. That wasn't without its dangers, either, both for him and for me. In terms of world politics and taking the long view of history, I still favor an alliance between the Soviet Union and Germany, believing as I do that a genuine, cordial alliance based on mutual trust would wipe even the—er—German Democratic Republic off the map. *We,* we are the ones the Soviet Union needs. But that's all in the future. Well, in Berlin I was looked upon as red—I suppose I was, too, still am—

and the only reason I am critical of the present West German Government's East European policy is that I find it too weak, too weak-kneed. Well, back to Bogakov—what happened was that one day an envelope was handed to me in my Berlin office and in it was a slip of paper containing only this message: 'Lev wants you to know B. has been taken prisoner by the Gers.' No use trying to find out who had brought the letter—didn't matter anyway, it'd been left with the porter downstairs.

"Now you can imagine how upset I was. I had developed a real affection for that intelligent, quiet, introspective boy whom I'd met a number of times—perhaps ten or twelve—in his father's apartment. I had given him the poems of Georg Trakl, the collected works of Hölderlin, suggested he read Kafka—I think I may claim to be one of the first readers, if not the first, of *The Country Doctor,* I had asked my mother to give it to me for Christmas in 1920 when I was fourteen. So now I discovered that this boy, who had always seemed such an introspective type, pretty much of a daydreamer, was in Germany as a Soviet prisoner of war. Do you suppose" (here, although not the object of so much as a hostile glance, he became downright militantly defensive, indeed aggressive), "do you suppose I didn't know what went on in those camps? Do you suppose I remained blind and deaf and unfeeling?" (All things the Au. had never maintained.) "Do you imagine" (here the voice became almost virulent!) "that I approved of all that? And here" (now the voice piano to pianissimo) "at last I had a chance to do something about it. But where was the boy? How many millions or at least hundreds of thousands of Soviet prisoners did we have at that time? Had he even been shot or wounded at the time he was captured? Just you try searching for a Boris Lvovich Koltovsky among all those" (the voice swelling again to truculence!). "I found him, but I tell you" (threatening gesture toward the *totally* innocent Au.), "I found him with the help of my SCA and SCAF friends" (Supreme Command of the Army, Supreme Command of the Armed Forces. Au.) "—I found him. Where? Working in a quarry, not exactly in a concentration camp but under concentration-camp conditions. Do you know what it means to work in a quarry?" (Having in fact at once time worked for three weeks in a quarry, the Au. found the implication that he did *not* know what it means to work in a quarry—to put it mildly—a bit much, especially since he was given no chance to reply.) "A death sentence, that's what it means. And have you ever tried to get someone out of a Nazi camp for Soviet prisoners of war?" (Reproach in the voice unjustified since, although the Au. has never tried, nor even been in the position of trying, to get anyone out of anywhere, he has had a few opportunities not to take prisoners in the first place or to let them run away, which in fact he did.)

"Well, even I needed four solid months to do anything effective for the boy. He was moved from one ghastly camp with a mortality rate of 1:1, first to a less ghastly camp with a mortality rate of 1:1.5, from the less ghastly camp to a merely terrible camp, mortality rate 1:2.5, from the terrible camp to a less terrible camp with a mortality rate of 1:3.5—and although this meant he was already in a camp that was way better than the overall average mortality rate, he was then shifted to a camp that may be regarded as relatively normal. Mortality rate extremely good: 1:5.8, and that's where I had him transferred because one of my best friends, Erich von Kahm, whom I had gone to school with and who had lost an arm, a leg, and an eye at Stalingrad, was the commandant of the Stalag" (Stalag? Stammlager—base camp. Au.) "where Boris now was; and do you imagine Erich von Kahm could have made that decision on his own?" (The Au. imagined nothing, his sole desire being for factual information.) "No indeed! Party bigwigs had to be roped in, one of them bribed—with a gas range for his mistress, gasoline coupons for a hundred gallons, and three hundred French cigarettes, if you want to know exactly" (the Au. did want to know exactly), "and finally this Party bigwig had to find another Party joker, that fellow Pelzer, who could be more or less given orders that Boris was to be handled circumspectly—but then there was the senior garrison officer who had to approve the daily guard for Boris, and that man, a Colonel Huberti, old school, conservative, humane, but cautious because the SS had tried several times to get him on grounds of 'misplaced humanitarian treatment,' this Colonel

Huberti had to be shown a certificate to the effect that Boris's work at the nursery was war-essential or 'of high intelligence value,' and now came a coincidence, or stroke of luck or, if you wish" (the Au. did not wish. Au.), "the hand of Providence. This Pelzer had once been a member of the Communist Party and had taken on a former woman comrade whose husband—or was it her lover, anyway free love or something—had fled to France with some top-secret documents, so Boris, totally ignorant, like Pelzer and that Communist woman, of what was going on, was officially detailed, as they say in their jargon, to watch this woman—and this was confirmed to me in turn by someone I knew in the 'Foreign Armies Eastern Europe' department—and the most important thing of all was to keep my own part in it a secret too, otherwise I would have achieved the very opposite: the SS would have become interested in Boris. How difficult do you imagine" (again the Au. imagined nothing. Au.) "it was to do something really worthwhile for a boy like that—and after July 20 things tightened up still more; the Party bigwig wanted more bribes—it hung by a thread. Who was there left to care about the fate of the Soviet Engineer Lieutenant Boris Lvovich Koltovsky?"

Relatively enlightened as to how difficult it was even for Mr. Exalted to do something for a Soviet prisoner of war, back again to Bogakov, armed with pickles and two tickets to *Ryan's Daughter.* Bogakov, who has meanwhile been supplied with rubber tubing from a hookah, clamped over the cigarette mouthpiece and thus enabling him to smoke "salubriously" because now he can hold the rubber tubing in his twisted hand ("Like this I don't have to keep fishing for the mouthpiece with puckered lips"), got quite carried away in his expansiveness and did not hesitate to mention intimate, indeed highly intimate, details concerning Boris.

"Now," in Bogakov's words, "there'd been no need for that martinet Viktor Genrikhov to point out to him the historical unlikelihood of his salubrious fate. What made the boy more uneasy than anything else was that manifest but invisible hand that moved him from camp to camp and finally to this nursery which, in addition to all its other advantages, had this one: it was warm, heated at all times, and in the winter of '43–'44 that was far from insalubrious. And when he finally found out, from my whispering it to him, *who* was shifting him around, he was a long way from being reassured, and for a time even suspected that dear girl, thinking she'd been sent there and paid by that person. And there was another thing that was a real ordeal for that boy's truly unearthly sensibility: the eternal firing going on near his otherwise most salubrious place of work. I'm not implying, not in the least, that the boy was ungrateful, no, far from it—he was overjoyed, but there it was: that eternal firing got on his nerves."

Here it must be borne in mind that, in late 1943 and early 1944, the burial of all categories of German dead represented a constant challenge: not merely to cemetery custodians, wreathmakers, priests, grandiloquent lord mayors, regional Party leaders, regimental commanders, schoolteachers, buddies, factory foremen—the soldiers of the guard battalion detailed to fire the salute had to be perpetually banging away at the sky. Depending on the number of victims, manner of death, rank, and function, between seven in the morning and six at night the main cemetery resounded with continuous banging. (Grundtsch's statement, quoted verbatim as follows:)

"It usually sounded as if the cemetery was a maneuver area or at least a rifle range. Obviously a salvo's supposed to sound like a *single* shot—in 1917 I was a sergeant myself and sometimes in command of a salvo party—but this wishful thinking rarely came off, it sounded like a fusillade, or as if they were trying out a new machine gun. And the bombs falling at intervals and antiaircraft guns banging away wasn't in the least amusing for people with sensitive ears, and sometimes when we opened the window and stuck out our noses we could actually smell it: gun smoke, even though it did come from blanks."

If the Au. may for once be permitted to comment, he would like to point out that probably from time to time young soldiers with little firing practice were assigned to salvo duty, and these men must have found it strange to fire over the heads of priests, mourners, officers, and Party bigwigs—and this may have made them nervous, for which it is to be hoped no one will blame them. We can be sure that many a T. flowed there, much W. was to be seen, P. was apparent, scarcely one of the bereaved remained steadfast in the self-confidence of his Being, and no doubt the P. so conspicuous on many a face, together with the prospect of one day being themselves buried to the accompaniment of a salvo, had anything but a reassuring effect on the soldiers. Proud grief was by no means always so proud, every day at the cemetery hundreds, if not thousands, of conjunctiva were active, brainstems could no longer be checked, for many a person present may have felt himself affected in his supreme life-assets.

Bogakov: "Suspicion of the girl didn't last long, of course, a day or two, and after she'd laid her hand on him, and it'd happened to him [??], well—I mean, you know what sometimes happens to men when they haven't had a woman for a long time and don't lay their own hand—right, right: that's what happened to him when the girl merely laid her hand on his hand, at the table where she took her wreaths. Right. That's how it was. He told me all about it, and though it'd happened to him a few times before, of course, only in dreams though, and never when he was awake, he was bewildered and filled with elation at how salubrious it was. I tell you, that boy was naive, he'd had a puritanical upbringing, and this business we call sexuality—he hadn't a clue. And now something came to light that I can only tell you provided you promise on your word of honor" (which he did! Au.) "that that girl will never get to hear of it" (The Au. is convinced that actually it would be all right for Leni to hear of it, she would not be embarrassed, most likely she would be glad to know about it. Au.) "—the boy had never visited with a woman." (Upon the Au. raising his eyebrows in astonishment, he went on:) "Yes, that's what I've always called it: visiting with a woman. Mind you, he didn't exactly want to know how it's done, he already knew there are certain physical conditions, of a salubrious nature, so to speak, that make it fairly clear where, in certain states of stimulation, you want to put what, when you love a woman and want to visit with her. Well, that much he did know, only—there was one detail—damn it all, I really loved that boy, if you want to know" (the Au. did want to know. Au.), "he saved my life, without him I'd have starved to death, never made it . . . without his trust in me too. Who could he talk to, damn it all! I was everything to him, father, brother, friend—and I used to lie there at night in tears, I was that scared, when he actually did have an affair with the girl. I warned him, I told him: 'O.K., it's all right to risk your own neck if you're so crazy about her—but how about hers? Just think for a moment of the risk she's running—she can't get out of it by saying you forced her or raped her, nobody's going to believe that under the circumstances. Be reasonable!' 'Reasonable,' he said. 'If you could see her you wouldn't be talking about reason, and if I talked to her about reason—she'd laugh in my face. She knows the risk I'm running, and she knows I know the risk she's running—but she won't be told that we should be reasonable. She doesn't want to die any more than I do, she wants to live—and she wants us to visit with each other as often as we can'—an expression he'd got from me, I admit. Then when I met her later and got to know her quite well, I realized that 'reason' had been a stupid word to use. No, but there'd been something else that had caused the boy a lot of anguish. As a little lad of two or three, during the civil war, his mother had hidden him in a village in Galicia, in the home of a woman friend, and this friend had a Jewish grandmother who took the boy when the friend was shot, and it seems that for a couple of years he toddled around the village with the Jewish kids, then that grandma died too and some other grandma took the kid, and by that time there was no one left who knew exactly where he came from. And one day this grandma discovers that little Boris hasn't been circumcised yet, and naturally she thinks the grandma who died has overlooked this and she just goes ahead and has it done—so, he was circumcised. I nearly had a fit. I asked him, I said, 'Boris, you know I'm not a man of prejudice but tell me: are you a Yid or not?' And he swore to me: 'No, I'm not, if I were I'd say so.' Well, I must say he didn't have the faintest suggestion of a Jewish accent—but that was bad news all right, for there were enough anti-Semites in our camp who would've teased him or even denounced him to the Germans. I asked him: 'How did you get by when they examined you and so forth, I mean, get by with your, well, let's say, altered foreskin?' And he told me he'd had a friend, a medical student in Moscow, who realized how dangerous this could be for him, and the friend temporarily sewed it on again with a piece of catgut, a very neat job but damn painful, before he had to go into the army, and it held till—well, until he kept getting so stimulated, and then the stitches gave way, came off. So what he wanted to know was whether women—and so on. Well, that was all the more reason for me to weep tears and sweat blood at night: not that about women—I don't know anything about that, what women and whether they notice—no, but that Viktor Genrikhovich was such a rabid anti-Semite, and there were a few others who would've denounced him to the Germans out of envy and suspicion: and then—well, the benefactor didn't exist who could've saved him then. That would've been the end of all the things that had been so salubrious."

The exalted personage: "I must admit I was pretty mad at him when I found out later that he had let himself in for a love affair. I really was. That was going too far. He should have known how dangerous that was and realized that all of us who were protecting him—and he knew he was being protected—would have been placed in an unpleasant position. That whole complicated coordination network would have been unraveled. I am sure you know that in a case like that no mercy would have been shown. Well, it turned out all right, it was only looking back on it that I got a scare and I made no attempt to disguise from Miss—Mrs. Pfeiffer my dismay at such ingratitude. Yes, ingratitude, that's what I call it. For God's sake, all because of a woman! Needless to say, my contact men were keeping me constantly informed as to how he was getting along, and every now and then I felt tempted to go there when I was on a business trip and have a look at him—but in the end I never did yield to the temptation. He had caused me enough trouble as it was by apparently provoking people in the streetcar, whether consciously or not I don't know—but the fact remained that complaints were received about him and his guard, and von Kahm had to follow this up. What Boris had been doing was singing in the streetcar in the early morning, usually humming but sometimes singing so that the words could be understood—and what do you suppose the words were? The second verse of 'Brothers, toward sunlight, toward freedom—See the procession of millions Surge forth without end from the night, Till your demands and your longings Flood the whole sky out of sight'—d'you think that was smart, to sing words like that to sleep-starved German workers early in the morning one year after Stalingrad, in an overcrowded streetcar, to sing at all in fact, considering how serious the situation was? Imagine if he'd sung—and I'm convinced there was no ulterior motive—the third verse: 'Shatter the yoke of the tyrants That cruelly tortures the world, Over the mass of the workers Let our banner blood-red be unfurled.' As you see, I'm not called 'red' for nothing. There was trouble, trouble. The guard was disciplined, von Kahm called me up—which he rarely did, otherwise we kept in touch by courier—and asked: 'What kind of an agent provocateur have you wished on me?' Well, it could be smoothed over, but the problems it caused! More bribes, another reminder of the instructions from the 'Foreign Armies Eastern Europe' department—but then the terrible thing happened: a worker spoke to Boris, whispered to him in the streetcar: 'Courage, Comrade, the war's as good as won.' The guard overheard this, and it was only with the utmost difficulty that he could be persuaded to retract his report—it would have cost the worker his life. No, gratitude is something I most certainly didn't get out of it. Just problems."

It proved necessary to pay another visit to the person who certainly is of a caliber to supplant Boris in the role of chief male protagonist: Walter Pelzer, aged seventy, in his yellow-and-black bungalow at the edge of the forest. Heavily gilded metal stags adorn one house wall, heavily gilded metal horses adorn the other. He has a saddle horse, a stable for the horse, he has a car (de luxe), his wife has a car (standard), and when the Au. went to see him for the second time (further visits will become necessary) he found him steeped in that defensive gloom of his that was close to being remorse.

"So you've given your kids an education, sent them to university: my son's a doctor, my daughter an archaeologist—in Turkey right now—and what do you get? Contempt for the home environment. Nouveau riche. Former Nazi, war profiteer, opportunist—you wouldn't believe the things I'm called. My daughter even talks to me about the Third World, and I ask you: what does she know about the first world? About the world that produced her? I've plenty of time to read, so I get to thinking. Look at Leni now, Leni who once wouldn't hear of selling her apartment house to me because she didn't trust me—so then she sold it to Hoyser, and what does he do with the help of that smart grandson of his? He's considering sending her an eviction notice because she sublets to foreign workers and for a long time now has been either late with the rent or unable to pay it at all. Would I ever once have dreamed of having her thrown out of her home? Never, no matter what the political system was. Never. I don't deny having fallen for her the very day she turned up, or that I've never been that particular about marriage vows and so on. Do I deny that? I don't. Do I deny having been a Nazi, a Communist, or that I took advantage of certain financial opportunities the war put in my way businesswise? I don't. To call a spade a spade—I cleaned up wherever I could. And I admit it. But after 1933 did I ever harm anyone in or outside my business? I didn't. O.K., so before that I was a bit rough, I admit. But after '33? Never harmed a living soul. Is there anyone who worked for me or with me who can complain? There isn't. And no one has complained either. The only one who might've done so was that fellow

Kremp, but he's dead. O.K., so I gave him a bad time, I admit, he was such a nuisance, such a fanatic, within an inch of turning my whole business upside down and ruining the atmosphere there for good and all. What that idiot wanted, the very first day the Russian came to work, was to get us all to treat the boy like some kind of subhuman.

"It all began with a cup of coffee that Leni took over to the Russian during coffee break just after nine. It was a very cold day, late December '43 or early January '44, and the routine was for Ilse Kremer to look after the coffee. The point was, if you ask me, that she was the most trustworthy of the bunch, and that dumb Kremp might have stopped to ask himself how come a former Communist was the most trustworthy person for a job like that. You see, we each brought our own coffee along in a little paper bag, and that coffee alone contained provocation enough. Some of us only had ersatz coffee, some had made a blend of 1:10, or 1:8, Leni's was always 1:3, and I sometimes allowed myself the luxury of 1:1, occasionally even straight coffee, the real stuff: in other words, there were ten individual coffee bags, ten individual coffeepots—so, with real coffee being that short, this was a position of the utmost trust for Ilse—who would ever have noticed anything or suspected if she had transferred just an eighth of an ounce from one good bag to hers, which was sometimes lousy? Nobody. That's what the Communists called solidarity, and Kremp and the Wanft and Schelf women, those Nazis, took advantage of that quite nicely. Never would it've occurred to a single one of us to trust Marga Wanft or the Schelf woman, let alone that archidiot Kremp with making the coffee; obviously they'd have switched coffees among themselves. Though I must say that, as far as Kremp was concerned, there would usually have been nothing to switch: he was much too dumb and too honest and mostly drank straight ersatz—and then the smells when the coffee was poured! In those days you could smell right away which coffee contained even a trace of the real thing—and it happened to be Leni's coffeepot that smelled the best—well, O.K. Can you imagine the envy, the ill will, the jealousy, yes even the hatred, the feelings of revenge, that were released as soon as the coffeepots were handed around at nine fifteen each morning? And do you think that, early in 1944, the police or the party could've afforded to prosecute or lay a complaint against every single person guilty of whatever they called it, 'Violation of the war economy'? I don't mind telling you, they were glad when people got their ounce or two of coffee, never mind where from.

"O.K.—so what does our Leni do, the very first day the Russian shows up for work? She pours him a cup of her own coffee—1:3, mind you, while Kremp was drinking his watery slops—pours the Russian some coffee from her own coffeepot into her own cup and carries it over to him, to the table where he spent his first few days working alongside Kremp making wreath frames. For Leni that was the most natural thing in the world, to offer a cup of coffee to someone who had no cup and no coffee—but do you think she had the faintest idea of how *political* it was? I could see even Ilse Kremer turning pale—*she* knew, you see, how political it was: to take a Russian a cup of 1:3 coffee with an aroma that was enough to kill all the other slop-blends right off. So what does Kremp do? He usually worked sitting down, without his artificial leg because it didn't fit properly yet, so he takes down the leg from the hook on the wall—you can imagine how attractive that looked, an artificial leg always hanging there on the wall—and dashes the cup from the bewildered Russian's hand.

"What came next? A deathly silence is what it's called, I believe, but even that deathly silence—that's the literary term for it, that's what it's called in the books I sometimes read nowadays—had its variations: deathly in a way that was approving in the case of the Schelf woman and Marga Wanft, neutral in the case of Helga Heuter and Miss Zeven, understanding in the case of Mrs. Hölthohne and Ilse. Well, we were *stunned,* I don't mind telling you, all except for old Grundtsch, who stood next to me leaning against the open office doorway and just laughed. It was all very well for him to laugh, he was considered an oddball anyway and didn't have much to be scared about, though he was a crafty old bastard, crafty as they come. So what did I do? Sheer tension made me spit from the office doorway into the workshop —and if such a thing exists, and I managed to express it, then that spit was pure irony and landed much closer to Kremp than to Leni. Damn it all, how can you explain politically significant details: like my spit landing closer to Kremp than to Leni, and how are you going to prove that the spit was meant to be ironical?

"Still that deathly silence, and what does Leni do during those tense moments, which were, you might say, breathless but fear-packed? What does she do? She picks up the cup, it had fallen on the peat moss lying around there so it wasn't broken, she picks it up, walks to the faucet, rinses it carefully—there was a kind of provocation in the care she took over this—and I believe that from that moment on she acted with deliberate provocation. Damn it all, you know how quickly you can rinse out a cup like that, and thoroughly too, but she rinsed it as if it was a sacred chalice—then she did something entirely gratuitous—dried the cup, carefully too, with a clean handkerchief, walked over to her coffeepot, poured the second cup from it—they were those two-cup pots, you know—and carried it over to the Russian, as cool as you please, without so much as a glance at Kremp. Not in silence either. No, she even said: 'There you are.' Now it was up to the Russian. He must've known how political the whole situation was—a high-strung, hypersensitive boy, I don't mind telling you, with a sense of tact that no one could hold a candle to, pale, with those quaint steel-rimmed spectacles and that very fair hair of his, a bit curly, there was a touch of the cherub about that boy—what does he, what did he do? Still that deathly silence, everyone felt this was a moment of truth. Leni's done her part—so what does he do? Well, he takes the cup, saying loud and clear, in impeccable German: 'Thank you, Miss'—and starts drinking the coffee. Beads of sweat on his forehead—mind you, it was probably years since he'd had as much as a drop of real coffee or tea—the effect on him was like an injection on an emaciated body.

"Well, luckily that put an end to that terrible tense deathly silence—Mrs. Hölthohne gave a sigh of relief, Kremp mumbled something about 'Bolsheviks—war widow—coffee for Bolsheviks,' Grundtsch laughed again, I spat again, with such lousy aim that I almost hit Kremp's artificial leg—and that, of course, would've been sacrilege. The Schelf woman and Marga Wanft snorted with indignation, the others with relief. And now, of course, there was no coffee for Leni—and what does my Ilse, Ilse Kremer, do? Takes her own coffeepot, pours Leni a cup, and carries it over to her, saying quite distinctly: 'You must have something to wash that bread down with,' and Ilse's coffee wasn't that bad either. She had a brother, you see, quite a Nazi and something high up in Antwerp, and he always brought her back raw coffee beans—oh well. That was it. That was Leni's decisive battle."

This decisive appearance of Leni's at the end of 1943 or early in 1944 seemed to the Au. of such importance that he wanted to collect further details on it and paid another visit to all the participants in the scene who were still alive. Above all it seemed to him that the duration of Pelzer's "deathly silence" had been represented as too long. In the Au.'s view, this was a case of literarization that needed to be clarified, for in his opinion and experience "deathly silence" can never last longer than thirty or forty seconds. Ilse Kremer—who, incidentally, by no means denies her Nazi brother and coffee-supplier!—estimates the deathly silence at "from three to four minutes." Miss Wanft: "I remember the scene very clearly, and I reproach myself to this day for the fact that we failed to remonstrate and thus gave a kind of approval to the things that happened—deathly silence? Contemptuous silence, I'd say—how long did it last? If it's so important to you: I'd say, a minute or two. The point is that we oughtn't to have remained silent, we had an obligation not to remain silent. Our boys out there, in the freezing cold, and always on the heels of the Bolsheviks" (in 1944 that was no longer the case, by that time it was the Bolsheviks who were "on the heels of our boys," historical correction by the Au.), "and there he sat in the warm getting 1:3 coffee from that tart."

Mrs. Hölthohne: "I must say, I had cold shivers down my

spine, regular goose pimples, I can assure you, and I wondered then as I so often did later on: Does Leni know what she's doing? I admired her, her courage and the naturalness and the staggering calm with which in the midst of that deathly silence she rinsed out the cup, dried it and so on, there was a—I'd say calculated—warmth and humanity about it, so help me—well, as to how long it lasted: I tell you, it was an eternity—I don't care whether it was three minutes or five or only eighty seconds. An eternity, and for the first time I felt something like sympathy for Pelzer, who was quite obviously on Leni's side and against Kremp—and that spitting seemed pretty vulgar, of course, but at that particular moment it was the only means of expression open to him—and it was clear what he was trying to express: he must have wanted to spit in Kremp's face, but of course he couldn't do that."

Grundtsch: "I wanted to shout for joy: that girl had guts. Damn it all, right at the outset she fought a decisive battle—probably without knowing it—and yet she must've had an idea: after all, she'd only known the boy for the hour and a half he'd been working at the wreath-frame table, at everyone's mercy—and no one, not even that Nosy-Parker Marga Wanft, could've accused her of carrying on with him. If you ask me, and if I may use a military term, Leni created an enormous firing zone for herself before there was anything to fire. No one could find any other explanation for what she did other than pure innocent humanity, the very thing that was forbidden to be shown to sub-humans, and yet, you know: even a fellow like that Kremp could see that Boris *was* human: he had a nose and two legs didn't he? and even spectacles on his nose, and he was more sensitive than that whole *mishpokhe* put together. Through Leni's brave deed Boris was simply made a human being, proclaimed a human being—and that was that, in spite of all the bad times ahead. As for how long it lasted: oh, it seemed to me like at least five minutes."

The Au. felt obliged to establish the possible duration of the deathly silence by way of an experiment. Since the workroom—now in Grundtsch's possession—is still in existence, it was possible to take some measurements: from Leni's to Boris's table—thirteen feet; from Boris's table to the faucet—ten feet; from the faucet to Leni's table (on which the coffeepot stood)—six feet; once more the thirteen feet to Boris's table—a total of forty-two feet, covered by Leni probably with outward calm but actually, we imagine, with dispatch. Unfortunately, the cup being dashed to the floor could only be simulated, the Au. having neither amputee nor amputee's prosthesis at his disposal; there was no need to simulate a cup being rinsed and dried, the coffee being poured: he—the Au.—performed the experiment three times in order to leave no room for doubt and to arrive at his objective: the factual mean value. Result: first experiment—45 seconds; second experiment—58 seconds; third experiment—42 seconds. Mean value—48 seconds.

Here the Au., having once again to depart from his rule and intervene directly, would like to describe this event as Leni's birth or rebirth, as a seminal experience, as it were. However, little material on Leni is available to him beyond that which permits the following summary: not overintelligent, perhaps, a blend of the romantic, the sensual, and the materialistic, a little Kleist-reading, a little piano-playing, a knowledge of certain secretory processes which, although amateurish, was far-reaching (or deep-seated); and even if we assume her to be (because of what happened to Erhard) a thwarted mistress, an unsatisfactory widow, three-quarters orphaned (mother dead, father in jail), even if we regard her as semi- or even grossly uneducated: not one of these dubious qualities, or their totality, explains the naturalness of her behavior at that moment which we will from now on call the "coffee incident." Granted, she had been touchingly, warmly solicitous of Rahel until the moment when Rahel was buried in a shallow grave in the convent grounds, but Rahel had been a bosom friend, after Erhard and Heinrich the dearest she had ever known—why, then, the coffee for a person like Boris Lvovich whom she was in turn placing in a highly conspicuous and dangerous position, for what was the situation of a Soviet prisoner of war who, on being offered coffee by a naive German girl, accepted it with the utmost *naturalness* and (so it seemed) equal naiveté? Did she even know what a Communist was if, as Margret believed, she never bothered to distinguish between Jews and non-Jews?

Miss van Doorn, who had known no more about the "coffee incident" (Leni had evidently not regarded it as worth telling her about) than Margret and Lotte, has a straightforward explanation to offer: "One thing, you know, had always been taken for granted at the Gruytens': everyone got a cup of coffee. Beggars, spongers, tramps, welcome or unwelcome business acquaintances. There was just no question, everyone got coffee, it was that simple. Even the Pfeiffers, and that's saying something. And—to be fair—he wasn't the one who committed the unpardonable sin, it was she. It's always reminded me of how it used to be taken for granted that anyone who knocked at a monastery door got a bowl of soup, without being asked about his religion or required to utter pious sayings. No, she would've offered coffee to anyone, Communist or otherwise . . . and I believe she'd have given some to even the worst Nazi. There was just no question about it—the thing was, that no matter how many other faults she may've had she was a generous person, and that's a fact. And warm and human—only, in one particular point, you know what I mean, she wasn't what he needed."

Now here we must at all costs avoid giving the impression that during that wartime period of late 1943 and early 1944 there was or could have been any such thing as Russophilia or Soviet euphoria at Pelzer's wreathmaking business. Leni's natural behavior can be assessed only relatively in historical terms, but in personal terms objectively. If we bear in mind that other

Germans (a few) risked and suffered prison, hanging, or concentration camp for far lesser favors rendered to Soviet individuals, we are forced to realize that this was not a deliberate display of humanity but—both objectively and subjectively—a relative one, to be seen only in the context of Leni's existence and the historical juncture. Had Leni been less unsuspecting (she had already demonstrated this aspect of her character apropos Rahel) she would have behaved—as is borne out by subsequent events and actions—in exactly the same manner. And had Leni been unable to express her naturalness in material form—by way of a cup of coffee, that is—the result would have been an inept, probably unsuccessful, stammering of empathy which might have entailed a worse interpretation than the coffee presented as if in a sacred chalice.

It is to be assumed that she derived a certain sensual pleasure from carefully rinsing the cup, carefully drying it: there was nothing pointed about that. Since in Leni's case reflection had always come later (Alois, Erhard, Heinrich, Sister Rahel, her father, her mother, the war), much later, we must expect her not to realize until later *what* it was she had done. She had not only given the Soviet individual a cup of coffee, she had positively presented him with it, she had spared the Soviet individual a humiliation and caused a German amputee to suffer one. Hence Leni was not born or reborn in the estimated fifty seconds of deathly silence, her birth or rebirth was not a finished process, it was a continuing one. In a nutshell: Leni never knew what she was doing until she did it. She had to materialize everything. It must not be forgotten that at this moment in time she was precisely twenty-one and a half years old. She was—we must reiterate—a person who was extremely dependent on secretion and hence digestion, totally unsuited for sublimating anything. She had a latent capacity for directness that had been neither recognized nor aroused by Alois, and which Erhard either never had the chance, or never availed himself of the chance, to arouse. The estimated eighteen to twenty-five minutes of sensual fulfillment she may have experienced with Alois had not fully mobilized her, Alois having also lacked the ability to grasp the paradox that Leni was sensual precisely because she was not altogether sensual.

There are only two witnesses to the next-most crucial experience: the laying-on-of-hands. Bogakov, who has already described it and its secretory consequences, and Pelzer, the only other person in the know.

Pelzer: "From then on, of course, the Russian got his coffee regularly, from her, and I can swear to it, when she took him his coffee the next day—but by then he wasn't with the wreath-frame group, he was already working at the final-trim table with Mrs. Hölthohne, I can swear to it—and by then it was no longer naive or unconscious, whichever you like, for she gave quite a little look around in case anyone was watching—she simply laid her left hand on his right, and it went through him, though it only lasted a second or two, it went through him like an electric shock. He shot up like a rocket taking off. I saw it, I can swear to it, and she didn't know I saw it, I was standing in my dark office with my eye on them because I wanted to see what was going to happen about the coffee. Do you know what I thought, it sounds vulgar, I know, but we gardeners aren't quite as namby-pamby as some people think; I thought: damn it all, she's rushing him—boy, is she rushing him, I thought, and I got really envious and jealous of that Russian. Erotically speaking, Leni was a progressive person, she didn't care that it's traditional for the man to take the initiative: *she* did it by laying her hand on him. And even though she obviously knew that in his position he simply couldn't take the initiative, still it was both things: it was, erotically and politically, a daring act, almost brazen."

Of both of them (of Leni through Margret, of Boris through Bogakov) it is known that each said, in identical words, that they were both "instantly on fire," and, as we know from Bogakov, Boris reacted as a man reacts and, as we know from Margret,

Leni had an experience that "was much more wonderful than that heather business I once told you about."

Pelzer on Boris's professional skills: "Believe me, I'm a good judge of people, and the very first day I knew that Boris, that Russian fellow, was a highly intelligent person with organizational ability. After only three days he became, unofficially, Grundtsch's deputy as final checker, and he got along fine with Mrs. Hölthohne and Miss Zeven, who were more or less under him but of course weren't supposed to notice they were under him. He was in his way an artist, and it didn't take long for him to catch on to the main point: economical use of materials. And no display of emotion when he had to handle ribbon-inscriptions that must surely have gone against the grain for him. 'For Führer, Nation, and Fatherland,' or 'Storm Trooper Company 112,' and although he was handling swastikas and eagles all day long he never batted an eyelid. So one day, when there were just the two of us in my office, where later he was in sole charge of the ribbon supplies and the ribbon accounts, I asked him: 'Boris, tell me frankly now, how do you feel among all those swastikas and eagles and things?' He didn't hesitate for a moment with his answer. 'Mr. Pelzer,' he said, 'I hope it won't hurt your feelings—since you ask me so openly—when I tell you: there's a certain comfort in not only suspecting and knowing but actually seeing that even the members of a Storm Trooper Company are mortal—and as for the swastikas and eagles, I'm fully aware of my historical situation.'

"As time went on, he and Leni became almost indispensable to me, I want to stress this, if I not only left him in peace but actually did him favors—and the same goes for the girl—there were business reasons for this too. I'm not really one of your starry-eyed philanthropists, never said I was. It was just that the boy had a fantastic sense of order and a gift for organization—he got along well with the staff too, even Marga and the Schelf woman didn't mind taking suggestions from him because he did it so skillfully. Believe me, in a free-market economy he'd have gone a long way. Well, he was an engineer of course, and most likely knew his math, but he was the first person to notice, though I'd been running the place for almost ten years and Grundtsch had been in the business for almost forty—not one of us had noticed, it hadn't even dawned on that clever Mrs. Hölthohne—that the frame—I mean the wreath-frame—group was understaffed in relation to the efficiency of the trimming table, and because he and Mrs. Hölthohne were the best checkers I could ever have wished for. So: regrouping. Miss Zeven back to the frame table, she grumbled a bit but I squared that with a raise, and the result: production rose, as the figures showed, by 12 to 15 percent. So are you surprised that I was keen to hold onto him and take care nothing happened to him? And then there were the Party comrades who let me know—sometimes directly, sometimes by hints—that I was to make sure nothing happened to him, that he had powerful protection. Well, it wasn't all that simple; a nasty little snooper like that Kremp, and that hysterical Wanft woman—they could've blown the whole place sky high. And not a soul, not even Leni or even Grundtsch, ever knew that in my own little greenhouse I let him have sixty square feet that'd been especially well manured, to grow his own tobacco, cucumbers, and tomatoes."

The Au. must confess that, as regards the surviving witnesses from the wartime wreathmaking business, he preferred to take the path of least resistance and so visited most frequently those witnesses who were most easily accessible. Marga Wanft having turned her back on him even more ostentatiously on the second visit than on the first, he excluded her. Pelzer, Grundtsch, Ilse Kremer, and Mrs. Hölthohne being equally accessible and equally loquacious—somewhat less so in the case of Ilse Kremer—the choice, or the selection, was rendered difficult; in Mrs. Hölthohne's case the lure was her superb tea and her meticulously furnished apartment, also her well-preserved and *soignée* attractiveness, as well as her open display of continuing Separatist feelings; the only things that made him hesitate with Mrs. Hölthohne were her tiny ashtray and her obvious dislike of chain smokers.

"Very well then, so our state" (meaning the state of North Rhineland-Westphalia. Au.) "has the highest tax income and supports other German states that have a low tax income—but does it ever occur to anyone to invite the people from the low tax income states—from Schleswig-Holstein and Bavaria, say—over here, so that for a change they can swallow not only our tax pennies but also our polluted air, the air that's one of the reasons we make so much money here? And drink our foul, dreadful water—and how about the Bavarians with their pristine lakes and the Holsteiners with their shoreline coming here one day for a dip in the Rhine, they'd certainly come out tarred and probably feathered too. And just look at that Strauss, a man whose whole career is made up of unsolved incidents, I say unsolved and I also say obscure because it means the same thing—the way he insults our state" (N.R.-W. Au.) "almost foaming at the mouth—why, I wonder? Well, simply because things are a little more progressive here. He should be compelled to live for three years in Duisburg or Dormagen or Wesseling, with his wife and children, so he can see where the money comes from and how it's earned—the money he gets for Bavaria and then has the nerve to insult because we have a state government here which, while far from entrancing, is *at least* not Christian Democrat, let alone Christian Socialist—do you see what I mean? Why am I supposed to feel 'togetherness,' why? Did I establish the Reich, was I ever in favor if its establishment? No. Why should we be concerned with all that, I'd like to know, up north and down south and in the middle? Just think for a moment of how we got into this crowd: all because of those damn Prussians—and what've they got to do with us? Who sold us down the river in 1815? Was it us? Was that what we wanted, was there such a thing as a plebiscite? No, I tell you. Why doesn't Strauss take a dip in the Rhine some day and breathe the Duisburg air—but no, he stays put in his wholesome Bavarian air, almost choking on his indignation when he starts spouting about 'Rhine and Ruhr.' What have these obscure provincial factors to do with us? Don't we have our own obscurity? Just think about it!" (Which the Au. promised to do.) "No, I'm a Separatist and always will be, and I'll accept a few Westphalians if you like, if there's no alternative, but what would we get out of them? Clericalism, hypocrisy, and maybe some potatoes—I don't really know what they grow there and I'm not all that interested—and their forests and fields, well, who cares, I can't take those home with me either—they'd stay nicely where they are, but very well, a few Westphalians. That's all. The trouble is, they're always taking offense, feeling slighted, grumbling and whining about 'equal time on radio' and nonsense like that. Nothing but trouble with those people.

"That's the marvelous thing about Leni, that she's so Rhenish. And I must tell you something, I'm sure you'll think it very odd: that Boris seemed more Rhenish to me than all the rest of them, except Pelzer, Pelzer had just that blend of criminality and humanity that's only possible here. It's true, mind you, he never did anyone any harm, except Kremp maybe, he did give him a bad time whenever he could, and Kremp being a Nazi you might say Pelzer wasn't such an opportunist after all, but that's where you'd be wrong—because the Nazis were outnumbered it was highly opportune to give Kremp, and only Kremp, a bad time—nobody liked him, you see, not even the two other Nazis, he was simply an unpleasant character, always after women in that nasty way of his. And yet, and yet, I must try and be fair to him, he was a young fellow and had lost a leg back in 1940 when he was only twenty—and who's willing to admit, or be forced to admit, that when you come right down to it, it was, or is, pointless? And we mustn't forget that during the first few months of the war those boys were treated like heroes, besieged by women—but then, the longer the war went on, losing a leg became more and more run-of-the-mill, and later on the ones with two legs simply had better luck than the ones with only one leg or none. I'm quite a progressive woman when it comes to thinking, and that's how I'd explain that boy's sexual and erotic status and his psychological situation. I ask you—what, in 1944, was a man who'd lost a leg? Just a poor bastard with a miserable pension—

and think for a moment what it's like when a fellow like that takes off his leg in a crucial sexual situation? Appalling, for him and his partner, even if she's a whore." (Oh, that glorious tea of hers, and is the Au. to take it as a declaration of partiality that on his third visit the ashtray had at least the dimensions of a demitasse saucer? Au.)

"And then there was that Pelzer, always the picture of health, whom you can take as a classic example of *mens sana in corpore sano,* something you find only among criminals, I mean among people totally devoid of conscience. Lack of conscience makes a person healthy, take it from me. Even the guards who brought Boris to work in the morning and picked him up in the evening, even with them he made deals on the side in brandy, coffee, and cigarettes—they used to drive pretty much every week to France or Belgium as convoy guards and bring back brandy, cigars, and coffee by the case, even cloth, you could even *order* goods from those fellows, like in a store. One of them, called Kolb, a rather dirty old man, once brought me enough velvet from Antwerp for a whole dress; the other was called Boldig and was younger, a cheery nihilist, the kind that emerged by the score from '44 on. A lighthearted lad if ever there was one, he had a glass eye and had lost a hand, quite a nice row of medals on his gallant chest, and he was quite cynical about using his lost eye, his lost hand, and the hardware on his chest to his advantage, the way you use counters to gamble with. He cared less about Führer, Nation, and Fatherland than even I did, for after all, though I could've managed without the Führer, I'm all for a Rhenish fatherland, for the Rhenish people. Well, he was casual as can be about going off with the Schelf woman—who, after Leni, was the snappiest of the lot—for short spells at the far end of the greenhouse and, as he called it, 'catching a wee mouse' or 'listening to a dickeybird,' on the pretext of having her pick him out a few flowers with Pelzer's consent. He had lots of names for it. Not a bad type—simply: with a cynicism and a nihilism that bordered on the macabre. And he was the one who used to try and cheer Kremp up a bit, he'd slip him a few cigarettes now and then, things like that, and clap him on the shoulder, and loudly proclaim the slogan you began hearing around that time: 'Enjoy the war, bud, peace is going to be terrible.'

"The other one, Kolb, was a nasty bit of work, always pawing and patting. As for Pelzer—to use a contemporary term: in view of the funeral-market situation, it was only natural for a black market to develop in everything—wreaths, ribbons, flowers, coffins, and naturally he got an allocation for the wreaths for Party bigwigs and heroes and air-raid victims. After all, who wants to have their dear departed buried wreathless? And because more and more soldiers, and civilians too, were dying, the coffins were eventually used not only over and over again but in the end as dummies: the body would be sewn up in canvas, later in sacking, then just wrapped up, more or less nude, and dropped through a flap into the bare earth, the dummy coffin was allowed to remain in place for a certain time, for appearances' sake, and some earth would be thrown on it to make it more convincing, but as soon as the mourners, the salvo parties, the lord mayors, and the Party bigwigs—well, let's say—as soon as the 'inevitable cortege,' as Pelzer called it, had moved far enough away, out of sight, the dummy coffin would be removed, dusted off, polished up a bit, and the grave hastily filled in—believe me, as hastily as at a Jewish funeral. One felt like saying: Next please, like at the dentist's. It wasn't long, of course, before it occurred to Pelzer, who missed out on the coffin rentals as well as the whole lucrative bag of tricks, that wreaths can be used over and over again too, and this double, triple, sometimes even quintuple use of wreaths was impossible without bribing and conspiring with the cemetery custodians. The number of times a wreath could be 'recycled' depended, of course, on the stability of the frame material and the tying greenery—at the same time it was a chance to have a good look at the methods and clumsy workmanship of the competition. Naturally this required organization, complicity—and a certain amount of secrecy; this was only possible with Grundtsch, with Leni, with me and Ilse Kremer—and I admit: we went along with it. Sometimes wreaths from nurseries out in the country would turn up, of truly prewar quality. So that the others wouldn't notice anything, the whole operation was known as the 'reworking group.' Eventually it extended even to the ribbons. It got to the point where Pelzer kept his eyes open and manipulated the customers when they placed their orders in such a way that the inscriptions became less and less personal, and this meant increased opportunities for recycling the ribbons. Inscriptions like 'From Dad,' 'From Mum,' can be used relatively often in wartime, and even a comparatively personal inscription like 'From Konrad' or 'From Ingrid' has some prospect when you give the ribbon a good press, freshen up the colors and the lettering a bit, and put the ribbon away in the ribbon closet, till once again a Konrad or an Ingrid has someone to mourn. Pelzer's favorite motto at this time, as at all times, was: Every little bit helps. Finally Boris hit on an idea that turned out to be quite a little gold mine, the idea—and he can only have known about this from his knowledge of second-rate German literature—of reintroducing an old-fashioned type of ribbon inscription: 'Gone but not forgotten.' Well, that turned out to be what today we'd call a best seller, and we could go on using that until the ribbon was finally past freshening up or pressing. Even highly individual inscriptions such as 'From Gudula' were saved."

Ilse Kremer on the same subject: "Yes, that's right, I did go along with it. We used to work special shifts so no one would notice. He always said that it wasn't desecrating the graves, that he got the wreaths from the rubbish heap. Well, I didn't care. It meant a nice bit of extra money for us, and after all: was it so bad? What was the good of the wreaths rotting on a rubbish heap? But eventually someone did lay a complaint, on the grounds of desecration and grave-robbing, because, of course, there were some people who were surprised to come back three or four days later and find their wreaths gone—but there again he was very nice about it, kept us out of the whole thing, went alone to the hearing, took the blame for everything, even kept Grundtsch out of it, and, according to what someone told me, he very cleverly used the argument of that national mumbo jumbo about the 'penny gobbler,' he admitted to 'certain irregularities' and donated a thousand marks to a convalescent home; what he said—it wasn't a regular court, you know, just a guild committee and later a Party court of honor—what he said was, so I was told: 'Gentlemen, Party comrades, I am fighting on a front that is unknown to most of you—and on the fronts that many of you know better than I, aren't there times when one is willing to stretch a point?' Well, after that he did drop it for a while, till the end of '44 in fact, and by that time the general confusion was so great that no one paid any more attention to such trivial things as wreaths and ribbons."

7 Since Grundtsch's invitations were both cordial and standing the Au. paid him several successive visits, enjoying with him the truly heavenly silence that reigns over a walled cemetery on warm late-summer evenings. The following passages represent the verbatim summary of some four sessions that all began harmoniously and all ended harmoniously. During these sessions, of which the first took place on a bench under an elderberry bush, the second on a bench under an oleander bush, the third on a bench under a syringa bush, the fourth on a bench under a laburnum tree (old Grundtsch likes variety and claims to have at his disposal other benches under other bushes), tobacco was smoked, beer was drunk, and street noises, distant and almost agreeable, were sometimes listened to.

Résumé of the first visit (under the elderberry bush): "It's really a joke, you know, Walt talking about financial opportunities—he's always taken advantage of them, even at nineteen, when he was with a quartermaster corps during the first war. Quartermaster corps?—well, let's say they clean up battlefields after the battle—there's quite a bit to collect, stuff the army might still use: steel helmets, rifles, machine guns, ammunition, cannon even, they pick up every canteen, every lost cap or belt and so on—and of course there are corpses lying around there too, and corpses usually have something in their pockets: photos, letters—wallets with money in them sometimes, and a buddy of Walt's once told me that he—Walt, that is—stopped at nothing, not even gold teeth, never mind the nationality of the gold teeth—and toward the end, of course, Americans also started turning up on European battlefields—and it was in dealing with corpses that Walt gave the first proof of his business sense. Needless to say, it was all strictly prohibited, but people—and I hope you're not one of them—usually make the mistake of thinking that what's prohibited isn't done. That's Sonny Boy's strong point: he doesn't care a rap about regulations and laws, he just makes sure he doesn't get caught.

"Well, the boy came home from World War I, at nineteen, with a respectable little fortune, a nice little packet of dollars, pounds, and Belgian and French francs—and a nice little packet of gold too. And he gave proof of his business sense by showing his instinct, his uncanny nose, for real estate, developed and undeveloped, he liked the undeveloped lots best, I mean undeveloped not in the horticultural sense but ones that hadn't been built on, but in a pinch he would take the developed ones too. At that time the dollars and pounds came in very handy, and fields, say on the outskirts of town, were dirt cheap, here an acre, there an acre, as close as possible to the main road leading out of town, and a few small buildings belonging to bankrupt tradesmen and business people in the center of town. Then off went Sonny Boy to do his peacetime work, if you like to call it that: he exhumed American soldiers and packed them in zinc coffins to be sent to America—and there was as much illegal business to be done there as legal, for some exhumed bodies also have gold teeth; with their mania for hygiene the Americans paid fantastic sums for this job, and again there were a lot of legal and illegal dollars at a time when dollars were few and far between, and again a few little properties for our man, tiny little lots, this time in the center of town where small grocers and tradesmen were going bust."

Résumé of the conversation under the oleander bush: "Walter was four when I began my apprenticeship, at the age of fourteen, with old Pelzer, and all of us, including his parents, called him Sonny Boy—and the name's stuck. They were nice folk, his parents, she overdid it a bit with her religion, was forever in church and so on, he was quite deliberately a heathen, if you've any idea what that meant in 1904. He'd read Nietzsche, of course, and Stefan George, and while he wasn't exactly a crackpot he was a bit of a crank; he wasn't specially interested in business, only in breeding, in experiments—to coin a new phrase: he was searching not only for the blue flower but the new flower. He'd been in the Socialist Youth Movement from the word go, and got me involved in it too: I can still sing you all the verses of 'The Workingmen'" (Grundtsch sang:) "'Who hauls the gold above ground? Who hammers ore and stone? Who weaves the cloth and velvet? Who plants the wine and grain? Who gives the rich their daily bread, Yet lives in poverty instead? It is the workingmen, the proletariat. Who toils from early morning Till far into the night? Creates for others riches, A life of ease and might? Who turns the world's great wheel alone, Yet rights within the state has none? It is the workingmen, the proletariat.'

"Well, anyway, as a lad of fourteen, coming from the wretchedest Eifel village you can imagine, I turned up at Heinz Pelzer's as an apprentice. He fixed up a little room for me in the greenhouse, with a bed and a table and a chair, right next to the stove—I got my board and a little money—and even Pelzer ate no better and had no more money than I did. We were communists, without knowing the word or really knowing what it means. Pelzer's wife Adelheid used to send me packages when I had to do my stint in the army from 1908 to 1910, and where did they send me? You guessed it, to coldest Prussia, to Bromberg, that's where; and where did I go when I got leave? Not home, that miserable priest-ridden hole, no, I went to the Pelzers'—well, Sonny Boy was always playing outside and forever getting under our feet in the greenhouse, a cute little fellow, quiet, not freindly but not unfriendly either, and you know, if I stop to think what made him so completely different from his father: it was fear. He was afraid. There was always trouble with the bailiffs and checks that bounced, and sometimes we few helpers would scrape our meager savings together to prevent the worst from happening. A nursery garden was never a gold mine, it's only become that since the flower craze has broken out all over Europe. And that Heinz Pelzer always after his new flower. He believed the new age needed a new flower, he had visions of something way out that he never found, though he spent years pottering over his flowerpots and flowerbeds, as secretive as any inventor, fertilizing, taking cuttings, crossing breeds: yet all he got for it was debased tulips or degenerate roses, ugly mongrels. Well anyway, when Sonny Boy got to be six and went to school, he had only one word in his head, 'baily'—that was his abbreviation of bailiff. 'Mum, is the baily coming today? Dad, is the baily coming again today?' Fear, I tell you, fear's what's made him the way he is.

"Not surprisingly, he never finished high school, dropped out in grade nine and became an apprentice right off, got his green apron, and that was the end, the year was 1914, and if you ask me: 1914 wasn't only the end for Walter and his education, it was the end of everything, everything, I was twenty-four, and I know what I'm saying: it was the end of any kind of socialism in Germany. The end. To think that those idiots let themselves be bamboozled by that soppy crappy Kaiser of theirs! Heinz, Walter's father, realized that too, and finally gave up his amateurish experiments. He had to join up, like me—and the two of us—out of rage, I tell you, out of fury and grief and rage—became sergeants. I hated them, those greenhorns, those new recruits, nicely brought up, servile, full of shit in both senses. I hated them and bullied them. Yes, I got to be a sergeant major, I sent them off by the score, by the battalion, from the Häcketauer barracks that were identical with the barracks in Bromberg, identical, down to the last detail—so that you could find the office of Company 3 in your sleep, like in Bromberg—I trained them by the score and sent them off to the front. In my pocket, in my wallet, a little photo of Rosa Luxemburg. I carried it around like a saint's picture, it finally got as dog-eared as a saint's picture. Anyway, I was *not* a member of a Soldiers' Council, no sir: in 1914 German history came to an end for me—and then of course they killed Rosa Luxemburg, *had* her killed, those gentlemen of the Social Democratic party—and then even our Sonny Boy got into the war, and maybe that was the only smart thing to do, collect gold teeth and dollar bills. His mother was a nice soul, Adelheid, she must have actually been pretty at one time, but then she soon turned sour, her nose got red and pointed, and she got that bitter, sour twist to her mouth that I can't stand in women: my grandmother had it, my mother too, those lovely faces left with nothing but *suffering,* sourpusses, listening to nobody but those damn priests and first thing in the morning off to early Mass and in the afternoon off again with their rosaries and in the evening once again with their rosaries—anyway, we had to go quite often to church or the cemetery chapel because we had a rental service for potted palms and such-like, and Adelheid's church connections came in nice and handy and at club evenings and office parties and so on—well, if I could've had my way I'd have spat at the altar, I didn't, though, because of Adelheid.

"Then to cap it all Heinz started drinking. . . . Well, I must say I could understand Sonny Boy staying away from home, digging up dead Yanks, then joining the Liberation Front for six months, in Silesia I think it was. After that he stayed in town for a while, took up boxing—professionally, but that wasn't very profitable, he did a bit of pimping—first with the really cheap tarts who would do it for a cup of coffee, later on the higher-class ones—and then he actually became a Communist, a card-carrying member, but that didn't last long either. He was never much of a talker, and it didn't bother him that he wasn't making much out of his real estate, he'd never done any gardening, your hands get pretty dirty from that, you see, the dirt eats into the creases of your skin—and our Sonny Boy was always spick-and-span and very health-conscious: went jogging every morning, then a shower, hot and cold, breakfast at home was too frugal for him, ersatz coffee and turnip jam, he'd head straight for his whores' cafes, order himself eggs, real coffee, and a brandy—all paid for later by the girls' beaus. And as soon as he could, of course, he got himself a car, even if it was only a Hanomag."

Résumé of the conversation under the syringa bush: "I must say, he was always nice to his parents, really nice, I fancy he really loved them. Never a harsh word to his mother, never even laughed at her, and Adelheid was getting more and more fretful, she didn't die of grief, she fretted her life away, went sour, it was too bad—she'd been as pretty as a picture at one time; in 1904, when I joined the business, she was a bonny woman. Then later, when Walter sometimes drove around with us delivering potted palms, you should've seen how convincingly he genuflected, dipped a hand in the holy-water stoup . . . as if to the manner born. Then in '32 he joined the Storm Troopers, and early in '33 he took part in the rounding up of prominent politicians, but he never turned any in, he cashed in instead and let them go in exchange for the family jewels and cash—that must've been pretty lucrative, right off there was a new car, new clothes, and by then, of course, there were cheap Jewish properties to be bought too, here a little shop, there a building site, and he calls that 'being a bit rough.'

"And all of a sudden he turned into a fine gentleman, manicured nails and all, he married at thirty-four, money of course, Prumtel's daughter Eva—you know, one of those girls who're always thinking of higher things; not a bad sort, just a bit hysterical; her old man had some kind of office where you could get credit for installment buying, and later a few pawnshops too—and the daughter, well, she read Rilke and played the flute. Anyway, her dowry contained a few properties and a pile of cash. After '34 he became an officer in an elite Storm Trooper commando, but he kept out of all the dirty goings-on, out of the brutal ones too, he can't be accused of that—of being brutal—just of having a sharp eye for property. The funny thing was that, the richer he got, the more humane he became, even that night when they broke the windows of every Jewish store in town he didn't join in the looting. All he did now was sit around in cafés, the kind where there's an orchestra playing, go to the opera (season ticket, of course), produce children, two cute kids he idolized, Walter and little Eva, then in '36 he finally took over the nursery garden, when Heinz had actually drunk himself to death, emaciated, bitter—well anyway, I became Sonny Boy's business manager, the orders placed by the Party got us started in the wreath business, and he made me a gift of that part of the nursery that still belongs to me, generous, one must say, and never a cross word, never petty. The business started looking up when Heinz and poor Adelheid were under the ground."

Résumé of the conversation under the laburnum tree: "Some

folk think it would be an insult even to a Nazi to call Walter a Nazi. The change in him came in the middle of '44, during that business with Leni and the Russian. The welfare of those two was constantly being hammered into him, by phone calls, in conversations. The change was that he started thinking, Walter did. Even he knew the war had been lost and that after the war it wouldn't do him any harm to have treated a Russian and the Gruyten girl decently—but: how much longer was the war going to last? That was the question that was driving us all crazy: how to survive those last few months, when every minute someone was being hanged or shot, you weren't safe either as an old Nazi or as a non-Nazi—and damn it, how long did it take for the Americans to reach the Rhine from Aachen? Almost six months. My belief is that Sonny Boy, always in the pink and worshipping his two kids, was now experiencing something he'd never known before: inner conflict. He lived out there in his villa, with two pampered dogs, two cute kids, his car, and more and more real estate. He'd sold the original properties for housing developments and barracks, not for cash, oh no, he didn't care that much about cash, what he was after was real values; he took payment in lots a bit farther toward the outskirts, double, triple the size of what he disposed of. He was an optimist, you see. He was a great one for keeping fit, still going for his regular morning jog through the park, taking a shower, having a hearty breakfast—at home now—and the odd time he had to go to church, still (or again) managing to bring off an impressive genuflection or a swift sign of the cross.

"But now there were those two, Leni and Boris, he liked them, they were his best workers, they were protected by higher powers, powers he didn't know—and then there were other higher powers at work, powers that could settle a person's hash very quickly, have him shot or sent to a concentration camp. Now let's have no misunderstanding, don't imagine that Sonny Boy suddenly discovered in himself the foreign body that some human beings call conscience, or that suddenly, quaking with fear or curiosity, he began to approach that outlandish word or continent, a mystery to him to this day, that's sometimes called morality. Oh no. Never at odds with himself but sometimes with others, he had run into occasional trouble with Party or Storm Troopers, he had achieved wealth. He had often been in tight corners, mind you, in all those activities of his from the quartermaster corps to the prominent politicians he let go in '33 in exchange for cash and the family jewels. Charges had been laid against him, in both Party and regular courts, especially when he overdid it with his wreath- and ribbon-recycling. There'd been plenty of those tight corners, and he'd faced them head on, never turning a hair and getting out of them by pointing out the national and economic importance of whatever he was doing in his capacity of tireless opponent of that national enemy known at the time as the 'penny gobbler.' Tight corners yes, but conflict with himself as to what was really to his advantage—that was something new to him. He cared no more about Jews than he did about Russians or Communists or Social Democrats, you name it—but how was he supposed to behave now, with one lot of higher powers opposing another lot, and with his fondness for Boris and Leni and—what a coincidence!—discovering that they were profitable? He didn't care a rap about the war being lost, he was no more interested in politics than he was in the 'German nation's struggle for existence'—but damn it all, who could tell in July 1944 how many eons it might take for the war to come to an end? He was convinced that the right thing to do was to switch horses and count on a lost war, but when should he, or could he, make that final switch?"

A kind of summary would seem to be in order here, as well as a few questions to be answered by the reader himself. First, the statistical and external details. To imagine Pelzer as a cigar-smoking, shifty individual would be mistaken. He was (and is) very clean, attired in custom-made suits, wore (and wears) the latest thing in ties, which do, in fact, still look good on the seventy-year-old Pelzer. He smokes cigarettes, was (and is) a perfect gentleman, and if he has once been described here as having spat, it must be added that he spits very seldom, almost never, and in that instance his spitting operates as historical punctuation, possibly even as an indication of partiality. He lives in a villa that he does not call a villa. He is six foot one, weighs—according to his son, who is a doctor and whose patient he is—171 pounds, with very thick hair that was once dark and is now just beginning to turn gray. Must we really regard him as the classic example of *mens sana in corpore sano?* Has he ever known S., or T. and W.? Although his sense of confidence in Being seems to be complete, not one of the eight adjectives listed in the paragraph on L. would be applicable to his L., and his occasional smile has always resembled the Mona Lisa's rather than Buddha's. Taking him as a person who does not shrink from external conflicts and knows no inner ones, who by 1944 has reached the age of forty-four without ever experiencing an inner conflict, has increased his father's business fivefold, and does not shrink from the "every little bit" that "helps," it must be realized that at the relatively advanced age of forty-four he was for the first time catapulted out of his total sense of confidence in Being and is now entering upon virgin territory with some trepidation.

Then if we take on of his most marked characteristics, an almost inordinately powerful sensuality (his breakfast habits are a perfect reflection of Leni's), the conflict in which he found himself from the middle of 1944 on may perhaps be imagined; and if we take a further marked characteristic of Pelzer's, an almost inordinately high vitality, the conflict in which he found himself after the events of July 1944 can be imagined. The Au. has in his possession some detailed information that may serve to typify Pelzer's behavior at approximately the end of the war.

On March 1, 1945, a few days before the Americans marched into the city, Pelzer announced, by way of registered letter, his resignation from both Party and Storm Troopers, dissociated himself from the crimes of this organization, and declared himself (the certified copy of this letter may be inspected at the Au.'s) to be "a decent German who was duped and led astray." He must actually have managed to find, almost on the eve of the arrival of the Americans, a German post office that was still functioning, or at least a responsible post-office official. The registration receipt, albeit disfigured by a Nazi ruptured vulture, is also on hand. When the Americans entered the city Pelzer could therefore truthfully assert that he was not a member of a Nazi organization. He obtained a permit to operate a nursery garden and wreathmaking business since burials still continued to take place, although in considerably reduced numbers. Pelzer's comment on the stability of his trade: "There'll always be people dying."

For the time being, however, he has to get through almost one whole additional war year in circumstances of increasing difficulty, and he took to saying, when asked for favors (vacation, advance, raise, special flowers): "I'm not a monster, you know." This expression, and the frequency with which it was used, is confirmed by all surviving and traceable witnesses from the wreath business. "It got to be almost a kind of litany" (Hölthohne) "that he rattled off, there was almost a kind of exorcism about it, as if he had to persuade himself that he really wasn't a monster, and sometimes he'd say it on occasions when it didn't fit at all, for example once when I asked him how his family was, he answered: 'I'm not a monster, you know,' and once, when someone—I forget who—asked him what day it was—whether Monday or Tuesday, he said: 'I'm not a monster, you know.' People began making fun of it, even Boris mimicked him, discreetly of course, and he'd say, for instance, when I handed him a wreath that was ready for its ribbon: 'I'm not a monster, you know.' It was interesting, I must say, from a psychoanalytical viewpoint, to observe what was happening to Walter Pelzer."

Ilse Kremer fully confirmed Pelzer's litanesque utterance both as to quantity and quality: "Oh yes, he used to say it so often you didn't even hear it any more, it was like the words in church 'The Lord be with you' or 'Have mercy upon us,' and later on he had two variations of it, 'I'm not a monster, you know,' and 'Do you take me for a monster?'"

Grundtsch (during a subsequent short visit that unfortunately did not permit a cozy session under elderberry or similar bushes): "Yes, that's true. Quite true. 'I'm not a monster, you know'—'Do you take me for a monster?'—sometimes he'd even mutter it to himself when he was alone. I often heard it and then forgot about it, because in time it came to him as naturally as breathing. Well anyway" (wicked laugh on G.'s part), "maybe those gold teeth were lying a bit heavy on his stomach, and the wreaths he pinched, and the ribbons and flowers, and those little parcels of land he kept on collecting even in wartime. By the way, just think for a moment how two or three or maybe four handfuls of gold teeth of assorted nationalities can be turned into real estate that looks unprepossessing at first but today, fifty years later, is a property with a large important building of the Federal Army standing on it that pays our Sonny Boy a pretty nice rent——"

It was even possible to pick up the trail of that high-ranking member of the Weimar Government, a trail which turned up again in Switzerland, where only the politician's widow was still to be found. A tall, extremely frail-looking lady in a Basel hotel remembers the incident exactly. "Well, for us what mattered most is that we owe our lives to him. I mean it. He saved our lives—but at the same time you mustn't forget how high or how low one's position had to be in those days in order to find oneself saving another person's life. This is the aspect of favors that is always forgotten: when Goring later claimed to have saved the lives of a few Jews, we must not forget: who could really save anyone's life, and what conditions of dictatorship are those in which a human life depends on a favor? What happened was that in February 1933 we were tracked down while staying with friends in a house in Bad Godesberg, and this person—Pelzer? Perhaps, I never knew his name—demanded all my jewelry, all our cash, even a check as well, as cold-bloodedly as a highwayman, not for a bribe, oh no, do you know how he put it? 'I'll sell you my motorcycle, you'll find it down by the garden gate, and I'll give you a tip: drive through the Eifel, not to Belgium or Luxembourg, then drive beyond Saarbrücken to the border and get someone to help you across. I'm not a monster, you know,' he said, 'and the question is, of course, whether my motorbike's worth that much to you and whether you can ride it. It's a Zündap.' Luckily my husband had been a motorcycle fan in his young days, but they—those young days—were twenty years back even then, and don't ask me how we drove to Altenahr and to Prüm and from Prüm to Trier, with me on the pillion—well, luckily we had Party friends in Trier who got us to the Saar territory—not they personally but through contacts. True, we owe our lives to him—but it's also true that he held our lives in his hand. No, don't remind me of it again please, and now go, if you don't mind. No, I don't wish to know the name of that person."

Pelzer himself denies almost nothing of all this: he merely has a different interpretation of it from everyone else's. Since he loves and needs to talk, the Au. is free at any time to call him up, go and see him, have a chat with him, for as long as he likes. Once again the reader is urged to remember: Pelzer seems in no way obscure or shifty or dubious. He is thoroughly confidence-inspiring: he would seem highly suitable as a bank manager, be accepted as chairman of the board and, were he introduced to one as a retired cabinet minister, the only cause for surprise would be that he has already retired, for he does not look in the least like a man of seventy, more like a man of sixty-four who succeeds in looking like sixty-one.

When asked about his job with the quartermaster corps, he did not try to change the subject, but he neither denied nor admitted anything, merely resorting to a quasi-philosophical interpretation: "You see, if there's one thing I've always hated, and still do, it's senseless waste: I emphasize the senseless—waste itself is a good thing so long as it has purpose and meaning: like splurging once in a while, giving a generous gift or something, but senseless waste really burns me up, and to my mind the way the Americans carried on with their dead came under the heading of 'senseless waste'—think of the cost in money, personnel, and material to send back to Wisconsin, in 1923 or 1922, the body of some Jimmy or other from—say, Bernkastel, where he died in a field hospital in 1919. What for? And does every gold tooth, every wedding ring, every gold amulet chain you find among the remains have to go along too? And you wouldn't believe what we collected—a few years earlier—in the way of wallets, after the battle of the Lys and after Cambrai—do you imagine that if we hadn't taken those dollars they'd have got much farther than the orderly room or the battalion office? And besides: the price of a motorbike is determined by the historical situation and the purse of whoever happens to need it in that historical situation.

"Good God, haven't I proved I can be generous too? And act contrary to my own interests when it's a matter of human concern? Are you in any position to judge the spot I was in from the middle of '44 on? Deliberately and knowingly I acted contrary to my duty as a citizen in order to make it possible for those two young people to enjoy their brief happiness. Didn't I see how she laid her hand on him, and later on watch how they would keep disappearing for two or three or four minutes at the far end of the greenhouse, where we kept the peat moss and straw and heather and the various tying greens—and do you think I didn't notice something that it seems the others actually didn't notice, that during air raids those two sometimes disappeared for an hour or more? And I acted not only contrary to my duty as a citizen but also contrary to my own sexual interests as a man, for I don't mind admitting—I've never made any secret of my interest in sex—that I'd cast an eye, two eyes, in Leni's direction myself. Even today, I don't mind your telling her, even today I'm still quite interested. We war veterans and gardeners can be crude fellows, and in those days we called what today is described so subtly and elaborately and sophisticatedly, we called that simply 'wrestling'—and to prove to you how honest I am I'll revert to my way of speaking and thinking in those days. I'd like to have had a 'wrestle' with Leni. So, not only as a citizen, as a boss, as a Party member, but also as a man, I made sacrifices. And while I object in principle to love affairs, lovemaking, wrestling if you like, between boss and employees, when the feeling came over me I used to throw those objections overboard and behave spontaneously and, well, go to it, and every so often I'd—to use another of our expressions for it—I'd lay one of them.

"Occasionally there'd be trouble with the girls, little troubles and big ones, the biggest was over Adele Kreten, she was in love with me, had a child by me and was dead set on marrying me, wanted me to get a divorce and so forth, but frankly I don't believe in divorce, I think it's the wrong solution for complex problems, so I set Adele up in a flowershop in the Hohenzollern Allee, supported the child, and now Albert's settled as a high-school teacher, and Adele's a sensible woman, very comfortably off. That starry-eyed Adele—she was one of those idealistic gardeners, as we specialists call them, always rhapsodizing about Nature and so forth—has become a good little business-woman. And that business with Boris and Leni made me start sweating blood even early in 1944, out of sheer panic, and I'd be obliged if you'd find somebody, anybody, who can justly claim that I was a monster."

As a matter of fact, not one of the persons involved has been able to claim with any conviction that Pelzer was a monster. However, it must be noted and remembered at this point that Pelzer was not economical in his sweating of fear and blood. He sweated six months too soon, and it is up to the reader to decide whether or not to give him credit for this.

Pelzer's glassed-in office (still there and used today by Grundtsch as a despatch room, where he sets out, ready to be picked up, the potted flowers and dwarf Christmas trees for the graves) was situated at the center of his whole operation: assuming an adjusted topographical position, from east, north, and south three greenhouses abutted in their entire width onto this office, where Pelzer kept accurate records (a job later delegated to Boris) of flowers grown in the greenhouses before passing some of them on to the trimming tables, others to Grundtsch (who was in sole charge of the perpetual-grave-care business, which in those days did not amount to much yet), and some to the relatively legitimate flower trade. On the west side of the office was the wreath workshop, which ran the width of the three greenhouses and had direct access to two of the three greenhouses, giving Pelzer an unobstructed view of every movement. What he may actually have seen is Leni and Boris sometimes going, one soon after the other, either to the toilet, which was not segregated as to sex, or to pick up material from one of the two greenhouses.

According to repeated statements by Mr. von den Driesch, the local air-raid warden, air-raid shelter conditions at Pelzer's were "criminal," the nearest shelter, which barely met requirements, being some two hundred and fifty yards away in the cemetery administration building, and the use of this shelter—again according to regulations—was prohibited to Jews, Soviet individuals, and Poles. The ones who insisted most vehemently on keeping to this rule were—predictably—Kremp, Marga Wanft, and the Schelf woman; where, then, was the Soviet individual to go when British or American bombs were falling, bombs which, although not directed at him, could hit him? The hitting of a Soviet individual was not that important. Kremp expressed it thus: "One less, what's the difference?" (Witness Kremer.) But then a further complication arose: who was to guard the Soviet individual while German life was being protected (if only fictitiously) in the shelter? Could he be left alone, unguarded, with a chance to make a bid for the condition that is known, if not familiar, to all: freedom? Pelzer's solution to the problem was a drastic one. He refused point-blank to so much as set foot in the shelter, disputing that it "offered even minimal protection. It's nothing but a coffin"—facts which even the civic authorities unofficially regarded as indisputable; during air raids he stayed in his office, guaranteeing that the Soviet individual would not find it "that easy" to make a bid for freedom. "I've been a soldier, after all, and know my duty." Leni, however, who has never in her life set foot in an air-raid shelter or cellar (a further instance of similarity between her and Pelzer) said she "used simply to go out into the cemetery and wait for the all-clear." What gradually happened was that "everyone simply went off somewhere, even the complaints of that fool von den Driesch had no effect, Sonny Boy simply saw to it that his written protests were intercepted by a good friend" (Grundtsch). "It was really a joke, that air-raid shelter in the administration building, an asphyxiation chamber, that's all it was, a mere fiction, an ordinary cellar reinforced by a couple of inches of cement, even an incendiary bomb would've gone through that." Result: when the air-raid siren sounded, anarchy ensued: work had to stop, the Soviet individual was not to be let out of sight, and all the others ran off "somewhere." Pelzer stayed in his office and assumed responsibility for Boris, glancing from time to time at the clock and bemoaning the passage of work time that was at his expense and totally unproductive. Since, moreover, von den Driesch was constantly finding fault with Pelzer's blackout blinds, he "eventually simply turned out the light—and darkness was upon the face of the deep" (Grundtsch).

So what happened in this darkness?

Early in 1944, while Pelzer was already sweating blood, was some "wrestling" already taking place between Boris and Leni?

Taking the statement of the sole witness whom Leni initiated into her intimate life—Margret—as a basis, it is possible to reconstruct with something like accuracy the state of the erotic relationship between Boris and Leni as follows. After the first laying-on-of-hands, Leni often spent her evenings with Margret, finally going to live with her, and once again she entered upon a "talkative phase"—corresponding to the "extremely talkative phase" she entered upon with Boris Bogakov. Granted that Boris Bogakov did not describe the erotic situation in such detail as Leni did to Margret, the result, if we use a somewhat coarser screen in our fact-finding, is nevertheless a synchronous picture. In any event, Pelzer, whose sense of reality has remained undisputed thus far, must have suffered considerable loss of reality if he was already "sweating blood" early in 1944. It was not until some time in February 1944—six weeks after the laying-on-of-hands—that the momentous words were uttered! Leni was able to whisper quickly to Boris outside the toilet: "I love you," and he quickly whispered back: "Me too." This grammatically incorrect contraction must be forgiven him. He should, of course, have said: "I love you too." Anyway: Leni understood, although "just then those damned salvos came to a climax" (Leni according to

Margret). About the middle of February the first kiss took place, sending them both into ecstasy. The first time they "lay together" (Leni's expression, verified by Margret), was, as we know, March 18, on the occasion of a daylight air raid that lasted from 2:02 P.M. until 3:18 P.M. and during which only one bomb was dropped.

At this point Leni must be cleared of a quite natural but entirely unfounded suspicion, the suspicion of anything platonic in her erotic behavior. She has the incomparable directness of Rhenish girls (yes, she is a Rhinelander, and a Rhinelander "endorsed" by Mrs. Hölthohne, which is saying something) who, when they are fond of someone, let alone feel they have found the right man, are instantly willing to engage in anything, in the "most daring caresses" and, moreover, without waiting for a marriage license from either church or state. Now these two were not only in love, they were "madly in love" (Bogakov), and Boris could feel Leni's enormous sensuality, which he described to Bogakov: "She's willing, willing—there's a—an incredible willingness to go along." It may be definitely assumed that the two of them wanted to lie together, or visit with each other, as soon as possible and as often as possible, only: the circumstances demanded a caution such as a couple might, by comparison, have to use when obliged to run from opposite directions across a mile-wide minefield, meet on an unmined area of three or four square yards, and have a "lay" or a wrestle.

Mrs. Hölthohne puts it this way: "Those two young people simply streaked toward each other like rockets, and it was only the urge for self-preservation or, even stronger, the urge to preserve each other, that saved them from behaving carelessly. In principle I am against 'affairs.' But given those historical and political circumstances I would have approved of special leniency in their case, and against my own moral principles I would have wished they could have gone to a hotel together, or at least to a park, I wouldn't even have minded a hallway or something—we know that in wartime quite sordid ways and places for a tête-à-tête become acceptable again—*at the time,* I must add, I would have found an affair dishonorable, *today* I am much more progressive about such things."

Margret verbatim: "Leni said to me: 'You know, everywhere I go, on all sides, I see a big sign: Danger!' And you must realize that the chances of communicating were very limited. It was really fantastic the way Leni knew as if by instinct that for a while she must keep the initiative in her own hands, in defiance of all convention, which in those days even I still adhered to. I would never have accosted a man. And not only were there words of love to be whispered, they also had to know, discover something, about each other. It really was enormously difficult ever to be alone together even for half a minute. After a while Leni simply hung up a piece of sacking between the toilet and the bales of peat moss, loosely, of course, with a bent nail stuck in it so the curtain could be drawn if necessary, and this made a little cubicle where they could stroke each other's cheeks sometimes, or exchange a kiss, and it was a real break when she could whisper 'my darling.'

"All the things they had to tell each other! Their background, their emotions, life in camp, politics, war, food. Then, of course, she also had contact with him on the job, she had to hand the finished wreaths over to him, and this handing over took, say, half a minute, and during maybe ten seconds of that they could quickly exchange whispers. And sometimes, with no prearrangement, they would both be busy at the same time in Pelzer's office, when Leni read out to him the quantities of flowers used or had to check something in the ribbon closet. So that would mean an extra minute. And then they had to communicate in abbreviations, but first they had to agree on those abbreviations. When Boris said 'two,' Leni knew that two men had died that day in camp. Then, too, they wasted a lot of time over questions that for all practical purposes are superfluous but for lovers are necessary, like 'Do you still love me?' and so forth, and that also had to be shortened. If Boris said, for instance: 'Still—as I do?,' Leni knew that meant, 'Do you still love me as I love you?,' and she could quickly say 'yes, oh yes'—and that way a minimum of time was wasted.

"Then, of course, there were times when she had to treat the Nazi amputee—I forget his name—to a few cigarettes, to keep in his good books, and that had to be done very, very carefully, so he wouldn't take it the wrong way: not as if she were trying to make advances or bribe him, just as a natural token of friendship among fellow workers, and after she had given the Nazi—over a period of, say, four weeks—four or five cigarettes, it was all right for her to give Boris a cigarette *openly,* and Pelzer would presumably say: 'O.K., kids, go outside for a few minutes and have a smoke in the fresh air,' and then it was all right for Boris to go out too and openly smoke one outside—and they could talk openly together for two or three minutes, but naturally in such a way that no one could make out the words. And every so often the Nazi would stay away sick, and that unpleasant female too, and sometimes both at once; occasionally they were in luck, and three or four would be off sick at the same time, and Pelzer away, and since Boris was doing part of the bookkeeping and Leni the other part, they could be officially in the office together for twenty minutes, or at least ten, and really talk, about their parents, their lives, Leni about Alois—it was ages, I believe they'd already 'lain together' as Leni called it, before she even knew his surname. 'Why,' she said to me, 'why did I have to know it any sooner, there were more important things to talk about, and I told him my name was Gruyten and not Pfeiffer as on the papers.' And the way Leni familiarized herself with what was happening in the war, so she could keep him posted on the situation at the front: she had an atlas, and in it she entered everything we heard on the British radio, and believe me, she knew exactly that at the beginning of January '44 the front was near Krivoi Rog, and that at the end of March there was an encirclement battle at Kamenets Podolsk, and that by mid-April '44 the Russians had already reached Lvov, and then she knew exactly who was advancing from the west after Avranches, St.-Lô, and Caen: the Americans, and in November, when she'd already been pregnant for some time, her constant rage at the Americans for being such 'slowpokes'—as she called them—and taking so long to get from Monschau to the Rhine. 'It's less than sixty miles,' she would say, 'why ever are they taking so long?' Well, we were all counting on being liberated by December or January at the latest, but things didn't go quite that fast, and she couldn't understand it. Then the awful gloom because of the Ardennes offensive and the long-drawn-out battle in Hürtgen Forest. I explained it to her, or tried to. That the Germans were fighting tooth and nail because the Americans were now on German soil, that the terrible winter was naturally hampering the advance. We went over this so often together that I still remember every detail. Well, you mustn't forget she was pregnant, and that we had to find a man we could trust who would pass himself off as the father of Leni's child. She didn't want to write down 'Father unknown' unless she absolutely had to.

"An unwanted complication—and I still say unwanted because we had other things to worry about, I can assure you—was that Boris added to the confusion by one day whispering the name Georg Trakl to her. We were both completely at a loss, hadn't the foggiest notion who he meant: could he be suggesting him as the father for Leni's child, and who was he, where did he live? Leni had understood Trakl as Trackel, and because she knew a little English she though it might even be Truckel or Truckle. I don't know to this day what Boris had in mind, in September 1944. Surely he must have realized that the lives of all of us were hanging by a thread. I spent the whole evening phoning around because Leni was so impatient and wanted the answer that very night. Nothing: not one of my friends reacted. Finally she went to her parents' home, late that same night, and picked all the Hoyser brains. Nothing. Rather a nuisance, because the following day she had to sacrifice precious seconds to ask Boris who it was. He said: 'Poet, German, Austria, dead.' Whereupon Leni made a beeline for the nearest public library and promptly wrote on her request slip: Trackel, Georg—arousing the explicit and overt disapproval of an elderly female librarian but ending up in possession of a slim volume of poems which she eagerly accepted and began to read the minute she got on the streetcar. I still remember a few lines because she used to read them aloud to me evening after evening: 'Ancestral marble has turned gray.' I liked that, in fact I liked it enormously, and the other one even better: 'Girls are standing at the gateways, Gazing out at life resplendent, Shyly, with moist lips a-quiver, And they wait there at the gateways.' I used to just bawl over that one, I still do, because it reminds me more and more, the older I get, of my childhood and youth: how expectant and gay I was—expectant and gay—and the other poem suited Leni so perfectly that we soon both had it off by heart: 'By the fountain, in the gloaming, Often is she seen enraptured, Drawing water, in the gloaming, Pail ascending and descending.' She learned those poems from the little book by heart, you see, and she would sing them softly to herself in the workshop to an improvised tune—to give him pleasure, and it did, but there was trouble too, with that Nazi, for one day he roared at her and asked what she thought she was doing, and she said she was only quoting from a German poet, and Boris was silly enough to interfere and said he knew that German poet, he was from the Ostmark—he actually said Ostmark instead of Austria!—and was called Georg Trakl, and so forth. That really infuriated the Nazi, a Bolshevik knowing more about German poetry than he did—so he inquired at Party headquarters or somewhere and asked whether this Trakl had been a Bolshevik, and they must have told him he was all right. And then he wanted to know whether it was all right for a Soviet Russian, a subhuman, a Communist, to know this Trakl so well, and they must have told him that the sacred German cultural heritage had no place in the mouth of a subhuman. And believe it or not, there was even more trouble because Leni—I must say, for a time she was cheeky and self-confident and looked absolutely marvelous because she was loved, as no one has never loved me, not even Schlömer—maybe Heinrich would've loved me like that—well, it so happened that on that particular day she sang the poem about Sonja: 'At eventide, in ancient gardens, Sonja's life, an azure silence'—the name Sonja occurs four times. And the Nazi shouted that Sonja was a

Russian name, and that was treason or some such thing. Leni retorted, quick as a flash: Sonja Henie was also called Sonja, and only a year ago she'd seen a movie called *The Postmaster,* full of Russians, and a Russian girl. This argument was presumably cut short by Pelzer saying that was all a lot of crap and of course Leni could sing while she worked, and if there was nothing anti-German in what she sang there was no objection, and they took a vote, and because she had such a sweet little contralto voice and everything was so depressing anyway, and no one ever simply started singing like that, every one of them, every single one, voted against the Nazi—and Leni could go on singing her improvised Trakl songs."

Mrs. Hölthohne, Ilse Kremer, and Grundtsch all testify, in differing formulations, that they had found Leni's singing pleasant. Mrs. Hölthohne: "Heavens above, in those cheerless days it was heartwarming: that child with her nice contralto, singing away—without being ordered to; well, it wasn't hard to tell that she knew her Schubert by heart, and what clever variations of him she produced with those beautiful, moving words." Ilse Kremer: "It was a regular ray of sunshine when Leni sang one of her songs. Not even Marga Wanft or the Schelf woman objected; you could see and hear and feel too, that she wasn't only in love but was loved in return—but who it was none of us would ever have guessed, with that Russian always standing there so quietly, stolidly working away."

Grundtsch: "I used to laugh myself sick, on the inside as well as on the out, over the fury of that Dirty Berty Kremp. Did he ever get mad about Sonja! As if there weren't hundreds, thousands of women called Sonja, and I must say that was pretty quick of Leni to come right back with Sonja Henie. It was like a sunflower bursting into bloom on a wintry cabbage field when that girl began to sing. Glorious, and we all, all of us, could sense that she was loved and that she loved in return—the way she blossomed in those days. Needless to say, apart from Sonny Boy no one had any idea of who the lucky man was."

Pelzer: "Of course I enjoyed her singing, I'd had no idea she had such a nice little contralto voice—but if I could only begin to tell you the trouble it gave me! The phone calls I got—and being constantly asked whether those were really Russian songs, whether the Russians were behind it, and so forth. Well, eventually things calmed down, but there was trouble enough, and not without danger either. I don't mind telling you: in those days nothing was without danger."

At this point it is necessary to correct an impression that may have mistakenly arisen, namely: that Boris and Leni spent their lives in a permanent state of gloom, or that Boris was overly concerned with testing or improving Leni's education in terms of German poetry and prose. As he told Bogakov every day at the time, he looked forward to his work and was always cheerful because, if there was one thing he could be sure of, it was that he would see Leni again and, depending on the war situation, air raids, and things in general, could hope for a "visit."

Following on the severe reprimand he had received because of his singing in the streetcar, he was smart enough to suppress, albeit with difficulty, any spontaneous desire to burst into song. He knew a number of German folk songs and nursery songs which he could sing in a melancholy voice, and that in turn meant trouble for *him* with Viktor Genrikhovich and some of his fellow camp inmates, who were not necessarily in the mood (understandably enough. Au.) for specimens of Germany's musical heritage. Eventually agreement was reached: since "Lili Marleen" was approved, in fact was in demand, and Boris's voice was acknowledged, he was allowed to sing one other German song for every "Lili Marleen" he sang (a song that, acc. to Bogakov, did not appeal to him. Au.). His favorite songs, acc. to Bogakov, were: "The Linden Tree," "The Boy and the Rose," and "Upon a Meadow Fair." It may be taken for granted that what Boris would have really liked to sing out over the heads of the gloomy-looking early-morning streetcar passengers would have been something like "Hark, What Enters from Without?" However, one consolation remained to him after that one occasion when his singing had been so painfully misunderstood, so rabidly suppressed: the German worker who had whispered words of comfort to him rode almost every morning in the streetcar. Naturally they could not exchange a word, they could merely look every so often deeply and honestly into each other's eyes, and only those who have been in a similar situation can gauge the meaning of a pair of eyes when they can be looked into deeply and honestly. So before starting to sing at work himself (Bogakov), he took some shrewd precautions. Since it was unavoidable for almost everyone in the workshop to *speak* to him occasionally, even Kremp and Marga Wanft—even if was only a "There" or "Hurry up" or "Well" growled in his direction; and since Pelzer was obliged from time to time to engage in lengthy dialogues with him—about ribbons, wreath- and flower-bookkeeping, about the work rhythm to be adopted, one day Boris approached Pelzer with a request for permission to "sing a song for them" now and again.

Pelzer: "I was staggered. I really was. That the boy should think of such a thing. Now this was a damn ticklish business, after that fiasco with the streetcar singing, though luckily nobody noticed at the time just what he was singing, only *that* he was singing. When I asked him why he was so keen on singing and explained that, in view of the war situation, a singing Russian prisoner of war was bound to be considered a provocation—don't forget it was June 1944, Rome was already in American hands and Sebastopol back in Russian hands—he said: 'I enjoy it so much.' Now I have to admit I was touched, I really was: he enjoyed singing German songs. So I said to him: 'Listen, Boris, you know I'm not a monster, and as far as I'm concerned you can belt out your songs like Chaliapin, but you remember, don't you, the commotion caused by Mrs. Pfeiffer's singing (I never called her Leni in his presence), so what's going to happen now if you . . . .' In the end I did risk it, made a little speech and said: 'Now listen, all of you, this Boris of ours has been working side by side with us for six months. We all know he's a good worker and a shy fellow, well it seems he likes German songs, in fact all German singing, and he'd like permission to sometimes sing a

German song at work. I suggest we take a vote, those in favor raise their hands,' and I was the first to put my hand up, right away—and lo and behold, that Kremp didn't exactly put his hand up, he just growled something under his breath—and I went on: 'What Boris wants to sing for us is part of our German cultural heritage, and I can see no danger in a Soviet Russian being that keen on our German cultural heritage.' Well, Boris was smart enough not to start singing then and there, he waited a few days, and then, I don't mind telling you, he sang arias by Karl Maria von Weber as well as I ever heard them at the opera house. And he sang Beethoven's "Adelaïde" too, flawless musically and in flawless German. Well, then he sang rather too many love songs for my taste; and then finally 'Off to Mahagonny, The air is cool and fresh, There's whiskey there and poker, And horse- and woman-flesh.' He used to sing that a lot, and it wasn't till later that I found out it's by that fellow Brecht—and I must say that even now, all these years later, I get cold shivers down my spine—it's a fine song, and later on I bought the record, I still listen to it often and enjoy it—but I get icy shivers down my spine just to think of it: that fellow Brecht being sung by a Russian prisoner of war in the fall of '44, with the British already at Arnhem, the Russians already in the outskirts of Warsaw, and the Americans almost in Bologna . . . you can get gray hair from just remembering a thing like that. But who'd heard of Brecht in those days? Not even Ilse Kremer—he could be sure of that, of nobody knowing Brecht and nobody knowing that Trakl fellow. I didn't tumble to it till later: they were singing love songs to each other, he and Leni! Real antiphonal singing, that's what it was."

Margret: "Those two were getting more and more daring, I got terribly scared. Leni was now bringing him something every single day: cigarettes, bread, sugar, butter, tea, coffee, newspapers that she folded into tiny squares, razor blades, clothing—winter was coming on, you see. You can figure that, starting in mid-March 1944, not a day went by without her bringing him something. She dug out a cavity in the bottom bale of peat moss and plugged it up with a chunk of peat moss, turned it against the wall, of course, and this is where he had to pick up the stuff; naturally she had to get on the right side of the guards so they wouldn't search him—that had to be done carefully, and there was this one cocky fellow, good fun but cocky, who wanted to take Leni dancing and so on and so forth, he called it 'going into a clinch'—a cocky young pup who probably knew more than he would admit. He insisted on Leni's going out with him, and finally there was no way out of it and she asked me to go along. So we went a few times to those honky-tonks that I knew so well and Leni not at all, and that cocky young fellow frankly admitted that I was more his type than Leni, that he found her too soulful and I was more of a 'swinger'—well, the inevitable happened, because Leni was terrified lest that fellow—Boldig was his name—should find out and raise the roof. I—how else can I put it—well, I can't say I exactly sacrificed myself, I simply took him over—took him upon myself, might be more accurate—but it wasn't that much of a sacrifice for me either, and at the end of '44 one more or less probably didn't make all that difference.

"He lived in style, that young fellow did: only the best hotels when he wanted to 'have a turn with me'—another of his names for it—champagne and all the rest of it, but the chief thing was that it turned out he wasn't only cocky, he also liked to talk big, and when he was a bit drunk he would blab the whole story. Dealt in anything you care to name: schnapps and cigarettes, that goes without saying, and coffee and meat, but his most profitable deals were in documents for medal awards, wound-tags, identification papers—during some retreat or other he'd taken along the stuff by the ton, and you can imagine that when I heard 'identification papers' I pricked up my ears, because of Boris and Leni. Well, first I let him rattle on, then I laughed at him till he *showed* me the stuff, and true enough: he still had a carton the size of an encyclopedia full of forms, all stamped and signed, as well as leave passes and travel permits. Good enough. I let it go at that—but now it was *we* who had a hold on *him,* while he still didn't know anything about us. I questioned him very carefully about the Russians, he looked on them as poor bastards, and sometimes, he said, he treated them to a few 'regulars'" (regular, i.e., not hand-rolled cigarettes. Au.), "and they always got his cigarette butts anyway, and he wasn't interested in making still more enemies. For an Iron Cross First Class Boldig charged three thousand marks and considered that 'a gift,' and for identification papers five thousand, 'after all, that could be a lifesaver'—he got rid of all his wound-tags during the massive retreat from France, when the deserters hid in the ruins, shooting one another—at a suitable distance, of course—in the leg or the arm so that then they were legalized with their wound-tags. At that time I'd already been working for two years in a military hospital, and I knew what happened to the fellows with self-inflicted wounds."

Pelzer: "That was the time when business began to decline for a while. Luckily for me, Kremp, who was always having trouble with his artificial leg, had to go into the hospital for a few months. I could easily have let two or three people go—reason: not that fewer people were dying, but the evacuation of the city was now being carried out more consistently and rigorously. Instead of the wounded all being brought into the city, they were now usually taken farther away across the Rhine. Well, luckily the Schelf woman and Miss Zeven chose to be evacuated to Saxony—and finally our select little group, if I may call it that. had the place almost to ourselves; but even to keep the rest of the staff reasonably busy was hard enough. I ended up putting them to work in the greenhouses—but even then business lagged, and I hardly made expenses. In '43 we'd had two shifts, sometimes a night shift, then came a slack period, then suddenly an upturn connected with the British stepping up their air raids—well, we do happen to be in the funeral business—and once again there were plenty of dead in the city. I took the workers out of the greenhouses again and reintroduced double shifts, and it was during this period that Leni hit on an invention, as it may fairly be called, which gave the business a real shot in the arm. She'd discovered a few broken pots of heather somewhere and simply began making wreaths from heather without frames, little tightly woven things which naturally revived the suspicion of romanizing—but after the events of July '44 there were only a few idiots left who still thought about such trifles—and Leni became a real expert at it, the wreaths were small, compact, almost metallic, later they were even given a coat of varnish, and Leni would weave the initials of the deceased or the donor into them—sometimes, when they weren't too long, the full names: there was just room for Heinz, or Maria, and this made for some attractive contrasts: like green on purple, and never, not once, did she break the rule of putting the trim in the top left third of the wreath. I was delighted, the customers were thrilled—and since we could still cross the Rhine, with no one to stop us and no particular risk involved, it was no problem to get hold of a cartload of heather. Sometimes she even outdid herself by weaving in religious symbols, and anchors, hearts, and crosses."

Margret: "I need hardly say that Leni had her ulterior motives when she started on the heather wreaths. The way she put it was: she wanted her bridal bed to be of heather and, since they were forced to remain within the cemetery grounds, they had no alternative but to decide on one of the huge family vaults for their rendezvous; their choice fell on the large private chapel of the Beauchamps, already considerably damaged by that time; it contained benches and a little altar that screened the heather behind it, and it was a simple matter to remove a stone from the altar and fix up a small cache of supplies, with cigarettes and wine, bread, candy, and cookies. At the same time Leni was getting craftier, for some time she'd only been bringing Boris a cup of coffee every four or five days instead of every day. Sometimes she skipped him when she handed in a wreath, she scarcely ever came near him at work, the whisperings had stopped, and the hiding place in the peat-moss bale was abolished and removed to the altar in the Beauchamp chapel. May 28 was their lucky day: there were two air-raid alarms, one right after the other, both daylight raids, between about one and four-thirty—not many bombs were dropped, just enough to make it a real air raid. Anyway, that evening she came home all smiles saying: 'Today was our wedding day—March 18 was our engagement day, and d'you know what Boris said to me? "Listen to the British, they don't lie."' Then there came a tough time, for more than two months there were no daylight raids, most of them being at night, a few just before midnight, and we'd lie in bed with Leni cursing under her breath: 'Why don't they come during the day, when are they going to come again during the day, why are the Americans such slowpokes, why is it taking them so long to get here, it's not that far, is it?' She was already pregnant, and we were worrying about finding a father for her child. At last, on Ascension Day, there was another big daylight raid, lasting two and a half hours—I believe—and plenty of bombs, some even fell on the cemetery, and a few splinters whistled through the glass windows of the Beauchamp chapel over the heads of those two. Then came the period Leni called 'glorious,' the 'month of the glorious rosary'—between October 2 and 28 nine major daylight raids. Leni's comment: 'I have Rahel and the Virgin Mary to thank for that, they've neither of them forgotten my devotion to them.'"

Here we must present, by way of a quick summary, a few facts of practical interest: Leni was twenty-two years old, and in bourgeois terms the three months between Christmas 1943 and the first "visit" on March 18, 1944, might justifiably be called the engagement period, while, starting with Ascension Day 1944, we must describe them as "newlyweds," as a couple that has placed its destiny entirely in the hands of Air Marshal Harris, then unknown to them. Infallible statistics are of more use to us here than Pelzer's and Margret's statements. Between September 12 and November 30, 1944, there were seventeen daylight raids, with approximately 150 aerial mines, slightly more than 14,000 explosive bombs, and approximately 350,000 incendiary bombs being dropped. It must be realized that the inevitable chaos favored the couple: by that time no one was looking that carefully to see who crawled in where and who crawled out with whom, even if it was the chapel of a family vault. Finicky lovers were stymied at such times and—obviously neither Leni nor Boris was finicky. Needless to say, they now had plenty of time to discuss parents, brothers and sisters, background, education, and the war situation. With the aid of air-raid statistics it is possible to calculate with almost scientific accuracy that, between August and December 1944, Leni and Boris spent almost twenty-four full hours together—three consecutive hours on October 17 alone. Should it occur to anyone to pity these two, let him quickly disabuse himself of this sentiment, for if we bear in mind how few couples, whether legally or illegally joined, whether at liberty or not, were able to spend that much time together in such close intimacy, we cannot but cite this as yet another instance of this couple's being favorites of Fortune—a couple that was shameless enough to long for daylight raids by the British Air Force in order to come together again in the Beauchamp chapel.

What Boris never suspected, and probably never found out, was that Leni was getting into considerable financial difficulties. Considering that her monthly wages were worth scarcely more than half a pound of coffee, that the revenue from her building was worth roughly a hundred cigarettes, but that her coffee consumption amounted to two pounds, her cigarette consumption—including those she constantly had to "slip" this person or that—to presumably three or four hundred, it will readily be seen that one of the simplest laws of economics was being manifested with the speed of an avalanche: increased expenditure coupled with reduced income. To be accurate, at least with a probability bordering on accuracy: Leni needed nearly four thousand, sometimes five thousand, marks a month to cover the cost of coffee, sugar, wine, cigarettes, and bread—taking the black-market prices for 1944. Her income (wages and rents) amounted to some one thousand marks a month; the consequences are obvious: debts. And if we further calculate that in April 1944 she discovered the whereabouts of her father and wanted to "see he got something too" from time to time, through devious channels, then from June 1944 her monthly budget rose to almost six thousand marks in expenses as compared to a thousand marks in income. She had never been one to economize, and even her own consumption—before Boris and her father made additional expenditures necessary—had far exceeded her income. In a nutshell: in September 1944 she is known to have already had debts of twenty thousand marks, and her creditors were becoming impatient. It was just at this time that her mania for extravagance assumed a new dimension: she craved such luxury items as razor blades, soap, even chocolate—and wine, an endless supply of wine.

Comment by Lotte H.: "She never borrowed from me, though, because she knew I was having a hard enough time as it was, with the two kids. On the contrary: every so often she'd slip me something, bread coupons and sugar, or occasionally tobacco or a few 'regulars.' No, no. She was all right. Between April and October she hardly ever came home, and you could tell she had someone who loved her and whom she loved. We didn't know who it was, of course, and we all thought she must be meeting him in Margret's apartment. By then I'd already been gone from the firm for a year, I was working for the Employment Bureau, later for the welfare department that looked after the homeless, making just enough to be able to buy my rations. The firm had been reorganized—after June '43 a new broom from the Ministry took over, a regular live wire, and because his name was Kierwind we all called him 'New Wind,' and he was always talking about 'airing the good old comfortable ways and letting the stuffy atmosphere out of the place'! My father-in-law and I were part of that stuffy atmosphere. He told me quite frankly: 'You two have been here too long, much too long—and I don't want any trouble with you if we now have to start building trenches and fortifications on the western frontier. It's going to be tough with

Russians, Ukrainians, and Russian women, and German penal units. That's not your cup of tea. The best thing you can do is quit voluntarily.' Kierwind was the classic go-ahead type, cynical yet not entirely unattractive—a familiar typc. 'You know, the whole place still smells of Gruyten.' So we quit, I went to the Employment Bureau, my father-in-law to the railway, as a bookkeeper.

"Well, I don't know how to put this—whether Hoyser was showing his true colors or whether those true colors had been affected by the circumstances. He turned quite nasty, and he's stayed that way ever since. To say that conditions in our apartment were hellish is putting it mildly. After Gruyten's arrest we started out with a kind of living and cooking commune in which we included Heinrich Pfeiffer, who was then still waiting to be called up. To begin with, Marja and my mother-in-law did the shopping and looked after the kids, and once in a while Marja would go out into the country, to Tolzem or Lyssemich, and bring back potatoes and vegetables if nothing else, and sometimes even an egg. For a time this worked quite well, till my father-in-law began bringing home the unrationed soup they got at noon at the railway station, and in the evening he'd warm it up and sip it with audible pleasure in front of our very eyes, in addition, of course, to what he got from the communal pot. Then my mother-in-law developed a 'gram mania,' as Marja called it, and began weighing everything; the next stage was when everyone locked up their own stuff in a locker with a heavy padlock—and needless to say they began accusing one another of stealing. My mother-in-law would weigh her margarine before locking it up and then again when she took it out—and every single time, without fail, she insisted that some of it had been pinched. What *I* found out was that she—my own mother-in-law—was even going for my kids' milk, she'd water it down so as to be able to make the occasional pudding for herself or the old man. So then I teamed up with Marja and left the shopping and cooking to her, and this worked out fine for me, neither Leni nor Marja was ever petty—but now the old Hoysers began sniffing around when something was cooking or appeared on the table, and a charming new variation was added: envy. Well, I must say I envied Leni, she could go off and hide away with her lover at Margret's —so I thought.

"But now, since being with the railway, old Hoyser began developing his connections, as he called it. He was in charge of the bookkeeping for the locomotive engineers, and in '43, of course, they were going into practically every corner of Europe, taking goods in demand *there* and bringing back goods in demand *here*. For a sack of salt they'd bring back a whole pig from the Ukraine; for a sack of semolina flour, cigars from starving Holland or Belgium, and wine from France of course, any amount of it, and champagne and cognac. Anyway, Hoyser was in a strategic position, and since he eventually took over the timetable coordination of all the transport trains he soon found himself in business in a big way. He'd make an exact analysis of what was in short supply in which part of Europe, and then see to it that the appropriate barter took place: Dutch cigars went to Normandy in exchange for butter—this was before the invasion, of course—and in Antwerp, say, butter would be exchanged for twice the number of cigars that had been given for the butter in, say, Normandy. And because he was then put in charge of routing, he gained control over the stokers and locomotive engineers and, needless to say, saw to it that those who collaborated best got the best routes, and of course on the domestic market, too, various items in various places brought various prices. In the cities everything fetched a good price: food and luxuries—coffee, of course, was more in demand than food in the rural areas—and through barter business, butter for coffee, say—it was possible to, as he put it, double one's investment.

"It was only natural for Leni to be the person he lent the most money to; he did warn her, it seems, but when she needed money he gave it to her. Eventually he became her source not only of money but also of goods, and he could make something on the side by charging her a bit extra, which Leni never noticed. She just kept right on signing IOU's.

"In the end he was the one who discovered old Gruyten's whereabouts: first he'd been a construction worker on the Atlantic coast in France, operating a cement mixer with a penal unit, later on in Berlin clearing rubble after air raids—and we finally found a way of getting the occasional parcel to him and getting news from him. The message was usually: 'Don't worry, I'll soon be back.' Then payments fell due again. The inevitable happened: around August '44 Leni owed Hoyser twenty thousand marks, and do you know what he did? He pressed her! He said, my transactions will come to a halt, my child, if I don't get my money back—do you know what the outcome was? Leni took a mortgage of thirty thousand marks on her building, gave the old man the twenty thousand, and was left with ten thousand for herself. I warned her, I told her it was madness to raise money on real estate in a time of inflation—but she laughed, gave me something for the kids and a package of ten 'regulars' for myself, and because just at that moment Heinrich slipped into the room looking for some extra goodies, she gave him something too and did a little improvised dance with the lad, who was completely baffled. I must say, it was fantastic the way she had blossomed, how lighthearted and gay she was, and I envied not only her but also the fellow she was so much in love with.

"Soon after that, Marja moved out for a time into the country, Heinrich was called up, and I was alone with old Hoyser, who I also had to leave in charge of my kids. As for Leni, the inevitable happened: the second mortgage fell due, and then, yes, then—I'm ashamed to tell you—he actually bought the building off her, a building that was only partially damaged, and in this location, at the end of '44, when it was already hard to get anything at all in exchange for money—he gave her a further twenty thousand marks, discharged the mortgages, which were in his name of course—and there he was, something he had apparently always aimed at being: a property owner, and now he owned the thing, a building that's easily worth nearly half a million today, and for the first time I realized his nature when he began right away on January 1, 1945, to collect the rent. That must've been his dream, to go around on the first of every month and collect—except that in January '45 there wasn't much to collect: most of the tenants had been evacuated, the two top floors were burned out, and it was really quite funny the way he put me on his rent list too, and the Pfeiffers of course, although they didn't come back till '52—and it wasn't until he collected the first rent from me—32 marks and 60 pfennigs for my two unfurnished rooms—that it dawned on me we'd been living all those years with Leni rent-free. Sometimes I've thought Leni behaved far from sensibly, I warned her too—but today I think she was sensible, to spend every penny she had with the man she loved. Besides, she never starved, neither then nor in peacetime."

Margret: "Now came what Leni herself called her 'second troop inspection.' She'd held the first one, so she told me, when the business with Boris began—she went through all her friends and relatives, had even gone down to the air-raid cellars in her building a few times to undertake tests there, she had 'inspected' the Hoysers and Marja, Heinrich, and all her fellow workers, and who emerged from this troop inspection as the only suitable lieutenant? Me. In her the world lost a strategist—when I think how she checked over each person, every single person, how she sensed a possible ally in Lotte but then eliminated her on grounds of 'jealousy,' old Hoyser and his wife as 'old-fashioned and anti-Russian,' Heinrich Pfeiffer as too 'biased,' and the way she was so sure that Mrs. Kremer was a potential ally and even went to see her so they could have a noncommittal talk, but then noticed she was 'just too timid, too timid and too tired, she's had enough, and I don't blame her.' She also considered Mrs. Hölthohne but had to reject her too 'on account of her old-fashioned moral code, for no other reason,' and 'then, then one had, of course, also to know who was strong enough to be told a thing like that and stick it out.' Well, she'd made up her mind to win the battle, and to her it was the most natural thing in the world to need money and strongpoints for carrying on the war, and the only strongpoint she could find when she first inspected the troops and summed up the situation was me—a great honor and also a great burden.

"So evidently I was strong enough. In the air-raid cellar, at home, and with the Hoysers and Marja, she systematically tested their attitude by departing from her usual reluctance to talk and offering a variety of stories: she began with a German girl who'd got involved with an Englishman, a prisoner of war, and though the outcome of her tests was devastating enough—most people were in favor of shooting, sterilizing, withdrawal of citizenship, and so on—she then tried it out with a Frenchman, who came off better 'as a person, as a lover worthy of consideration' " (probably because of the French talent *pour faire l'amour.* Au.) "and prompted a smirk, but then was totally rejected as an 'enemy.' But she persisted and produced her Poles and her Russians, or should I say threw them to the lions, and there was only one opinion there, nothing less than 'off with her head.' Within the family circle itself, if you include the Hoysers and Marja, people expressed themselves more openly, more honestly, less politically. Surprisingly, Marja was in favor of Poles because she saw in them 'dashing officers,' Frenchmen she considered 'depraved,' Englishmen 'probably useless as lovers—Russians inscrutable.' Lotte thought as I did, that it was all a lot of crap, or shit I might've called it. 'A man's a man,' was her comment, and Lotte said she thought that, while Marja and her parents-in-law weren't free of national prejudices, they certainly had no political ones. Frenchmen were described as sensualists but parasites, Poles as charming and temperamental but faithless, Russians as faithful, faithful, very faithful—but the situation being what it was everyone, including Lotte, thought it was 'at the very least dangerous to start something with a western European and risking one's very life to do so with an eastern European.' "

Lotte H.: "Once, when she happened to be at our place to transact some financial business with my father-in-law, I opened the bathroom door to find Leni standing naked in front of the mirror, considering the firm lines of her body; I threw a bath towel over her from behind, and as I went up to her Leni turned crimson—

I never saw her blush before—and I put my hand on her shoulder and said: 'Be glad you can love someone again, if you ever did love that other one, forget him. I can't forget my Willi. Take him, even if he is an Englishman.' I wasn't so dumb that I didn't have a notion, in February 1944, that there was something going on with a man, and probably with a foreigner, when she started coming out with her funny make-believe stories. To be honest, I'd have advised her strongly, very strongly, against a Russian or a Pole or a Jew, that would've meant risking your very life, and to this day I'm glad she never told me about it. It wasn't safe to know too much."

Margret: "Even Pelzer had emerged as a potential ally from Leni's first troop inspection. Grundtsch might have been a possibility too, but he talked too much. Now came the second inspection, and again I was the only reliable one when it came to Leni's pregnancy and its consequences. We ended up by bearing Pelzer in mind as a kind of strategic reserve and eliminating the older of the two guards, the one who usually brought Boris to work, because he couldn't keep his hands to himself or his mouth shut, and then we considered Boldig the swinger, I was still seeing him on and off and his business was flourishing—but not for long, he overdid it and got picked up in November '44—with his entire stock of forms and stationery—and shot on the spot behind the railway station where they'd caught him red-handed in a deal, so he was out, and his sets of identification papers too, sad to say."

In order to be fair to Leni and Margret, a few comments must be interjected here relating to prevailing social attitudes. Strictly speaking, Leni was not even a widow, she was the bereaved lover of Erhard, with whom she occasionally even compared Boris. "Both of them were poets, if you ask me, both of them." For a woman of twenty-two who had lost her mother, her lover Erhard, her brother, and her husband, who had gone through approximately two hundred air-raid warnings and at least a hundred air raids, who, far from spending *all* her time carrying on with her lover in the chapels of family vaults, was obliged to get up in the morning at five thirty, wrap herself up against the cold and walk to the streetcar to go to work through darkened streets —for this young woman, Alois's victory-prattle, still faintly audible in her ear perhaps, must have seemed like some fading sentimental hit tune to which one might have danced some night twenty years ago. Leni—contrary to all expectation and in defiance of the circumstances—was provocatively gay. The people around her were petty, morose, despondent, and if we bear in mind that Leni might have sold her father's fine-quality clothing with considerable profit on the black market but chose instead to give it not only to *him* but also to the cold and needy members of a declared enemy power (a Red Army commissar was running around in her father's cashmere vest!)—then even the most skeptical observer of the scene is bound to approve the word "generous" as a second adjective for Leni.

A word or two more on the subject of Margret. It would be a mistake to call her a whore. All she had ever done for money was get married. Assigned since 1942 to a huge reserve military hospital, she had far more trying days and trying nights than Leni, who could carry on undisturbed making her wreaths, was constantly in her beloved's company, and was protected by Pelzer's benevolence. From this point of view Leni is by no means *the* or even *a* heroine: it was not until she was forty-eight that she treated a man with compassion (i.e., the Turk by the name of Mehmet, whom the gentle reader may possibly recall); Margret never did anything else, even when on duty at the hospital as day or night nurse she treated "anyone who looked nice and seemed down in the mouth with total compassion"—and the only reason she carried on with a cocky cynical fellow like Boldig was as a cover for Leni's blissful hours on a couch of heather in the Beauchamp cemetery chapel, to divert Boldig's attention from Leni. Let us allow justice to prevail and take note of what

Margret herself has noted after a long life of total and compassionate dedication: "I've been loved a great deal, but I've loved only one person. Only once did I feel that insane joy I saw so often on the faces of others." No, Margret is not to be classed among Fortune's favorites, she has had far more bad luck then Leni—like the embittered Lotte, yet neither of these two women has shown any sign of envying Leni.

8 The Au., by now totally engrossed in his role of researcher (and always in danger of being taken for an informer while his sole purpose at all times is to present a taciturn and reticent, proud, unrepentant person such as Leni Gruyten Pfeiffer—a woman as static as she is statuesque!—in the right light), had some difficulty in gaining, or searching out, from those involved a reasonably factual picture of her situation at the end of the war.

There was only one point in which all those presented and quoted here in greater or lesser detail were in agreement: they did not want to leave the city; even the two Soviet individuals Bogakov and Boris had no desire to move eastward. Now that the Americans (Leni to Margret: "At last, at last, what ages they've taken!") were approaching, they alone guaranteed what everyone was longing for but could not believe: the end of the war. *One* problem was solved starting January 1, 1945: Boris's and Leni's—for simplicity's sake let us use the term "visiting days." Leni was seven months pregnant, still quite "perky" (M.v.D.) albeit somewhat hampered by her condition, but—"visiting," lying together, wrestling, whatever we decide to call it, "was now simply out of the question" (Leni according to Margret).

But where and how to survive? It sounds simple enough if we disregard who had to hide from whom. Margret, for instance, ought—like any soldier she was subject to orders and regulations—to have crossed the Rhine eastward with the hospital. But she did not, nor could she take refuge in her apartment, from which she would have been forcibly removed. Lotte H. was similarly placed, being an employee of a government department that was likewise shifting to the east. Where was she to go? If we recall that as late as January 1945 people were being evacuated to almost as far as Silesia, i.e., were being transported directly into the path of the Red Army, a brief geographical reminder will not be amiss: in mid-March 1945 that German Reich to which frequent allusion has been made was still some five to six hundred miles in width and scarcely more in length. The question of where to go was of the most pressing urgency for the most varied groups. Where were the Nazis to be sent, the prisoners of war, the soldiers, the slave workers? There were, of course, tried and true solutions: execution, etc. Yet even that was not always a simple matter since the executioners were not all of one mind and some were inclined to play a rather different role, namely that of rescuer. Many a man who was in principle an executioner became a nonexecutioner, but how, for instance, were the potential victims of execution—let us call them the executees—to behave? It is not that simple. One is inclined to think that all of a sudden there occurred something called the end of the war, that at some point there was a date, and that was it. How was a person to know whether he had fallen into the hands of a reformed or unreformed executioner, let alone into the hands of a specimen of that emerging breed whom we might call the "now-more-than-ever executioners," many of whom had previously belonged to the nonexecutioner group? There were even branches of the SS that disclaimed their reputation as executioners! Correspondence ensued between the SS and the glorious German Army in which each side tried to palm off the dead onto the other, like so many rotting potatoes! "Elimination" and "disposal" were expected to be carried out by honorable persons and institutions which—like their correspondents—were bent on arriving with reasonably clean hands at that state which it would have been wrong to call peace but right to call the end of the war.

The Au. reads, for example: "The commandants of the concentration camps complain that some 5 to 10 percent of the Soviet Russians marked for execution arrive at the camps either dead or dying. This gives rise to the impression that the POW base camps use this method to dispose of such prisoners.

"In particular it has been noted that on foot marches, e.g., from railway station to camp, a not inconsiderable number of prisoners of war collapse dead or dying from exhaustion and have to be collected by a truck bringing up the rear.

"It is impossible to prevent the German population from noticing these occurrences.

"Despite the fact that the delivery of prisoners to concentration camps is as a general rule carried out by the Army, the population will nevertheless hold the SS responsible for this state of affairs.

"In order as far as possible to prevent a repetition of such occurrences, I hereby order, to take effect forthwith, that in future any condemned Soviet Russians already manifestly moribund (e.g., from starvation-typhoid), hence no longer equal to the exertions of even a short foot march, be excluded from transportation to concentration camps for purposes of execution.
(Signed): Müller (Deputy)"

It is left to the reader to meditate on the phrase "not inconsiderable" as applied to those marked for death. This had been a problem as early as 1941, at a time when the German Reich was sufficiently large in extent. Four years later the German Reich was, God knows, much smaller, and there were not only Soviet Russians, Jews, and the like, to be eliminated and disposed of, but also a sizable number of Germans, deserters, saboteurs, and collaborators; furthermore, concentration camps and towns had to be emptied of women, children, and the aged, the intention being to leave nothing but ruins for the enemy.

Not surprisingly, problems of morality and/or hygiene arose. For example, the following:

"It is not unusual for the district chiefs and/or village elders (many of whom are corrupt) to cause the skilled workers whom they have selected to be taken at night from their beds and locked up in cellars awaiting transportation. Since the male and/or female workers are frequently allowed no time to pack their belongings, etc., many of them arrive at the assembly camp with totally insufficient equipment (without shoes, two dresses, eating and drinking utensils, blanket, etc.). Hence in extreme cases new arrivals must be immediately sent back in order to collect the bare necessities. Threats and beatings administered by the aforesaid village militiamen to the skilled workers in cases where the latter do not immediately obey orders to accompany them are common practice and have been reported from most communities. In numerous cases women were beaten until incapable of participating in the march. One particularly flagrant case has been reported by me to the head of the military police (Colonel Samek) for severe punishment (Village of Zotsolinkov, District of Dergachi). The excesses of the district chiefs and militiamen are of a particularly serious nature in that, in order to justify their actions, the persons cited usually maintain that everything was undertaken in the name of the German Army. The truth is, however, that in almost every case the latter has behaved with exemplary consideration toward skilled workers and the Ukrainian population. However, this cannot be said of many administrative departments. As an illustration of the above: in one instance a woman arrived wearing not much more than an undershirt."

"With reference to reports received, it must also be pointed out that it is irresponsible to keep the workers locked up for many hours in railway cars so that they are not even able to relieve themselves. Opportunity must as a matter of course be given at intervals to allow these people to fetch drinking water, wash, and relieve themselves. Railway cars have been shown in which workers have bored holes in order to relieve themselves. It is to be noted, however, that when trains are approaching large railway stations the opportunity to perform bodily functions must, wherever possible, be given beyond the limits of such stations."

"Reports of impropriety have been received from delousing stations, where some male staff or other male persons have been employed or have circulated among the women and girls in the shower rooms—even to the point of soaping such females!—and, vice versa, female persons among the men, and in some cases men have spent protracted periods taking photographs in the women's shower rooms. Since most of those transported during recent months emanate from the Ukr. rural population, whose female portion has a strong moral sense and is accustomed to a strict code of behavior, such treatment must inevitably be regarded by them as a national degradation. The first-named improprieties have meanwhile to our knowledge been eliminated by the action of those in charge of transportation. The photographing was reported to us from Halle, the instances of soaping from Kievertse."

Can it be that the sex wave had already begun, and that many photographs being pressed upon us today were taken at delousing stations for slave workers from Eastern Europe?

Now it is important to realize that the conquest of continents or worlds is by no means easy, that those people had their problems too, and that they tried to solve them with German thoroughness and to document them with German meticulousness. Whatever you do, don't improvise! Nature's calls remain Nature's calls, and it simply won't do for people destined for execution to turn up on delivery as corpses! It is an outrage and must be severely punished, and it won't do either for men to soap women or for women to soap men during the delousing process, and as for taking photographs! It simply won't do. Then no one's hands remain clean. Have libertines and fiends infiltrated a procedure that is "in itself" perfectly proper?

Now that disputes over corpses and/or partial corpses have become a hallmark of modern conventional warfare, and libertines and fiends—in uniform!—admit to assaulting women and even taking photographs in the process, there is no further need to bore the reader with similar examples.

The only thing was: how and where were they to survive, the

pregnant Leni, the hypersensitive Boris, the strong-minded Lotte, the overly compassionate Margret, Grundtsch—that grubber in the soil—and Pelzer, who was never a monster? In March 1945, what became of our Marja, of Bogakov and Viktor Genrikhovich, of old Gruyten, and so many others?

First of all, in late December '44 or early January '45 Boris was the cause of a totally unnecessary complication about which Leni tells nothing, Margret everything, and of which Lotte and Marja were ignorant.

Margret, now under the strictest supervision to prevent the Au. slipping her an occasional something (The doctor to the Au.: "She simply has to starve now for four or five weeks, that'll give us at least half a chance to restore her endocrine and exocrine balance: she's in such a mess right now that tears might come out of her nipples and urine out of her nose. So talking's O.K., but no gifts."). Margret, already used to asceticism, in fact hoping it would cure her: "But you can give me a 'regular'" (which the Au. did), "well, I was furious with Boris at the time, really angry, and that didn't let up until later, when we were all living in one another's pockets and I got to know him—saw how wise and sensitive he was, but at the end of '44, around Christmastime, or it may've been early in '45, around the first week in January but certainly no later, that Leni came home one day with a name in her head, though this time she at least knew it was a writer, and a dead one at that, so at least we didn't have to start phoning around.

"Again it was all about a book, and the author was called Kafka, Franz Kafka; the book: *In the Penal Colony.* I asked Boris later whether he'd really had no idea of the trouble he was causing by recommending a Jewish writer to Leni at the end of 1944 (!), and he said: 'I had so much on my mind, so much to think about, that I never thought of *that.*' So: off goes Leni again with the request slip to the public library—there was still one functioning, and luckily for Leni it was quite a sensible older woman who tore up Leni's slip, took her aside then and there and spoke to her exactly as the mother superior had done when Leni had pressed her for information about Rahel: 'My child, have your wits deserted you? Who sent you here with such a request?' But believe me, once again Leni was persistent. That woman in the library must've seen right away that Leni was no agent provocateur, so she took her aside and explained to her in great detail that this Kafka was a Jew, that all his books had been banned and burned and so on, and no doubt Leni once again countered with her shattering 'So what?,' and the woman must have explained to her with great thoroughness, although belatedly, all about the Jews and the Nazis, and she showed her a copy of *Der Stürmer*—for of course she had it right there in the library—and explained the whole thing to her, and Leni was horrified when she came to see me. At last she was beginning to understand. She still wouldn't give up though, she just wanted her Kafka, she wanted to read him and she got him! She actually went to Bonn and looked up a few of the professors her father had once worked for, men she knew had large libraries of their own, and she actually found one who was already a grandfather by then, past seventy-five and living in retirement surrounded by his books, and do you know what he told her: 'My child, have your wits deserted you? Why Kafka of all people—why not Heine?' He must've been very nice to her then, he remembered her and her father, but he didn't have the book himself so he in turn had to go first to one colleague and then to another till he found one who could trust him and whom he could trust and who also had the book. It wasn't that easy, it took a whole day, believe me, she came home in the middle of the night with the book in her handbag, it hadn't been all that easy, for they'd had to find someone who could not only trust the professor and whom the professor could trust, he had to be able to trust Leni too, and not only did he have to have the book but he had to be willing to part with it! It seems they found two who had the book, but the first one didn't want to let it out of his hands. It was really crazy, the things she and that Boris of hers were worrying about, while all the time it was our bare lives, our bare naked lives, that were in danger.

"To add to my troubles, it was just at that time that Schlömer, whom I was married to, turned up. It was his house we were living in, and in this Schlömer all trace of the man of the world, of former elegance, was gone, he was on his beam-ends, was suddenly in army uniform but without papers and he'd got away by the skin of his teeth from the French partisans who'd been just about to shoot him. I don't know, somehow I'd always been fond of him, he was always kind and generous to me, and in his way I suppose he was fond of me too, maybe he even loved me. Now he was a mere nothing, in a pitiful state, and he told me: 'Margret, I've done things that will cost me my neck everywhere, wherever I go, with the French, with the Germans—the pro-Nazis and the few who are anti—with the British, the Dutch, the Americans, the Belgians, if the Russians get me and find out who I am it's curtains—and it's also curtains if the Germans get me, the ones who're still running the show. Help me, Margret.' You should've seen him in the old days, the kind of man who went everywhere by taxi or turned up in an official car, went on leave three times a year bringing gifts back by the score, always dashing and gay, and now here he was like a pitiful little mouse, scared of the cops and of the Americans, of everyone.

"So then I hit on an idea I might've thought of before. Men were dying all the time in the hospital, and naturally the identification papers were collected, registered, and sent back to the unit or wherever; anyway, I knew where the identification papers were, and I also knew that many soldiers hadn't handed theirs in or that they hadn't been found, in cases where the men had been brought in seriously wounded and their tattered bloody rags had been thrown away. So what did I do? That very night I stole three sets—there were plenty lying around there, enough for me to pick some with photos resembling Schlömer and Boris in age and appearance; so I took two of men with fair hair and glasses, about twenty-four or twenty-five years old, and one of a slender dark type without glasses, in his late thirties, like Schlömer, and gave it to him. I took his pack and stowed away all the money I had in it, and butter and cigarettes and bread, and sent him on his way with his new name: Ernst Wilhelm

Keiper, I even made a note of it and the address because I wanted to know what happened to him. After all, we'd been married to each other for almost six years, though rather sporadically, and I told him the safest thing to do would be to go to the Army, to the deployment center or some such place, since everyone was on his tail. And that's what he did. He cried, and if you didn't know Schlömer before 1944 you don't know what that means: a weeping, begging, grateful Schlömer who kissed my hand. He whimpered like a puppy—and off he went. Never saw him again. Some time later I went out of curiosity to see the wife of that Keiper, in the coal-mining area, near Buer, I wanted to find out, you see. She'd already remarried, and I told her I'd nursed her husband in hospital, and that he'd died and asked me to look her up. Well, that was a cheeky little baggage all right, she asked me: 'Which of my husbands d'you mean—Ernst Wilhelm? He died twice, you know, once in hospital and a second time in some godforsaken hole called Würselen.' So Schlömer was dead too, and I won't deny I was relieved. Maybe he was better off that way than being hanged or shot by the Nazis or the partisans. Well, it turned out he'd been a regular war criminal—in France and Belgium and Holland he went around recruiting forced labor, right at the beginning, in 1939; he'd had a business training, of course. I've been interrogated quite a few times on his account, and then they took away the house from me and everything in it, all I could take along was my clothes. It seems that Schlömer had been stealing in a big way and, to put it bluntly, taken bribes—so there I was in 1949 out on the street, and I've been more or less on the street ever since. Yes, on the street, although Leni and the others have tried to get me back on my feet again. I lived with Leni for six months, but in the long run that didn't work out because of my men friends, what with her son getting to be a big boy and asking me one day: 'Margret, why does Harry'—that was a British corporal I was going with at the time—'why does he always want to go into you so deep?'" (Margret blushed again. Au.).

Schirtenstein's whereabouts at the end of the war are already known to the reader: he was strumming "Lili Marleen" on the piano for Soviet officers, somewhere between Leningrad and Vitebsk; a man for whom even a Monique Haas had respect. "I had one relentless, terrible desire" (S. to the Au.), "I wanted to eat and stay alive. And I would even have played 'Lili Marleen' on the mouth organ."

Dr. Scholsdorff spent the end of the war in a way that almost stamps him as a hero: he had "retired to a little village on the right bank of the Rhine where, since I had genuine papers and no political stigma, I waited for the end of the war, unmolested by the Nazis and without having to be afraid of the Americans. In order to complete my camouflage, I took over the command of a home-guard group of about ten men, of whom three were over seventy, two were under seventeen, two had lost a leg above the knee, one below the knee, one had lost an arm, and the tenth was mentally defective, in other words, the village idiot; our weapons consisted of a few cudgels and for the most part of white bed sheets cut in four; we also had a few hand grenades with which we were supposed to blow up a bridge. Well, I marched off with my unit, we fastened our cut-up sheets to poles, left the bridge unharmed—and surrendered the village intact to the Americans. Until two years ago I was always very welcome in the village" (the hamlet of Ausler Mühle in Bergisch Land. Au.) "and had a standing invitation to the fair and other similar festivities; but I must say that in the last two years I've noticed a change of mood, from time to time I hear the word defeatist—and that after twenty-five years, and in spite of my having also saved the church spire by pledging my life to an American lieutenant, Earl Wittney, that it was unoccupied and not used for military purposes. Well, there's been a swing to the right, no doubt about that. Whatever the reason, I don't feel quite so relaxed when I go there these days."

Hans and Grete Helzen need only a brief alibi: Hans was not born until June 1945; it is not known to the Au. whether he demonstrated Werewolf sentiments in his mother's womb. And Grete was not born until 1946.

Heinrich Pfeiffer, aged twenty-one at the end of the war, his (left) leg having just been amputated above the knee, was in a baroque convent near Bamberg that had been turned into a military hospital. He had—in his own words—"just come round from the anesthetic and was feeling quite lousy enough when the Yanks showed up—luckily they left me in peace."

Pfeiffer, Sr., who gives his and his wife's whereabouts "on the day of defeat" as "not far from Dresden," has now been dragging his paralyzed leg for twenty-seven years (or, taking today's date, thirty-five years), the leg that Leni's father, before he had to go to jail, in 1943, was still calling "the phoniest leg I've ever known."

Miss van Doorn: "I thought I was being the smartest of the lot, and by November 1944 I'd already moved out to Tolzem, where I'd bought my parents' home and the property belonging to it with the money Hubert had given away in such quantities. I kept telling Leni she should move out to my place and have her baby—we still didn't know whose it was—in peace in the country, and I told her, the Americans are sure to be two or three weeks earlier out here than in town where you are, and what actually happened? It was lucky Leni wasn't with me. They razed Tolzem to the ground—that's what they call it, isn't it?—we had half an hour to get away, and they took us in cars across the Rhine, and afterwards we couldn't go back across the Rhine because over there the Americans were in control and on our side it was still the Germans. How lucky Leni didn't take my advice! Talk about the peace and quiet and fresh country air and flowers—and so forth: all we could see was a huge cloud of dust—what had once been Tolzem—it's been rebuilt now, of course, but I tell you: one great cloud of dust!"

Mrs. Kremer: "After they'd taken away the boy I thought: where do I go now, east or west, or should I stay here? I decided to stay: no one was allowed to go to the west, only soldiers and labor detachments—and east? For all I knew, they might go on playing at war there for months or even a year. So I stayed in my apartment until the Second" (i.e., March 2, 1945, which among certain circles who stayed behind in the city is known simply as "the Second." Au.). "Then came the air raid when so many people went crazy, or almost; I went across the street into the brewery cellar, thinking: the world's coming to an end, the world's coming to an end, and I tell you quite frankly, though I'd never set foot in a church since I was twelve, since 1914, never bothered with all that mumbo jumbo, and not even when the Nazis were *apparently*" (stress not the Au.'s) "against the priests was I in favor of them: by then I'd swallowed that much dialectic and that much materialistic interpretation of history—though most of the comrades thought of me as just a stupid harmless little hen—believe me, I prayed: that was all I did. It all came back to me: 'Hail Mary' and 'Our Father' and even 'Beneath the Shelter of Thy Wings'—I just prayed. It was the worst, the heaviest raid we ever had, and it lasted exactly six hours and forty-four minutes, and sometimes the ceiling of the cellar moved a little. Rather like a tent in the wind, it trembled and moved—and all that on a city that was practically depopulated, down it came, more and more and again and again.

"There were only six of us in the cellar, two women, me and a young woman with a little boy of three, she just sat there with her teeth chattering—and for the first time I saw what that means, what you so often read about: someone's teeth chattering; it was purely mechanical, she couldn't help it, she didn't even know she was doing it—finally she'd bitten through her lips till they bled, and we stuck a piece of wood between her teeth, some smooth little piece we found lying around, probably from a barrel stave; I thought she was going nuts, that I was going nuts—it wasn't all that noisy, it was the shaking, and the ceiling sometimes looking like a rubber ball, when it's broken and you can press it in or out; the little boy was asleep: he just got tired, fell asleep, and was smiling in his dream.

"There were three men there too, an elderly warehouse helper in a Brownshirt uniform—on the Second, imagine!—well, he simply shit in his pants till they were full, he was trembling all over as if he had the shakes—and he peed all down his pants too and then ran outside, just ran outside yelling—out onto the street; not so much as a collar button did they find of him, believe me. Then there were two younger men too, in civvies, Germans, deserters I think, who'd been lurking around in the ruins but then got the daylights scared out of them during this raid; first they were very quiet and pale, and suddenly, after the older fellow had run outside, they got—well, I'm sixty-eight now and it must sound terrible when I tell it like this, the way it really was, I was forty-three then, and the young woman—I never saw her again, never, not one of the four, neither the young fellows nor the child, no one—the young woman was in her late twenties maybe—well anyway, these young fellows, who were at most twenty-two or three, suddenly started—how shall I put, getting randy, pestering us, no that's all wrong, and after all, for three years, ever since they tortured my husband to death in the concentration camp, I hadn't looked at another man—well the two of them, you can't exactly say they fell on us and we didn't put up much of a fight either, they didn't rape us—anyway: one of them came over to me, grabbed me by the breast and pulled down my underpants, the other one went over to the young woman, took the piece of wood out from between her teeth and kissed her, and suddenly there we were, going at it together, or however you want to call it, with the little boy sleeping right there in the middle, and I know it must sound terrible to you, but you simply can't imagine what it's like when for six and a half hours the planes come over and drop bombs, aerial mines and nearly six thousand bombs—we simply closed in together, the four of us, the little boy in the middle; and I can still feel how the young fellow, the one who'd picked me, had his mouth full of dust when he kissed me, and I can still feel that dust in my mouth—it must've all come trickling down from that swaying ceiling—and I can still feel how glad I was, how I calmed down, went on praying, and I can remember how the young woman suddenly got quite quiet, her fellow was lying on top of her and she stroked the hair back from his forehead and smiled at him, and I stroked my fellow's hair back from his forehead and smiled at him, and then we got dressed again, fixed ourselves up a bit, and sat there quietly; without discussing it we'd taken everything out of our pockets, cigarettes and bread, and the young woman had some preserves in her shopping bag, pickles and strawberry jam—and together we ate the lot, not saying a word and, as if by common consent, we didn't ask one another's names—didn't say a word, and dust was gritting in our teeth, the young fellow's dust in mine, and mine in his, I suppose—and then it was all over, about four thirty. Silence. Not quite. Somewhere a thud, somewhere a wall collapsed, somewhere there was an explosion —nearly six thousand bombs. Well, when I say silent I mean no more planes—and we all ran out, each for himself—no goodbyes. Well, there we all stood in an enormous cloud of dust reaching right up to the sky, in a cloud of smoke, in a cloud of fire—I passed out, and a few days later I woke up in the hospital and was still praying—well, that was the last time. I was lucky they didn't just bury me in the rubble, how many people d'you think got buried like that by mistake? And what do you imagine happened to the brewery cellar? It collapsed, two days after we left it—I imagine the vaulted ceiling went on bulging like a rubber ball and then caved in. I went there because I wanted to see what happened to my apartment: nothing left, nothing, nothing—not even what you might call a decent pile of rubble, and the next day, when I left the hospital, the Americans arrived."

We know that Marga Wanft was evacuated. Evidently she suffered terrible, dreadful things (since she remains silent, the Au.

is unable to determine whether these things were objectively or merely subjectively terrible or dreadful). She said only one word: "Schneidemühl." As for Kremp, we know that he died for the *Autobahn,* beside the *Autobahn,* possibly with a word such as "Germany" on his lips.

Dr. Henges "withdrew" (H. on H.) "with my aristocratic boss to one of the villages where we could be sure that the farm people wouldn't give us away. Disguised as woodsmen, we lived in a log cabin but were fed and looked after like true gentlemen; even amorous services were not only not refused but positively offered us by the women devoted to the Count's family. Quite frankly, the erotic practices and sexuality of Bavaria were too coarse for my taste, and I longed for the refinements of the Rhineland, and not only in that department either. Since I didn't have too many black marks against me, it was safe for me to go home in 1951, the Count had to wait until 1953, then placed himself voluntarily at the disposal of the courts, but at a moment when the fuss over the war criminals was being tacitly called off. He spent the next three months in Werl and soon after that reentered the diplomatic service. I preferred not to expose myself politically again, but merely to offer my knowledge of philology to any who might care to use it."

Hoyser, Sr.: "I felt I had to stay on because of my properties. You see, I didn't only own the Gruyten building: in January '45 and again in February '45 I managed to acquire buildings belonging to people who were in great political danger. Anti-Aryanization, or re-anti-Aryanization you might call it; two buildings that had once belonged to Jews and were sold to me by two former Nazis, legally, everything notarized, payment by check, all quite legal. It was a perfectly proper transfer of property. After all, there was no law against buying or selling property, right? I was spared 'the Second' because I happened to be out in the country —but I saw the dust cloud twenty-five miles away—a gigantic dust cloud—and when I cycled back the next day I found an apartment on the west side of town that was in perfect shape, and I didn't have to get out till the British arrived. Those British, I must say, took good care to see no damage was done to the parts of the city they wanted to live in later. The others—Leni and Lotte and the others—left me nicely in the lurch and didn't tell me a thing about the little Soviet paradise they'd set up in the burial vaults. Well, I was an old man—sixty, after all—and they didn't want me around.

"In fact Lotte behaved pretty badly all round, considering my wife had died the previous October. She kept moving from place to place in town with the children, first to her relatives, then to that whore Margret, then to friends, simply to avoid being evacuated, and why? Because she was dead set on looting, and she knew exactly where the army supplies were. Needless to say, nobody let old Grandpa in on it when they looted the warehouse near what used to be the Carmelite convent. Oh no, they went there with handcarts and old bicycles and derelict burned-out cars that were standing around on the streets but which you could still get moving somehow by pushing, and they looted eggs and butter, bacon and cigarettes, coffee and clothing, by the sackful—and they were so greedy they fried eggs for themselves right there on the street, using the lids of gas-mask containers, and schnapps and whatever they wanted—regular orgies, like during the French Revolution, and women always out front, our Lotte leading the way like a virago! Regular battles were fought—there were still German soldiers in the city, remember.

"I found all this out later and was glad I'd moved out of that apartment in time, for it soon became a kind of bordello when they had to get out of their Soviet paradise in the vaults and Hubert began his affair with Lotte. You wouldn't have recognized Lotte: mind you, she's always been a bitter, brittle kind of woman, sarcastic and shrewish, but she was absolutely beside herself, a different woman. During the war we'd put up with her socialist cant, though it was dangerous for us, the things she used to say at the time, and her dragging our son Wilhelm into that Red nonsense, that hurt but we forgave her, she was a decent, conscientious wife and mother after all, but then, on March 5, she must've thought socialism had broken out and everything would be divided up, goods and real estate, the works. In fact for a time she actually ran the municipal housing department, first by simply usurping the position, the authorities having fled of course, and then legally because it was quite true she hadn't been a Fascist, but it just isn't enough not to have been a Fascist.

"Anyway, she ran the place for a year and arbitrarily put people into empty villas, people who scarcely knew how to flush a toilet and did their laundry in the bathtub and raised carp and made a kind of sugar-beet jam in the bathrooms. It's a fact that bathtubs were found afterwards half full of sugar-beet jam. Well, fortunately this confusion between socialism and democracy didn't last long, and she eventually settled down quite nicely to being what she actually was: a minor employee. But at the time, during the days of wholesale looting, she lived down there with all the rest of them in that vault paradise, with the children, and though she knew where I was, knew perfectly well, she never got in touch with me, not once. Oh dear me no, no question of gratitude from that quarter, yet actually, if you stop to think of it, she owes her life to us. We'd only have had to hint, just hint, about all the things she used to say about the war and the war aims, just that one little word 'crap,' and she'd have been in it up to her neck, in jail or concentration camp, maybe even hanging from a gallows—and then that."

There may be a reader who cares to know that B.H.T.'s urine manipulations, inspired by Rahel, did not exactly come to naught, they continued to be successful right up to the end, only —they ceased to benefit him. Late in September 1944 he was called up and assigned to a stomach-ulcer battalion, regardless of the fact that stomach ulcers require a different diet from diabetes. B.H.T. took part in several battles: the Ardennes offensive, Hürtgen Forest, was taken prisoner by the Americans near a place called Würselen, and it is not impossible that he "fought shoulder to shoulder" with the Schlömer who had been transformed into a Keiper. In any event, the end of the war saw B.H.T. in an American POW camp near Reims in the "company of some 200,000 German soldiers of all ranks, and believe me, it was no picnic, in terms either of the company or the food situation, especially in regard to—if you will permit the expression—the prospect of female company—it was a disaster." (A remark that surprised the Au. He had assumed B.H.T. to be sexually neutral.)

Although the Au. felt embarrassed at questioning M.v.D. on Gruyten's death, in order to get at the facts he made a few cautious attempts that ended in angry complaints about Lotte, apparently the object of M.v.D.'s jealousy on account of "certain things that happened." "It was all because I hadn't got back yet when he came home, otherwise I'm absolutely sure he'd have looked to me for the consolation—and found it, what's more—that she offered him, though I'm thirteen years older than her. But you see, I'd landed up on the other side of the Rhine, almost beyond the Wupper I'd say, and there I was, stuck in that hole in Westphalia, where they looked on us Rhinelanders as hard to please, picky eaters, and generally spoiled and weren't what you might call friendly toward us—and the Americans didn't show up there till the middle of April, and you've no idea how difficult, how impossible, it was to cross westwards over the Rhine at the time. So I had to stay put till the middle of May, and Hubert was back home again by early May, and it seems he crawled into bed with that Lotte right off. So there was nothing I could do about it when I got home. It was too late."

Lotte: "Sometimes I get mixed up about the period February to March '45 and then the time from March '45 to early May. There was too much going on, you couldn't see the woods for the trees. Of course I joined in the looting in the Schnürer Gasse near the old Carmelite convent, I took whatever I could, and at the time I preferred to make use of Pelzer's help rather than my father-in-law's. The problems we had to solve! I had to get out of the apartment, you see, the only one who could've stayed there was Leni, but the baby was due in a few days and we couldn't leave her alone, of course, so we all moved in together into what he calls the Soviet paradise in the vaults. The secret was out now, that the father of her child was a Russian, but she'd been silly enough to register the name of another Russian, because of course she'd been getting special mother's rations since September or October of '44—Margret had put her up to it by simply giving her the name of a soldier who had died in the hospital: Yendritsky it was. They'd been a bit too hasty about it, those two, and hadn't realized that the deceased Yendritsky had been married—there might've been all kinds of trouble with his widow and, to my mind, nasty trouble, it's not right to saddle a dead man with something like that. Well, I managed to repair the damage when I took over the housing department for the military government in mid-March. We had all the rubber stamps and stuff we wanted, and access to all the other authorities, so we were able to give the child its rightful father: Boris Lvovich Koltovsky—when you remember that all the authorities were squeezed together in three offices you can well imagine there wasn't much difficulty about taking away the paternity of Leni's child from that poor Yendritsky and fixing the whole thing up.

"This all happened, of course, after 'the Second,' and when those German idiots had finally all left—they were still hanging deserters in the city on March the sixth, you know, before they finally made off, blowing up the bridges behind them. It was only then that the Americans arrived, and at last we could leave the Soviet vault-paradise and go back to the apartment; but even the Americans couldn't make head or tail of the confusion, even they must've been shocked when they saw what the city actually looked like, and I saw some of them in tears, especially a few women outside the hotel across from the Cathedral—and you wouldn't believe all the types that suddenly showed up: German deserters, Russians who'd been in hiding, Yugoslavs, Poles, Russian women workers, escaped concentration-camp inmates, a few Jews who'd been in hiding—and how were the

Americans to tell who'd been a collaborator and who not, and who belonged in what camp? They must have imagined it was going to be simpler, a bit too simple, to decide between Nazis and non-Nazis and all that; and it turned out to be less simple than their childlike mentality had led them to believe. Everything had to be sorted and classified—and when Hubert finally turned up, around the beginning of May, things had been at least partially sorted out, I say partially, and I don't mind admitting it—with my rubber stamps and certificates I took a pretty generous hand in quite a few destinies; what else are rubber stamps and certificates good for, I'd like to know?

"Hubert, for instance, turned up in an Italian uniform that had been given him by some of his buddies in Berlin, fellows he'd been clearing out fortifications and subway tunnels with. They'd thought it all out very carefully: to move westward as a German convict was too risky; between Berlin and the Rhine there were still quite a few Nazi pockets where they might have hanged him; he was too young to go as a civilian: at forty-five he might've landed up in some POW camp: with the Russians, the British, or the Americans. So he went as an Italian, not that this was any kind of insurance, mind you, but it was quite smart: they had nothing but contempt for the Italians and didn't always string them up on the spot, and that was the whole object: not to get strung up or shot, that was the tricky part, and with his Italian uniform and his 'No speaka da German' he was lucky—only there again it wasn't exactly the best kind of insurance—to be taken to Italy wearing an Italian uniform and identified there as a German! That could've cost him his neck too.

"Well, he made it, and he turned up here as cheerful as you please, it's the truth, you never saw anyone so cheerful in your life. He said to us: 'Well, my dears, I've made up my mind to spend the rest of my life smiling, smiling.' He embraced us all, Leni, Boris, was thrilled to death with his grandson, he embraced Margret and my kids and me of course and said to me: 'Lotte, you know I'm fond of you, and sometimes I think you're fond of me too. Why don't we shack up together?' So we took three of the rooms, Leni, Boris, and the baby took three, Margret one, and we shared the kitchen. Problems just ceased to exist among so many sensible people, we had everything we needed, after all, the whole inheritance from the glorious German Army's Schnürer Gasse warehouse, and Margret had managed to liberate a good supply of medicines from the hospital; and we felt it was best to have Hubert go on running around in his Italian uniform—the only trouble was that unfortunately I couldn't get him any Italian papers, and he got some from the military government with an Italian name that Boris thought up for him: Manzoni, that was the only Italian name he knew, he must've read a book by this Manzoni. After all, he couldn't very well say he was a discharged German convict because actually he'd been in jail not for political reasons but as a criminal, and the Americans were quite fussy about such things. Naturally they didn't want criminals running around loose, and how could we explain to them that his crime had *actually* been a political one? So it was better for him to be Luigi Manzoni, Italian, who was living with me. You had to be careful as hell not to get into any kind of camp, even one for returning Germans. Better not to risk it. You never knew where the transports would end up. And that worked quite well till early 1946, by that time the Americans weren't so keen any more on sticking every German into some camp or other, and soon the British arrived, and I managed to cope quite well with both, the British and the Americans.

"Naturally lots of people asked why we didn't get married, what with me being a widow and him a widower, and some people say I didn't because of my pension, but that's simply not true. It was just tiresome, that's really all it was, to tie oneself as irrevocably as, let's face it, marriage does. Today I regret it, because later on my kids got swallowed up in my father-in-law's sphere of influence. Leni would have liked to marry her Boris, and vice versa, but obviously that was impossible since Boris had no papers; he didn't want to admit to being a Russian, there were some cushy jobs to be had, mind you, but most of the Russians were simply packed up and sent home to Papa Stalin against their will and without knowing what they were in for, and Margret had given him some German papers that had the name Alfred Bullhorst, but a healthy German male of twenty-four, suffering only from slight undernourishment, do you know what was in store for him? Sinzig or Wickrath, those hellish POW camps—and naturally we didn't want that. So that was no insurance either.

"He spent most of his time at home anyway, and you should've seen how those two carried on with their little son: like the Holy Family. He stuck to his belief that a woman is not to be touched for three months after her confinement nor from the sixth month of pregnancy on—so for six months they lived like Mary and Joseph with now and again a kiss of course, but other than that only the child! They fondled him and spoiled him and they sang songs to him, and then one evening they jumped the gun a bit, in June '45, they went for a walk beside the Rhine, until curfew time. We all warned them, all of us, Hubert and I and Margret, but there was no stopping them: every evening beside the Rhine. And it was wonderful, I must say, Hubert and I often went along, too, and we'd sit there and feel something we actually hadn't felt for twelve years: peace. No ships on the Rhine, wrecks all over the place and the bridges smashed—just a few ferries and the American army bridge—sometimes, you know, I think it'd have been best not to build any more bridges across the Rhine and let the German West finally be the German West.

"Well, things turned out differently- and for Boris too; one evening in June he was picked up by an American patrol, and stupidly enough he had his German papers in his pocket, and there wasn't a thing we could do: my American officers couldn't help, and Margret's American boy friends couldn't help, nor my going to the city commandant and telling him the whole involved story about Boris: Boris was gone, and at first things didn't look too bad; all that happened was that he'd been taken prisoner by the Americans and would come home as Alfred Bullhorst—seeing he didn't want to go to the Soviet Union. It was no paradise, mind you, an American POW camp—but what we didn't know was that during the summer the Americans began to, well let's say, hand over German prisoners to the French—it could also be called selling them, because they got themselves reimbursed in dollars for the cost of food and accommodation—and we also didn't know that this was how Boris ended up in a mine in Lorraine, in his weakened condition—the truth is that, thanks to Leni, or shall we say, thanks to Leni's mortgage, the boy hadn't exactly starved, but then he wasn't that strong either—and now—you ought to have seen Leni: she took off right away, on an old bicycle. She got across all the zone borders, even across all the national frontiers, into the French Zone, into the Saar Territory, right into Belgium, back again into the Saar Territory, from there to Lorraine, going from camp to camp and asking each of the commandants after Alfred Bullhorst, pleading for him, courageously and stubbornly, I tell you, but she didn't know that in Europe there were probably fifteen to twenty million German POW's; she was on the road with her bike till November, coming home at intervals to replenish her supplies—and then she'd be off again. To this day I don't know how she managed to get across all the frontiers and back again, with her German papers, and she never told us either. Just the songs—sometimes she'd sing them to us, and over and over again she'd sing them to the boy: 'On Christmas Eve, this very day, We poor folk sit here as we pray, The room is cheerless here within, Outside winds blow and enter in, Lord Jesus come, be with us here, We truly need Thy presence dear'—oh the songs she used to sing! It brought tears to our eyes. Several times she rode her bike clear across the Eifel and on through the Ardennes and back again, from Sinzig to Namur, from Namur to Reims, and to Metz again and to Saarbrücken again, and once again to Saarbrücken. It wasn't the best kind of insurance, I can tell you that, crossing and recrossing that corner of Europe with German papers. Well, believe it or not, she found her Boris, her Yendritsky, her Koltovsky, her Bullhorst—pick any name you like. She found him, she found him in a cemetery, not in a Soviet paradise in the vaults, no, in a grave, dead, killed in an accident in an iron mine between Metz and Saarbrücken in some remote village in Lorraine—and she'd just turned twenty-three and, if you want to be exact about it, had been widowed for the third time. After that she really did become a statue, and we'd go hot and cold all over when she sang to the boy in the evening, the songs his father had loved so much:

> Ancestral marble has turned gray
> We sit around this place today
> In a darkly heathen way
> The snow falls coldly on our skin
> The snow insists on coming in
> Come join us, snow, we welcome you
> In Heaven you are homeless too . . .

And then suddenly, in an impudent voice: 'Off to Mahagonny, the air is cool and fresh. There's whiskey there and poker, and horse- and woman-flesh, shine for us, fair green moon of Mahagonny, for today we have folding money under our belts for a big laugh from your big stupid mouth'—then suddenly, solemn enough to make your flesh creep, in a loud chant: 'When I was a boy a god often rescued me from the shouting and the rod of men, then, safe and good, I played among the flowers of the grove, and the gentle airs of Heaven played with me, and just as Thou gladden'st the heart of the plants when they stretch out their frail arms to Thee, so didst Thou gladden my heart.' Fifty years from now I'll still know that by heart, we got to hear it so often—almost every evening and several times a day, and you must picture it: Leni speaking in a strict, stilted High German, whereas otherwise she spoke only in her marvelous dry Rhenish dialect. Believe me, that's something you never forget, never, and the boy never forgot it either, nor did any of us, not even Margret, and there were some of her English and American boy friends who could never have enough of it, watching and listening to Leni recite and sing, and especially when she recited the Rhine poem to her little boy . . . well, she was a wonderful girl, she's a wonderful woman and, I think, a wonderful mother too, the fact that in the end things didn't work out for the boy isn't her fault, it's the fault of those crooks, and I'm including those rotten sons of mine, the 'united Hoysers'—and their fiendish behavior, especially the old man, my father-in-law; Hubert knew how to fix him all right, when he came to collect his rent, his forty-six marks and fifteen pfennigs for our three rooms—Hubert would laugh every time, laugh like a maniac, every time without fail—till finally thcy only communicated by letter, and old Hoyser brought up the usual pettifogging argument that the onus was on the tenant to bring the rent to the landlord, not on the landlord to collect the rent from the tenant—well, then Hubert started *taking* the rent to him in his villa out there on the west side, every first of the month—and he'd laugh his maniac's laugh there too, till old Hoyser couldn't stand it any more and insisted on having the rent sent to him. Then Hubert started a lawsuit over whether rent is a debt to be paid by bringing, collecting, or sending—he couldn't be expected, he said, to spend ten or twenty pfennigs on a postal money order or even on a remittance to a post-office account, he was only an unskilled worker, he said, which was true enough. Well, they actually appeared in court together, and Hubert won his case, so now Hoyser could choose whether he wanted to hear that maniac's laugh at our place or at his: he'd been hearing it now on the first of the month for forty months, till he finally hit on the idea of employing a rent collector—but believe me, Hoyser still has that maniac's laugh in his bones, and it's Leni who has to pay for it today; he's tormenting her to death, and he'll have her kicked out if we don't do something about it." (Sighs, coffee, cigarette—see above: hand passed over gray cropped hair.)

"For us it was a happy time, till 1948, till Hubert Gruyten got killed in that frightful accident—it was madness, and since then I haven't been able to stand the sight of Pelzer, I never want to hear of him again, I really don't; it was too awful; and it was soon after that, of course, that the kids were taken away from me, the old man just wouldn't let up, he accused me of carrying on with every man who happened to be staying with us or even just came to see us, every one of them, so he could take the kids away from me, first hand them over to the welfare, then take them over himself; he even suspected me of carrying on with that poor Heinrich Pfeiffer, that poor boy who in those days was still hobbling around without an artificial leg and used to stay with us whenever he had to go into the hospital or to the relief agency.

We had to rent out rooms, you see, we had to because he raised the rent and wouldn't let up—and it so happened that the social worker came a few times, well actually she came several times, and always without warning, and damn it all, you can think what you like, yes damn it all, she happened to catch me three times with a fellow in what she called an 'unequivocally equivocal situation,' that's to say, in plain English I was in bed with Bogakov, who'd been a buddy of Boris's and sometimes came to see us. Yes, and the third time she caught me in an 'equivocal situation' with Bogakov standing by the window in his undershirt, shaving, and using my pocket mirror and a wash basin that stood on the windowsill. 'Such situations,' she wrote in her report, 'would indicate an intimacy not conducive to the upbringing of growing children.' Well yes, Kurt was nine, of course, and Werner fourteen, maybe it wasn't right, especially as I wasn't in the least in love with Bogakov, not even particularly fond of him, we just crawled into bed together; and needless to say they questioned the kids—and then I lost them, lost them for good; at first they cried when they had to leave, but later on, when they moved from the nuns to their grandfather's, they had no further use for me; then I was not only a whore, I was a Communist and all that, but I must say this for the old man: he saw to it that they finished high school and went on to university, and he speculated so cleverly with the piece of land Mrs. Gruyten made over to Kurt when he was a baby that today, thirty years later, with four blocks of buildings on it and stores at street level, it's easily worth three million, and the revenue from it would be enough for us all to live on, including Leni, and at the time it was given to Kurt it was meant as a kind of gilded teacup or something—I need hardly say that's rather different from a tired worn-out old mum who still goes to the office every morning for eleven hundred and twelve marks a month before taxes. And I must say this for him: I'd never have been—never could have been—that smart. Yet that business with Bogakov didn't mean a thing, not a thing, I was so tired and depressed after Hubert died in that terrible way, and poor Bogakov, he was always in tears and didn't know whether or not to go home to Little Mother Russia and so on and sang his sad songs, like Boris—my God, all we did was crawl into bed together a few times.

"Later on I found out it'd been Hoyser who'd squealed on us to the German auxiliary police, telling them we had a supply of black-market goods. He just couldn't get over the fact that he hadn't got a thing from the Schnürer Gasse, and so one day, it must've been early '46, those slimy German snoopers turned up at our place and of course they found our supplies in the cellar: the salt butter, the bacon, the cigarettes and coffee, and piles of socks and underwear—and they confiscated the lot; enough to see us through another two or three years, and quite nicely too. Mind you, there was one thing they couldn't stick us with: we hadn't sold a single gram on the black market, at most an occasional swap, and we'd even given a lot away, Leni saw to that. Our British-American connections were no help, this was a matter for those German snoopers, and they even searched the house and at Leni's they found those comical diplomas of hers stating she was the most German girl in the school. One of those stinkers actually wanted to squeal on her, denounce her as a Nazi, all because of those crappy diplomas she'd been given at the age of ten or twelve, mind you, but this fellow was one I'd happened to see in Storm Trooper's uniform, and I must say he shut up quickly, otherwise it would've been awkward for Leni: just try and explain to an Englishman or an American that you can get a diploma for being 'the most German girl in the school' yet not be a Nazi. When all this happened Pelzer was really very decent, he'd stowed away his share from the Schnürer Gasse in a safe place, you see, and nobody'd squealed on him, and when he heard that all our stuff had been confiscated he gave us some of his without waiting to be asked: not for money, or services rendered, most likely to get into Leni's good books. Whatever the reason, that gangster was nicer than old Hoyser. It was later, much later, 1954 I believe, that I found out from one of those policemen that it was my own father-in-law who'd squealed on us."

❋

Mrs. Hölthohne, whom the Au. had arranged to meet this time at a very fashionable little café—not only out of gallantry but also to avoid exposing himself to any internal or external limitations on his consumption of cigarettes—had found herself at the end of the war in one of those former Carmelite convents, in the cellar of the former convent church, "in one of those crypts where at one time, no doubt, the nuns spent their periods of incarceration. I noticed nothing of the looting, and to me 'the Second' was merely a remote, terrible, endless dull roar, bad enough but very far away, and I was bound and determined not to leave that cellar until I was positive the Americans had arrived; I was scared. So many people were being shot and hanged, and though my papers were all right and had stood up to many tests, I was scared: I was scared some patrol might get it into their heads to be suspicious and shoot me.

"So I stayed down where I was, finally all alone, and let them get on up there with their looting and celebrating. I didn't come out till I heard the Americans were actually there, then I breathed again and wept, for joy and pain, joy at the liberation and pain at the sight of that totally and senselessly destroyed city—then I wept for joy when I saw that all the bridges, every last one of them, had been destroyed: at last the Rhine was Germany's frontier again, at last—what an opportunity that was, it should have been taken advantage of. Simply build no more bridges, just let ferries, subject to constant inspection of course, cross back and forth.

"Well, I immediately got in touch with the American military authorities, after some phoning around located my friend the French colonel, was allowed to travel freely between the British and French Zones, and was lucky enough two or three times to be able to help the little Gruyten girl, Leni, out of rather ticklish situations, when she was naively cycling all over the countryside looking for her Boris.

"By November I already had my permit, I rented a bit of land, knocked together some greenhouses, opened a store, and right away took on Leni, the Gruyten girl. It was a crucial moment for me when I got my permit and my new papers: should I become

Elli Marx from Saarlouis again, or should I stay Liane Hölthohne? I decided to stay Liane Hölthohne. My passport says Marx, alias Hölthohne. I must say you get a better cup of tea at my place than in this pseudo-topnotch establishment." (Which the Au. confirmed, with both gallantry and conviction.) "What's really good here is the petits fours, I must remember that.

"Now to the subject of what certain informants have described to you as the Soviet paradise in the vaults: we were invited to this paradise too, Grundtsch and I, but we were scared, not of the dead but of the living and because the cemetery was right in the planes' bombing path, between the old part of town and the suburbs; as for the dead, there was nothing about them to bother me in that paradise, after all people have been meeting and celebrating their feast days in catacombs for centuries. The cellar adjoining the crypt of the Carmelite convent seemed safer to me—the military police were welcome to come and ask me for my papers there, but in the cemetery, in the burial vaults: that was rather a suspicious place to be, wasn't it, and toward the end you really never knew what was the safest thing to be—a Jewish woman in hiding, a Separatist in hiding, a German soldier who had not deserted or who had, a convict who had escaped or who had not, and of course the city was swarming with deserters, and with them around it was anything but pleasant, all of them trigger-happy, both sides.

"Grundtsch had the same fears, though he had hardly left the cemetery, so to speak, for the past forty or fifty years, but now, around mid-February '45, he did, and for a while he moved out into the country, and he even ended up joining the Home Guard somewhere, and he was right: for that particular period some form or other of legality was the best protection, and my own motto was—don't overdo it, lie low somewhere with reasonably good papers, play possum, and wait. Quite deliberately—and it wasn't easy, believe me, for there were things there we hadn't even dared dream about—quite deliberately I'd taken no part in the looting, for naturally it was illegal, it carried the death penalty, and while the looting was going on the Germans were still officially in control of the city, and I had no wish to run around even for two or three or four days with a crime like that around my neck. I wanted to live, live—I was forty-one and wanted to live, and that life wasn't something I wanted to gamble with in the final few days. So I kept as quiet as a mouse and even three days before the Americans marched in I didn't dare talk about the war being over, let alone lost. There it had been in black and white, ever since October, on billboards and leaflets, that the entire German nation would be relentless in demanding just atonement for alarmists, defeatists, pessimists, lackeys of the enemy—and this atonement had but one name: death. They were getting crazier and crazier: somewhere they shot a woman who had washed her sheets and hung them out to dry—they thought she'd run up the white flag and they shot her—simply shot her through the window with a machine gun. No, better to go a bit hungry and wait, that was my motto, that orgy of looting on 'the Second' after the raid—that was too risky for me, and it was as much as your life was worth to then go and cart all that stuff to the cemetery; the city was still in German hands, you know, and they claimed they were going to defend it.

"Once the Germans had finally left, I didn't hesitate another moment, I went straight to the Americans and got in touch right away with my French friends; I had a nice little apartment allocated to me and got my first permit for a nursery garden. As long as old Grundtsch still hadn't returned I used his facilities and duly paid rent into an account for him, and when he got back in '46 I duly handed his place back to him, in good order, and opened my own business, and then by August '45 Friend Pelzer was already there wanting his character reference, though he'd started out so cleverly, and who was it gave it to him? Who was it spoke for him at the tribunal? Leni and I. Yes, we gave him a clean bill of health, and I did it against two convictions: against my conscience, because in spite of everything I considered him a scoundrel, and against my business interests, because it was only natural for him to become my competitor, and he continued to be till the mid-fifties."

My informant, Mrs. Hölthohne, suddenly looked very old, almost decrepit, the previously firm skin of her face suddenly became slack, her hand unsteady as it toyed with the teaspoon, her voice quavering, almost shaking.

"I still can't make up my mind whether it was right to get him cleared—and get him through the tribunal, but, you know, from the age of nineteen to the age of forty-two I'd been a persecuted person, since that battle near the Ägidienberg till the Americans marched in, for twenty-two years I'd been persecuted, politically, racially, call it what you like—and I'd deliberately picked Pelzer because I thought the safest place for me would be working for a Nazi, all the more so if it was a corrupt and criminal Nazi. I knew the kind of things that were said about him and that Grundtsch used to tell me, and now suddenly there he was in front of me, chalk-white with fear, he turned up with his wife, who really was innocent and knew nothing of what he might have done prior to '33, and he brought along his two really adorable young children too, the boy and the girl, they must've been between ten and twelve or so—delightful, and his pale, slightly hysterical wife, who'd really been completely in the dark, I felt sorry for her too—and he asked me whether, during the ten years I'd worked for him, I could accuse him of, or prove, a single, even the tiniest inhuman act directed at me or anyone else, either within the business or outside of it, and whether there wasn't a point at which a person's youthful transgressions—that's what he called them—had to be forgiven and forgotten.

"He knew enough not to offer me a bribe, he merely exerted gentle pressure by reminding me that he had included me in his wreath-recycling group, in other words, had taken me into his confidence—a hint, of course, that my slate hadn't been all that clean either, for it hadn't been very nice, had it, the way we spruced up stolen wreaths and even used the ribbons over again—well, I ended up by giving in and letting him have the character reference he wanted, gave my French friends as guarantors for myself, and all the rest of it.

"He did the same thing with Leni, at that time she had plenty of political prestige, Leni did, just like her friend Lotte, those two could've gone right to the top—but Leni happened to be like that, she didn't give a damn about getting ahead; Pelzer offered her a partnership—just as I did later on—then he offered her father a partnership, but he had no more use for it than she had, he was suddenly quite the proletarian, would have nothing more to do with business, just laughed and advised Leni to give Pelzer his 'thing,' his clean bill of health, and she did, without taking anything in return of course. This was all after Boris's death, when she had turned into a statue. Well, she gave it to him—just as I did. And that saved him, for we both counted for something. And if you ask me whether I regret it I'll say neither no nor yes nor perhaps, I'll only say: I feel sick at my stomach to think that we had him in our power—understand? In our power, with a piece of paper, a pen, a few phone calls to Baden-Baden and Mainz, and it was that crazy time when Leni was flirting a bit with the Communist Party, and a Communist Party man was on the tribunal, of course, and so on.

"Well anyway: we gave him his character reference and got him out—and I must say, whatever he did as a businessman as a speculator, and whatever shady deals he put over with his predatory instincts, he never was and never became a Fascist, not even later, when it would have been quite useful, and once again became quite useful, to be able to do even *that.* No. Never. I must say that for him, I must give him credit for that, and he never competed unfairly with me, nor against Grundtsch—I must say that for him. And yet—I feel sick at my stomach to think that we had him in our power. And finally even Ilse Kremer went along with it too—he talked her into it, she was a victim of political persecution, and could prove it, and her voice was worth as much as Leni's and mine, and though we two would have been enough he wanted a reference from her too, and got it—and the Kremer woman didn't give a damn either, neither about Pelzer's offer nor about mine nor about the fact that her old Party comrades were now showing up again. She had only one phrase in her head, even in those days: 'I've had enough, I've had enough,' and she'd certainly had enough of her former comrades—she used to call them the Thälmannites who had betrayed her husband or her lover in France, during the year and a half when the Hitler-Stalin pact was in force, which she was against, right from the start.

"So what became of her, Ilse Kremer? Once again an unskilled worker, first for Grundtsch, then back to Pelzer after all, till I took her on myself, and then she started working with Leni at the job we'd done during the war: making wreaths, trimming them, putting ribbons on them, making bouquets, till it was time for her to retire. Somehow or other I felt them both to be a kind of living reproach: although they neither thought it nor expressed it nor even hinted at it, they'd derived no profit, no advantage, and it was all exactly the way it'd been during the war—Ilse Kremer making the morning coffee, and the coffee proportion was for a time a fairly long time, even more miserable than during the war. And they came to work with their head scarves and their sandwiches and their coffee in little paper bags just as they'd always done. Ilse Kremer till '66 and Leni till '69, fortunately she'd been paying in her unemployment contributions for over thirty years, but what she doesn't know and mustn't ever find out is that I took the entire responsibility for her pension affairs and made additional payments out of my own pocket, so that now she at least has a little something. She's as healthy as can be, mind you—but what's she going to get when the pension plan really comes off? Less than four hundred marks, give or take a few. Can you understand—though it makes no sense at all—that I feel her to be a living reproach? Although she never reproaches me, just comes to me from time to time shyly asking for a loan because they're threatening to seize something of hers that she's fond of. I happen to be quite efficient and able to organize, even to rationalize, and I enjoy keeping a tight hand on my chain of stores and expanding it—and yet: there's always something there that makes me very sad. Yes. The fact, too, that I couldn't help Boris, couldn't save him from that ridiculous fate: arrested like that on the street as a German soldier, and he of all people to be killed in a mining accident? Why? And why couldn't I do anything about it? After all, I *had* those good friends among the French, and for me they'd have got not only Boris out but even a

German Nazi if I'd asked them to, but when it finally became clear that it was no longer the Americans who were holding him but the French, it was too late, he was already dead—and they weren't even sure of his fictitious German name—whether he'd been called Bellhorst or Böllhorst or Bull- or Ballhorst, neither Leni nor Margret nor Lotte knew for sure. And why should they? For them he was Boris, and naturally they hadn't looked all that closely at those German identification papers, let alone made a note of the name."

A number of conversations and some extensive research were needed to obtain precise information on the Soviet paradise in the vaults. But at least its duration could be accurately ascertained: from February 20 to March 7, 1945, Leni, Boris, Lotte, Margret, Pelzer, and Lotte's two sons Kurt and Werner, then aged five and ten, lived in catacomblike conditions in a regular "vault system" (Pelzer) under the municipal cemetery. Whereas Boris and Leni had previously been able to spend their "visiting days" above ground in the Beauchamp chapel, now they had to "go underground" (Lotte). The idea originated with Pelzer, who contributed the psychological rationale, as it were.

Cooperative as ever, he received the Au. on a further (and still not final) occasion in his rumpus room adjoining his wreath museum, at the swivel-top built-in bar, where he served highballs and placed an enormous ashtray as big as a fair-sized laurel wreath at the Au.'s elbow. The Au. was struck by the melancholy of a person who had come unscathed through highly contradictory periods of history. A man of seventy who, while not having to worry about a heart attack, still plays his two weekly games of tennis, goes for his regular morning jog, took up riding "at the ripe age of fifty-five" (P. on P.) and, "confidentially" (P. to Au.), "man to man, all I know of potency problems is from hearsay"; this melancholy, so it seemed to the Au., increases from visit to visit, and the truth is—if the Au. may be permitted this psychological conclusion—that the reason for this melancholy of Pelzer's is a surprising one: unrequited love. He still desires Leni, he would be willing "to take the stars down from the sky for her, but it seems she'd rather carry on with unwashed Turks than grant me a few favors, and presumably all because of something for which I was genuinely not to blame. What had I done, after all? If you get right down to it, I actually saved Boris's life. What good would his German uniform and his German papers have done him if he'd had no place to hide, and who was it who knew how scared the Americans are of corpses and cemeteries, of anything to do with death? Yours truly. My experiences in the first war and during the inflation, when I'd worked for that exhumation outfit, had taught me they'd look everywhere but most certainly not in burial vaults—and that goes for the cops, too, the whole pack—they weren't going to be in any hurry to search the nether regions of cemeteries. Obviously Leni couldn't be left alone, with the baby expected any day, and since Lotte and Margret were forced to go into hiding anyway it was clear that Leni couldn't stay behind alone in the apartment.

"So what did I do? After all, I was the only able-bodied man in the group, and my family was somewhere in Bavaria—and I had no wish to join the Home Guard or be taken prisoner by the Americans. So what did I do? I did a regular mining job, digging and propping, digging and propping, till I'd made galleries joining the Herriger vault, the Beauchamp vault, and the extensive von der Zecke burial chambers. That made altogether four little underground rooms, clean and dry as a bone, each measuring about six by eight, a regular four-room apartment. Next I installed electric current, taking it through from my own place, not more than fifty or sixty yards away. I got hold of some small heaters, because of the kids and Leni being pregnant, and—why hide it—there were also recesses for coffins, hollowed out but not yet occupied, reserved seats, so to speak, for the Beauchamps, the Herrigers, and the von der Zeckes. And these, of course, were ideal for storage. Straw on the floor, then mattresses, and, just in case, a little coal stove—for nighttime, of course, it would've been madness to light the thing during the day, as Margret later once tried to do—that girl had no conception of camouflage.

"Now during all this tunneling Grundtsch had been a great

help—all those family burial vaults, of course, were on our list of permanent-care customers—but he refused to live in them, he had a complex about being buried alive, brought back from the first war, you could never get him into any cellar or basement bar, so I had to hand up the baskets of earth to him, he'd never have gone down into a vault, and he refused to live down there with us. Above ground, fine, there the dead didn't scare him, but underground he was scared of his own death. So when things began to get dicey he moved out to his native village west of the city, somewhere between Monschau and Kronenburg—at the end of January '45, if you please! No wonder he walked right into the trap, became a Home Guardsman and, old as he was, landed up in a POW camp.

"So anyway, by about the middle of February I'd got this four-room apartment in the vaults ready, and February was a quiet month, only one air raid, just once for half an hour or so, a few bombs you could hardly hear. So one night I moved in there with Lotte and her two kids, then Margret joined us, and if anyone tells you I made a pass at her I'd say: I did and I didn't. There we were, us two in the two von der Zecke rooms, Lotte next door with her kids at the Herrigers', and of course for Leni and Boris we'd reserved their original love nest, the Beauchamp vault, with mattresses and straw and an electric heater, some crackers, water, milk powder, a bit of tobacco, methylated spirit, beer—just like in an air-raid shelter. Sometimes we could hear the sound of artillery from the Erft front, that's where at the last moment they'd sent the Russians to build fortifications—Boris with a German uniform in his pack, complete with medals and decorations, all the things that went with those damn papers—so anyway, the Russians were still building fortifications and gun emplacements, living in barns and no longer quite so strictly guarded, and one day Leni turned up on her stolen bike with Boris riding on the crossbar. I must say the German uniform looked pretty good on him, and the phony bandage looked great—he even had a wound-tag, all stamped and signed, that's how they got past the cops, and they moved into their own little home in the cemetery around February 20, and it turned out I was right: no patrols, either German or American, dared go down into the vaults, and we lived an idyllic existence there, sometimes hearing nothing, seeing nothing, for days on end, and for appearances' sake I worked during the day at my place, for naturally people were still dying and had to be buried, no longer quite so elaborately, no more salvos, no more proper wreaths but still a few branches of fir, sometimes a flower—it really was madness. In the evening I'd walk back toward home, later I rode there on Leni's stolen bike—but part-way there I'd turn around and go back to the cemetery.

"I need hardly say that those Hoyser brats were a regular nuisance, the cheekiest little bastards imaginable, crafty and unscrupulous, the only thing that kept them quiet was: learning, and what they wanted to learn was obvious: how to make money. They'd pick my brains on costing and bookkeeping and so forth. Even in those days they treated their mother like a doormat, and if there'd been such a game as Monopoly we could've kept those cheeky little brats quiet for weeks on end. They understood, mind you, that they had to be quiet and not show themselves outside, for they had no wish to be forcibly evacuated, oh no, that much they grasped, but the things they got up to inside! I mean, there are limits, surely, I mean a bit of respect for the dead and all that, surely that's in everyone, even in me—but those brats dreamed of treasure in the graves, and sometimes they were on the point of unscrewing the tablets from the niches, looking for that damn treasure. If anyone says I made money from the gold teeth of the dead—I'll say of those kids that they'd have made money from the gold teeth of the living. If Lotte says now that her kids were taken out of her hands, then I say she never had them in her hands. They'd been trained by their grandmother, who was dead, and by their grandfather, who was still alive, for one thing only: to take every last advantage and to accumulate assets. One thing I never did—something all the others did, Margret, Leni, Lotte, even Boris—I never collected my own cigarette butts, let alone other people's, I find that absolutely disgusting. I've always liked everything neat and clean, and anyone will back me up when I say I used to go outside in the cold, break open the ice in the water tank we used for watering the graves—watering the flowers, I mean—and wash myself from head to foot, and if it was at all possible I'd go for my regular morning jog, even then, though later on it became my nightly jog, and that damn butt-collecting was something I hated.

"Well, anyway, toward the end of February, just before we went for our great haul to the Schnürer Gasse on 'the Second,' we found ourselves running pretty short in that Soviet paradise in the vaults—we had miscalculated, that was all, we'd expected the Americans a week earlier—and even the crackers were beginning to get low, and the butter too, and even the ersatz coffee, and needless to say the cigarettes; and along came those brats with neatly rolled cigarettes that they'd rolled with their mother's cigarette machine, they'd got the paper from that good-natured Margret—and they sold me, as it turned out later, my own butts as freshly rolled cigarettes! And in their eyes ten marks apiece was a fair price!

"Those women laughed and thought the boys' realistic approach was great, but I felt cold shivers up and down my spine as I haggled with those cute little devils. It wasn't the money, mind you, I had plenty of that, and I'd have paid fifty for a cigarette—it was the principle of the thing! The principle was all wrong. To be amused at such young kids' being so mercenary, and to laugh at it! Only Boris shook his head, later Leni did too, when, after 'the Second,' the kids began building up a little stock they called their capital. A can of lard here, a package of cigarettes there—we were all much too much on edge to pay proper attention. Leni's baby, remember, was born on the evening of 'the Second,' and she didn't want to have it—and I can understand that—in a burial vault, and her Saint Joseph didn't want that either. So they walked across the cemetery, all full of bomb pits it was, to the nursery garden, Leni already in labor, Margret with the medical supplies, and they proceeded to make her a bed of peat moss and old blankets and straw matting, and that's where she had her baby, probably right where it was conceived.

"It was a boy, weighing nearly eight pounds, and since it was born on March 2 it must, if I can still count, have been conceived around June 2—and you won't find a single daylight raid around that time, not one! Nor was there any night shift worked that date, my payroll sheets prove that, and certainly not by Boris—so that must mean they took advantage of some opportunity in broad daylight.

"Well, O.K., it's all past history now, but it was a far cry from being a Soviet paradise. You should have seen the cemetery after the raid on 'the Second': heads of angels and saints knocked off, graves torn up, with and without coffins, take your choice, and us totally exhausted after the horribly dangerous job of lugging and carting our loot away from the Schnürer Gasse, and, to cap it all, the baby being born that evening! It all went quickly and smoothly, by the way. Talk about Soviet paradise though! Do you know who was the only person to teach us how to pray again? That Soviet fellow! That's right. Taught us to pray, he did. A fine lad, I don't mind telling you, and if he'd listened to me he'd be alive today. It was madness, it really was, to move so soon—on the afternoon of the seventh—back into town with the women and kids, carrying those lousy German army papers in his pocket and nothing else. The boy could have stayed down there in the vault for months, reading his Kleist and his Hölderlin and I don't know what all—I'd even have got hold of a Pushkin for him—till he'd been able to produce some discharge papers, genuine or forged. Farm workers were already being discharged from American POW camps that summer, and all he lacked was some decent British or American discharge papers. Those women never thought of that, they were all caught up in the excitement over the peace and in sheer joy at being alive, but it was a bit premature for that. And talk about those evenings and afternoons sitting by the Rhine, for months on end, with the baby and those Hoyser brats and Grandpa Gruyten with that perpetual smile of his: the boy could be sitting by the Rhine today, or the Volga, if he'd wanted to.

"That's what I'd got hold of for myself, before I showed up officially in early June: discharge papers, in my own name with a proper POW number, the camp rubber stamp—after all, our trade could be classified as agricultural—it was all quite logical and proper, and God knows there was enough to do in my line, I mean, people didn't even have to die, enough had died already, and somehow or other they all had to be got under the ground. That was something Lotte and Margret never thought of, either of them, in spite of all their connections, getting proper discharge papers for the boy—Margret could have done it with a wiggle of her hips, and Lotte would only have had to think of it, with all her rubber stamps and forms and connections. It was plain irresponsible not to legalize the boy after May or June, even if he'd had to call himself Friedrich Krupp. I'd certainly have been prepared to pay a price for that—I wasn't only fond of the lad, I loved him, and you may smile: but it was he who taught me that all that stuff about subhumans and so forth is just so much crap. Talk about subhumans—they were right here."

Were Pelzer's tears genuine? Before he had even finished one highball there were tears in his eyes, tears that he wiped away with a furtive gesture. "And am I to blame for the death of Leni's father? Me? Must I be avoided like the plague because of that? Tell me, what did I do other than give Leni's father a real opportunity? Any child could see he wasn't even a good plasterer, he couldn't do a decent job even with the best materials, and as for his work gang, people used them because there weren't any others, but then all the people he worked for found that their ceilings fell down again or the plaster crumbled off the walls—he simply hadn't learned how to plaster, he didn't know how to cast the stuff, didn't know how to swing his arm properly, and all that about not wanting to be a businessman any more and deliberately pretending to be a proletarian, that was nothing but a fantasy he'd thought up in jail or in camp, or been inoculated with by other inmates who were Communists. I don't mind telling you, that was a real disappointment, the great man with the great scandal in his past turning out to be a regular duffer who didn't even know how to fix up a wall properly. And it was just a kind of snobbishness, you know, suddenly starting to go from house to house with an old pushcart, a few galvanized tubs, and a trowel, a spatula, and a shovel, offering his services as a plasterer in return for potatoes, bread, and the occasional cigar.

And that sitting by the Rhine with daughter and grandson and son-in-law, singing ditties and watching the ships—that wasn't the right thing for a man with such terrific organizational talents and guts.

"I made him several fair offers, I told him: 'Gruyten,' I said, 'look, I've got three or four hundred thousand marks which, try as I might, I wasn't able to invest in firm or even reasonably safe assets: take it, use it to start a business, and when the inflation's over give it back to me, not one to one, not two to one, no, three to one and no interest. You're smart enough to realize that this cigarette-currency is kid stuff, it's all right for returning nihilists who had nothing to smoke in camp, it's all right for kids and nicotine addicts like bombed-out women or war widows, you know as well as I do that one day cigarettes are going to cost five pfennigs again or at most ten, and if you invest five marks fifty today in a cigarette which you sell at the next corner for six fifty, that's just kid stuff, and if you intend keeping the cigarettes till the currency gets hard again, then I'm willing to bet that for your five marks fifty you'll get five pfennigs, provided the cigarettes haven't gone moldy by then.' He laughed, he thought I was suggesting he go into the cigarette business, whereas I was just using that as an example.

"Now naturally I thought he'd start up a construction business, and if he'd been a bit smarter he could have passed himself off as a victim of political persecution. But no, he didn't want to do that. I ended up having to invest my money after all, and in those days there wasn't much doing in real estate. If Leni had sold me her building earlier for half a million I'd have undertaken to provide her with a rent-free apartment for the rest of her life. What did Hoyser give her for it? Four times the unit value: all of sixty thousand, and that in December of '44—it's beyond belief!

"Well, there I sat with my money. I had invested where I could, in furniture and pictures and rugs, I even bought books, but I was still left with that chunk of three or four hundred thousand that I had at home in cash. And then I got an idea, everyone laughed and said: 'That Pelzer's become human after all, for the first time in his life he's doing business that makes no sense.'

What did I do? I bought scrap, not any old scrap, only steel girders of the best quality, legally of course, I even got myself wrecking permits wherever I could—most people were glad to get their properties cleared of rubble that way. As for the girders—it was merely a matter of storing them, and for that I had plenty of land: so what was to stop me!

"Do you know what the wages of a nursery-garden worker like Leni or the Kremer woman were at that time? All of fifty pfennigs an hour. And an unskilled construction worker, well, he might've got one mark and, if he was lucky, one mark twenty, but the real plums were the supplementary ration cards for heavy manual labor, with these you got fat, bread, sugar, and so forth, and in order to get those you naturally had to found a company. So I did, my company was called 'Demolition Inc.,' and half the town laughed their heads off when I began collecting steel girders, there were miles and miles of them, of course, all Europe was buried under steel, and for a shot-up tank you didn't even get two packages of cigarettes—well, I let them laugh. I employed four gangs, supplied them with tools, got my wrecking permits, and systematically collected steel girders. Because I thought: laugh away, steel's steel and always will be. Those were the days when you could get old battleships, tanks, and airplanes for a song, if you'd only cart them away, and I did that too: carted away tanks, I had plenty of land not yet built on.

"So that was how I managed to invest my entire capital between 1945 and 1948: over three hundred thousand feet of steel girders of the very finest quality, neatly stacked up and stored, and right from the start I didn't pay according to the regular wage scale, I didn't let those men work for eight or ten marks a day, I paid by piecework, a mark a foot, and some of them, depending on the location, easily made as much as a hundred and fifty marks a day or more, and in addition to that they all got their manual workers' rations. That was a fringe benefit.

"We moved systematically from the outskirts of the city in toward the center, where the big stores and office buildings were. It got a bit more difficult there because so much concrete was still clinging to the girders, and sometimes a whole tangle of reinforcing rods had to burned off. In cases like that, of course, I had to pay a mark fifty or two marks a foot, even as high as three fifty, a thing like that has to be negotiated, the way you negotiate in a mine depending on the location of the coal. Fair enough. Leni's father was in charge of one of these gangs, and naturally he took a hand too, and depending on how many feet of steel were delivered to me in the evening, so and so much cash would be paid: into the open palms went the bills, and some fellows would take home three hundred marks at the end of the day, some of course only eighty, but never less than that. And that at a time when the workers in my nursery were earning barely sixty a week. And still half the town was laughing at my girder collection as it lay rusting on my lots on Schönstätter Strasse, at a time when blast furnaces were being dismantled! Anyway: I hung on, if only out of stubbornness.

"Now I'll admit the work wasn't entirely without its dangers, but after all I never forced anyone to do it, never: it was a straight offer, a straight business deal, and I just ignored whatever else they found lying around in the ruins: furniture and junk, books and household utensils and so forth. That was their own business. People were laughing themselves sick, and whenever they walked past my lots they'd say 'There's Pelzer's money, rusting away.' And among my pals in the Mardi Gras club, the 'Evergreens,' there were even some wits—construction engineers and so forth—who calculated for my benefit exactly how much money was actually being eaten up by rust: they had their conversion tables from bridge-building and stuff like that, all the figures, and to tell the truth, by that time even I was beginning to doubt whether I'd make a good investment. But the funny thing was that in 1953, when the stuff had been lying there between five and eight years and I had to get rid of it—and wanted to, what's more, if only to be able to build on the lots because of the housing shortage, and I cleared a million and a half marks for it, they all called me a scoundrel, a speculator, a profiteer, and I don't know what all. Suddenly even the old tanks were worth something too and the trucks and all that extra junk I'd had carted away—all quite legally of course—merely because those two huge lots of mine had been empty and I had all that money lying around.

"Well, it was then that the terrible thing happened, the thing those women have never forgiven me. Leni's father was killed in an accident while getting out scrap metal from the ruins of what was once the Health Department. I never doubted that this work might be dangerous, some of it highly dangerous, and I used to give the men supplementary risk-pay, that's to say I raised the fixed rate per foot, which was the equivalent of risk-pay, and I warned old Gruyten when he began waving the cutting-torch around, and I ask you, how was I to know he had so little sense of statics that he would burn the ground from under his feet, so to speak, and go crashing twenty-five feet into the ruins? Good God, he was a construction man, wasn't he, he had an engineering degree, didn't he, and he must have used ten times as many steel girders in the course of his career as I'd managed to get out of the ruins in five years—how was I supposed to know he would bring about his own downfall, so to speak? Could I foresee that, am I to blame for that? Didn't everyone know it's a risky business, burning out steel girders from a bombed concrete building in a ruined city, and didn't I pay for this risk accordingly? And, to be honest, not once on the job, either collecting those girders or cutting or burning them out did that almost mythical construction man Gruyten prove particularly skillful, or even theoretically technically informed—I paid him a bit extra on the q.t. because of Leni, since what was going to happen to her and Boris mattered a good deal to me."

Pelzer's tears were now flowing so fast that it would have been a crime to doubt their physical genuineness, whereas it is beyond the Au.'s competence to pass an opinion on their emotional genuineness. On he went, in a low voice, clutching his highball glass, looking around as if his rumpus room, his bar, his wreath collection in the next room, were unfamiliar to him: "It was a terrible fate, to be impaled like that on a bunch of reinforcing rods that was sticking up out of a concrete slab, transfixed, not mangled, just transfixed, transfixed in four places through his neck, through the abdomen, through the chest, and again through the right arm above the elbow, and—it was terrible, awful I tell you—smiling. Still smiling—crazy, he looked like a crucified madman. Madness. And then to blame me for it! And" (hesitation in P.'s voice, anguish in his eyes, trembling hands. Au.) "and the cutting-torch hung hissing, spitting, steaming from the remains of the projecting girder that Gruyten had just burned off. It was crazy, the whole thing, one month before the currency reform, when I was just about to wind up my girder-collecting and anyway my entire Reichsmark capital had been used up.

"Needless to say, right after the accident I liquidated the whole business, and if those women say I did that because I'd wanted to wind it up anyway, that's a monstrous lie: I tell you, I'd have stopped even if it'd been the middle of 1946. But just try and prove a 'would have, if,' just try and prove that. But as it happened, in actual fact, one month before the currency reform—that's how it was, and there I sat, those women breathing hatred down my neck and with scorn in their faces all on account of my scrap pile, which went on steadily rusting away and continued to lie there for another five years. And because old Gruyten hadn't been insured—I'd taken him on as a kind of free-lance colleague after all, not as a worker or as an employee, but more or less as a subcontractor—I volunteered to pay Leni and Lotte a small pension: nothing doing—Lotte spat at me once as I was leaving her place. 'Bloodsucker,' she screamed, and 'crucifier' and worse. Yet I saved her life in that Soviet paradise in the vaults, I shut her mouth with my own hand when she suddenly began yelling socialist slogans like a madwoman during that looting in the Schnürer Gässe. I put up with her brats, bought my own cigarette butts back as freshly rolled cigarettes from those cunning little devils, when we started to run low at the end of February, in our vaults—we spent almost seven hours cooped up together on 'the Second,' clinging to one another, our teeth chattering, and believe me, even that atheist Lotte was murmuring her Our Father after Boris as he recited it for us, even the Hoyser brats were quiet, scared and awed, Margret was crying, we had our arms around one another like brothers and sisters as we crouched there thinking our last moment had come. I tell you, it was as if the world were coming to an end. It didn't matter any more whether one person had once been a Nazi or a Communist, the other a Russian soldier, and Margret an all-too-merciful sister of mercy, only one thing mattered: life or death. Even if you'd more or less kept out of the churches they still meant something to you, they were part of the scene, after all, part of life—and in one single day they were reduced to dust, for days we'd still be gritting dust between our teeth, feeling it on our gums—and when the raid was over, out we rushed, the moment we could, to take possession together—together I tell you—of our legacy from the German Army—and that same day, just as it was beginning to get dark, to help bring Leni's and Boris's son into the world."

Still tears, and the voice softer, still softer: "The only person who understood me, who was fond of me, whom I'd taken like a son to my heart, into my family, my business, anything you like, who was closer to me than my wife, closer than my kids are to me today—you know who that was? Boris Lvovich—I loved that boy, although he robbed me of the girl I still hanker after today—the fact is, he really knew me, knew me for what I was, he insisted on my baptizing the little boy. Me. With these hands, yes—and I don't mind telling you, a kind of shock of horror ran through my body when I thought in a flash of all the things those hands had been responsible for, what they'd done to the living and to the dead, to women and to men, with checks and with cash boxes, with wreaths and ribbons and so forth—and he wanted me, me, with these hands, to baptize his little boy. Even Lotte shut her trap then, she'd been on the verge of making her usual remark about crap—she was flabbergasted, speechless, when Boris said to me: 'Walter,' he said—after what we'd been through together we all used first names—'Walter,' he said, 'I ask that you now perform an emergency baptism for our son.' And I did—I went into my office, turned on the faucet, waited till the rust and dirt had run out and the water ran clearer, rinsed out my tumbler, filled it with water, and baptized him, the way I'd so often seen it done when I was an altar boy—and because I couldn't be godfather too, of course, that much I knew, young Werner and Lotte held the baby, and I baptized him with the words: 'In the name of the Father and of the Son and of the Holy Ghost I baptize thee Lev'—and at that point even that little rascal Kurt burst into tears and even that shrew Lotte, and Boris, and Margret was in floods anyway—only Leni didn't cry, she lay there, radiant, her eyes open and inflamed with dust, and at once put the baby to her breast. Yes, that's how it all happened, and now, would you mind leaving—its stirred up too much inside me."

The Au. frankly admits that all this had stirred him considerably too, and that he had a hard time suppressing a tear or two that welled up as he seated himself at the wheel of his car. To avoid giving way to excessive sentimentality he drove straight to Bogakov, whom he found in pleasant circumstances: sitting in a wheelchair on a glass-roofed terrace, wrapped in blankets, looking pensively out over an extensive garden-allotment colony toward the intersection of two railroad tracks, between which a gravel pit, a nursery garden, and a scrap yard were squeezed. Somewhere among all this, the incongruous sight of a tennis court, with puddles still visible on its faded red surface, Starfighters in the air, traffic noise from a bypass, children playing hockey with empty cans on the paths between the allotment gardens. Bogakov, likewise in sentimental mood, without his smoking gallows, alone on the terrace, declined the proffered cigarette and took hold of the Au.'s wrist as if he—Bogakov—wanted to feel his—the Au.'s—pulse.

"You know, I left a wife back there, and a son who I imagine would be about your age if he has survived the twenty thousand possibilities of coming to a sticky end. My boy Lavrik was nineteen in '44, and they're sure to have taken him—who knows where—and sometimes, you know, I think of going back and dying there, never mind where—and my wife Larissa, I wonder if she's still alive? I was unfaithful to her as soon as I got a chance in February '45 when they sent us to the Erft front to dig ditches and foxholes and gun emplacements. That was the first time in four years that I'd laid hands on a woman and visited with her—in the dark, we were lying there in a barn every which way, Russians and Germans, soldiers, prisoners, women —and I couldn't tell you how old she was—well, I can't say she resisted, only later she cried a bit, because I suppose neither of us was used to it, adultery if you can call it that, in that darkness, in that madness, with no one knowing where they belonged—there we lay among the straw and the sugar beets, in Grossbüllesheim, a real rich kulak village—my God, we both cried, I did too—it was really more of a crawling close together in fear and darkness and dirt, we fellows with mud on our feet, and maybe she took me for a German or an American since there were a few half-frozen wounded American boys lying around there too, someone was supposed to get them to a hospital or to an assembly point, but I guess he deserted and just left the boys lying there, and about all they could say at that point was 'fucking war' and 'fucking generals' and 'shit on the fucking Hürtgen Forest'—that wasn't hands across the Elbe, it was hands across the Erft, and it was along a pitiful little river like that, one you could've spat across, that the Erft front was to be formed, between the Rhine and the western frontier—a boy of ten could've pissed across it. Well, sometimes I think of the woman who opened up to me—I stroked her cheek and her hair, it was thick and smooth. I don't even know whether it was fair or dark or whether she was thirty or fifty or what her name was.

"We got there in the dark and left again in the dark—all I saw was those big farms, fires burning where men were cooking their meals, soldiers, those frozen Americans, and us in the middle of it all, Boris was there too, Leni following him like the girl with the seven pairs of iron shoes—I hope you know that nice little fairy tale. Darkness, mud on our feet, sugar beets, a woman's cheek, her hair, her tears—and, well yes, the inside of her body. Marie or Paula or Katharina, and I hope it never occurred to her to tell her husband about it or to whisper it to some father confessor.

"No my boy, don't take away your hand, it's good to feel the pulse of a human being. The pickle-eater and the world-weary

Russian from Leningrad have gone off to the movies. To see a Soviet film about the battle of Kursk. That's fine with me. I was taken prisoner by the Germans back in August '41, my boy, in some lousy battle not far from Kirovograd. Anyway, that's what the town was still called in those days, who knows what it's called today, considering what they did to Kirov—that was my man, our man, Kirov—well O.K., so he's gone.

"It wasn't very salubrious, that German POW camp of yours, my boy, and if you tell me that ours weren't salubrious either then I'll tell you that our people were going through just as bad a time as the German prisoners—for three days, four days, we marched through villages and across fields and went almost crazy with thirst—whenever we saw a spring or a little stream we'd lick our lips with thirst and quit thinking about eating—five thousand of us stuck into a cattle yard on a kolkhoz, out in the open, and still thirsty. And when peaceful civilians, our own people, tried to bring us something to drink or eat they weren't allowed near us—the guards just fired right into them—and if one of our own lot approached the civilians: machine gun, my boy, and that was the end of him. One woman sent a little girl, maybe five years old, toward us with some bread and milk, a really sweet little Natasha—she must have thought they wouldn't do anything to a sweet little kid like that, carrying milk in a jug and bread in her hand, but nothing doing—machine gun—and our little Natasha was as dead as any of the others, and there was milk and blood and bread on the ground.

"So we went from Tarnovka to Uman, from Uman to Ivan-Gora, from Ivan-Gora to Gaizin, and from there to Vinnitsa, then to Shmerinka on the sixth day and on to Rakovo, that was near Prokurov; twice a day some thin pea soup—they just set the soup kettles down among the crowd, and the crowd consisted of twenty to thirty thousand men; then came the rush to the kettles—we used our bare hands to scoop the soup out of the pot and we lapped it up like dogs, if we got any—sometimes there were half-cooked sugar beets, cabbage or potatoes, and if you ate any of that stuff you got stomach cramps, diarrhea—and you kicked off at the roadside. We stayed there till almost March

'42; and sometimes there'd be eight or nine hundred dead a day—and at intervals beatings and taunts, taunts and beatings, and now and again they'd fire into the crowd—and even if they had nothing for us to eat, or claimed they hadn't, why didn't they let the peaceful local inhabitants get near us, the ones who wanted to bring us things?

"Then I worked at Krupp's in Königsberg, in a plant that made caterpillar treads—you worked eleven hours night shift and twelve day—and slept in the urinals, and if you were lucky you managed to get a dog kennel, it was cramped but at least you were alone for once. The worst thing was to get sick, or for them to think you were loafing—the loafers were handed over to the SS, and when you got sick and couldn't work any more there were only the mass hospitals, which actually were nothing more than extermination camps, death camps, disguised as hospitals, crowded to four times their capacity, run down and filthy, and the daily ration consisted of 9 ounces of substitute bread and two quarts of Balanda soup: the substitute bread consisted mostly of substitute flour, and the substitute flour was nothing more than coarsely chopped straw, chaff, and even wood fibers—the chaff, the husks, irritated your guts, and it wasn't nourishment, it was systematic undernourishment—and then the constant beatings and taunts, and the constant swinging of the club. Eventually even the chaff must have been considered too good for us, and there was sawdust in the bread, up to two thirds, and the Balanda soup consisted of rotten potatoes mixed with every conceivable kind of kitchen garbage flavored with rat droppings—sometimes a hundred men would die in one day.

"It was virtually impossible to get out of there alive, you really had to be one of Fortune's favorites, and I guess that's what I was: I simply stopped eating the stuff, I was hungry, but at least I wasn't sick, I realized right off that it was poisonous—and it was better to spend another twelve hours assembling caterpillar treads for Mr. Krupp. Now you see what a bit of luck it was to be sent into a city to collect corpses and clear ruins, and how Boris seemed to us like a fairy-tale prince who ends up by becoming king after all. He was allowed to make wreaths at a nursery without even having learned how to be a gardener, a special guard came to pick him up in the morning and brought him back in the evening, he didn't get beaten, he even got things given to him, and—something really nobody knew but me—he even had a girl he loved and who loved him. He was a prince all right! And the rest of us, while we weren't exactly princes, we were certainly favored by Fortune. Not that we were worthy, mind you, of handling and removing German bodies, oh no, but we were allowed to shovel rubble into trucks and repair railroad tracks, and sometimes while we were digging into the rubble the inevitable happened: some Russian hand, a shovel directed by a Russian, would come upon a body and that always meant a break, an undeserved bit of luck—till the bodies had been removed, bodies for which Boris was making wreaths somewhere and arranging flowers and choosing ribbons. And sometimes there'd be smashed kitchen cabinets and buffets in among the ruins, and there might be something in there that you could use, and of course there would be times when by some lucky coincidence the guard happened not to be looking *when* you found something to eat, and days when you got a triple break: you found something, the guard wasn't looking, and you didn't get searched. If a fellow got caught, he had a bad time: not even the Germans were allowed to take anything, and if you as a Russian slipped something into your pocket, well, you suffered the same fate as Gavril Ossipovich and Alexei Ivanovich, they were handed over to the SS for punishment, and the next thing was rat-a-tat rat-a-tat. Your best bet, when you found something, was to eat it then and there, and you had to take care how you chewed, for though it wasn't forbidden to eat while on the job for the simple reason that there was no need to forbid it—the question was, how could the likes of us ever get hold of anything to eat? You had to have stolen it.

"I must say we were lucky with our camp commandant, he'd have us locked up when we were reported, and only if the sergeant insisted on handing one of us over to the SS would he do it, anyway he insisted that we at least get our rations properly. Once when I was being searched I listened in while he was on the phone to some higher-up and arguing about whether or not the work we were doing was to be classified as *of any significance;* for work of *some* significance, you see, we got roughly 11 ounces of bread, three quarters of an ounce of meat, half an ounce of fat, and an ounce and a quarter of sugar a day, for work of *no* significance the rations were only 8 ounces of bread, a third of an ounce of fat and meat, and not quite three quarters of an ounce of sugar—he was arguing away with someone in Berlin or Düsseldorf about having our work classified as of some significance; after all, my friend, after all—it meant a difference of 3 ounces of bread, an eighth of an ounce of fat, a quarter of an ounce of meat, and half an ounce of sugar more or less—he was a pretty forceful fellow, that major of ours, he had an arm, a leg, and an eye less than a complete man should have. He was roaring away there while I was being searched, and later on he really did save our lives, the lives of the twelve camp survivors. Thirty had already got away, during the heavy air raids, they'd crawled away into the ruins or made off to the west in the direction of the Americans, led by our tireless Viktor Genrikhovich—that was the last we heard of them, and the rest of us, including Boris, who was cheerfully waiting to be taken off to his nursery garden, woke up one morning to find that all our guards had deserted as one man and in a body; no sentry, the guardroom open, the gates open, only the barbed wire was still there—and the view we had was exactly the same as the one from here, from the terrace: railway tracks, allotments, gravel pit, scrap yard—and so there we were with our freedom, and believe me, it was a lousy feeling. What were we to do with this freedom and where were we to go in it? It wasn't the safest thing in the world, simply to roam the countryside as a released Soviet prisoner of war—and that action of the guards had been their personal end to the war, not the official one, and most likely some of them were picked up too, and strung up or stood against a wall.

"We went into a huddle and decided to inform the camp authorities on the state of affairs; if that major hadn't deserted, he would help us to get rid of this freedom which, just at the moment, was highly inopportune and dangerous—there was no sense in simply running off into the arms of the next patrol, the cops; for there's one very simple method of getting rid of people whom it's too much trouble to watch, lock up, and sentence: you shoot them and, as I'm sure you'll understand, we weren't too keen on that.

"Now we could already hear the artillery at times, and it did sound like a bit of genuine freedom—but just to be set free like that was too risky for our taste. Viktor Genrikhovich's action had been carefully planned, with maps and provisions and a few addresses he'd got hold of through his satellites or his mail drops; they went off in groups, arranging to meet in Heinsberg on the Dutch border and to go on to Arnhem, good enough. But we fellows, we were totally taken aback by this freedom that had been presented to us overnight. Five had the guts to make use of it, they scraped up some old duds, changed a bit, and off they went across the railway tracks, disguised as a work gang with shovels and pickaxes, not a bad idea. But the seven of us who were left were scared, and naturally Boris didn't want to leave Leni. And naturally he couldn't go and see her alone without his nursemaid Kolb, so Boris went straight to the phone, managed to reach the nursery garden, gave the alarm, and half an hour later the girl was waiting with her bike down there at the corner of Näggerath and Wildersdorfer Strasse. Next, Boris phoned the camp and informed them we had no guards, and in less than half an hour the one-armed, one-legged, one-eyed major turned up with a few soldiers in his car and first marched through the hut without a word; he had a very well-fitting marvelous artificial leg, he could even ride a bike with it—then he went into the guardroom, came out again, summoned Boris and thanked him, with a proper handshake, man-to-man and all that. Proper German behavior, and not so ridiculous as it may sound. Damn it all, that was two weeks before the Americans reached the city, and what did he do, that major, he sent us off in their direction! To the Erft front, which they'd already reached. And to Boris he said: 'Koltovsky, I regret to say that I am obliged to regard your gardening duties as hereby terminated.' But I saw the girl talking to the major's driver, and it must have been from him that she found out where we were going, and it was plain as could be that she was pregnant, like a sunflower when the seeds are just ready to burst, and I drew my own conclusions.

"So twenty minutes later we followed in a truck, first to Grossbüllesheim, then to Grossvernich, then on again at night to Balkhausen, and by the time we'd been taken as far as Frechen, again at night, Boris and I were the only ones left, the others had cottoned on to the major's hint and had crawled across the sugar beet fields at night to the Americans, and our prince was dressed up by his princess in a German uniform, bandaged with gauze, smeared with chicken blood, and transported to the cemetery.

"As for me, I did something utterly crazy: I went back to town, alone, at night, at the end of February, to that ruined, devastated city where I'd spent a whole year shoveling rubble and uncovering bodies, where I'd been insulted and taunted but also where some passerby had now and then tossed a butt or a whole cigarette and sometimes an apple or a slice of bread at my feet, when the guard wasn't looking or chose not to look—I went back into town and hid in a bombed-out villa, in the cellar, which had half collapsed so that the ceiling formed a sloping roof for me, and there in that sheltered corner I waited. I'd pinched some bread and eggs from the farmers and I drank rainwater from a puddle in the laundry room, during the day I collected wood, hardwood flooring, that burns so well, and I rummaged around among the splintered furniture till I finally found something to smoke: six fat expensive cigars in a proper capitalist-type leather cigar case, imprinted with the words: Lucerne 1919, I still have it, I can show it to you—and six expensive fat cigars, if you're not too extravagant that makes thirty-six quite passable cigarettes, and if you have matches as well it's a fortune, and not only matches but cigarette paper, in the form of a prayer book from Grossvernich, printed on India paper, five hundred pages and the name on the flyleaf was: Katharina Wermelskirchen, First Communion 1878—and naturally before rolling my cigarettes I'd read what was on each page: 'Examine thy conscience and see wherein thou hast offended God in thought, word, or deed. I have sinned, O Father, mightily have I sinned against Heaven and against

Thee. I have strayed like a lost lamb, I am not worthy to be called Thy child.' I owed the poor old paper at least that much before it went up in smoke.

"So there I was, bundled up in whatever bits of stuff, rags or otherwise, I found lying around: drapes and remains of tablecloths, women's slips and bits of rug, and at night my little fire of hardwood flooring—that's where I was on 'the Second,' that thunder from Heaven, that Hell, that Last Judgment, and now I'll tell you something I've never told anyone, I haven't even told myself yet, I fell in love with this city, with its dust that I had eaten, with its earth that had rocked and with the church spires that collapsed, and with the women I crawled in with afterwards during those cold, cold winters when there was nothing to warm you up but the nearest woman you could crawl in with. By that time there was no way I could leave this city, may Lavrik and Larissa forgive me, and may she forgive what I read in that prayer book: 'Hast thou conducted thyself in the holy state of matrimony according to thy duty? Hast thou sinned against it in thought, word, or deed? Hast thou deliberately or consentingly—even if in fact no act took place—desired to sin with the spouse of another or with a single person?" Questions put to Katharina Wermelskirchen that I am obliged to answer in the affirmative but which she, let's hope, could answer in the negative, and perhaps this is the best way of approaching prayer, using prayer books as cigarette paper and promising yourself to read each page carefully before rolling your cigarette. And now leave your hand in mine and say nothing" (which the deeply disturbed Au. did, noting that Bogakov gave evidence of T. and W., also of P. and, with a probability bordering on certainty, of S.).

At this juncture, as a modest supplement to Bogakov's factual information and for purposes of illustration, the Au. takes the liberty of quoting a brief selection of documented quotations, some directly from the lips of certain high-placed personages, some from depositions and reports of such personages.

"ALFRED ROSENBERG: "Some of them seem to imagine that

being sent to Germany is something like being sent to Siberia.

"I am aware that when 3½ million people are brought here it is impossible to provide them with luxury accommodation. For thousands of people to be badly accommodated or badly treated is only to be expected. There is no need for us to lose sleep over that. But it is a very down-to-earth question—and I assume that Gauleiter Sauckel has already discussed it or intends to do so later: these people from the East [Eastern Europe] are being brought to Germany to work and to achieve the utmost in productivity. This is a perfectly natural state of affairs. In order to achieve high productivity it is obvious that they must not be brought here three-quarters frozen or allowed to stand for ten hours; on the contrary, they must be given enough to eat so they may have reserves of energy. . . ."

"The right to disciplinary action is accorded every supervisor of Polish agricultural workers. . . . In such cases, such a supervisor may not be called to account for his actions by any authority.

"Agricultural workers of Polish origin are to be excluded as far as possible from the domestic environment and can be accommodated in stables, etc. No qualms must be permitted to stand in the way of this."

"ALBERT SPEER: In view of modern conveyor-belt production methods, working hours should remain constant throughout the month. Air raids have caused interruptions in deliveries from plants supplying parts and raw materials. As a result, hours of work in the plants have fluctuated from eight to twelve hours a day. According to our statistics, the average must have been approximately 60 to 64 hours a week.

"DR. FLÄCHSNER: What were the working hours of the workers in factories staffed by concentration-camp inmates?

"SPEER: Exactly the same as those of other workers in the plant. The workers from concentration camps usually formed only one segment of the work force, and that segment was not required to work any harder than any of the other workers.

"DR. FLÄCHSNER: What was the reason for that?

"SPEER: It was a stipulation of the SS that the inmates of the concentration camps form a separate body in one section of the factory. Supervisory personnel consisted of German head workers and foremen. The hours of work had to match those of the whole plant because, as is well known, all work in a plant must proceed at the same rate.

"DR. FLÄCHSNER: From each of two documents which I shall produce in another context the fact emerges that, in the munitions industries of the Army, Navy, and Air Force, workers from concentration camps worked an average of 60 hours a week.

"In that case, Mr. Speer, why were special concentration-camp quarters established at the plants and known as work camps?

"SPEER: Those work camps were established in order to avoid long distances for the inmates and thus ensure that the worker was *fresh and eager to work when at the plant* (italics are the Au.'s).

"Bolshevism is the mortal enemy of National Socialist Germany. . . . Consequently the Bolshevik soldier has forfeited all claim to treatment as an honorable soldier and according to the Geneva Convention. . . . The sense of pride and superiority of the German soldier who is ordered to guard Soviet prisoners of war must at all times be apparent to the public. . . . Hence orders are for ruthless and forceful action at the slightest sign of resistance, particularly toward Bolshevik agitators. . . . In dealing with Soviet prisoners of war, disciplinary reasons alone require that weapons be used at the slightest provocation.

"The German Army must forthwith eliminate all those elements among prisoners of war that may be considered Bolshevik agitators. Hence the special position of the Eastern campaign demands special measures which are to be carried out unhampered by bureaucratic or administrative influences and with a keen sense of responsibility."

"Shooting of Soviet Russian prisoners of war. (POW Ord.)

"The shooting of and fatal accidents to Soviet Russian POW's are henceforth no longer to be reported by telephone to the commandant in charge of prisoners of war as being exceptional occurrences."

"Prisoners of war who meet their quota in a full day's work are to receive a basic daily remuneration of

Reichsmark 0.70 non-Soviet prisoners of war
Reichsmark 0.35 Soviet prisoners of war.

The lowest daily renumeration, however, is to be:
Reichsmark 0.20 for non-Soviet prisoners of war
Reichsmark 0.10 for Soviet prisoners of war."

While we are about it, let us offer a further document, this one turned up by that tireless and agreeably corruptible (by Camel nonfilter cigarettes!) Marja van Doorn. Miss van Doorn came across this document among the jumble of objects in Leni's chest during further investigations occasioned by Leni's finally having consented to move to the country—a hitherto undiscovered letter written by the deceased Heinrich Gruyten which the Au. has no hesitation in describing as a "posthumous example of concrete poetry."

"Space-allocation is to be on a purely mathematical basis. Its purpose is to establish the minimum number of rooms, and specifically which of any existing living quarters, are required for the accommodation of the garrison strength while adhering strictly to the most economical use of space. (Column 'Regulation Occupancy-Capacity' in the Accommodation Plan.) The actual use of the living quarters made by the troop unit within the limits set by the Accommodation Plan may be disregarded. Apart from the single rooms provided for by the Plan, the remaining rooms are to be included in the calculations in order of size until the garrison strength has been reached. Rooms not required to be occupied within the terms of regulation room-use, viz., pursuant to the Accommodation Plan, are to be disregarded in space-allocation. Rooms for orderlies in officers' quarters and accommodation for the quartering of noncommissioned officers and men in officers' living quarters are to be debited to the annual budget of the troop unit and hence listed as permanently occupied.

"*In the event that due space cannot be provided, viz., that the barracks are overoccupied, all available accommodation must be taken into consideration in calculating the annual budget for materials consumed and the annual budget for wear-and-tear of utensils. Hence in such cases space-allocation for the garrison strength is to be calculated not according to regulation occupancy-capacity pursuant to the Accommodation Plan but in terms of actual occupancy.*

"Space-allocation is subject to readjustment when the garrison strength is recalculated.

"The allocation, maintenance, and financing of government-owned buildings and rooms for the holding of church services in garrison parishes (garrison churches and churches at Army Bases) and of garrison cemeteries are functions of the Garris. Admin. In large military hospitals a room for prayer is to be provided.

"Approval of the ASC or NSC is required for the construction of new garrison churches and for the establishment of new garrison cemeteries with ancillary structures, and for the equipping of individual rooms for the holding of church services, and for any alterations to existing structures of this nature. Bishops attached to the Armed Forces are to be consulted. In garrisons where government-owned rooms suitable for the holding of church services are not available, the right to use or share in the use of civilian churches is to be secured. *Efforts are to be made during negotiations to obtain a share in the use of ceremonial utensils in civilian churches. Where this cannot be achieved, these utensils are to be provided by the Administration pursuant to II 113 (a).* The contract to be entered into by the Garris. Admin. requires the participation of the Army (Navy) garrison chaplain and of the Army Corps District (Nav. Station) chaplain, together with the approval of the Army or Nav. Admin. Cf. A. Dv. 370 (A.B.) No. 29.

"For confirmation (First Communicants) classes, suitable

accommodation in churches or other buildings is to be provided. If necessary it may be rented by the Garris. Admin. with the approval of the Army or Nav. Admin. In certain cases it may be left to the religious instructor to supply such accommodation himself. In such cases an appropriate reimbursement is to be established by the Army or Nav. Admin.

"The cost of maintaining garrison churches, special accommodation pursuant to Para. 150, and garrison cemeteries with ancillary structures, as well as of maintenance and replacement of the regulation accommodation utensils (incl. those for religious services—viz., II 113 (a)—), together with the costs of heating, lighting, and janitorial services for churches and cemetery chapels and for the maintenance and laundering of church linen, are to be defrayed out of the appropriate budgets classified under 'Accommodation.'

"In cases where the disposal of stable manure is handled by the troop unit concerned, one half of all net yield (i.e., gross revenue less turnover tax, cf. Para. 69 (2) R.A.O.) from the disposal of manure is to be posted by the accounting departments of the troop unit concerned to the item 'Miscellaneous Income,' whereas the remaining half is to be retained by the troop unit concerned and pursuant to Para. 244 is to be posted in the 'S' ledger under the special heading: 'Manure Revenue.'

"In return the troop units concerned must undertake:

"(a) the cleaning of manure locations—II 408 (d);

"(b) the maintenance and replacement of their own fodder vehicles;

"(c) improvements to the equipment of stables, indoor riding rings (e.g., by the installation of riding mirrors), outdoor rings, and jumping courses over and above regulation furnishing and equipment (179 [3] and 246);

"(d) the providing of supplemental fodder and other expenditures for the benefit of the horses.

"Other expenditures may not be defrayed from the 'S' account 'Manure Revenue.' It is incumbent upon the troop unit concerned to dispose of the accruing stable manure to the best possible advantage and with the approval of the Garris. Admin. The latter is required to ascertain the most advantageous sales opportunities. When stable manure is exchanged for fodder, this barter transaction is to be broken down into purchase and sale but without the necessity of notifying the other party to the transaction of this procedure. The monetary value is to be shown in the ledgers as income and expenditure, and one half of the monetary value of the stable manure is to be posted as Manure Revenue to 'Miscellaneous Income'; the troop unit is to be reimbursed for the value of manure used by the unit itself, e.g., for fertilizing grassland. Half of the monetary value is to be posted to 'Miscellaneous Income.'

"The management of stable manure is the function of the administrative unit (cavalry regiment, battalion, etc.). It can also be left to individual squadrons, batteries, and companies for independent handling. To be entered in 'S' ledger pursuant to Paras. 244 and 261.

"Any balance under 'Manure Revenue' in the 'S' ledger is to remain to the credit of the troop unit concerned even when the latter is transferred to another barracks or another garrison. In the event of transfer of individual sections of a troop unit, an appropriate amount may be transferred to the new troop unit. In the event of the dissolution of a troop unit, etc., the balance of Manure Revenue is to be posted to 'Miscellaneous Income' after defrayment of all outstanding costs. In such cases any equipment purchased from the proceeds of Manure Revenue is to be surrendered to the Administration without compensation and against a receipt and is to be posted by the Administration in its equipment inventory."

For the sake of certain information and amplification, and in order to verify a few items, it was impossible to avoid imposing once again on the exalted personage. When requested by telephone for an interview, as soon as he learned of the Au.'s request he instructed the call to be switched through and agreed without hesitation to a further interview "and if necessary still further ones." This time his voice sounded friendly, almost jovial, and this time the Au. embarked on the train journey of some thirty-six minutes without trepidation. He decided to indulge in a taxi, thereby missing the Bentley of the exalted personage which the latter had of his own accord sent to the station with his chauffeur for the express purpose of meeting the Au. Since the Au. had not only not expected such attention but had received no advance notice of it, this lack of communication cost him some DM.17.80, including tip DM.19.50, since the exalted personage lives at a considerable distance from town. The Au. greatly deplores having thereby deprived the income-tax department of approximately DM.1.75 to 2.20. Once again the occasion seemed opportune to invest in further gifts. He decided on a view of the Rhine, similar to those whose jewellike clarity had struck him so agreeably at Mrs. Hölthohne's. Cost: DM.42.00, or 51.80 with frame; the personage's wife, to be referred to henceforward *tout court* as Mimi, was—and not only verbally—"delighted at his thoughtfulness." For the personage himself the Au. had managed to pick up a first edition of the Communist Manifesto, although only in facsimile (in actual fact it was merely a photocopy with a few added graphic touches, but this also drew a gratified smile from the personage).

This time the atmosphere was more relaxed. Mimi, no longer suspicious, served tea approximately of the quality described by Mrs. Hölthohne in the café as not especially good; there were cookies, dry, sherry, dry, and cigarettes, and on the faces of those two sensitive people there prevailed a delicate melancholy that precluded tears but not moist eyes. It turned out to be a pleasant afternoon, without covert aggression, not quite without overt aggression. The parklike grounds have already been described, as has the room, the terrace not yet: it was curved in the baroque style, ornamented at either end with pergolas, its central portion extending well out into the grounds; on the lawn, croquet paraphernalia. First blossoms (forsythia) on the shrubs.

Mimi: brunette and, although fifty-six, *genuinely* looking like forty-six, long legs, narrow mouth, normal bosom, in a rust-red knit dress, her complexion given an artificial pallor that went well with her type.

"That's a lovely story of yours, about the girl riding her bicycle from camp to camp, looking for her lover and finally finding him in the cemetery; when I say lovely, I don't mean the cemetery of course, and her finding him there, all I mean is: a young woman bicycling across the Eifel, across the Ardennes all the way to Namur, managing to get as far as Reims, back to Metz, and home, again right through the Eifel and across zone boundaries and national frontiers.

"Well, I know this young woman, and if I'd known it was she you were talking about I'd have—well, I'd have, I don't quite know what I'd have done—well, I'd have tried to do something nice for her, although she's quite a reserved kind of person. We went to see her, you know, in 1952, right after my husband was finally released, after we'd tracked down the gardener and got her address from him. A person of remarkable beauty, whose appeal for men even I as a woman can appreciate" (?? Au.). "And that boy of hers, just as beautiful, with his long fair straight hair. My husband was quite moved—the child reminded him so of young Boris, though Boris had been extremely thin and had worn glasses, but the child did look like him, didn't he?" (A nod from the personage. Au.).

"She brought him up all wrong, of course. She shouldn't have refused to send the boy to school. After all, the boy was seven and a half then, and the way she carried on with him was completely unrealistic. Singing songs and telling fairy tales and that incongruous mixture of Hölderlin, Trakl, and Brecht—and I don't really know whether Kafka's *Penal Colony* is the right reading for a boy of barely eight, and I don't know either whether the naturalistic depictions of all, and I do mean *all,* the human organs doesn't lead to, well let's say, to a somewhat too materialistic outlook on life. And yet: there was something quite wonderful about her, in spite of the pure anarchy that prevailed. I must say, those pictures of human sexual organs, and enlarged at that: I don't really know whether that wasn't a bit premature—today, of course, it would already be almost too late" (laughter from both. Au.). "But he was adorable, that child, adorable and quite natural—and what that young woman had gone through, she must have been just thirty at the time, and she'd lost you might say three husbands, and the brother, the father, the mother, and proud! No, I didn't have the courage to go and see her again, she was that proud.

"We did correspond with her later, when my husband went to Moscow with Adenauer in '55 and actually managed to find one—repeat one—person at the Foreign Ministry whom he'd known during his Berlin days, and he barely had time on his way out to ask him about Koltovsky. Result: negative, grandmother and grandfather of that adorable child—dead; and his aunt Lydia—no trace."

The personage: "I am not exaggerating when I say that it is the fault of the Western allies that Boris is no longer alive. By that I don't mean that unfortunate and foolish subterfuge with the identification papers, and the fact that he was killed in a mining accident. No, that's not what I mean. The fault of the Western allies lay in the fact that they arrested me and interned me for seven years, that's to say, put me under lock and key, even if the locks didn't lock that well and the keys weren't always turned. You see, I had arranged with Erich von Kahm that he was to warn me as soon as the situation became acute for Boris, but when his entire guard personnel deserted he lost his nerve, and he did the best thing he could under the circumstances: sent him to the Erft front where he would have had no difficulty going over to the Americans at the first opportunity. Our plan had been a different one: Kahm was to get him a British or American uniform and put him into a POW camp for British or Americans—by the time the mistake was cleared up the war would have been over. It was madness, of course, to stick him with German papers, a German uniform, even a faked wound-tag. Madness. Naturally neither Kahm nor I could have had any idea that there was a woman behind it! And a child on the way, and the air raids! Lunacy! At the time I didn't get much response out of the girl, she thanked me when she found out it had been I who had wangled Boris a job at the nursery, but thanked—well, you might say the way a reasonably well-brought-up girl would thank you for a bar of chocolate. That girl had no idea what I had risked, and how an affidavit by Boris would have helped me at Nuremberg and so on. I made an utter fool of myself in court and before my fellow defendants by stating that I had saved the life of one Boris Lvovich Koltovsky, aged so and so much. The Soviet prosecutor said: 'Well, we'll try and locate this Boris since you even know his POW-camp number.' But a year later he still hadn't been found! At the time I thought it was all just a pretense. Boris could certainly have helped *me* if he had lived and if he had been allowed to.

"They accused me of making the most horrible statements, and while it is true that they were made at conferences I took part in, they were not made by me. Would you credit me with the following?" (Pulling out his notebook he read aloud): "'Leniency is not called for even toward the Soviet prisoner of war who shows willingness to work and docility. He will interpret it as weakness and draw his own conclusions.' I am also supposed to have suggested, during a meeting that took place in September '41 with the head of the army munitions industry, that some RLS" (Reich Labor Service. Au.) "barracks which had housed a hundred anf fifty prisoners be adjusted to house eight hundred and forty prisoners by installing tiered bunks. In one of my plants Russians are said to have come to work in the morning without bread or work clothes and to have begged German workers for bread—there are also supposed to have been punishment cells. Yet I was the one who in March '42 complained that the Russians being sent to us had been so weakened by the atrocious camp diet that they were no longer able to operate a lathe properly, for instance. During a discussion with General Reinecke, the man responsible for all prisoners of war, I protested personally against the regulation mixture for what was known as Russian POW bread, this had to consist of 50 percent rye husks, 20 percent chopped sugar beets, 20 percent ground cellulose, and 10 percent ground straw or leaves. I managed to get the percentage of rye husks raised to 55 percent and that of chopped sugar beets to 25 percent, which meant that the horrible ingredients of ground cellulose, ground straw or leaves, dropped correspondingly, at least in our plants—and at the expense of our plants.

"It is all too easily forgotten that the problems were not of the simplest. I pointed out to Backe, the Secretary of State in the Reich Ministry for Food, and to Moritz, the ministerial director, that work in the munitions industry must not be tantamount to a death sentence, and that such work required strong men. Finally it was I who pushed through what later became the famous 'thick soup days.' I had a row with Sauckel, who threatened me with jail and literally waved under my nose all the ordinances of the AHC and AFHC and CORSD" (Army High Command, Armed Forces High Command, Central Office of the Reich Security Department. Au.). "And because that utterly inhuman feeding system had to be kept from the German public, I made use of deliberate indiscretions to smuggle news of it out to Sweden and exposed myself to considerable danger in my efforts to alert world public opinion, and what thanks did I get? Two years' internment, five years' imprisonment, on account of our subsidiary plants in Königsberg, for which I *really* was not responsible.

"Well, all right, all right, others died, others were treated even worse than I was, and after all I am in good health and not particularly impaired" (?? In what way? Au.). "Let's forget about it, and the whole hypocritical claptrap of the trial, when they held documents under my nose and accused me of statements that quite honestly I never made, I wanted so much to get that boy safely through the war, and I failed—I failed to find his parents and his sister after the war, and I completely failed to exert any influence on his son's upbringing. Didn't I prove that my cultural influence on Boris had not been all that bad? Who was it introduced him to Trakl and Kafka, and ultimately Hölderlin too, tell me that? And couldn't that obtuse woman have eventually, through me, incorporated those poets into her inadequate cultural background and then passed them on to her son? Was it really so presumptuous of me to feel an obligation to become a kind of sublimated godfather to the sole known survivor of the

Koltovskys? I am convinced that Boris himself would not have turned down such a sincere offer, and did they really have to treat me with such contempt? Especially that impudent creature who was living there too—I've forgotten her name—with her vulgar socialist notions, who insulted me so rudely and finally threw me out—judging by what I've heard she hasn't even been able to handle her own sons properly and has been living constantly on the periphery of society, not to say prostitution. And as for Gruyten, the father of that strangely silent woman and later on the lover of that impertinent pinko floozy, would anyone claim that during the war he was as innocent as a babe unborn? What I'm getting at is: there was no reason to turn me away so snootily and to accept without question the sentences passed by a court whose dubiousness is by now a household word. No indeed, I certainly got no thanks out of that affair."

All this was delivered in a low voice, more injured than aggressive, and every so often Mimi would take his hand to calm him down when his veins began to swell.

"Money orders returned, letters not answered, advice not followed, when one day that impertinent creature, the other woman, I mean, told me point-blank in a letter: 'Can't you get it into your head that Leni wants nothing to do with you?' Very well then—from that day on I kept entirely in the background, but of course I made it my business to find out what was going on, for the boy's sake—and what has he turned out to be? I won't say a criminal, for I am above accepting *any* legal concept without questioning it. I was a criminal myself, it was a crime for me to decide on my own that the rye-husk and chopped sugar-beet content of Russian POW bread be raised by 5 percent and the cellulose and leaf content correspondingly lowered, so as to make the bread more digestible: I might have gone to concentration camp for that. And I was a criminal simply because I was associated with factories and, because of complex family and financial involvements, was among the major industrialists whose empire, or I should say extent, became so vast that a detailed overview was impossible. So you see I myself was enough of a criminal, during the most varied epochs, not to want simply to call the boy a criminal, but he went wrong, there's no doubt about that—it's madness, and the outcome of a crazy upbringing, for someone of twenty-three to try and restore certain property relationships by forging checks and promissory notes, relationships that happen to be legal though painful, irrevocable though the result of the perhaps embarrassing shrewdness, if you like, of the present owners. A deed of land is a deed of land, and a sale is a sale. In terms of psychoanalysis, the boy is suffering from a dangerous attachment to his mother as well as from a father-trauma. That woman had no idea what she was starting with that Kafka of hers—nor did she know that such widely different authors as Kafka and Brecht, when read so intensively, are bound to lie side by side indigestibly—and on top of everything else the extreme pathos of Hölderlin and those fascinating, decadent poems of Trakl: the child drank all that in just as he was learning to talk and listen, and there was that corporealist materialism, too, with its mystical overtones: naturally I am against taboos too, but was it right to pursue that biologism in such detail, that glorification of all the organs of the human body and their functions? After all, we are divided, aren't we, divided in our nature? I tell you, it's bitter when you are not allowed to help, it hurts to be rejected."

Here again, something the Au. would have considered impossible in this case; T. as the result of W., the latter in turn as the result of hidden S.—and just then the dogs came bounding across the sumptuous lawn, Afghan hounds of regal beauty who briefly sniffed the Au., turned aside from him as being obviously too low-class, and proceeded to lick away their master's tears. Damn it all, was everyone suddenly beginning to get sentimental: Pelzer, Bogakov, the exalted personage? Hadn't even Lotte's eyes glistened suspiciously, hadn't Marja van Doorn likewise wept openly—and hadn't Margret already dissolved in tears, while Leni herself permitted her eyes just exactly as much moisture as was necessary to keep them clear and open?

The parting from Mimi and the exalted personage was friendly, their voices were still wistful as they asked the Au. to see if he could not intervene as mediator, they were still, and always would be, prepared to help Boris's son—just because he was Boris's son and Lev Koltovsky's grandson—"get back on his feet."

Grundtsch's situation, physical and psychic as well as geographical and political, remained unclarified, almost unclear, at the end of the war. A visit to him was readily arranged: telephone call, appointment, and there was Grundtsch, after cemetery closing hours, standing by the rusty gate that is only opened when the pile of those discarded wreaths and flowers which are of plastic, hence useless for compost, is carted away. Grundtsch, hospitable as ever, pleased by the visit, took the Au. by the hand to guide him safely past "the specially slippery bits."

His situation inside the cemetery had meanwhile improved considerably. Now the holder of a key to the public toilet as well as to the shower rooms of the municipal cemetery workers, and equipped with a transistor radio and a television set, he was enjoying to the full (It was around Eastertime. Au.) the imminent hydrangea boom expected for Low Sunday. On this cool March evening, although sitting about on benches was not possible, a peaceful stroll through the cemetery was, this time to the main path called by Grundtsch the main road. "Our best residential area," he said with a chuckle, "our most expensive lots, and in case it should ever occur to you not to believe our Sonny Boy, I'll show you a thing or two that prove his story. He never lies, you know, no more than he was ever a monster" (chuckle). Grundtsch showed the Au. the remains of the electric cable laid by Pelzer and Grundtsch in February 1945: pieces of inferior-grade cable, with black insulation, leading from the nursery to an ivy-covered oak tree, thence through an elderberry bush (the clips attached to it, although rusty, still visible), through a privet hedge to the family tomb of the von der Zeckes. On the outer wall of this imposing burial place, more clips, more remains of inferior-grade cable with black insulation—and then the Au. was standing (not without a slight shiver, it is true) facing the solemn bronze door that had once formed the entrance to the

Soviet paradise in the vaults but which on this nippy evening in early spring unfortunately was locked.

"Here's where they went in, see?" said Grundtsch. "Then inside over to the Herrigers', and from there on over to the Beauchamps'." The von der Zecke and Herriger tombs were very well tended, planted with moss, pansies, and roses. Grundtsch's comment: "That's right, I took over the two annual contracts from Sonny Boy. After the war he had the passages bricked up again and plastered over, rather a botched job I'm afraid, done by old Gruyten, but he said the cracks that showed up later, and the crumbling plaster, were due to the bombs, and that wasn't so far from the truth either, what with all the banging that went on during 'the Second,' it must have been quite something. Over there you can still see an angel with a bomb splinter in its head, as if someone's battle-ax had got stuck in it." (Although dusk was falling, the Au. could make out the angel and is able to confirm Grundtsch's statement.) "And some of that sentimental art-stuff at the Herrigers' and the von der Zeckes' got wrecked, as you can see. The Herrigers had it restored, the von der Zeckes had theirs modernized, while the Beauchamps, that's to say old Beauchamp, is just letting the grave fall to pieces. The boy—well, by now he's close on sixty-five too, but back in the early twenties I used to see him in his sailor suit crying his eyes out and praying all over the place here, and he looked pretty funny, for even in those days he was a bit too old for a sailor suit, but he refused to give it up—and for all I know he's still running around in it, down there in that sanatorium near Merano. Periodically his attorney'll send a check so that at least the worst of the weeds can be taken care of, and this attorney's insisting on burial rights for the funny old gentleman in the sailor suit who's still living off the cigarette-paper factory. Otherwise, I guess, the city would probably pull the whole thing down. So there's a regular lawsuit going on about a burial plot!" (Chuckle. Au.) "As if the old boy couldn't just as well be buried down there in the Tyrol. Here we are at the chapel, the door's fallen to pieces, you can have a peek if you like and see whether Leni and Boris left any of their heather behind."

And indeed the Au. did enter the rather dilapidated little chapel, observing with some concern the crumbling sentimental frescoes in the charming (architecturally speaking) shell-shaped niches. It was dirty inside the chapel, cold and damp, and in order to have a good look at the altar, which had been robbed of all its metal ornamentation, the Au. indulged in a few matches (whether he can charge them to his income tax has not yet been determined; since he is a heavy smoker his consumption of matches is considerable, and an audit—by highly paid public and private experts—has still to be made to decide whether some thirteen to sixteen matches can be written off to expenses). Behind the altar the Au. found some dust of vegetable origin that still had a strangely reddish-purple tinge and could unquestionably have derived from decomposed heather; the nature of the female garment normally worn under a dress or sweater on the upper part of the body was explained to him, as he left the chapel in a daze, by Grundtsch as the latter puffed away at his pipe. "Oh well, I guess they go in there sometimes, a few couples wandering off this way and desperate for somewhere to go, no doorway, no money for a room, ones who aren't scared of the dead."

It turned out to be a nice long walk in the nippy air, the evening just right to be rounded off with a kirsch at Grundtsch's place.

"What happened was," Grundtsch went on, "that I simply lost my nerve when I heard there was all that heavy fighting going on back home, and I wanted to go back and see my mother again and be there if she needed me. She was getting on for eighty after all, and it was twenty-five years since I'd been to see her, and though she'd spent her life running after the priests that wasn't her fault, it was the fault of certain" (chuckle) "structures. It was crazy, but off I went, much too late, relying on my knowledge of the countryside. After all, as a kid I used to herd the cows there, and sometimes I'd go through the forest and along the edge of the forest as far as the White Wehe and Red Wehe rivers. But as luck would have it those donkeys caught me just beyond Düren, stuck a rifle in my hand, gave me an armband, and sent me off with a party of half-grown youths into the forest, Well, what I did was simulate a scout party—I remembered all that crap from the last war—and took those few lads along—but my knowledge of the countryside was no use to me now, it wasn't countryside any more, it was nothing but craters, tree stumps, mines, and if the Yanks hadn't picked us up pretty soon we'd have had it—they were the ones, of course, who knew which paths weren't mined.

"Luckily at least those lads came through, so did I, though it was quite a while before they let me go, four months of empty stomachs and tents, muck and cold, well, it wasn't exactly a picnic with the Yanks, I've had rheumatism ever since and I never saw my mother again. Some German blockhead shot her dead for running up a white flag—the little place lay between the lines, sometimes the Yanks, sometimes the Germans, and my old woman didn't want to leave. And the Germans actually let my old mum have it with a machine pistol though she was nearly eighty, most likely the same bastards who're now getting monuments put up to them. And still the priests are doing damn all about stopping those fucking monuments from being put up. I tell you, I'd just about had it when the Yanks finally let me go in June, with the agricultural workers. I had quite a time getting out, what's more, though I genuinely did belong in that category. The word about agricultural workers, see, had been kept dark in camp by members of the Catholic Guild, and they passed it on as a tip to their buddies. Well, I made like old Father Kolping himself, like a Christian worker, rattled off a few pious sayings, and that way I got out by June.

"When I got back here I found a nice little business, all cleaned up and running properly and duly handed over to me by Mrs. Hölthohne, together with the lease. I've never forgotten that, and to this day she still gets her flowers from me at cost. Sonny Boy never asked *me* for a reference—I'd have let him sweat it out for a few months at least, I don't mind telling you, seeing as how he came through all those bad times without a scratch. Just as a kind of therapy of course, a bit of squirming wouldn't have done him any harm. Well, he treated me right too, he worked out my share of the business and gave me a loan so I could finally start up my own business. We divided up the accounts between us, the ones for perpetual grave care, and he was generous, I must say, in helping me out with seed, but I still say that six months or so locked up some place would've done that fellow good."

The Au. stayed on a while (about an hour and a half) at Grundtsch's, the latter giving not the least sign of tearfulness and from then on maintaining a soothing silence. It was nice and cozy at his place, there was beer and kirsch, and here in Grundtsch's quarters the Au. was permitted something that Grundtsch had forbidden him to do while in the cemetery ("You can see a cigarette for miles."): to smoke.

As Grundtsch accompanied the Au. outside, again guiding him past the slippery rubbish, Grundtsch said, in a voice full, if not of tears, of emotion: "Something drastic must be done to get Leni's boy out of clink. All he did was make a fool of himself, after all. He was only trying to get some kind of personal restitution from that Hoyser gang. He's a fine lad, just like his mother, like his father too, and don't forget he was born right where I live and he worked for me for three years before going to work for the cemetery and then becoming a street cleaner. A fine lad, and not nearly as close-mouthed as his mother. We have to do something for that lad. He used to play here as a kid, when Leni came to help Pelzer out, and later myself, during the busy season. If necessary I'd hide him here in this very cemetery where his father was hidden. Not a soul would ever find him here, besides, he doesn't have my fear of vaults and cellars."

The Au. bid him a cordial farewell and promised—a promise he intends to keep—to come again; he also promised to give young Gruyten, if he managed to escape from jail, what Grundtsch called the "tip about the cemetery." "And what's more," Grundtsch called out after the Au., "tell him there'll always be a cup of coffee and a bowl of soup and a smoke for him at my place. No matter what."

The following is a summary of the few extant quotations direct from Leni:

"to walk the streets" (to save her piano from seizure)

"creatures with souls" (in the universe)

"impromptu little dance" (with E.K.)

"when the time comes, to be buried in it" (in her bathrobe)

"Come on now, tell me! What's all this stuff coming out of me?" (Leni as a little girl, referring to her excrements)

"spread-eagled and in total surrender"; "opened up"; "taken"; "given" (experience in the heather)

"Please, please give me this Bread of Life! Why must I wait so long?" (statement that led to her being refused First Communion)

"And then that pale, fragile, dry tasteless thing was placed on my tongue—I almost spat it out again!" (referring to her actual First Communion)

"muscle business" (referring to her "paperless status" in connection with bowel movements)

"whom I mean to love, to whom I can give myself unreservedly"; "dream up daring caresses"; "he is to find joy in me and I in him" (referring to "the right man")

"The fellow" (does not have) "tender hands" (first rendezvous)

"so I could have a little cry in peace" (visits to the movies)

"so sweet, so terribly sweet and nice" (her brother Heinrich)

"scared of him because he was so terribly well educated" (her brother Heinrich)

"then surprised because he was so awfully, awfully nice" (her brother Heinrich)

"managed quite well to keep his head above water"; "wrecker" (referring to her father after 1945)

"even in those days probably represented a genuine temptation for Father, by which I don't mean she was a *temptress*" (referring to Lotte H.)

"awful, awful, awful" (referring to the family coffee gatherings with her brother H.)

"Our poets never flinched from cleaning out a john" (after *she* had cleaned out Margret's plugged john, referring to H. and E.)

"It (mustn't and shouldn't happen) in bed." "In the open, in the open. This whole business of going to bed together is not what I'm looking for" (speculations in Margret's presence regarding an activity commonly known as intercourse)

"as far as I was concerned (he) was dead before he was killed" (referring to her husband A.P., after he had forced her to the above-described activity)

"too embarrassing for words" (referring to the escapade with A.)

"She wasted away there, starved to death, although toward the end I always took her some food, and then when she was dead they buried her in the garden, just in shallow earth, with no gravestone or anything; as soon as I got there I sensed that she had gone, and Scheukens said to me: 'No use now, Miss, no use —unless you want to scratch open the ground?' So then I went to the mother superior and asked very determinedly for Rahel, and they told me she had gone away, and when I asked where to the mother superior got nervous and said: 'But child, have your wits deserted you?'" (re Rahel's death)

(nauseating) "sight of those stacks of freshly printed money" (re her office job during the war)

"revenge" (motive assumed by Leni for her father's Dead Souls manipulation)

"instantly on fire" (laying her hand on Boris)

"much more wonderful than that heather business I once told you about" (see above)

"just then those damned salvos came to a climax" (the moment when Boris declared his love)

"lying together" (Leni to Margret re an otherwise more crudely described activity)

"You know, everywhere I go, on all sides, I see a big sign: Danger!" (re her situation after they had first lain together)

"Why did I have to know it any sooner, there were more important things to talk about, and I told him my name was Gruyten and not Pfeiffer as on the papers" (Leni to Margret re a conversation with Boris)

(that the Americans were) "such slowpokes"

"It's less than sixty miles, why ever are they taking so long?" (see above)

"Why don't they come during the day, when are they going to come again during the day, why are the Americans such slowpokes, why is it taking them so long to get here, it's not that far, is it?" (re the American air raids and their—to Leni—dilatory advance)

"month of the glorious rosary" (re October '44, during which there were many daylight raids permitting Leni to lie with Boris)

"I have Rahel and the Virgin Mary to thank for that, they've neither of them forgotten my devotion to them" (referring to the glorious month)

"Both of them were poets, if you ask me, both of them" (re Boris and Erhard)

"At last, at last, what ages they've taken!" (again re the American advance)

(lying together) "was now simply out of the question" (Leni in her pregnant condition)

9 The Au. would have been only too glad to skip a period in Leni's life already touched upon by some of the informants: her brief political activity after 1945. He finds himself deserted here not by his visionary powers, merely by his credulity. Is he nevertheless to give credence to what is reported with such credibility? Here the theme of the author's dilemma, beloved of professionals and nonprofessionals alike, rears its head with a vengeance!

The fact that Leni is not uninterested in politics has been attested to by Hans and Grete Helzen, who have been sharing many an hour before the television set with her, in a manner that would prompt neither a notary nor a reporter to withhold his verification. Leni prefers (and this has been specifically confirmed by both Helzens after almost two years of joint viewing in front of Leni's black-and-white set) "to watch the faces of the people who talk about politics" (one of the few direct Leni-quotes!). Her opinions of Barzel, Kiesinger, and Strauss cannot be reproduced here: it would prove too costly for the Au. He cannot afford it, and he finds himself, as regards those three gentlemen, in a situation similar to that regarding Mr. Exalted. He—the Au.—could invoke his journalistic responsibility, quote Leni, lay the burden of proof upon her, drag her into court, and, although convinced that she would let neither him nor the Helzens down, he still prefers to hint rather than quote. For one simple reason: he would be sorry to see Leni haled into court. Leni has enough problems, he feels: her one and only, dearly beloved son in jail, now even her piano threatened with seizure; her fear or apprehension—her uncertainty as to whether she has "conceived" from the Turk (Leni according to Hans and Grete H.); whereby a biological detail is confirmed: she is still subject to the conditions of womanhood; the threat of being gassed, of which no one knows whether it can be carried out—uttered by a retired civil servant in the neighborhood who is definitely known to have made unsuccessful advances (flagrant attempts to molest her in the dark hallway of the building, pawings at the bakery, an act of exhibitionism, also in the dark hallway); the whole jungle of seizures and threatened seizures that "you couldn't begin to cut your way through even with a machete" (Lotte H.). Is she to be haled into court and made to repeat her devastating comments, so exquisite in their pregnancy (literarily speaking), on Barzel, Kiesinger, and Strauss? There is but one answer to this question: no, no, a thousand times no.

But now without further ado: Yes, Leni "became associated with" the German Communist Party (Lotte H., Margret, Hoyser, Sr., M.v.D., and a onetime functionary of this party, all used the same expression!). Now we are all familiar with posters displaying the words "in association with . . ."; this usually refers to prominent persons who in fact never appear, nor have they ever been asked, or consented, to do so, persons who are merely credited with drawing power. Was Leni credited with drawing power? Apparently yes, although mistakenly.

The onetime functionary, now temporarily running a busy newsstand in a favorable downtown location, describes himself as a "sixty-eighter"; this—to the Au., at least—likable fellow, in his mid-fifties, seemed resigned, not to say embittered, and when asked if he would mind enlarging on the cryptic term "sixty-eighter" all he said was: "Well, since 1968 I've had nothing more to do with them. No sir, not me."

The following report by this informant (who wishes to remain as anonymous as the exalted personage) is reproduced here without a break, although in fact it was given in bits and pieces, the informant being constantly interrupted by customers. The

Au. was thus able to witness the highly intransigent sales policy of this "sixty-eighter" who, when asked for porno products at least fourteen or fifteen times in less than half an hour, replied brusquely, if not morosely: "I don't sell that stuff." Even relatively harmless press organs—such as highbrow and lowbrow daily papers and illustrated weeklies of a *semi* or *moderately* harmless nature—were, so it seemed to the Au., parted with reluctantly by the "sixty-eighter."

The Au.'s cautious prognosis that, in view of such a sales policy, he had doubts as to whether the kiosk would show a profit, was given a straight rebuttal by this informant. "As soon as I've wangled my old-age pension I'm going to close up shop anyway. So far all I've got is a small reparations pension, and when that was approved I was made to feel in no uncertain terms that they'd have preferred it if I hadn't survived. It would've been cheaper for them too. No, I'm not going to sell that humiliating bourgeois crap, that porno-imperialism, no matter how hard they try to make me—like: 'A kiosk in such a key location is morally obliged to maintain a stock for potential customers that conforms to popular demand' (Quotation from a submission by a city councillor, member of the Christian Democratic Union party). No sir, that's not for me. Let them finally get around to selling their filth where it belongs: in church doorways, along with those religious pamphlets and their hypocritical pussyfooting around about chastity. No sir, that's not for me. Sticks and stones may break my bones—but never mind, let them go on boycotting me and suspecting me, I'll carry on with my own censorship. I'm not going to sell that humiliating bourgeois crap if it kills me."

By way of amplification it may be added that this informant is a chain smoker, with the complexion and eyes that betoken a diseased liver, with thick whitish-gray hair, glasses with very thick lenses, trembling hands, and on his face such a concentrated expression of contempt that the Au., try as he might, could not pretend to be excluded from that contempt.

"I might've known, back then when they took Ilse Kremer's husband Werner out of the camp in France, those Vichy Fascists, and handed him over to the Nazis, as I found out later. No one can have any idea of how we felt during that year and a half during the time of the Hitler-Stalin pact. Well, they shot Werner, and they circulated a rumor that he'd been a Fascist traitor and that in order to get rid of Fascist traitors it was all right to make use of the Fascists. And I went on believing that crap till '68. 'Root out the Fascists from your ranks by denouncing them to the Fascists as spies!' Well, naturally, that way the hands of the dictating proletariat stayed clean at least. O.K. That was enough for me. No sir. I should've listened to Ilse in '45, but I didn't. For twenty-three years I went on working, legally and illegally, letting myself be denounced, arrested, spied on, laughed at. Now as soon as I close up this place I'm off to Italy, maybe there's still a few human beings there, and a few who aren't arse-lickers like us.

"As for that business with the Pfeiffer girl, the Gruyten girl—at the time even I found it embarrassing, though I was still as bigoted as a whole clutch of cardinals. We'd just found out that, at the risk of her life, she'd had a love affair with a Red Army soldier, that she'd smuggled food to him, maps, newspapers, war reports, she even had a child with a Russian first name by him. We wanted to make her look like a Resistance fighter, and do you know what that Red Army soldier had taught her? How to pray! What madness! Well, she was very attractive, a lovely-looking wench, and that looked good at those pitiful functions of ours, seeing as how we had to put up some sort of fight against the crazy goings-on of an allegedly Socialist army in East Prussia and so on. If only I'd listened to Ilse, she told me: 'Fritz, be honest with yourself, admit things can't be done this way any more, not this way. This isn't what we wanted in '28, now is it, when maybe we did still have to support Teddy Thälmann for tactical reasons. Be honest with yourself and admit that Hindenburg won, even in '45. And leave that nice girl alone, you'll get her into trouble without doing yourselves any good.'

"True enough, but the fact is she was a worker, a genuine worker, even if she did come from a bourgeois family that had once seen better days, and, let's face it, a few times we got her to carry the red flag and march with us through the city, though we had to get her almost drunk to do it because she was so painfully shy, and then a few times she sat very decoratively on the platform while I made a speech. I still feel embarrassed whenever I think about it." (Was the plainly visible darkening of Fritz's already dark skin a kind of blush? Surely a legitimate question. Incidentally, the name Fritz is fictitious; "Fritz's" true first name is not known to the Au.)

"The thing was, she was so gloriously proletarian—totally incapable of adopting, let alone practicing, the bourgeois profit mentality—but Ilse was proved right: we did her harm and ourselves no good, for the couple of times she actually did answer reporters when they asked her about Boris and what she had learned from him 'underground' she told them: 'How to pray.' Those were the only words she uttered, and needless to say the reactionary press made hay out of them and couldn't resist devoting a headline to us: 'Learns to pray with German Communist Party. Delacroix blonde a Trojan horse.' Quite unnecessarily, she had at some time or other actually become a party member and forgotten to resign, so she promptly had her apartment searched when we were banned, and then she dug in her heels and, as she put it, 'just to show them,' refused to resign, and when I asked her once why she had gone along with us in the first place she said: 'Because the Soviet Union has produced people like Boris.' A person could go crazy at the thought that in some very roundabout way she actually did belong in our world but we didn't belong in hers—and then, yes, then you really get confused because that makes you realize why the world proletarian movement has been such a total flop in Western Europe.

"Oh well, never mind. I'm off to Italy soon, and I'm sorry to hear she's having such a thin time. I'm not someone she'd like to be reminded of, otherwise I'd ask you to say hello to her for me. I should've listened to Ilse and old Gruyten, the girl's father—he just laughed, laughed and shook his head when Leni marched off with her red flag."

It should perhaps be added that Fritz and the Au. took it in turns to offer each other cigarettes, while Fritz sold the bourgeois newspapers he found so contemptible with an almost voluptuous contempt. He did it with gestures and in a manner that a perceptive customer might have felt to be insulting. Fritz's comment: "Now they'll go off and read that claptrap, that feudalistic blarney, the kind of stuff that, when you read it, you can hear just the right amount of condescension in the writers' voices. And they gobble up sex and hash the way they used to gobble up all that priests' hogwash, and they wear their minis and their maxis as dutifully as they used to wear their chaste little white blouses. I'll give you some good advice: vote for Barzel or Köppler, then at least you'll get liberal baloney first hand. Personally, I'm learning the language of human beings, Italian, and I'm spreading the slogan: Hash is opium for the people."

It was a load off the Au.'s mind to have at least a partial explanation for this embarrassing episode in Leni's life, but he had no luck when it came to confronting further potential informants as soon as they opened their front doors and greeted him with the question: "Are you for or against '68?" Since the Au., riddled with the most varied motivations, torn this way and that between the most varied emotions, did not immediately, at least not the first time, understand why he should opt in favor or otherwise of an entire year in the twentieth century, he pondered too long over this particular year and finally decided, on the basis of what he frankly admits to being an almost habitual compulsion to the negative, on the reply: "Against"—thereby closing those doors to himself for all time.

Nevertheless, he managed to find among some archives the newspaper quoted by Fritz apropos Leni. It was a Christian Democrat paper, published in 1946, and Fritz's quotation was verified as "word for word correct" (Au.). Of interest and hence perhaps worth passing on were two items: the wording of the article itself, and a newspaper photo showing a speaker's platform, decorated with Communist Party flags and emblems, on which Fritz is to be seen in practiced rhetorical pose—astonishingly young: in his middle or late twenties, as yet without glasses. In the background, Leni holding a banner with Soviet emblems aslant over Fritz's head, a pose vividly recalling to the Au. the part played by banners during certain liturgical ceremonies that demand the lowering of banners at the most solemn moments. As she was in this picture, Leni made two distinct impressions on the Au.: she seemed both appealing and out of place, not to say—something that cannot be said lightly—phony. Actually the Au. wishes he could concentrate his visionary powers on this photograph by means of an as yet uninvented lens, so as to burn Leni out of it. Fortunately, in this poorly reproduced newspaper picture she is recognizable only to the initiated, and it is to be hoped that no archives exist containing any negative of this photo. As for the article itself, it may be as well to quote it verbatim. Under the aforesaid photo caption appears the headline:

"Young woman with Christian upbringing taught by Red hordes to pray. It is almost unbelievable, yet a proven fact, that a young woman, of whom one scarcely knows whether to call her Miss G. or Mrs. P., claims to have been taught how to pray again by a Red Army soldier. She is the mother of an illegitimate child whose father, she proudly claims, is a Soviet soldier with whom, two years after her husband P. had sacrificed his life in the native land of the illegitimate father, she entered upon a sexual relationship that was both illegal and illegitimate. She is not ashamed to make propaganda for Stalin. Our readers require no warning in the face of such madness, but perhaps it is legitimate to ask whether certain manifestations of pseudo-naiveté should not be classified as political criminality. We know where we learned how to pray: while being taught Religion at school, and in church; and we also know what we pray for: for a Christian Western world, and readers to whom this report has given food for thought might perhaps utter the occasional silent prayer for Miss G. alias Mrs. P. She can use it. In any event, the prayerful former Lord Mayor Dr. Adenauer has, in our view, greater power of conviction than could be contained in the little finger of this duped, possibly mentally disturbed woman (girl?) who is said to come from a family which, while once respected, has from every point of view gone steadily downhill."

The Au. fervently hopes that Leni was just as sporadic a newspaper reader then as she is today. He—the Au.—would be very sorry to see her hurt in such Christian Democrat style.

Meanwhile it has been possible to verify another important detail: the notches cut by Marja van Doorn when the Pfeiffers were asking for Leni's hand on behalf of Alois have been discovered by Grete Helzen on the door frame—and it is clearly evident that on that occasion the word honor was uttered sixty times. This in turn proves two further details: M.v.D. is a reliable informant, and: Leni's door frame has not been painted for thirty years.

After some devious efforts (which turned out to be superfluous) it was also possible to verify that strange word "Crystalation." The Au. made some attempts (superfluous, see above) to obtain an explanation from more youthful clerics, this word, despite its mineralogical ring, having been uttered by the unimpeachable Grandma Commer in an ecclesiastical context. Result: negative. The pastoral agencies to which he made a number of telephone calls felt (unjustifiably!) that the Au. was having fun at their expense, and while they listened—reluctantly and with extreme caution—to his explanation, they showed a complete lack of interest in the linguistic context, simply hanging up (or replacing the receiver). Hence these calls turned out to be merely an annoyance and a waste of time, until the thought occurred to him—which it might have done earlier, the word having reached him from the geographical triangle Werpen-Tolzem-Lyssemich—to ask M.v.D. She instantly identified it as a dialect term for "Christian lessons," a service that "was actually designed for children as a kind of extra religious instruction but we grown-ups sometimes went too, as a sort of refresher course; mind you, it was usually held at a time when our family was having a nap after a heavy midday dinner: around three on Sunday afternoons" (M.v.D.). More than likely it is a Catholic parallel to the Protestant "Sunday school."

The Au. (who had fallen behind in his research because of the Clay-Frazier fight) felt some twinges of conscience over the financing of his investigations and the related question of how much the income-tax department was bound to lose. Should he indulge in the trip to Rome, so that by investigating the archives of the Order's motherhouse he could find out the truth about Haruspica? Although his encounters with the two Jesuits in Freiburg and Rome had had their human value, from the reportorial standpoint they had turned out to be unprofitable and—incl. telephone, telegram, postage, and traveling expenses—an unquestionably poor investment; virtually all he had derived from them was a little saint's picture, whereas Margret, for all her malfunctioning exocrine and endocrine glands, to visit whom had cost him merely a few bunches of flowers, a bottle of modest dimensions that he had filled with gin, and the occasional few cigarettes—not even a taxi (since for reasons of health he usually preferred to walk there)—had made him the richer by a few significant and unexpected details about Heinrich Gruyten. Besides, apart from the matter of income-tax deductions, were there not also humanitarian aspects to be considered: would he not be getting the kindly Sister Cecilia into trouble, causing embarrassment to Sister Sapientia, and possibly provoking yet another disciplinary transfer for the less than likable Alfred Scheukens?

So that he might reflect in peace on all these problems, the Au. began by undertaking a journey to the Lower Rhine, traveling second-class on a train without a dining car—in fact without even a snack bar—through the pilgrims' mecca of Kevelaer, through the home town of Siegfried, arriving shortly thereafter at the town where Lohengrin lost his nerve, and thence by taxi another three miles or so, past the home of Joseph Beuys, to a village that seemed almost unrelievedly Dutch.

Tired, and rendered somewhat irritable by the uncomfortable

three-hour journey, the Au. decided on some immediate light refreshment. This he consumed at a snack-stall where an attractive blonde served him French fries, mayonnaise, and meatballs (hot), and then directed him for his coffee to an inn across the street. It was a foggy day, mist curling in the air, and it was easy to believe that Siegfried had not only ridden through Nifelheim on his way to Worms but had actually come from this nebulous-sounding place.

Inside the inn all was warm and quiet; a sleepy innkeeper was serving schnapps to two sleepy male customers and pushed a large schnapps toward the Au. with the words: "Best thing for this weather, takes away the shivers; besides, after French fries with mayonnaise it's a must," continued to chat quietly with his two customers in a guttural dialect that sounded positively Batavian. Although the Au. was now only some sixty miles from his home base, he felt by comparison like a southerner; he liked the lack of curiosity on the part of the two sleepy men and the innkeeper, who was already pushing a second schnapps across the counter toward him; the main topic of conversation seemed to be "the kirk," in concrete, architectural, and organizational terms as well as in the abstract, almost metaphysical sense; much shaking of heads, some muttering, then some remarks about the *Paapen,* by which they cannot possibly have meant the embarrassing German Reich Chancellor von Papen; no doubt these three dignified men would not have found him worthy even of mention. Was it possible, he wondered, that one of these three, who for once, although they were Germans in a bar, were not talking about the war, might have known Alfred Bullhorst? Probably all three did, it was even possible, or very likely, that they had been in the same class at school, had gone to confession with him on Saturdays, fresh from the tub and hair slicked down, and on Sundays to Mass, and on Sunday afternoons to that form of instruction that somewhat farther south was called Crystalation, had slid in clogs along icy gutters, had made the occasional pilgrimage to Kevelaer and smuggled cigarettes from Holland. Judging by their age, they must have, might well have, known him, the man who late in 1944 died in Margret's military hospital after a double amputation and whose papers had been lifted in order to provide a Soviet soldier—temporarily, at least—with legitimate status.

The Au. declined a third schnapps and asked for some coffee to prevent the pleasant somnolence from putting him to sleep. Was it here in Nifelheim that on just such a foggy day Lohengrin had lost his nerve when Elsa finally put the question; was it somewhere here that he had boarded the swan which later generations have so casually adopted as a symbol for a brand of margarine? The coffee was very good, passed through the hatch by a female person of whom only the plump pink-white arm was vouchsafed to the Au.'s view, the innkeeper heaped a generous portion of sugar onto the saucer, and the mandatory little jug contained not milk but cream. Church and priests, mild anger in the still subdued voices. Why, why had Alfred Bullhorst not been born a couple of miles farther west and, in that case, whose papers might Margret have pinched for Boris on that particular day?

Reasonably refreshed, the Au. proceeded first to the church, where he consulted the Roll of Honor: there were four Bullhorsts but only one Alfred—and that Alfred was reported as having died (aged twenty-two) not in 1944 but in 1945. That was puzzling. Wasn't this case like Keiper's, for whom Schlömer had died a second death? Shouldn't a double death have been reported? The sacristan who, on his way to carrying out some liturgical preparations or other (were they green, purple, or red, those cloths being spread out somewhere?) emerged from the sacristy nonchalantly smoking his pipe, knew the answer. The Au., hopeless at either lying or inventing (he is almost painfully dependent on facts, as any reader will have gathered by now), mumbled something about an Alfred Bullhorst he had run into during the war, whereupon the sacristan, skeptical although not suspicious, immediately told him that "their" Alfred had died in a mining accident while a prisoner of war of the French and had been buried in Lorraine; that an annual fee for permanent grave care was paid to a nursery in St. Avold; that his fiancée—"a slim pretty girl, blond, kind, intelligent—had entered a convent, and that Alfred's parents were still inconsolable because he "got it" when the war was already over. Yes, he had been employed at the Swan Margarine factory, a good lad, quiet, with no desire to be a soldier, and where had the Au. met him? Still not suspicious but nevertheless curious, the bald-headed sacristan gave the Au. such a penetrating look that the latter, after an awkward genuflection, took his leave with all possible speed. He would have been reluctant to correct the date of Alfred's death, reluctant to tell Alfred's parents that their annual payments were benefiting the bones, the ashes, the dust of a Soviet individual, not becuase he—the Au.—would have begrudged such care of that dust, those ashes—no, but one does like to know, after all, that the person assumed to be in a grave is in fact in it, and it did seem that in this instance this was not the case, and the most disturbing factor of all: it was obvious that here the German bureaucracy of death had failed completely. It was all very puzzling. And no doubt the sacristan had already been given enough to puzzle him.

The difficulty of finding a taxi will not be gone into here, nor the lengthy wait at Cleves, nor the return trip of almost three hours in a most uncomfortable train that again passed through Xanten and Kevelaer.

Margret, asked that same evening for information, swore "up and down" that this Alfred Bullhorst had died in her care: blond, sad, asking for a priest, both legs gone—only, before reporting his death, she had hurried to the orderly room, which had already closed for the night, opened the wall closet with an extra key, and extracted his identification papers, hiding them in her purse, and only then had she reported Alfred's death. Yes, he had told her about his fiancée, a lovely girl, quiet, blond, had also mentioned his village—the very one which the Au., in the service of truth, had visited at such sacrifice of time and energy, but she admitted the possibility that, in all the hurry of relocating the hospital, the "formalities" had been overlooked, by which she meant not the funeral but the reporting of his death to his relations.

Only one question remains to be asked: did German bureaucracy really fail, or would it have been the Au.'s duty to seek out the elderly Bullhorst couple and make no bones about the bones in whose memory they were having heather or pansies planted year after year on All Saints' Day, and to ask them whether they had never noticed that from time to time a bouquet of crimson roses lay on the grave, placed there by Leni and her son Lev whenever they came to visit it; or might the Au. have found at the Bullhorsts' that pink printed card filled out by Boris, telling them he was now safe and sound in an American POW camp? These questions must remain unanswered. Not everything can be clarified. And the Au. frankly admits that, when confronted by the curious, skeptical look of a sacristan so Lower Rhenish as to be almost from the Low Countries, not too far from Nijmegen, he too—like Elsa von Brabant and Lohengrin—lost his nerve.

To the Au.'s surprise, an explanation—although only partial—could be found, if not for Haruspica's death, at least for one stage of her life: her future, not as she saw it but as others see it. This time the trip to Rome, which the Au. finally did decide to take, turned out to be well worthwhile. For information on the city of Rome the Au. refers the reader to the appropriate travel folders and guidebooks, to French, English, Italian, American, and German movies, as well as to the extensive literature on Italy to which he has no intention of adding; he wishes merely to admit that—even in Rome—he understood what Fritz was looking for; that he had a chance to study the difference between a Jesuit monastery and a nuns' convent; that he was received by a truly delightful nun, who could not have been more than forty-one and whose smile was not patronizing but genuinely kind and understanding when she heard such flattering accounts from the Au. of Sisters Columbanus, Prudentia, Cecilia, and Sapientia.

Even Leni was mentioned, and it turned out that she was known at this Order's motherhouse, situated so gloriously on a hill in the northwest sector of Rome. To think they know about Leni there! Beneath pines and palms, among marble and brass, in a cool room of considerable elegance, seated in black-leather Morris chairs, tea of a far from indifferent quality on the table, the burning cigarette perched on the saucer being not studiously, not graciously, but *genuinely* ignored, a truly charming nun who had written a graduation thesis on Fontane, was just embarking on a doctoral thesis on Gottfried Benn (!!), even if only at a college of the Order; a highly cultured Germanist who wore a simple habit (that suited her marvelously) and even knew all about Heissenbüttel—*she* knew about Leni!

Imagine it: Rome! Shadows of pine trees. Cicadas, ceiling fans, tea, macaroons, cigarettes, the hour about six in the evening, a person of seductive charms both physical and intellectual, who at the mention of *The Marquise of O*___ showed not the faintest hint of embarrassment, who, when the Au. lit a second cigarette after offhandedly stubbing out the first one in a saucer (imitation Dresden, but good imitation), suddenly whispered huskily: "For Heaven's sake, let me have one too, that Virginia tobacco—I can't resist the smell"—inhaled in a manner that can only be described as "sinful," and continued in a whisper that now sounded downright conspiratorial: "If Sister Sophia comes in, it's yours."

This person, here at the center of the world, deep in the heart of Catholicism, knew Leni, even as Pfeiffer, not only as Gruyten, and this celestial person now proceeded with scholarly detachment to look through a green cardboard box, surface dimensions: standard letter-size, height: approximately four inches, and, with only occasional recourse to various papers and bundles to refresh her memory, produced information on "Sister Rahel Maria Ginzburg from the Baltic States; born near Riga in 1891, matriculated at Königsberg in 1908; attended university in Berlin, Göttingen, Heidelberg. Graduated from the last-named in 1914, majoring in biology. Jailed several times during World War I as a pacifist socialist of Jewish origin. In 1918 studied under

Claude Bernard for her thesis on the beginnings of endocrinology, a work that was hard to place on account of its medical, theological, philosophical, and moral dimensions but was eventually accepted by an internist as a medical work. Practiced medicine in working-class areas in the Ruhr. Converted to Catholicism in 1922. Lectured extensively to Youth Movement groups. Entered the convent after much difficulty, due not so much to her pseudomaterialistic teachings as to her age, in 1932 she was forty-one after all and had not—to put it mildly—lived an entirely platonic life. Intercession by a cardinal. Entered the convent; was barred from teaching after six months. Well"—at this point the lovely Sister Klementina calmly reached for the Au.'s package of cigarettes and "stuck a fag between her lips" (Au.)—"the rest you know, at least a bit of it. But I must correct any impression that they terrorized her at the Gerselen convent. On the contrary: they hid her. She was reported as 'escaped' and, to tell the truth, Miss Gruyten's (or Mrs. Pfeiffer's) charitable and possibly even slightly homoerotic association with her, her solicitude for her, posed a real threat to Sister Ginzburg, to the convent, to Miss Gruyten. Even Scheukens, the gardener, behaved most irresponsibly in letting Mrs. Pfeiffer in. Never mind, it's past history now, we survived it, though painfully, though with mutual recrimination, and since I assume you have some small measure of insight into the dialectics of motivation I needn't explain that if one wishes to save a person from concentration camp one is more or less obliged to hide that person under concentration-camp conditions. It was cruel, but wouldn't it have been crueler still to have left her to her fate? One must face the fact that she was not much liked, and there was some harassment, some nastiness, on both sides, for she was a stubborn person.

"Well, to cut a long story short: now comes the terrible part. Will you believe me when I tell you that the Order has not the slightest interest in creating a saint but that, because of certain—certain phenomena which the Order would much rather suppress, it is being virtually forced on a course that is anything but popular? Will you believe me?"

To the Au. it seemed that the interrogative form of the future tense as applied to the verb "to believe," issuing from the lips of such an eminent Germanist, of a nun "sinfully" inhaling Virginia cigarettes who, whenever she looked in the mirror, could not fail to be gratified by the sight of the classic line of her firm but delicate dark brows, the flattering effect of her nun's coif, the intensely seductive line of her firm, frankly sensual mouth; who was quite well aware of the effect of her uncommonly attractive hands; whose chaste habit nevertheless "hinted at" a faultless bosom beneath it—to hear from such lips the interrogative form of the future tense as applied to the verb "to believe" seemed to the Au. most unfair! A simple question in the future tense such as "Will you go for a walk with me?" or "Will you propose to me?" is perfectly permissible in such circumstances, but the question of whether a person *will believe* what he has not yet even heard—! The Au. was weak enough to nod his assent and moreover, penetrating looks having already challenged him to verbal utterance, to breathe a Yes such as is otherwise breathed only at the marriage altar. What else could he—the Au.—do?

From this moment on there could be no further doubt that the journey to Rome had been worthwhile, this compulsion to breathe a Yes having given the Au. some insight into a highly sophisticated, celibate-platonic eroticism such as Sister Cecilia had no more than hinted at. Even Sister Klementina seemed conscious of having gone a shade too far; she withdrew a good deal of the intensive charm of her eyes, her—there is no getting away from it—rosebud mouth took on a sour little twist, and the Au. reacted to her next remarks as to a deliberately administered psychological cold shower. She said—and far from not fluttering an eyelash, her eyelashes (which, surprisingly and soberingly, were short and straight, rather like little brooms) fluttered considerably as she spoke:

"Incidentally, nowadays when we discuss the problems of *The Marquise of O*___ our pupils coolly come back at us with: 'She should've taken the pill, even if she was a widow'—in this way even the lyricism of a writer of Kleist's eminence is dragged down to the level of a cheap tabloid. But I won't digress. The bad part about the Ginzburg case is not, as you might suppose, that miracles are being contrived. On the contrary: we can't get rid of the miracles. We can't get rid of the roses that bloom in midwinter where Sister Rahel is buried. I admit we have prevented you from talking to Sister Cecilia and Scheukens—who, by the way, has been excellently taken care of, you don't have to worry about him—but not because we are manipulating a miracle, rather because the miracle is manipulating us, and we want to keep news-hungry outsiders away from it, not because we desire the beatification process but because we don't! Now do you believe what you promised to believe?"

This time, before answering, the Au. gave her a thoughtful and "searching" look: Sister Klementina suddenly looked so—there is no other way to express it—haggard, upset, she adjusted her coif, thereby causing—unfortunately this also is true—a wealth of auburn hair to become visible; she fished another cigarette out of the package, this time with the weary routine of a chain-smoking co-ed who at four in the morning realizes in despair that her paper on Kafka which she is to read six hours from now is a complete mess.

She poured some more tea, added milk and sugar in exactly the proportions preferred by the Au., even stirred it for him, shifted his cup closer to him, and looked at him—there is no other word for it—imploringly. Again one must visualize the situation: late on a sunny afternoon in spring. Rome. Scent of pines. The sound of cicadas dying away—church bells, marble, leather Morris chairs, wooden tubs with peonies just coming into bloom, everything positively vibrating with that Catholicism which now and again sends Protestants into raptures; the sudden wilting of Klementina's beauty, only a few minutes before in full bloom; her sobering remark about *The Marquise of O___*. With a sigh she turned to the green box and took out paper after paper, little bundles secured by paper clips or rubber bands, five, six, ten, eighteen—a total of twenty-six: "A report for each year, and always the same: roses suddenly sprouting out of the ground in December. Roses that don't begin to fade till roses normally begin blooming! We have gone to the most desperate lengths, lengths you might even feel were macabre, we have exhumed her, transferred—er, her remains, which were unquestionably in a state of decay corresponding to the time of her death, to other burial grounds in the convent; then, when those terrible roses started blossoming there too, we exhumed her again, put her back where she came from, exhumed her once more, had her cremated, placing the urn in the chapel, where it is true to say that there wasn't even a speck of Mother Earth anywhere near: roses! They came welling up out of the urn, grew rampant all over the chapel; back into the earth with her ashes—and again: roses. I'm convinced that if the urn were dropped from a plane roses would grow out of the ocean, out of the desert!

"So that's our problem. Not telling the world but keeping it dark, that's our problem, and *that's* why we had to keep you away from Sister Cecilia, why we had to promote Scheukens and make him manager of a big farming estate near Würzburg, that's why we are worried about Mrs. Pfeiffer, not because she disputes the—er—phenomenon, but because, judging by what I know of her from the additional information you have now given me, she would most likely regard it as perfectly natural for roses to blossom from the ashes of her friend Haruspica, year after year around the middle of December, a dense, thorny rose thicket such as I have never imagined outside of Sleeping Beauty. If only all this were happening in Italy—in this country we'd have nothing to fear even from the Communists, but in Germany! That would be a regression into Heaven knows what century. What would become of liturgical reform, of recent demonstrations of the physico-biological plausibility of so-called miracles! And besides: who could guarantee that the roses would go on blossoming if the affair were publicized? What kind of fools would we look like if they suddenly stopped? Even quite reactionary circles in Rome are advising us, with due courtesy, to close our files. Botanists, biologists, and theologians have been asked to inspect the phenomenon with assurances of absolute discretion. Do you know who it was that claimed to be moved by it, who introduced the supernatural element? The botanists and biologists, not the theologians. And think of the political dimensions: from the ashes of a Jewish woman who converted, became a nun and was promptly banned from teaching, who then—let's face it—died under highly unpleasant circumstances—from the ashes of this woman, roses have been blossoming since 1943! It's like witchcraft. Magic. Mysticism. And I, I of all people, I who have been outspokenly critical of Benn's biologism, *I* am saddled with this file! Do you know what an eminent prelate said to me with a chuckle on the phone yesterday? 'Paul supplies us with enough miracles, please don't give us any more. He is all the Little Flower we want, we don't need any more flowers.' Are you going to keep quiet about it?"

Here, instead of nodding, the Au. shook his head vigorously, reinforcing this movement by a clearly enunciated "No," and because Klementina now smiled, wearily, and with the aid of the empty cigarette package swept the butts from her saucer into the Au.'s to consolidate them with his, then, still wearily and again using the empty package, swept the smokers' traces into a blue plastic wastebasket, then, smiling, remained standing as a sign that it was time to leave, the Au. is not sure whether the purpose of denying a miracle is not in fact an attempt to contrive that miracle.

Klementina, chatting about books, accompanied the Au. to the gates. It was quite a distance, nearly a quarter of a mile across the extensive grounds. Cypresses, pines, oleanders—all familiar enough. When they reached the street, with the view of the gold-red Eternal City, the Au. handed Klementina his unopened reserve package of cigarettes, and with a smile she hid it in the sleeve of her habit, tucking it inside the shirtlike garment whose elasticized cuffs rendered it suitable for hiding more than cigarettes. And here, while waiting for the bus that was to take him into town in the direction of the Vatican, the Au. felt the moment had come to break the platonic spell; he drew Klementina between two young cypress trees and kissed her with perfect naturalness on the forehead, the right cheek, then on the mouth. Not only did she not resist, she said with a sigh: "Mm, yes," smiled and was silent for a few seconds until she in turn kissed him on the cheek and said, as she heard the bus approaching: "Come back—but please don't bring any roses."

The fact that the Au. found this journey worthwhile will be readily understood; his desire not to delay his departure and thus avoid thrusting a variety of people into conflict-situations may be understood with equal ease; and since the principle of making haste slowly did not apply in his case, he chose to return by air—inwardly racked, as he still is, by the problem of whether (and if so, to what degree) professional and private interests had combined (in terms of expenses) in this trip, and furthermore racked, if only partially, by a problem of both professional and private dimensions: had K. been subtly angling for publicity for the Gerselen miracle of the roses, or had she, with equal subtlety, been trying to prevent it? And, assuming he managed to interpret from the expression of the woman he now loved which it was that she wanted, how was he to conduct himself: objectively, as dictated by duty, or subjectively, as dictated by inclination and the desire to please K.?

Preoccupied with this quadruple problem, on edge, or perhaps one should say irritable, he found the winter of his own country, following immediately upon the Roman spring, indeed hard to take: snow in Nifelheim, slippery streets, a bad-tempered taxi driver who was forever wanting to gas, shoot, kill, or at least beat up somebody, and—a sharp disappointment—an unfriendly reception at the convent gates in Gerselen, where he was turned away with a few brusque words by a grouchy old nun who remarked cryptically: "We're fed up with journalists!"

However, there was nothing to stop him from walking around the convent walls (total length approximately five hundred yards around all four sides), he could still look at the Rhine, village church closed (where the altar boys had served who had once gone into ecstasies over Margret's skin). Here Leni had lived, here Haruspica was buried, dug up, buried again, once more dug up, cremated—and nowhere, nowhere a gap in the convent wall! He was left with the village inn, and, once inside, the atmosphere was a far cry from the peaceful somnolence of Alfred Bullhorst's village. No, here it was noisy, the Au. was eyed suspiciously, here he noticed strangers of an unmistakable category; journalists, in fact, who, when he asked the innkeeper at the counter for a room, chimed in like some mocking chorus. "A room in Gerselen, today! And maybe"—the mockery was intensified—"maybe even a room with a view of the convent garden, eh?" And when he naively nodded, a regular howl went up, a Hahaha and a Hohoho from smartly dressed men and women who, when he was taken in by further mock-friendliness and confirmed that he did indeed want a view of the snow-covered convent garden, finally accepted him into the ranks of the simpletons, became more friendly and—while the innkeeper poured and tapped, tapped and poured, put him wise: didn't he know what everyone was talking about?—that in the convent garden a hot spring had been discovered that had caused an old rose bush to blossom; that the nuns, invoking their rights to control their own territory, had screened off the spot in question with their own hands; that, because the door to the church tower was locked, someone had sent to the neighboring university town (the very one where B.H.T. had had his tête-à-têtes with Haruspica! Au.) to borrow a seventy-foot extension ladder from a demolition firm in order to "sneak a look at what the nuns were up to"?

Now they were all crowding around the Au., who no longer knew whether he had been naive, and if so to what extent—the people from UPI, from dpa, from AFP, and even one representative of Novosti who, together with a CTK man, was determined "to tear the mask from the face of clerical Fascism and expose this election gimmick of the Christian Democratic Union. You know," went on the Novosti man, otherwise a nice enough fellow, as he held out a beer to the Au., "in Italy the madonnas shed tears during election time, and now the latest thing is for hot springs to emerge in convent gardens in the Federal Republic of Germany, roses grow where nuns were buried, nuns, so they would have us believe, who are supposed to have been raped during the Soviet occupation of East Prussia. Anyway, it's being claimed that this business has some Communist angle or other, and what else can Communists have done to nuns but rape them?" The Au., better informed than most of those present, having five hours previously (a view of Rome spread before him) kissed a cheek that was anything but parchment-skinned, decided to capitulate and await the newspaper reports. It was futile to continue a search for the truth here. Had Leni in some twisted way been mixed up in the story, had Haruspica been transformed into heat? He left the inn, and just as he was closing the door he heard the mocking voice of one of the women journalists starting up the old carol: "Oh see the rose that's blossomed!"

The very next day, in the morning edition of the newspaper already quoted, he found a "definitive report":

"The strange occurrence, sarcastically described in the Eastern European press as the 'Gerselen Hot Springs Miracle of the Roses,' has turned out to be due to natural causes. As indicated by the place name itself, in which the word 'geyser' is concealed (Gerselen may at one time have been called Geyslrenheim), there were hot springs in Gerselen as long ago as the fourth century A.D., which explains why during the eighth century the place was for a time the site of a small imperial residence that was maintained until the springs dried up again. The nuns have emphatically stated, as we have been informed in an exclusive interview with the mother superior, Sister Sapientia, that they have never at any time thought in terms of a miracle and have spread no such reports; that the word may quite possibly have found its way into the reports via a former pupil whose connection with the long-standing Gerselen high school can only be described as ambivalent and who at a later date was associated with the German Communist Party. The fact of the matter is, she went on, that, as has meanwhile been confirmed by experts, the eruption—unexpected, she must admit—of some hot springs had indeed caused a number of rose bushes to bloom. Nothing, nothing whatever, declared Sister Sapientia in the down-to-earth manner of a modern, open-minded, and enlightened member of a religious order, permitted the assumption of any supernatural element."

While he did not hesitate for a moment to tell Margret about the miracle of the roses and the hot springs and the story behind them (she was all smiles, believed everything, and urged him not to neglect Klementina), and even exposed himself to the acerbic ridicule of Lotte, who naturally said it was all a fraud and relegated him to the embarrassing category of nun-chasers ("And I mean that literally as well as symbolically." Lotte), the Au. hesitated to acquaint Leni with the strange happenings in Gerselen or give even an outline of the state of his investigations in Rome. B.H.T.—the Au. felt—also had a right to know the effect being attributed, after twenty-seven years, to the ashes of the Sister Rahel whom he had unquestionably held in such high esteem. Meanwhile geologists of repute, supported by a number of prospectors from an oil company that had no scruples about exploiting the affair of the miracle of the roses for publicity purposes, had expressed their unshakable opinion that the event was of "exclusively natural origin," yet a section of the Eastern European press still clung obstinately to the version that the "Gerselen electioneering support for reactionary forces" had "collapsed merely because of indefatigable pressure from socialist forces, and it has now retreated behind the opinions of pseudoscientific experts who are entirely subservient to capitalism. This is but one more proof of the extent to which capitalist science can be manipulated."

It may be that the Au. has not measured up here; he should have intervened, he should have climbed over the wall in Gerselen, possibly supported by the bald-headed B.H.T., should have mobilized Leni, at least picked a few roses for her and delivered them at her door; they might well have been a most fitting adornment to her ambitious painting "Part of the Retina of the Left Eye of the Virgin Mary alias Rahel." But just at this moment events came thick and fast, becoming so involved that the Au. had no time to yield to a private nostalgia that was pulling him toward Rome. Duty called, it called in the form of Herweg Schirtenstein, who had set up a kind of "Leni Needs You—Help Leni Committee" and was planning to round up everyone to give her support, both moral and financial, against increasing pressure from the Hoysers, and possibly even to contemplate political measures.

Over the telephone Schirtenstein sounded agitated yet determined, the sensitive huskiness of his voice, whose vibrations in previous conversations had sounded as thin as veneer, now sounded metallic. He asked for the addresses of all "persons interested in this astounding woman," was given them, and called a meeting for that evening. This gave the Au. time finally—for the sake of objectivity, justice, and truth, and to avoid as far as possible adopting a purely emotional stance, also from a sense of duty to obtain information—to invade the headquarters of the opposition. The Hoysers, likewise interested in presenting their point of view in this unfortunate affair, probably also from fear of certain planned actions, were at once prepared "to put aside some very urgent business." The only difficulty turned out to be the choice of a meeting place. The choice was between: the apartment of old Mr. Hoyser in that combination of luxury hotel, retirement home, and sanatorium already described; the office or apartment of his grandson Werner, the proprietor of the betting office; the office or apartment of the "Building Development Manager" (title is an exact quotation from his own definition. Au.), Kurt Hoyser; and the conference room of Hoyser, Inc., a corporation in which "we jointly represent our various interests and investments." (All quotations as given over the telephone by Kurt Hoyser.)

It was not entirely without self-interest that the Au. suggested the conference room of Hoyser, Inc., situated on the twelfth floor of a high-rise building beside the Rhine and, as initiates know but the Au. had not yet discovered, offering a fantastic view over both landscape and cityscape. On the way there the Au. felt some qualms: when confronted by the truly prestigious, his lower-middle-class nature always reacts with trepidation; his extremely lower-middle-class background causes him to enjoy being there yet to feel out of place. With a quaking heart he entered the lobby of that exclusive building whose penthouse apartments are so popular. A doorman, not exactly in uniform, nor even in livery, yet somehow giving the impression of being in both uniform and livery, eyed him not exactly disdainfully, merely appraisingly, and the definite impression was given: his footwear did not pass muster. Silent elevator: familiar enough. In the elevator a brass plate inscribed with the words "Floor Directory," a quick glance —an intensive and detailed study was not possible owing to the disconcertingly silent speed of the elevator—revealed that the forces at work in this building were almost exclusively creative: architects, editorial offices, fashion agencies, one plate—because of its width—being particularly noticeable: ERWIN KELF, CONTACTS WITH CREATIVE PEOPLE.

Still mulling over the question of whether these contacts were physical or intellectual, or possibly merely social (without obligation), or whether the allusion was to a camouflaged call-man or call-girl ring, he found himself already at the twelfth floor where the door slid silently open and a pleasant-looking fellow awaited him, introducing himself simply with the words: "I'm Kurt Hoyser." Without the slightest sign of familiarity, condescension, let alone contempt, with an agreeable neutral friendliness by no means exclusive of cordiality, in fact presupposing it, Kurt Hoyser led him into the conference room which was strongly reminiscent of the one in which, two days before, he had been sitting opposite Klementina: marble, metal doors and windows, leather Morris chairs—and a view, not exactly of the gold-red city of Rome, merely of the Rhine and some of the little places along its banks, at the precise geographical point where the still majestic river enters upon its very, very filthiest state, approximately thirty to forty miles upriver from the point where the whole filthy river, or river filth, is discharged onto the innocent Dutch towns of Arnhem and Nijmegen.

The room, which, apart from the furniture, seemed unexpectedly pleasant, was shaped like the segment of a circle and contained nothing but a few tables and those very Morris chairs that were directly related to the ones at the Order's motherhouse in Rome. The reader will no doubt concede that the Au. found new nourishment here for his nostalgia, and will understand why he was momentarily so taken aback that he paused on the threshold. He was assigned the best seat, by the window with a view of the Rhine and right across half a dozen bridges; arranged on the table, whose graceful curves corresponded to the sweep of the picture window, were: a variety of alcoholic drinks, fruit juice, tea in a Thermos jug; there were also cigars and cigarettes, their quantity and selection being far from vulgarly nouveau riche, on the contrary, in sensible moderation. Here one may with propriety use the words "quiet elegance."

Both old Mr. Hoyser and his grandson Werner seemed much more likable than he had remember them; as befitted his situation, the Au. hastened to correct and lay aside his prejudices and to assume the ominous Kurt Hoyser, whom he was meeting for the first time, to be a likable, quiet, modest fellow who had endowed his otherwise carefully chosen apparel with that soupçon of casualness that suited his quiet baritone voice. He bore a striking resemblance to his mother Lotte: the hairline, the round eyes. Had this man once really been the infant born under such dramatic circumstances who at the insistence of his mother had not been baptized; born in the very room where a Portuguese family of five now slept, and had he really, together with the far tougher-looking Werner (now thirty-five), rolled Pelzer's own cigarette butts in new cigarette paper when they were all living in the Soviet paradise in the vaults, subsequently palming them off as "regulars" on the still resentful Pelzer?

A few moments of embarrassment ensued, it being obvious that the Au. was regarded as some kind of emissary, and some unavoidable explanation on the part of the Au. was needed in order to explain his visit. To *obtain information,* to obtain *facts.*

There was no question—thus the Au. in his concise explanation—of sympathies, partisanship, offers, counteroffers. Only the actual state of affairs was of interest here, no ideology, no proxy, of any kind; he—the Au.—had been in no way empowered, nor was he interested in being empowered; the "person under discussion" had never once been introduced to him, he had merely seen her two or three times on the street, had never exchanged a single word with her, his desire was to conduct a research into her life, a piecemeal research perhaps, but no more piecemeal than necessary, his mission emanated from neither a terrestrial nor a celestial authority, it was *existential:* and noting for the first time on the faces of all three Hoysers, who had barely managed to listen to his discourse with polite attention, something approaching interest because, as was quite obvious, they appeared to sense in the word "existential" a purely material interest, the Au. felt obliged to present *all* aspects of the existential elements in the matter. Then, asked by Kurt Hoyser whether he was an idealist, he vigorously denied it; asked whether in that case he was a materialist, a realist, he denied this with equal vigor; all at once he found himself the target of a kind of cross-examination being conducted in turn by old Mr. Hoyser, Kurt, and Werner: they asked him whether he was an intellectual, a Catholic, a Protestant, a Rhinelander, a Socialist, a Marxist, liberal, for or against the sex-wave, the pill, the Pope, Barzel, a free economy, a planned economy; and finally, since—it being a sort of vocal barrage that forced him constantly to swivel his head in the direction of each questioner—he consistently and categorically answered all these questions in the negative, a secretary emerged without warning from a hitherto invisible door, poured him some tea, moved the cheese biscuits closer to him, opened a cigarette box and, by pressing a button, caused one of the apparently seamless walls to slide back; from the aperture she extracted three file folders and placed them on the table in front of Kurt Hoyser, with notepad, paper, and pipe beside them, before—a person of neutral prettiness who reminded the Au. of the businesslike efficiency with which in certain movies the requirements of bordello customers are attended to—she vanished, blond, medium-bosomed, once again through the door.

Finally old Mr. Hoyser was the first to break the silence: he lightly tapped the files with his crook-handled cane, letting it lie on the files to enable him to supply periodic rhythmic punctuation. "This means," he said, and his voice held an undeniable note of wistfulness, "this means the end of a link, an association, an era that for seventy-five years has seen me closely associated with the Gruyten family. As you know, I was fifteen when I became Hubert Gruyten's godfather—and now I, and with me my grandsons, am severing all ties, destroying the whole fabric."

For once, a certain condensation is called for, since old Hoyser dilated a good deal—beginning roughly with the apples he used to pick at the age of six (ca. 1890) in the garden of Leni's parents' house, proceeding to a fairly minute description of two world wars (emphasizing his basically democratic stance), describing Leni's various (political, moral, financial) mistakes and stupidities, and the lives of virtually all the characters presented here—a discourse lasting approximately an hour and a half that the Au. found somewhat tiring in view of the fact that he was already in possession, although via other channels, of most of the information. Leni's mother, Leni's father, the young architect with whom she had once gone away for the weekend, her brother, her cousin, the Dead Souls, everything, the lot—and it seemed to the Au. that not even the grandsons were listening with undivided attention—also "certain transactions that had been one hundred percent legal"—was hashed over with aggressiveness that was defensive rather than one-dimensional, almost in the style of Mr. Exalted; the piece of land given to Kurt in his infancy—here the Au. pricked up his ears—"when Mrs. Gruyten's grandfather acquired it in 1870 from an emigrating farmer, had cost ten pfennigs a square yard in those days, and that was a charitable price, he could have got it for four pfennigs, but of course *they* always had to be the generous ones and, being a lunatic, he even rounded the price upward and instead of some five thousand marks planked down six thousand, which meant he was paying twelve pfennigs a square yard. Is it our fault if today each square yard is worth three hundred and fifty marks? If we take into consideration certain—as I believe—temporary inflationary trends, you might say the figure was actually five hundred, not counting the value of the building, which you can safely take as being equal to the value of the land. And believe me, if you brought me a buyer tomorrow who offered me five million, cash on the nail, I—we wouldn't part with it, and now come here and look out the window."

At this point he calmly used his cane as a grappling iron, hooking it into the loosely buttoned jacket of the Au., who at the best of times is in a constant state of anxiety over his loose buttons, and pulled him, not without unwarranted force and—it is only fair to say—not without a shake of the head from his grandsons, brusquely toward him, thus compelling the Au. to look out at the surrounding buildings which, with their nine, eight, and seven floors, were stacked around the twelve-story building. "Do you know," this in an ominously soft voice, "do you know what they call this part of the city?" Head shake from the Au., who is not that observant of topographical changes. "They call this part of the city Hoyseringen—and it stands on land that for seventy years was simply allowed to lie fallow, until someone was good enough to present it to that young gentleman over there" (cane waved in Kurt's direction, voice now mocking) "when he was an infant, and it was I, I, I who saw to it that it didn't continue to lie fallow, in accordance with the saying that used to be preached to our forefathers: 'Replenish the earth, and subdue it.'"

It was at this juncture that the old gentleman, who was, after all, of a venerable age, began to show signs of senility; although now openly aggressive himself, he interpreted the Au.'s attempts to disengage himself from the walking cane/grappling iron as aggressiveness on the *Au.'s* part, although the latter proceeded gingerly enough and, out of his concern for his buttons, with great restraint. Hoyser, Sr., suddenly turned brick-red and actually ripped off the button, thereby putting paid to a sizable fragment of well-worn tweed, and brandished his cane menacingly over the Au.'s head. Although the Au. is at all times prepared to turn the other cheek, this seemed to be an occasion calling for self-defense: he ducked out of reach and barely managed to weather the situation with dignity. Meanwhile, Kurt and Werner intervened appeasingly and, apparently summoned by the pressing of an invisible button, the blond, medium-bosomed efficiency-machine went into action: with a sangfroid both indescribable and inimitable she lured the old gentleman out of the office by whispering something into his ear, a procedure that prompted both grandsons to remark in one voice: "Trude, you're the perfect Girl Friday!" Before leaving the sanctum (the Au. is not going to risk using the word "room" in this context for fear it might lead to libel charges), the old gentleman called back over his shoulder: "Hubert, that laugh of yours is going to cost you a pretty penny, and he who laughs last laughs longest."

Mr. Werner and Mr. Kurt Hoyser seemed affected by these events from the insurance angle only. An embarrassing trialogue ensued on the subject of the damaged jacket. A spontaneous attempt by Werner to offer compensation for the jacket by an immediate and overgenerous cash payment was, so to speak, nipped in the bud by a glance from Kurt; Werner's hand had already gone to his wallet in the universally familiar gesture but was then withdrawn in astonishment. Such phrases were uttered as: "It goes without saying that we will reimburse you for a new jacket, although we are under no obligation to do so." Such phrases as: "Compensation for pain and suffering," "shock supplement"; insurance companies were named, policies quoted with their numbers, finally the poker-faced Trude, on being summoned, asked the Au. for his business card, and when it turned out that he did not possess one she made a note of his address in her stenographer's notebook with a look of open disgust, her expression implying that she was being forced to handle a type of excrement whose stench was of a particularly revolting nature.

Here the Au. would like to say something about himself: he was not interested in a new jacket worth as much or even twice as much as his old one, he wanted his old jacket back again and, peevish though it may sound, he was genuinely attached to it and insisted that his garment be restored to its former condition; consequently, when the Hoyser brothers tried to talk him out of this by indicating the decline in the tailoring trade, he indicated that he knew of an invisible-mending expert, a woman who had already done several excellent jobs on his jacket. We all know the kind of people who, although no one has ever forbidden them to speak or ever would, suddenly say: "I'd like to say something," or "May I say something?"—this was the kind of situation in which the Au. found himself, for at this stage of the negotiations he was finding it hard to preserve his objectivity; he refrained from mentioning the age of his jacket, the journeys he had made with it, the numerous scraps of paper he had stuffed into its pockets and taken out again, the small change in the lining, the bread crumbs, the fluff, and should he actually tell them that, scarcely forty-eight hours ago, Klementina's cheek had rested, albeit briefly, against his right lapel? Should he expose himself to the suspicion of sentimentality, when actually all he cared about was that concrete concern of the Western world expressed by Vergil in the phrase *lacrymae rerum?*

The atmosphere was not nearly as harmonious now as it had been and might have been had the two Hoyser brothers showed the remotest understanding of the fact that a person is more attached to an old object than to a new one, and that there are some things in this world that cannot be assessed from the insurance angle. "If," Werner Hoyser said at last, "someone drives into your old VW and, though he's only obligated to reimburse you for its used-car value, offers you a new VW and you don't accept it, I can only call that abnormal." The mere suggestion that the Au. drove some ancient VW was an affront, although an unconscious one, an allusion to income bracket and taste which, not objectively perhaps, but subjectively, was of the nature of a humiliation. Will anyone find it offensive to learn that he—the Au.—emerged from his objectivity and stated in no uncertain terms that they could stuff their VW's, whether old or new?—all he wanted was for his jacket, which had been ruined by a senile old roué, to be restored to its former condition.

Obviously such a conversation could lead nowhere. How can

you explain to a person that you happen to be attached to your old jacket, and that you can't take it off—as was being demanded, in order to assess the actual extent of the damage—because, damn it, life's like that sometimes, you have a hole in your shirt, a tear caused by a Roman youth in a bus with his fishhook; also because the shirt is by now something less than clean, damn it, since in the service of truth you are forever moving about, forever making notes with pencils and ball-point pens, and at night, dog tired, you fall into bed without taking your shirt off? Isn't restoration an easy enough word to understand? It may well be that people after whom parts of a city are named which they have built on their own land suffer a well-nigh metaphysical exasperation when obliged to acknowledge that there are apparently some things, even jackets, for which the owner cannot be compensated in money. There may well be a sad provocation in this—but those who have thus far been reasonably convinced of the Au.'s strictly rational attitude will also credit him with something that may sound incredible: in this confrontation *he* was the rational one, the quiet, courteous, albeit immovable element, whereas the two Hoysers became irrational, their voices exasperated, on edge, hurt, their—toward the end of this painful scene even Kurt's—hands twitching continually in the direction where one might suppose their wallets to be—as if from in there they could extract jackets, beloved twelve-year-old jackets that are dearer to a person than his own skin and less replaceable, for skin is transplantable whereas a jacket is not; to which one is attached *without* sentimentality, simply because, in the final analysis, one is a member of the Western world and the *lacrymae rerum* have been drummed into one.

A still further provocation was seen in the Au.'s going down on his hands and knees on the parquet floor and slithering about in search of the scrap of material that had been ripped out with one of his buttons, for obviously he was going to need this when he went to the invisible mender's. His final rejection of any kind of compensation and his offer to have the jacket invisibly mended at his own expense while indicating that this might be classified as a business expense, since he was here on business, wasn't he, was also taken as an affront; money was no object, etc. Oh what a chain of misunderstandings! Is it really so impossible to believe that a person merely wants his jacket back, his jacket and nothing else? Must this immediately place one under suspicion of fetishistic sentimentalism? And finally, is there no higher economy which should make it an offense simply to discard a jacket that has been darned, invisibly mended, is still eminently wearable, and gives pleasure to the wearer, simply because one has a bulging wallet and wishes to avoid annoyance?

At last, after this annoying interlude that had noticeably impaired the initial harmony, they got down to business: to the three file folders that evidently constituted Leni's dossier. Again some condensation is merited of all the things that were dished up again about "Aunt Leni's sloppy ways," Aunt Leni's unrealistic attitude, Aunt Leni's faulty child-rearing methods, the company Aunt Leni kept—"and so that you won't think we're prudish or old-fashioned, or not progressive, the point here is not the lovers, not even the Turks or the Italians or the Greeks—the point is that the property is showing a profit of almost 65 percent less than it should; the proceeds from a sale alone, if wisely invested, could yield an annual revenue of forty to fifty thousand marks, probably more, but we wish to be fair so we will take the lower figure as a basis for argument—and how much does the building yield? If we deduct repairs, costs of administration, and the consequences of the asocial occupancy of the ground floor, where Aunt Leni lives and positively scares away a better class of tenant—thereby ruining the rent level—how much does the building yield? Less than fifteen thousand, barely thirteen or fourteen." Thus Werner Hoyser.

Followed by Kurt Hoyser (condensed, verifiable from the Au.'s notes), who maintained they had nothing against foreign workers, they had no racial prejudices, but one must be consistent, and if Aunt Leni were to declare her willingness to *accept* rents at the going rate, then one would be prepared to discuss opening up the whole building to foreign workers, space to be rented by the bed, by the room, Aunt Leni to be appointed manageress and even supplied with rent-free accommodation and a monthly cash allowance; the trouble was that she was collecting—and this really was madness and contrary to the conclusions reached even by socialist economic doctrine—she was collecting in rents exactly what she was paying out herself; it was only for her sake that the rent had been kept at DM.2.50 a square yard and not in order that others should profit by it; for instance, the Portuguese family was paying DM.125 for 50 square yards, plus DM.13 for use of bath and kitchen, the three Turks ("Of whom one, of course, more often than not sleeps with her, which means that their room is occupied by two persons only") are paying DM.87.50 for 35 square yards, whereas the Helzen couple are paying DM.125 for 50 square yards, plus the DM.13 each, "and then she's crazy enough to calculate her share of kitchen and bath at double-occupancy rate because she's keeping the extra room for Lev who, as we know, is being temporarily housed free of charge." And the last straw was the fact that she was charging the unfurnished rate for furnished rooms; and that, mind you, was nothing as harmless as some anarchistic-Communist experiment—that was undermining the market; without being too unfair, one could easily squeeze 300 to 400 marks a room, with use of bath and kitchen, out of the building. Etc. Etc.

Even Kurt Hoyser seemed embarrassed to bring up a subject "that I must touch on if we're going to be businesslike": the fact was that, of the ten beds, only seven actually belonged to Leni, one still belonged to Grandfather, a second one to the deeply injured Heinrich Pfeiffer, and the third to his parents, the Pfeiffers, "whose very hair stands on end when they think of what may be going on in those beds." In other words, Leni was violating not only incontestable economic laws and usage rights, but also ownership rights, and since by this time the Pfeiffers found it quite impossible to negotiate directly with Leni, they had designated Hoyser, Inc., as trustees of their ownership rights to the beds: there were therefore not only personal but legally assigned rights to be preserved, in other words the affair had acquired an additional dimension in which matters of principle were at stake. Granted, of course, that the bed belonging to Heinrich Pfeiffer was the one given him by Aunt Leni's mother during the war "while he was waiting to be called up," but a gift was a gift; moreover, in the eyes of the law a gift was an irrevocable transfer of property. Furthermore—the Au. was free to make what use he liked of this—it was hard to see why all the tenants and/or subtenants should be employed by the city garbage-collection and/or street-cleaning departments.

Here the Au. intervened by pointing out that the Helzen couple were *not* employees of the garbage-collection department: Mr. Helzen was a municipal employee in a fairly senior position, Mrs. Helzen pursued the honorable calling of cosmetician, and the Portuguese lady Ana-Maria Pinto was employed at the counter of a self-service restaurant in a reputable department store; he had personally picked up meatballs, cheesecake, and coffee at her counter and checked her calculation of the cost, which had turned out to be accurate. With a nod Kurt Hoyser acknowledged this correction but added that there was a further point in which Aunt Leni had not behaved in a financially responsible manner: she was in perfect health and fit to work for another seventeen years or so, but at the foolish promptings of her mixed-up son she had given up her job in order to look after the three Portuguese children, singing to them, teaching them German, letting them help in her "daubings," keeping them all too often—as the records proved—out of school, just as she had done with her own son. The fact was, there was a whole "raft" of delinquencies to be taken into account, and it so happened that anyone coming into conflict with the law was regarded by his fellows as suspect, and it also so happened that garbage collecting and street cleaning were regarded as the lowest occupations, a fact that had a debasing effect on the social attractiveness of the building and, in consequence, on the rents.

All this was delivered in a quiet tone of voice, with reasonable argumentation, and made sense. The annoyance over the jacket had long been forgotten, merely continuing to smolder in the Au. who, involuntarily fingering his beloved garment, found there was considerable damage to the interlining and, furthermore, could feel that the tear in his shirt caused by the Italian boy had got bigger. But for all that there were good tea, cheese pastries, cigarettes, there was still the superb view through the picture window, and there was something reassuring about the fact that Werner Hoyser was constantly confirming his brother's statements by means of rhythmic nods, in a kind of scansion of the periods, commas, hyphens, and semicolons—the result being a blend of psychedelic and jazz elements that seemed to harmonize remarkably well.

Here we must comment on the empathy of Werner Hoyser, who no doubt felt that the Au., brimful as he was of such lower-middle-class motivation as discretion, would dearly like to broach a topic that was on the tip of his tongue: Lotte Hoyser, who was, after all, the mother of these two self-assured young men.

So it was he—Werner—who did not shrink from broaching the subject of this "regrettable and unfortunately total estrangement"; there should be no pretense, he felt, one should analyze the fact in a businesslike manner, perform a psychic if painful operation, since he knew that contact existed between the Au. and his mother, possibly even mutual understanding, whereas the mutual understanding between him, his brother, Grandfather, and the Au. was, as a result of a "regrettable but in fact trivial occurrence," now "out of balance." He wanted to make the point that he was totally incapable of understanding why a person should prefer a worn-out tweed jacket from a third-rate manufacturer, but he had been brought up in the tradition of tolerance and was prepared to exercise that tolerance, even if only because of the Rhineland motto "Live and let live"; he was also incapable of understanding the very obvious antipathy toward such a popular and ubiquitous automobile as the VW, he had himself acquired a VW for his wife as a second car, and when his son Otto, now twelve, graduated in another six or seven years and started going to university or began his military service, he was going to buy a VW as a third car. Well, never mind all that, now about his mother.

She had—and this was where she had been mainly at fault—

if not exactly falsified the image of the father killed in the war, belittled the historical background against which he had been killed by vulgarly representing it all as crap. "Even such whiz-kids as we must have been were bound one day to demand some image of their father." That had not been denied them, their father had been represented to them as a kind and sensitive man who in some way had been a failure, certainly professionally, nor could there ever have been any doubt of their mother's love for their father Wilhelm, nevertheless their father's image had been systematically, if perhaps not deliberately, destroyed by the continual use of the word crap in every historical context; and even worse was the fact that she had had lovers. Gruyten, well, that had not been too bad, though the irregularity of the relationship had earned them derision and annoyance, but then she had "even" had Russians in her bed, and also from time to time one of "that dreadful woman Margret's discarded Yanks"; and thirdly, her antireligious and antichurch pose—not at all the same thing, as he no doubt knew—had had devastating consequences; in her case both poses had "coincided disastrously"; she had insisted on their attending a nondenominational school that had been most inconveniently located, she had grown steadily more morose and embittered after "Grandpa Gruyten's" accident, and what had been lacking was the counterbalance; this—the counterbalance—he had to admit it, and to this day held it greatly to her credit—was something they had found in Aunt Leni, who had always been warm and kind and generous, had sung them songs, told them fairy tales, and the image of her deceased—well, one might after all say—husband, even though he had been a soldier in the Red Army, this image had remained undefiled, and Leni had refused to participate in the countless interpretations of history as garbage or crap; for years, yes literally for years, she had sat with them and Lev in the evening beside the Rhine, "her hands badly pricked by rose thorns"; and it was Lev who had been baptized, not Kurt, he had been seven years old before the nuns had baptized him when Grandfather Otto had succeeded, "thank God," in rescuing them from "those surroundings," and the reason he said thank God was that

Aunt Leni was marvelous for small children but a disaster for adolescents; she sang too much, spoke too little, although it was soothing and had had a soothing effect that Aunt Leni "never ever carried on with men, while with our mother we were never sure, and that dreadful woman Margret carried on as if in a cathouse." Marja van Doorn also came in for praise from Werner Hoyser, and he even found a kind word for Bogakov, "though he sometimes sang a bit too much too."

Well, in the end they had got onto the right track, had entered upon a Christian way of life, had been raised to standards of achievement and responsibility, had gone to university, he studying law, Kurt political economy, "while Grandfather was carrying on what can only be called the inspired management of his fortune, which enabled us to apply our expertise immediately to our own enterprises." He could understand that some people might regard the operation of a betting office, which to him was merely a side line, as a less than serious undertaking, but the fact was, it was his hobby, a business enterprise designed to indulge his gambling urge. But in the final analysis it must be realized that Aunt Leni was more of a menace than his mother, whom he described as "simply a frustrated pseudosocialist" who could do no harm. Aunt Leni, on the other hand, he regarded as being reactionary in the truest sense of the word: it was inhuman, one might even say monstrous, the way she instinctively, stubbornly, inarticulately, but consistently, refused—not only rejected, that presupposed articulation—every manifestation of the profit motive, simply refused to have anything to do with it. She emitted destruction and self-destruction, it must be a Gruyten element, for it had also been inherent in her brother and to an even stronger degree in her father. Personally, Werner Hoyser said in conclusion, he was not a monster, he was broad-minded, liberal to the utmost limits taught him by his education; he was an open supporter of the pill and the sex-wave, yet considered himself a Christian, he was, if you like, a "fresh-air fiend," and that was what had to be done with Aunt Leni, she needed some fresh air. She was the inhuman one, not he, for a wholesome striving after profit and property—as had been demonstrated by theology and was being increasingly acknowledged even by Marxist philosophers—was part of human nature.

Finally, and this was what he found it hardest to forgive, Leni had on her conscience a human being whom he not only *had* loved but still loved: Lev Borisovich Gruyten, his godson, "who was entrusted to me under such dramatic circumstances that I look on it as a mission, though I may for a time have regarded that mission somewhat cynically, but it so happens that I *am* his godfather, and that is not merely a metaphysical or socioreligious status, it is also a legal status that I intend to observe." It had been interpreted as hatred that he and his brother had laid charges against Lev which had resulted in his being sent to jail, on account of "a few foolish actions that were, after all, of doubtful legality," but to tell the truth this had been an act of affection calculated to bring him to his senses and purge him of what "is surely regarded as the worst of all sins: his pride, his arrogance." He still remembered Lev's father very well, a kind, sensitive, quiet man, and he was convinced that he also would not have liked to see his son become what he had, by a circuitous route, eventually become: a garbage-truck driver. He certainly had no wish to dispute the fact that garbage collecting should be regarded as of great significance and a social function of prime importance, but Lev—there was no arguing about this—was "destined for higher things." (The quotation marks are the Au.'s, who could not be quite sure in listening to Werner Hoyser's words whether he was citing, reciting, or merely citing as his own the words of someone else; it must remain an open question whether the quotation marks are justified. They are to be regarded as merely tentative.)

It must be realized that up to this point almost three hours, from four until seven, had elapsed. So much had happened, so much had been said. Girl Friday had not reappeared, the tea in the Thermos jug had turned bitter from concentration; the cheese pastries had lost their freshness and turned leathery in what was, frankly, a somewhat overheated room and although Werner Hoyser had called himself a fresh-air fiend he made no move to introduce some fresh air into the room, filled to capacity as it was with various types of tobacco smoke (Werner Hoyser: pipe, Kurt Hoyser: cigar, the Au.: cigarette); an attempt by the Au. to open the center section of the window (indicated as openable by a separate brass rim and a handle) was frustrated by Kurt Hoyser with a smile and gentle firmness, not without an allusion to the complex air-conditioning system that only permitted "spontaneous individual airing" at the lighting up of a certain signal that regulated the "climatological system" in the building; this being the hour—thus Kurt Hoyser in a kindly voice—at which the offices and editorial rooms were closing and which might be called the critical hour, one must expect it to be another hour and a half before the magic eye set into the window would light up and give permission to let in fresh air; at the same time the air-conditioning system was so overloaded that it was incapable of introducing sufficient fresh air. "This building, you must remember, is a building unit of forty-eight—twelve times four—individual structural units which at this time, with letters being dictated, vital telephone calls being made, important conferences taking place, are all considerably overloaded. Figure forty-eight units at four rooms each, figure for each room an average of two and a half smokers—shown by statistics to consist of an average of one chain cigarette smoker, half a pipe smoker, approximately three quarters of a cigar smoker—and you will see that at this hour of the day this building contains an average of four hundred and seventy-five smokers—but I interrupted my brother, and I feel we should finish up now for I am sure your time is limited too."

Yes, now it was Werner Hoyser's turn again (greatly condensed here): this was not a matter—as merely superficial observers (by which he on no account meant the Au.) might suppose—of money. Aunt Leni had been offered a rent-free apartment in an excellent location, *rent free,* offers had been made to enable Lev, whose release was imminent, to matriculate at night school and go on to university, but all this had been refused because, so it seemed, one felt at home in the society of garbage collectors, because, so it seemed, one refused to make even the most minimal adjustment; no amenity could tempt her or tempt her away, one was attached, so it seemed, to one's old-fashioned range to one's stoves, to one's habits—there was no doubt about who was the reactionary party here. It was a matter of—and he was using the word, he said, in his dual capacity as a Christian leading the Christian way of life and as a tolerant political economist and jurist who was familiar with constitutional principles—it was a matter of progress, and "in striding forward one must leave many a person behind in one's stride. It's all over with that romantic stuff, 'When we're marching side by side,' the song our mother used to sing to us ad nauseam. *We* can't do whatever we like, either—we are not even permitted to open the windows in our own building whenever we like." Needless to say, it would not be possible to offer Aunt Leni two hundred and eleven square yards in one of the new Hoyser building complexes, that would represent a revenue-loss of almost two thousand marks, nor would it be possible to permit stoves, and windows "that can be flung open at will," and naturally, as far as her tenants, subtenants, and lovers were concerned, certain "very minor social" restrictions would have to be imposed. "But damn it all," and here for the first time Werner Hoyser became, although only momentarily, aggressive, "I wouldn't mind Aunt Leni's easy life myself for a change." For this and other reasons, but mainly on account of higher interests, it was necessary for what seemed like relentless machinery to go into action.

At this juncture the Au. would have dearly liked to speak a few simple and conciliatory words, he would even have been prepared to admit the relative unimportance of the annoyance over the jacket in view of the weighty problems of these tormented people who were not even allowed to fling open the windows in their own building; when one got right down to it, it was not as important as he had first thought. The person who prevented him from speaking these simple words which, if not conciliatory (for there really had been no quarrel between him and the two informants), would at least have been sympathetic, was—Kurt Hoyser. He it was who delivered a kind of summing-up as he blocked the exit in a manner that, far from being threatening, might rather be called pleading, when the Au., topcoat over his arm and cap in hand, briefly took his leave and walked toward the door.

As for the Au., he had had to correct a great many prejudices, for, after all the details he had been given about Kurt Hoyser, he had imagined him to be a blend of hyena and wolf, a ruthless financial baron; yet on closer inspection Kurt H.'s eyes turned out to be downright gentle, only resembling his mother's in their shape, not in their expression; certainly Lotte's mocking asperity and almost lachrymose bitterness were softened in those round, gentle, brown—one might safely say—doe's eyes by elements that could only have come from his father Wilhelm, or at any rate from that side of the family, although not from the latter's father, Kurt's grandfather. When we consider that all the genes of the numerous people directly associated with Leni originated in the geographical triangle of Werpen-Tolzem-Lyssemich, perhaps we must spare a word of praise for those sugar-beet fields after all, despite the fact of their having also produced the Pfeiffers. There was no doubt about it: Kurt Hoyser was a sensitive person and, although time was getting on, he must be given a chance to express this.

He even went so far as to place his hands on the Au.'s shoulders, and here again this gesture contained nothing of familiarity or condescension, merely a certain brotherly affection that no one should be denied. "Look," he said in a low voice, "you mustn't go away with the impression that, as far as Aunt Leni's concerned, some brutal sociohistorical process of automation is under way, a relentless process that destroys obsolete structures and to which we too are subject; certainly that would be the case if we allowed this eviction to proceed without consciousness, without reflection, and entirely without scruple. But that's not how it is. We are doing this consciously and not unscrupulously, at any rate not without having examined our consciences. I will not dispute the pressure being exerted on us by adjacent property-owners and real-estate groups. But we would be powerful enough to shake that off, or at least to get a postponement. Nor will I dispute that our grandfather is motivated by powerful emotional pressures, but those too we could deal with; we could continue, as we have been doing for years, indeed almost for decades, to make up Aunt Leni's rental account out of our own pockets, thus acting as peacemakers and conciliators. When all's said and done we love her, we owe a great deal to her, and we find her whims and fancies endearing rather than unpleasant. I will make you the following promise, and I authorize you to pass on the content of this promise: if by tomorrow the eviction has gone forward, the apartment has been vacated, we, Kurt and I, will immediately settle all accounts, see that all threats of seizure are discontinued; a most attractive apartment in one of our building complexes is already at her disposal, though not, I should say, one in which she can accommodate ten subtenants. Not quite. But there is room enough for her son and possibly her lover, from whom we have no wish to separate her.

"Our action is something I am not ashamed to call a corrective measure, an affectionate guidance, that unfortunately has had to make use of somewhat brutal means of execution. There is simply no such thing as private means of execution. So it will all happen swiftly and painlessly, by noon it will all be over, and if she doesn't get all wrought up over it—which in her case, I am sorry to say, is liable to happen—by evening she will be installed in the apartment that has been readied for her. All preparations have been made to redeem or buy back her beloved old pieces of furniture. The action we are taking is based upon corrective, affectionately corrective, principles.

"Possibly you underestimate the sociological insights of a group such as building and real-estate owners, but I can tell you this much: it has been known for a long while now that it is precisely these large old-fashioned apartments, which are relatively cheap, have certain amenities and so on, in which the cells are formed that are declaring war on our achievement-oriented society. The high wages of the foreign worker in this country are only justifiable, in terms of the national economy, when part of them is skimmed off in rent and thus, in one way or another, remains in the country. The three Turks together earn approximately two thousand and some marks—it is simply unwarrantable that they should only pay roughly a hundred marks in rent out of this, including use of kitchen and bath. That is 5 percent, compared to the 20 to 40 percent a normal working person has to pay. Of the barely two thousand three hundred marks earned jointly by the Helzen couple, they pay roughly a hundred and forty marks, *furnished.* With the Portuguese the situation is similar.

"This is quite simply a case of the competitive situation being falsified in such a way that, were it to spread, it would actually, like some infectious disease, undermine, erode, disintegrate, one of the basic principles of our achievement-oriented society, of the free democratic constitutional state. This represents a violation of the principle of equal opportunity, do you understand? Side by side with this economic antiprocess—and this is central to the issue—there is a moral antiprocess. It so happens that conditions like those in Aunt Leni's apartment foster communal, not to say communistic, illusions which, not as illusions but as idylls, are disastrous, and they also foster, well, not exactly promiscuity—but promiscuitivism, which slowly but surely destroys modesty and morality and makes a mockery of individualism. I could advance still further, probably half a dozen, aspects that make sense. In a nutshell: this is not an action directed personally against Aunt Leni, there is no hatred involved, no revenge, on the contrary, understanding and, to tell the truth, a certain nostalgia for that endearing anarchism, yes, I admit it, a touch of envy—but the deciding factor is this: these types of apartment—and our association has reached this conclusion after a precise analysis of the situation—are the breeding grounds for a—let us say the word without emotion—communalism that fosters utopian idylls and paradisiacal notions. I appreciate your patience, and should you ever run into any housing problems we are—without obligation on your part, merely on the basis of an understanding tolerance—we are at your disposal."

10 In Schirtenstein's apartment the same sort of things were going on as may have gone on in October 1917 in some of the lesser rooms of the Smolny Institute in St. Petersburg. In the various rooms various committees were meeting. Mrs. Hölthohne, Lotte Hoyser, and Dr. Scholsdorff constituted what they called the Finance Committee, whose job it was to examine the extent of Leni's financial plight, records of seized articles, notices of eviction, etc. With the cooperation of the Helzens, Mehmet the Turk, and Pinto the Portuguese, it had been possible to get hold of letters, etc., that Leni had wickedly hidden, unopened, in the drawer of her bedside table and later, when that was full, in the lower section of her bedside table. Pelzer was attached to this triumvirate as a kind of general chief of staff.

Schirtenstein's function, together with Hans Helzen, Grundtsch, and Bogakov (who had been brought along by Lotte in a taxi), was to deal with "social action." M.v.D. had taken on the catering, which meant preparing sandwiches, potato salad, hard-boiled eggs, and tea. Like so many samovar-laymen she was under the impression that tea is actually made in a samovar, but Bogakov familiarized her with the functions of a samovar, a giant apparatus that had been delivered to Schirtenstein's apartment, so he told them, by an unknown donor, with a typed note saying: "For the many thousands of times you have played 'Lili Marleen.' From someone you know." M.v.D., like all housewives in her age group, with no experience in tea-making, had to be persuaded almost forcibly to use at least four times as much tea as she had intended. She turned out, incidentally, to be wonderfully resourceful, and as soon as she found herself with a head start on her food preparations she took the Au.'s jacket, looked—for a long time in vain but then, with Lotte's help, successfully—in Schirtenstein's chest of drawers for his sewing kit, and began, with consummate skill and no glasses, to mend the jacket's painful wounds from inside and out, with a skill that, while not certified by any diploma, was tantamount to invisible mending.

The Au. took himself off to Schirtenstein's bathroom, whose opulent dimensions and enormous bathtub delighted him no less than Schirtenstein's supply of fragrant toiletries. Lotte having discovered, before he could prevent it, the tear in his shirt, Schirtenstein lent him a shirt which, despite a certain discrepancy in chest and collar measurements, was thoroughly acceptable.

One is fully entitled to describe Schirtenstein's apartment as ideal: an old-fashioned building, three rooms facing the courtyard, one of them containing a grand piano, his library, and his desk, the second room, almost warranting the term enormous (dimensions—merely paced out, not measured with a tape: twenty-three by twenty), containing Schirtenstein's bed, clothes closet, chests of drawers, with scattered files containing his collected reviews; the third room was the kitchen, none too large but adequate, and then that bathroom which, compared with a bathroom in any modern building in terms of both spaciousness and fittings, seemed extravagant, not to say luxurious. The windows were open to the courtyard, overlooking trees that were at least eighty years old, an ivy covered wall, and while the Au. was prolonging his bath a sudden silence fell in the adjoining rooms, a silence that had been commanded by a vigorous "ssssh" from Schirtenstein.

And now something happened that temporarily distracted the Au.'s thoughts from Klementina, or rather, considerably intensified them, painfully in a way. Something wonderful happened: a woman was singing—it could only be Leni. Those who have never wondered what the lovely young Lilofee was like would perhaps do best to skip the next few lines; but those who have ever invested a little imagination in the lovely Lilofee, to those we say: only thus can she have sung. It was a girl's voice, a woman's voice, yet it sounded like an instrument, and what was she singing out into the quiet courtyard, through the open window into open windows?

> I made my song a coat
> Covered with embroideries
> Out of old mythologies
> From heel to throat;
> But the fools caught it,
> Wore it in the world's eyes
> As though they'd wrought it.
> Song, let them take it,
> For there's more enterprise
> In walking naked.

From an existential point of view, the effect of that voice singing those words out into the courtyard into which it had probably sung—unheard and with unheard-of beauty—more than forty years ago, was such that the Au. had difficulty restraining his T., and finally, because he asked himself why one should always hold them back, allowed them to flow unimpeded. Yes, here he was overcome by W., yet he felt B. and, since he finds it extremely difficult to keep himself from thinking in literary terms, he suddenly felt doubtful of the information he had been given regarding Leni's books; was it possible that a search had been made, with all due care, in trunks, shelves, closets, but that a few books once belonging to Leni's mother might have been overlooked, books by an author whose name had been withheld for fear of mispronouncing it? There was no doubt that among Leni's books there were still riches to be discovered, hidden treasures known to her mother as a young girl back in 1914, or at the latest 1916.

While the Finance Committee had still not clarifed their problems, the Social Action Committee had suddenly realized that, while those brutal measures were to get under way at seven thirty in the morning, the offices in which it might be possible to have these measures stayed would not open until the same hour; that—in this connection Schirtenstein had made some fruitless telephone calls to a number of attorneys, even district attorneys—it was impossible to have these measures stayed during the night. The question therefore was how to gain time, the almost insoluble problem: how could the forced evacuation of the apartment be delayed until nine thirty or so?

Pelzer temporarily placed his expertise and useful connections at the disposal of the Social Action Committee, made telephone calls to a number of moving companies, bailiffs, fellow members of his Mardi Gras club, the "Evergreens," and since it turned out that he was also a member of a male choral society "which was swarming with lawyers and people like that," he did at least manage to ascertain that it was virtually impossible to get a legal stay of proceedings. Once more at the telephone, he suggested to a person whom he addressed as Jupp the possibility of a truck breakdown which he—Pelzer—"would be quite prepared to pay for," but Jupp, who was apparently supposed to do the moving, would not bite, it seemed, thus prompting Pelzer's bitter comment: "He still doesn't trust me, still doesn't believe in my purely humanitarian motives."

However, now that the magic word "breakdown" had been uttered, Bogakov had what amounted almost to an inspiration. Wasn't Lev Borisovich a garbage-truck driver, and weren't Kaya Tunç the Turk, and Pinto the Portuguese, garbage-truck drivers too, and mightn't garbage-truck drivers have something like solidarity with their jailed buddy and his mother? How—thus Pinto, who looked just as rustic as Tunç and, since he did not appear to be needed on either the Finance or the Social Action Committee, was peeling potatoes in the kitchen while Tunc was in charge of the samovar and preparing the tea—how—thus both now—could mere solidarity do any good? Were they supposed—in hurt and contemptuous tones now—to demonstrate solidarity in empty bourgeois phrases (they expressed it differently: "Words, words, nothing but words from them bourgeois"), while ten human beings, including three children, were being legally evicted?

But here Bogakov shook his head, obtained silence by a painful gesture of his arm, and told them that many years ago, in Minsk, when he was a schoolboy, he had seen how reactionary forces had prevented some prisoners from being driven away. Half an hour before the trucks were due to leave, a false fire alarm had been turned in, care being taken, of course, to see that the fire trucks were being driven by reliable comrades; then, outside the school where the prisoners were locked up, the fire trucks were made to collide in such a way that even the sidewalk was blocked, causing a simulated pile-up. This way time had been gained, and the prisoners—all accused of desertion and armed mutiny, soldiers and officers in real peril of their lives—were freed through the rear exit.

Since Pinto and Tunç, as well as Schirtenstein and Scholsdorff (the latter having hurriedly joined the group), still did not understand, Bogakov proceeded to explain. "Garbage trucks," he said, "are pretty heavy objects which even at the best of times are not particularly salubrious to have around in traffic. You know how they're always causing traffic jams; now if two, or better still, three garbage trucks collide here at the intersection, this whole part of town will be impassable for at least five hours, and that fellow Jupp won't get within five hundred yards of the building with his truck, and since he would only be able to get to the building by driving the wrong way down two one-way streets, if I know anything about Germans we'll have an official stay of execution long before he gets here. But just in case he does cover every angle, that's to say gets permission to use the one-way streets on emergency grounds, just in case that happens two garbage trucks must collide at the other intersection."

Schirtenstein pointed out that there were bound to be repercussions, especially for foreign truck drivers, if they were found responsible for all this, and that some thought should be given to whether it would not be better to persuade Germans to do the job. To this end, Salazar was given streetcar fare and sent on his way, while Bogakov, equipped by Scholsdorff with pencil and paper, drew a map on which, with Helzen's help, he marked in all the one-way streets. It was decided that a collision of two trucks would be enough to create such total chaos that Jupp's vehicle would get hopelessly stuck half a mile or so from the apartment. Since Helzen knew something about traffic statistics and, in his capacity as an employee of the highways department, the exact size and tonnage of a garbage truck, he came to the conclusion, working side by side with Bogakov over the strategic sketch map, that "it would almost be enough if a single garbage truck drove into that lamppost or this tree." But it would be better to have a second truck cause a further accident by ramming the first one. "What with the police and all that rigmarole, that'll take at least four to five hours."

Thereupon Bogakov was embraced by Schirtenstein, and when asked if there was anything Schirtenstein could do for him Bogakov replied that it was his dearest, perhaps his last wish—for he really was feeling lousy—to hear "Lili Marleen" one more time. Since he had never met Schirtenstein before, malice cannot be suspected here, merely a certain Russian naiveté. Schirtenstein turned pale but proved himself a gentleman by immediately going over to the piano and playing "Lili Marleen"—probably for the first time in about fifteen years. He played it through without a mistake. Apart from Bogakov, who was moved to tears, those who showed pleasure in the song were Tunç the Turk, Pelzer, and Grundtsch. Lotte and Mrs. Hölthohne held their hands over their ears, M.v.D. emerged grinning from the kitchen.

Tunç, once again businesslike, said he would be responsible for the fake accident, he had a record of eight years' accident-free driving to the satisfaction of the city truck pool, he could afford an accident, but he would have to change, or rather exchange, his route; this would require some prior arrangement which, though difficult, would not be impossible.

Meanwhile the Finance Committee had achieved some results. "But," said Mrs. Hölthohne, "let's face it, the results are staggering. The Hoysers have got their hands on everything, they've even bought up the debts to other creditors, including the gasworks and waterworks accounts. The whole sum amounts to—brace yourselves—six thousand and seventy-eight marks and thirty pfennigs." Incidentally, the deficit coincided almost exactly with the loss of income caused by Lev's arrest, thus proving that Leni was perfectly capable of balancing her budget; so what was needed was not a subsidy, in other words money down the drain, merely a loan. She took out her checkbook, placed it on the table, made out a check, and said: "Twelve hundred to start with. That's the best I can do at the moment. I'm overextended in Italian long-stems—Pelzer, you know how it is." Pelzer, before drawing out his checkbook too, could not refrain from a moralizing comment: "If she'd sold the building to me this whole trouble would never have happened, but never mind, I'll give fifteen hundred. And"—with a glance at Lotte—"I hope I won't be considered a pariah the next time someone needs money." Lotte, ignoring Pelzer's hint, said she was broke, Schirtenstein assured them convincingly that with the best will in the world he could not drum up more than a hundred marks; Helzen and Scholsdorff contributed three and five hundred respectively, Helzen stating that he would reduce the balance of the debt by paying a higher rent.

Scholsdorff now declared, with a blush, that he felt under an obligation to assume the balance, since he had been to blame—only to a greater or lesser degree, it was true, but causatively one hundred percent—for Mrs. Pfeiffer's financial plight; the trouble was that he had a vice which imposed a constant restriction on the liquidity of his assets, he was a collector of Russiana, especially holographs, and only the other day he had acquired at great expense some letters of Tolstoi's, but he was prepared to start taking the necessary steps with the authorities first thing in the morning and to speed things up, and because of his connections he was sure he could get a postponement, particularly if he took out a loan against his salary—which he would do as soon as the bank opened in the morning—and went with the whole amount, in cash, to the proper authorities. Incidentally, he felt sure half would be enough to go on with if he promised the rest by noon. After all, he was a civil servant, known to be trustworthy, and besides, after the war he had made Leni's father several personal offers of private restitution which had been declined, but now here was a chance for him to atone for his philological sins, whose political dimensions he had not realized until it was too late. One really had to see Scholsdorff: the complete scholar, not unlike Schopenhauer in appearance—the T. in his voice were unmistakable. "But what I need, ladies and gentlemen, is at least two hours. I do not approve of the garbage-truck action, I will accept it as a final resort and, despite the conflict with my oath as a civil servant, I will say nothing about it. I assure you that I too have friends, influence; a spotless record of service, contrary to my inclinations yet apparently not to my talents and now extending over a period of almost thirty years, has earned me friends in high places who will speed up the stay of execution. All I ask of you is: give me time."

Bogakov, who had meanwhile been studying the city map with Tunç, felt that the only possibility would be in a detour, a faked breakdown, or a wait in a quiet side street. In any event Scholsdorff was promised the time he requested. Schirtenstein, even before he could begin to speak, interrupted himself with a vigorous "ssssh"—Leni was singing again.

Like your body swelling fair,
Ripening vines make gold the hill,
A distant pond gleams smooth and still,
The reaping scythe rings through the air.

Pelzer's comment on this, after an almost awed silence broken only by Lotte's derisive titter: "So it's true then, she really is pregnant by him." Which only goes to show that even exalted poetry has its grass-roots communication value.

Before leaving the company, which by this time was in festive mood, the Au. broke his neutrality for the first time by adding his mite to the Leni Fund.

Next morning around ten thirty the Au. was informed by Scholsdorff of the success of the postponement, and the day after that he read the following report in a local newspaper under the headline: "MUST IT ALWAYS BE FOREIGNERS?":

"Was it sabotage, coincidence, a repetition of the controversial 'garbage happening,' or was there some other explanation for the collision yesterday morning, just before seven, between a garbage truck with a Portuguese driver, which at that hour should have been operating two miles farther west on Bruckner Strasse, and a second garbage truck, this one with a Turkish driver, which should have been operating four miles farther east on Kreckmann Strasse? The collision occurred at the intersection of Oldenburg Strasse and Bitzerath Strasse. And how was it that a third garbage truck, this one with a German driver, ignoring the one-way-street sign, also entered Bitzerath Strasse, where it rammed into a lamppost? Business circles which enjoy a high reputation in our city and have rendered many services to our city have conveyed information to our editorial offices which permit the conclusion that this was a case of a deliberately planned action. For, *mirabile dictu:* the Turkish and Portuguese drivers both live in a house of ill repute in Bitzerath Strasse which, after consultations had taken place with the social-welfare department and the morality squad, was to have been evacuated yesterday. 'Patrons' of a certain lady said, to be a 'practitioner of the supplied arts,' managed by means of inordinately large 'loans' to prevent the evacuation which, as a result of the indescribable traffic chaos (see photo) was sabotaged. Perhaps a more thorough checkup should be made of the two foreign drivers, described by the embassies of their respective countries as politically unreliable elements. Have there not been numerous cases recently of foreigners operating as procurers? We repeat—as a *ceterum censeo*—must it always be foreigners? This manifestly scandalous affair is being further investigated. A hitherto unknown person who, on the threadbare pretext of being an 'existentialist,' infiltrated the above-named business circles and to whom certain information was imparted in good faith, is assumed to have master-minded the action. Preliminary estimates set the material damage at approximately six thousand marks. What the cost of the many hours of traffic chaos may have amounted to in terms of lost man-hours is almost beyond computation."

The Au. flew, not from cowardice but from longing—no, not to Rome but to Frankfurt, whence he took a train to Würzburg, Klementina having been transferred there as a disciplinary measure after she too had come under suspicion of being indiscreet in her conversations with him on the subject of Rahel Ginzburg. She—Klementina—is no longer wavering, she has decided to lay aside her coif and allow her coppery hair to come into its own.

It might be as well to make a splendidly banal pronouncement here: that the Au., although trying, like a certain doctor, to drive along his tortuous paths "with an earthly vehicle, unearthly horses," is also only human; that he does indeed hear in certain literary works the sigh "with Effi up there on the Baltic" and, with a clear conscience, there being no Effi around whom he might take to the Baltic, simply takes Klementina to—shall we say—Veitshöchheim, where he discusses existential matters with her; he resists making her "his" because she resists becoming "his"; she has a definite bridal complex for, having spent almost eighteen years as a bride of the Church, she has no wish to become a bride again; what are known as honorable intentions are in her eyes dishonorable; incidentally, her eyelashes prove to be longer and softer than they had at one moment appeared in Rome. For many years an early riser, she enjoys being able to sleep late, have breakfast in bed, go for walks, take an afternoon nap, and she delivers fairly lengthy discourses (which might also be called meditations or monologues) on the reasons for her fear of crossing north over the River Main in the company of the Au.

Her pre-Veitshöchheim life is never mentioned. "Suppose I were divorced or a widow—I'd tell you nothing about my marriage either." Her real age is forty-one, her real name Carola, but she does not mind still being called Klementina. On closer acquaintance, after a number of conversations, it turns out she has been spoiled: she has never had to worry about rent, clothes, books, food—hence her fear of life; even the cost of a simple afternoon cup of coffee—possibly also in Schwetzingen or Nymphenburg—is a shock to her, each time the wallet is taken out she becomes alarmed. The continual telephoning that is necessary to the "country beyond the Main"—this is what she calls it—upsets her because she regards everything she hears about Leni as fictitious. Not Leni herself, whose existence has, after all, been documented in the Order's dossier; although she has not been able to locate and read the famous essay on *The Marquise of O__* she has received written confirmation from Sister Prudentia of its form and content. Any mention of Rahel Ginzburg upsets her, and when asked by the Au. whether she would not like to go to Gerselen with him and pick some roses, she responded with a catlike pawing movement of her left hand; she doesn't "want to know about any miracles."

Perhaps it is permitted to point out that she—unconsciously—fails to appreciate the difference between faith and knowledge; there can be no doubt that Gerselen is likely to become a spa; the water there has a temperature of 100 to 102 degrees, which is regarded as ideal. Nor can there be any doubt that (as was ascertained over the telephone) Scholsdorff is deeply committed (acc. to Schirtenstein), that the newspaper quoted above is being sued to retract such expressions as "house of ill repute" and "practitioner of the supplied arts," the only difficulty being to convince the court that the "courteous expression 'practitioner of the supplied arts'" is to be regarded as an insult; furthermore: Lotte is for the time being occupying Lev's room, the two Turks, Tunç and Kiliç, are probably going to take over Lotte's apartment (provided the building owner, who is said to be a "Levantinophobe," agrees) because Leni and Mehmet have decided to set up housekeeping together, a temporary description, for Mehmet is married although, being a Muhammadan, he is permitted a second wife—in his own eyes if not in those of the law of his host country, unless Leni were to become a Muhammadan too, which is not altogether out of the question since the Koran also has a niche occupied by the Madonna.

In the meantime the shopping problem has also been solved, now that the oldest of the Portuguese children, eight-year-old Manuela, picks up the breakfast rolls. Helzen is "under temporarily gentle pressure" from his superiors (all this according to Schirtenstein). Leni has meanwhile faced the "Help Leni Committee," she has blushed (probably for the fourth time in her life. Au.) "with joy and embarrassment" at the gynecologist's confirmation that she is pregnant, and she now spends a great deal of time with doctors, having tests "from top to bottom and side to side" because she "wants to prepare a good home for the baby" (Leni's own words according to Schirtenstein). The findings of the internist, the dentist, the orthopedist, and the urologist are a hundred percent negative; only the psychiatrist has a few reservations, he has noted some quite unfounded damage to her self-esteem and considerable damage arising from her environment, but regards all this as curable as soon as Lev is released from prison. When that happens she is to—"and this is to be taken as a prescribed medication" (the psychiatrist acc. to S.)—go for walks as often as possible, and quite openly, arm in arm with Mehmet Şahin and Lev. What the psychiatrist has not understood, any more than Schirtenstein has, is the nightmares in which Leni appears to be haunted by a harrow, a board, a draftsman, and an officer, even after falling asleep in Mehmet's comforting arms. This he calls (an oversimplification and inaccurate at that, as the Au. would be able to prove) a "widow complex," and is also attributed (equally inaccurately) to the circumstances in which Leni conceived and bore Lev. These bad dreams, as Klementina knows too, have nothing whatever to do with vaults, air raids, or embraces during such air raids.

Gradually, by planning the journey in easy stages and by stopping over first in Mainz, then in Koblenz, and finally in Andernach, the Au. managed to lure Klementina north across the river into that "country beyond the Main." Her encounters with people were as carefully thought out as those with the countryside: first Mrs. Hölthohne, because of her library, the cultured atmosphere and almost nunlike quality of her home; cultured people are also entitled to consideration. A successful meeting that Mrs. Hölthohne ended with a hoarse whisper "Congratulations" (on what? Au.). Next came B.H.T. who, with a fabulous onion soup, an excellent Italian salad, and grilled steak, made an outstanding impression and avidly drank in every single detail regarding Rahel Ginzburg, Gerselen, etc.; who, since he does not deign to read the papers, knew nothing of the scandal that must meanwhile have subsided, and who whispered as they left "You lucky fellow." Grundtsch, Scholsdorff, and Schirtenstein were each a smashing success: the first because he was so "completely natural" but probably also because the seductive melancholy of old cemeteries never fails to have its effect; Scholsdorff because he happens to be an out-and-out charmer, who could resist him? He is so much more at ease now that he has discovered a real way of being of service to Leni; besides, as a philologist he is a colleague of Klementina's, and over tea and macaroons the two of them quickly got into a passionate argument regarding a Russian/Soviet cultural epoch that K. spoke of as formalism, Scholsdorff as structuralism. Schirtenstein, on the other hand, did not do quite so well, he complained rather too much about the intrigues and Wagnerianism of certain pseudoyouthful composers, complained openly too, with a wistful look at K. and a still more wistful look out into the courtyard, that he had never tied himself to a woman and never tied a woman to himself; he cursed the piano and music, and in an attack of masochism went to the piano and hammered out "Lili Marleen" almost self-destructively, then apologized and with a dry sob asked to be "left alone with his suffering."

Of what nature this suffering might be became clear during the indispensable visit to Pelzer, who meanwhile—in the space of the approximately five days in Veitshöchheim, Schwetzinger, and Nymphenburg—had become quite haggard; he was with his wife Eva, who with a weary but appealing melancholy served coffee and cake, made an occasional, usually resigned, remark, failed to look entirely genuine in her paint-daubed artist's smock, and carried on an elegiac conversation—on such topics as Beuys,

Artmann, the "meaningful meaninglessness of art," quoting liberally from one of the more high-toned papers—then had to go back to her easel, "I just have to, please excuse me!" Pelzer's appearance gave cause for concern. He looked at Klementina as if considering her as "a bird in the hand," and when she disappeared for a while, for urgent and understandable reasons (between three and six o'clock she had drunk four cups of tea at Scholsdorff's, three at Schirtenstein's, and so far two cups of coffee at Pelzer's), Pelzer whispered: "They thought at first it was diabetes, but my blood-sugar level is completely normal, so is everything else. It's the truth, though you may laugh, that for the first time I'm conscious of having a soul and that this soul is suffering; for the first time I'm finding that not just any woman, only one woman, can cure me; I could wring that Turk's neck—what can she see in that country bumpkin reeking of mutton and garlic, besides, he's ten years younger than she is; he's got a wife and four kids, and now he's got her pregnant too—I—you've got to help me."

The Au., who has developed a certain liking for Pelzer, pointed out that in such desperate situations the mediation of a third person always turns out to be a mistake, in fact even has the opposite effect, *this* was something the injured party had to cope with alone. "And yet," thus Pelzer, "every day I fork out a dozen candles for the Madonna, I—just between us men—seek consolation with other women, I don't find it, I drink, go to casinos—but *rien ne va plus* is all I can say. So there you have it."

To say here that Pelzer made a pathetic impression is not to imply even a trace of irony, especially since he supplied a very apt comment on his condition himself: "I've never been in love in my life, I've always played around with bought women, yes, I've always gone to whores, and my wife, well, I was very fond of her, still am in fact, and I don't want her to suffer as long as I live—but I was never in love with her, and Leni, well, I desired her from the first moment I saw her, and some damn foreigner is forever coming between us, I wasn't in love with her, I've only been that since I saw her a week ago. I . . . I'm *not* to blame for her father's death, I—I love her—I've never said that about a woman before." Just then Klementina returned and made it clear, discreetly yet unmistakably, that it was time to leave. Her comment was rather disdainful, at any rate cool and quite matter-of-fact: "You can call it whatever you like, Pelzer's disease or Schirtenstein's disease."

The expedition to Tolzem-Lyssemich provided an occasion to kill two birds with one stone: Klementina, who consistently calls herself a dedicated mountain-lover and a Bavarian and only reluctantly admits that congenial people live north of the Main too, could be introduced to the charms, indeed the fascination, of the flat country, such *wide* flat country, which would remind her enthusiastically; she admitted to never having seen such *flat* flat country, such *wide* flat country, which would remind her of Russia "if I didn't know that here this only extends for two or three hundred miles whereas in Russia it's in the thousands, but you must admit it reminds one of Russia." She would not allow the qualification of "except for the fences," in the same way that she rejected any lengthy meditations on fences, hedges, in fact all border markings, as too "literary," any allusion to their Celtic origin as "too racial," but eventually, albeit again reluctantly, she did admit that "it has a horizontal pull whereas where I come from it's a vertical pull; here you always get the feeling you're swimming, even in a car, and probably on a train too, and you're afraid you're never going to reach the other shore, or is there such a thing hereabouts as another shore?" A reminder of the visible elevations of the foothills and the first slopes of the Eifel drew from her merely a disdainful smile.

Marja van Doorn, on the other hand, was a total success. *Pflaumenkuchen* with whipped cream (Comment: "You people eat whipped cream with everything."), coffee, freshly roasted and ground by M.v.D. ("the only proper way") proved irresistible, "fabulous, the first real coffee I've ever tasted, now at last I know what coffee is," etc., etc. And: "You people know how to live, I must say." M.v.D. had her farewell comment to make too: "A bit late but not too late, and God bless you," then in a whisper:

"She'll teach you how." (Correction, blushing, also whispered:) "I mean, she'll bring a bit of order into your life and so on." Then tears: "A real old maid, that's all I've ever been and all I'll ever be."

At the home, Bogakov was reported as "moved away" and, surprisingly, "with no forwarding address." All he had left behind was a note saying: "Don't have them look for me, thanks for now, I'll get word to you," but in four days this word had not come. Belenko thought Bogakov had started "whoring around again," while Kitkin thought he had most likely been sent off somewhere as a "Red informer"; the kindly sister frankly admitted to missing Bogakov and told them casually that this happened almost every spring. "He simply has to take off then, all of a sudden, only it's getting more and more difficult, you see, because he needs his injections. Let's hope he's warm enough."

Although she had now heard of and about Leni from such many-angled perspectives, some forceful, some direct, some indirect (e.g., B.H.T., who had at least been able to confirm her existence), K. was now all agog to meet her "in the flesh, to touch her, smell her, see her." The time was now ripe for this encounter with Leni, and it was with some trepidation that the Au. asked Hans Helzen to arrange it. It was agreed, since Leni was so "uptight" about it, to allow only Lotte, Mehmet, and "you'll be surprised who" to be present at this encounter.

"Ever since the first few walks with Mehmet," said Hans Helzen, "she's been in such a state of tension that she can't bear the presence of more than five people. That's why neither my wife nor I will be there either. What upsets her especially is the presence of someone in love and the erotic anticipation or tension that goes with that, the kind that emanates from Pelzer and Schirtenstein and is even slightly noticeable in Scholsdorff."

Since K. interpreted the Au.'s own tension as jealousy, he explained to her that while he did know all about Leni he knew almost nothing about her—K.; indeed, on the basis of much intensive and tedious research he was familiar with Leni's most intimate spheres of intimacy, making him feel like a traitor or a conniver; but that while she—K.—was close to him, Leni, despite his affection for her, seemed like a stranger.

It is freely admitted that the Au. was glad of K.'s company, of her philological and sociological curiosity, for without her—for whom, when you came right down to it, he had Leni and Haruspica to thank—he would certainly have been in danger of succumbing to the incurable Schirtenstein or Pelzer disease.

Fortunately his agitation and anticipation were distracted by a surprise: who should be sitting there on the sofa, openly holding hands with a delightfully blushing Lotte Hoyser, so embarrassed that he was not smiling but grinning? None other than Bogakov! One thing was certain: the kindly sister at the home from which he had fled had no need to worry about him, he was warm enough! And lest there be anyone who doubts that Lotte is capable of radiating warmth, let him stand corrected.

And there sat the Turk too, surprisingly, almost disappointingly unoriental-looking; rustic, stiff, not embarrassed, wearing a dark-blue suit, starched shirt, unobtrusive (mid-brown) tie, there he sat, holding Leni's hand in a pose that suggested he was sitting, about the year 1889, opposite the giant camera of a portrait photographer who had just pushed in the plate and asked them not to move, before he pressed the rubber ball that clicks the shutter. Leni—well, there was still much trepidation before the Au.'s eyes turned toward her and then fastened fully on her: it must not be forgotten that in the course of his tireless research the Au. had set eyes on her only twice, a mere fleeting glimpse on the street, from the side, never *en face,* had admired her proud walk, but now evasion was no longer possible, reality must be looked in the eye, and the simple understatement: it was worth it! must be permitted here. It was a good thing K. was present, otherwise jealousy of Mehmet might have been a distinct possibility; some vestige remained anyway, a slight pang of regret that it was in his arms and not the Au.'s that she dreamed of harrow, draftsman, and officer. She had cut her hair and tinted it slightly gray and could easily have passed for thirty-eight; her dark eyes were clear, not without sadness, and although she is known to be five foot six and a half she seemed more like six foot two, although at the same time her long legs prove that she is equally beautiful standing and sitting down.

It was charming the way she took charge of the coffeepot, while Lotte put cake onto the plates and Mehmet distributed the inevitable whipped cream, "One spoon? two? three?" according to taste. Leni, it became clear, was not only taciturn and reticent, she was downright laconic, and so shy that her face wore a constant "nervous smile." Her expression—something that filled the Au. with pride and joy—as she looked at K. was one of satisfaction and benevolence; asked by K. about Haruspica, she pointed to the picture on the wall, which was indeed impressive and—not colorful but colored—hung, five feet by five, over the sofa, and—although still incomplete—radiated an indescribably cosmic force and tenderness; the design of her uncompleted life's work was not merely multilayered but (they could be counted) eight-layered—of the six million cones she had by now entered perhaps thirty thousand, of the one hundred million rods perhaps eighty thousand—instead of taking a cross-section she had designed it horizontally, like an endless plain over which one might march toward a still unformed horizon. Leni: "There she is, maybe a thousandth part of her retina, when it's finished." She waxed almost talkative in adding: "My great teacher, my great friend." That was all she said during the thirty-five minutes the visit lasted.

Mehmet seemed rather humorless, even when he was serving the cream he did not let go of Leni's hand with his free hand, and when Leni poured coffee he forced her to do it with one hand by hanging on to her free hand. This hand-holding was so infectious that finally K. started holding the Au.'s hand, as if she were keeping her fingers on his pulse. There was no doubt about it: K. was moved. All trace of her academic arrogance had vanished, it was quite obvious that she had known about Leni but not believed in her; she figured in the Order's dossiers, but the fact that she existed and, what was more, genuinely existed, stirred her profoundly. She gave a deep sigh and transmitted her heightened pulse to the Au.

Has the impatient reader noticed that quantities of happy endings are now taking place? Holding hands, alliances formed, old friendships—such as that between Lotte and Bogakov—being renewed, while others—Pelzer, Schirtenstein, and Scholsdorff, for example—thirsting and hungering, were getting nowhere? That a Turk who looks like a farmer from the Rhön mountains or the central Eifel has won the bride? A man who already has a wife and four children at home and on account of polygamous rights, of which he is aware but of which he has so far never been able to make use, has shown not the remotest trace of a guilty conscience, in fact may well already have acquainted some Suleika with the situation? A man who, compared with Bogakov and the Au., appears maddeningly clean, positively scrubbed: with creased pants, a tie; who finds bliss in a starched shirt because for him it is all part of the solemnity of the occasion? Who continues to sit there as if the imaginary photographer in artist's beret and artist's cravat, a painter *manqué* somewhere in Ankara or Istanbul about the year 1889, still had his finger on the rubber ball? A garbage collector who rolls, lifts, empties garbage cans, bound in love to a woman who mourns three husbands, has read Kafka, knows Hölderlin by heart, is a singer, pianist, painter, mistress, a past and future mother, who causes the pulse of a former nun who has spent her life wrestling with the problems of reality in literary works to beat faster and faster?

Even the glib Lotte was silent, as if she too were touched, moved, deeply stirred; bit by bit she told them about Lev's imminent release and the resultant accommodation problems, the owner of the building having refused to accept "Turkish garbage-truck drivers," while the Helzens, since Grete Helzen "earned a bit on the side" in the evenings as a cosmetician in one of their rooms, could not relinquish a room, and it was impossible to "squeeze their five Portuguese friends into one room," yet she wanted to, must, remain—with Bogakov, whom she frankly called "my Pyotr"—close to Leni, all of which meant that she was forced to "stand up to" her sons and her father-in-law. "It's merely a postponement, it's not over yet." That she was willing to marry Bogakov and he her but that there was no evidence of his being either a widower or divorced.

Eventually Leni did contribute to the conversation by murmuring "Margret, Margret, that poor Margret," her eyes first moist, then weeping. Until finally Mehmet, by an indefinable movement causing him to sit even more upright than he already was, made it unmistakably clear that he regarded the audience as at an end.

The good-byes—"not final, let's hope," K. said to Leni, who responded with such a sweet smile—followed and were protracted in the usual manner by the guests' commenting kindly on the photos, the piano, the apartment in general, enthusiastically on the painting, and the group continuing to stand around for a while in the hall, where Leni then murmured, "well, we must just try and carry on with the earthly vehicle, the unearthly horses," an allusion that not even K., with her apparently inadequate education, understood.

Finally, outside on Bitzerath Strasse, which seemed very ordinary, K. lapsed into her inevitable, incorrigibly literary pose by saying: "Yes, she exists, and yet she doesn't. She doesn't exist, and yet she does." A pose of skepticism which, the Au. feels, is far below K.'s level.

However, she did add: "One day she will console all those men who are suffering because of her, she will heal them all."

Shortly after that she added: "I wonder whether Mehmet is as fond of ballroom dancing as Leni is."

11 To his relief, the Au. finds that almost all the remainder of the report needs only to be quoted: a psychologist's opinion, a letter from an elderly male nurse, the deposition of a police officer. The manner in which he came into possession of these documents must remain a professional secret. Granted it was not always done entirely legally or entirely discreetly, but in this case trivial infringements of legality and discretion serve a sacred purpose: to get at the facts. What does it matter, surely, if, as regards the psychologist's opinion (which, by the way, contains nothing discriminatory), one of the Hoyser office staff (not Girl Friday!) quickly runs a few typed pages through the photocopier; for the Hoysers this meant (bearing in mind the five million that cost the Au. a button) a loss of approximately DM.2.50 (although not allowing for a proportion of the overhead). Is this not compensated for by a box of chocolates worth DM.4.50? The letter from the male nurse, holograph, was procured by the indefatigable M.v.D. and left with the Au. long enough for him to photocopy it personally in a department store for DM.0.50 per page. Total cost (incl. cigarettes for M.v.D.) approximately DM.8.00. The police officer's deposition was acquired by the Au. gratis. Since the deposition contains no police (let alone security) secrets, being merely a kind of unintentional yet successful sociological study, the only misgivings that might have arisen would have been of a theoretical and not practical nature, and these misgivings were simply washed overboard with a few glasses of beer—beer, incidentally, for which the young police officer insisted on paying, an understandable wish that the Au. respected and

did not like to infringe upon even with flowers for the police officer's wife or a nice toy for his eighteen-month-old son ("cute," as he was able to confirm, without need of pretense, after one look at the photo. The wife's picture was not shown him! And indeed he would have been hard put to it to call another man's wife "cute" in the presence of her husband).

Let us therefore begin with the psychologist's opinion. Education, background, age, etc., of this expert remained anonymous, all that the young lady in question would say was that he was esteemed equally by functionaries of the German Labor Federation and members of labor tribunals.

"The expert (hereafter abbreviated to E.) knew Lev Borisovich Gruyten (hereafter L.B.G.) from an introductory interview that took place four months prior to L.B.G.'s arrest and at the instigation of the personnel manager of the municipal sanitation department. The first interview dealt with the possible promotion of L.B.G. to a post in internal administration at which he would work half the day as spokesman for the numerous foreign workers and the other half as a time-and-motion adviser. At that juncture L.B.G. was recommended by the E. for both positions; however, both positions were declined by L.B.G. At the time, L.B.G.'s psychological development could be only superficially assessed, on the basis of certain data; meanwhile, however, with the cooperation of the prison administration, four further interviews, each of one hour's duration, were made possible, allowing of a considerably more intensive examination, although still not in sufficient detail to do justice in scientific terms to a person of such complex structure. There is no doubt that L.B.G. would be a worthy subject for a detailed and intensive scientific study. The E., now instructor of psychology at a technical college, is therefore contemplating recommending L.B.G. to one of his students as a subject for a graduate thesis.

"Hence this attempt at a psychogram of L.B.G. must, despite the approximately accurate picture it may convey, be accepted with due reservation in terms of scientific usefulness. It is of use only for internal administrative purposes as a possible means of facilitating further association with L.B.G. and, with the above-named reservations, can serve as an attempt to explain L.B.G.'s motives during his 'criminal' behavior.

"L.B.G. grew up in extremely unfavorable circumstances in terms of his extra-family environment, in extremely favorable circumstances in terms of his family environment. If the word 'favorable' used in the latter case requires a qualification that could be appropriately described as 'indulgence'—then it is this very 'indulgence,' looking at the twenty-five-year-old man today, that accounts for the fact that L.B.G. is to be considered, despite the presence in him of considerable social disturbance, an undeniably useful, indeed agreeable, member of our society.

"What was extremely unfavorable for L.B.G. was the fact that, growing up as he did as an illegitimate and fatherless child, he had no claim to the status of orphan (let alone war orphan) that is so important to psychological development. For the illegitimate child, the deceased father is not an orphan-alibi. Since, furthermore, on the streets and in school he was called 'the Russian kid,' and his mother was sometimes abused as 'the Russian sweetie,' he was constantly being made to feel—if not specifically nevertheless unconsciously—that the fact of his having been conceived not by rape but in voluntary surrender was particularly disgusting and humiliating. He had been conceived in circumstances that for his father and mother might have resulted in severe penalties, if not the death penalty. In this sense he was, in addition to everything else, a 'convict's kid.' All the other children, the illegitimate ones, had, as the 'children of dead heroes,' the psychological advantage of regarding themselves as socially one rank higher than L.B.G. Expressed in popular terms, matters got even worse for him: to an increasing extent he became a victim of that problem-fraught institution (as demonstrated by the E. in numerous publications!) known as the denominational school. Although he had been baptized, and baptized a Catholic, and although this baptism was confirmed by a certain Pelzer under whom at a later date he served a temporary apprenticeship, as well as by other persons, the church authorities insisted on the repetition of this 'emergency baptism' to make it a formal baptism. The intensive, pedantic, and embarrassing research carried out in this connection earned for L.B.G. a further and highly macabre nickname, for he was also called a 'graveyard kid,' a 'vault kid,' he had been 'conceived and born among corpses.' In short: his mother refused to have him baptized again since she cherished the memory of the baptism in which L.B.G.'s father had participated; she did not want the memory of that baptism to be wiped out by 'just any baptism,' on the other hand she did not want to send her son to the nondenominational school some ten miles away and even less to the 'Protestants' (although there was no certainty as to whether the latter might not also have insisted on a new baptism), and so L.B.G. acquired the last, the ultimate taint: was he a 'Christian,' was he a 'Catholic,' or wasn't he?

"Seen against this background, the word 'indulgence' acquires a relativity that almost nullifies it. L.B.G. also had plenty of 'aunts': Aunt Margret, Aunt Lotte, Aunt Liane, Aunt Marja, above all he had his mother, all women who 'indulged' him; in addition he had 'uncles' and 'cousins,' father- and brother-surrogates, his uncles Otto and Pyotr, his cousins Werner and Kurt, he had the living memory of his grandfather, with whom he had 'sat for years beside the Rhine.' Retrospectively it may be said that his mother's instinctive reaction to keep him out of school as often as possible—based though it sometimes was on flimsy pretexts—was a thoroughly sound one. Despite the fact that L.B.G. displayed an astonishing psychic strength by voluntarily absenting himself from the 'sphere of indulgence,' going out to play on the street, shunning neither passive nor active blows, it is doubtful whether he would have been able to stand up to the daily pressures of school. Had there been—this as a hypothesis—even a suggestion of deformity or sickliness in L.B.G. he would not have withstood those massive multiple environmental pressures beyond his fourteenth year; suicide, incurable depression, or aggression-criminality would have been the result. L.B.G. has indeed overcome a great deal, he has also repressed a great deal. What he could neither overcome nor repress was the fact that his 'Uncle' Otto, previously always so friendly, ended by depriving him of the society of his two 'cousins' Werner and

Kurt who, respectively five and ten years older than he, represented for him the protection that he did not have to contrive, on which he could rely. It is therefore quite clear that the social rift that developed between him and his cousins, coupled with feelings of revenge and defiance, are the motivations for his 'criminality.' This 'criminality' consisted in the clumsy forging of two checks, although after a total of five interviews it is still not clear to the E. whether the clumsiness with which the checks were forged is to be interpreted as a conscious or unconscious provocation of the uncle and cousins. Since, although these forgeries occurred several (four) times, were hushed up three times and only on the fourth occasion prompted a charge against him, all four forgeries contained the same mistake (error in filling in the line marked: In Words), one is tempted to assume that this was a conscious provocation to be viewed within the context of that wartime shift in the financial circumstances of the Gruyten and Hoyser families of which he had by this time been made aware.

"Now, how did L.B.G.—as a child and as an adolescent—compensate for this grievance? The fact that the intra-family compensation described here under the general heading of 'indulgence' was inadequate, that L.B.G. had also to develop his own initiative, that, especially after the removal from the scene of the two 'cousins,' he could not rely on his mother and his numerous aunts, must have been instinctively clear to him; but that in the final analysis he would have to be 'the man of the house' must have been borne in on him at an early age in view of the helplessness and vulnerability of his mother.

"It is now necessary to introduce the concept of deliberate underachievement (hereafter called d.u.a.). First: d.u.a. in school, where for a while he was faced with possible removal to a special 'school for slow learners.' Contrary to his indisputable talents and intelligence he behaved as society expected him to in its automatic assessment of a boy burdened with so many antisocial attributes. As a pupil he was far worse than he need have been, even simulating to some extent the behavior of a mental defective. He avoided being required to repeat a year only when this prospect brought the 'special school' dangerously close, and this—relegation to the special school—he avoided simply because his mother was worried about the special school's being so far away. He admitted to the E. that he 'would have liked to go to the special school,' but that at the time it was located in a remote suburb and, since his mother was working and L.B.G. had household chores to perform even at an early age, the distance alone would have been enough to disrupt 'the running of the home.'

"Parallel with the d.u.a. in school was a deliberate, defiance-motivated overachievement (hereafter called d.o.a.) that, scholastically speaking, 'brought no returns.' Because of the generosity of a person known to his mother and grandfather who gave him lessons three times a week, he was able at the age of thirteen to read and write Russian fluently. Note: the language of his father! He—one would like to be able to say—surprised his teachers but, in view of the fundamental psychological outlook of the average elementary-school pedagogue during the period in question, it must unfortunately be said that he annoyed his teachers by quoting Russian poetry from Pushkin to Blok while at the same time clinging obstinately to a level in German grammar that would have warranted his transfer to a special school. However, it must have been more than annoying, it must have been taken as an outright provocation that this boy—who at the age of thirteen had progressed no farther than Grade 5!—furthermore confronted his teachers—and uninvited at that!—with Kafka, Trakl, Hölderlin, Kleist, and Brecht, as well as with the poems of an as yet unidentifiable English-language poet, probably of Irish descent.

"Enough of examples. The E.'s findings: an extreme polarization toward society manifested in the practice of d.u.a. in school, where achievement might 'bring some return,' but simultaneously of d.o.a. outside of school, where achievement can 'bring no return.'

"This extreme polarization remains the determining factor in L.B.G.'s life. Now that he is getting older and, motivated by healthy reaction, is liberating himself from 'indulgence,' it represents the tension from which he draws his powers of resistance and survival. Until the age of fourteen, shortly before being dismissed from school, L.B.G. becomes for the first time 'criminal' in a context which the E. can unfortunately only report but not precisely analyze, since he lacks internal and external access to the aforesaid experience-material, and a precise analysis would require an extensive religio-psychological and historical study. Hence experience-data only will be quoted here:

"L.B.G., whose participation in religious instruction was only sporadic and generally under circumstances that were annoying for both him and the priests, was refused—I use his own expression—'the sacraments of confession and Communion, by then it was no longer so much a matter of my inadequate baptism but because I was considered obstinate, arrogant, presumptuous, in any event not sufficiently meek, and also because I had taken an interest—only a layman's, of course, but still with a real desire for knowledge—in religious literature. That irritated the teachers, I mean the priests who taught us religion, since the "administration of the sacraments" was made dependent on one's "subjection" to them.' However, L.B.G., who—as he admitted—now insisted on having them administered to him, if only on principle and for mystical considerations, finally, by resorting to 'a sacrilegious act, to robbery, or, to be exact, altar desecration,' gained possession of the consecrated Eucharist, which he consumed. There was a scandal. If it had not been for the intervention of an enlightened priest with some experience in psychology, L.B.G. would have been placed under detention as a juvenile delinquent. 'From then on,' L.B.G. verbatim to the E., 'the only way I took Communion was with my mother at breakfast.'

"A further d.u.a. becomes apparent by the age of fourteen: an almost anankastic trait, a heightened love of order, a compulsion to tidiness, that is doubtless related to incipient puberty. Not only does he sweep the street outside the building, the front yard, the apartment—even when out for a walk he engages in tidying activities by picking up leaves, and although his preponderantly female environment hinted that this was 'womanish' or 'girlish,' his favorite toy between the ages of eight and thirteen is a broom of any kind. As an additional explanation for this psychological phenomenon it might be said that this is one way of demonstrating and practicing cleanliness—again as an aid to polarization—vis-à-vis an environment that consistently abuses and defiles him.

"Dismissed from school in Grade 6, L.B.G., with his not especially charitable report card, had no chance of finding a normal apprenticeship. For a time he worked—again mainly with a broom!—in a nursery garden owned by a certain Pelzer, later at the same type of work for a certain Grundtsch, was then taken over by the cemetery administration, later transferred to the municipal sanitation department, at whose expense he obtained his driver's license. He has been employed there for six years, and apart from a certain inclination to extended weekends and holidays, and discounting the quite understandable resentment of his obvious d.u.a., his present employer is perfectly satisfied with him. During the past six years, L.B.G.'s d.o.a. was directed exclusively toward his mother, whom he advised to give up her employment although she is still a relatively young and productive person. He found subtenants for her among foreign workers and their families. The fact that one of these workers finally became her lover evoked suspiciously little conflict in L.B.G., about whose extremely strong attachment to his mother there can be no doubt. Even the news that his mother was now known to be pregnant by a foreigner of Oriental descent evoked a spontaneous, the E. would like to maintain, suspiciously spontaneous, 'Thank God, at last I'll have a little brother or sister,' an utterance in which, although only to the trained ear, a certain forced element was clearly audible.

"It would be erroneous to regard this forced element as being rooted solely in the oedipal sphere. It is unquestionably also based on a certain understandable fear of renewed environment problems, problems into which L.B.G. no doubt sees his future sibling drawn and with whose anticipated environment problems he doubtless identifies on the basis of his own experience.

"While it is true that the obvious suspicion of jealousy cannot be discounted, it may be reduced to a minimum. Investigations among L.B.G.'s age-peers and fellow workers show that he not only is popular with women and girls but also does not evade the consequences of this popularity.

"It must be accepted as a fact that the workers in the sanitation department occasionally fulfill special requests of garbage-overloaded householders, resulting in unscheduled contacts. Such 'infractions'—special requests of householders to remove garbage in excess of the allotted quantity, usually in return for a tip—are tolerated by the administration in view of the extreme inadequacy of available garbage-truck tonnage.

"Relatively harmonious though the picture of L.B.G. to date may seem, certain social conflicts are nevertheless quite clearly present, conflicts which, although explainable in terms of polarization-compulsions developed in self-defense, can still only be described as such.

"Even for a layman in the field of psychology the following are apparent in L.B.G.:

"*1. A solidarity complex* that is accounted for by the constant compulsion to identify with his father and mother but which, in the boy who has meanwhile become a man, is fixated on foreigners and, after three months of imprisonment, also on his fellow prison inmates. Assuming prison inmates to be likewise 'aliens in society,' the solidarity complex gives rise to a further and related complex, *2. xenophilia,* of which one manifestation is *3. xenophilology,* the desire to learn the languages of foreigners. (For several months now, L.B.G. has been taking a course in Turkish.) A person (here the E. is rather inclined than disinclined, despite some misgivings, to speak of a personality) such as L.B.G., whose highly developed sensitivity and intelligence permit only two alternatives: either to adjust and 'betray' himself and his identity fixation points or (in a perpetual state of nonadjustment) to confirm himself and his identity fixation points, finds himself in perpetual conflict between the socially achievable and his talents. Hence this person (personality?) requires an increasing number of new (later artificial) resistances in order to demonstrate confirmation vis-à-vis himself and his environment. Assuming that this person derives advantages (using the word in its generally accepted sense) therefrom (e.g., prolonged stay in hospital, wangling of pensions or leaves of absence, etc.), L.B.G. is a *4. simulator* who—in exaggerated terms—simulates for the sake of disadvantages rather than advantages in order thereby to satisfy his solidarity complex and his xenophilous inclinations. To this extent even the check-forging is to be interpreted as a 'simulation' rather than as 'criminal per se.' The fact that some simulations ultimately brought him advantages (e.g., the proofs of confidence on the part of foreign workers that border on veneration) is part of the dialectic of such an experiment in existence which a social model —or social principle, as my Marxist colleagues would put it—then 'makes manifest.'

"An explanation must also be given for the fact that L.B.G. displayed d.u.a. Meanwhile promoted to the rank of truck-column leader ('That's as high as I want to go!'), he had displayed an astonishing organizational talent. Once familiarized with conditions of garbage-collection and traffic in the series of streets assigned to him, he succeeded in planning the readying and emptying of garbage cans in such a way that his team, without undue haste, reached their appointed target two or sometimes three hours ahead of time. L.B.G. and his team were then caught enjoying surprisingly long breaks which had no adverse effect whatever on productivity. When required to place his organizational experience at the disposal of the planning section, he refused and went back to performing the work according to rule, complaints from householders over the protracted breaks, especially of foreign workers, having been received and even taken up by the press.

"Such was the behavior that led to the initial interview between the E. and L.B.G., since at that time consideration was being given to some disciplinary action. However, on the advice of the E. the idea was dropped.

"(Here the E. refers to the case of H.M., an employee of the municipal administration, a case in which the E. was also professionally involved and used for the first time the term d.u.a., which has since been adopted by the literature on labor legislation. H.M., who in two and a half hours completed the work assigned to him for eight hours but then, since he was (to this extent unlike L.B.G.) working out a model for his colleagues and was then frustrated by their machinations, became seriously mentally ill; then, fit to work again, this time in a different department, forced to spend six and a half hours 'doing nothing' in the office, sued for the 'restitution of six and a half hours of wasted time daily' which he claimed as time off. When this action was dismissed, H.M.'s condition deteriorated still further, and since his case aroused some interest he was then employed by an industrial concern where, now fully recovered, he contributes significantly to the firm's d.o.a. In the case of H.M., in which the E. was also consulted, the reproach of d.u.a. was directed solely at his refusal to sit out the prescribed work period. D.u.a. is a steadily increasing phenomenon that will burden our achievement-oriented society with serious problems.)

"In L.B.G.'s case, the d.u.a. consists in the fact that, although he reaches the target expected of him, his innate intelligence, his organizational talent, are not—even after a considerable increase in wages—placed fully at the disposal of his employer. Granted that the achievement-oriented society can have its minima and maxima and/or averages calculated by computers; nevertheless, the working out of special factors—which in the case of garbage collection are very complex since the unforeseeable (e.g., traffic congestion and traffic accidents, as well as tendencies thereto) varies topographically—can only be performed by an experienced employee, such as L.B.G., who is capable of abstract thinking. Furthermore, if it is remembered that in such a case not only local but also regional and extra-regional garbage problems might be considerably rationalized, the damage caused by L.B.G. to the total economy is almost beyond computation. To this extent we may speak of the presence of considerable d.u.a.

"Since it was important for the E. to know that all L.B.G.'s physical functions had been checked out, he caused the prison doctor to check his height, weight, and all organic functions.

Result: one hundred percent negative. L.B.G.'s consumption of alcohol and nicotine is also normal, at least there is no evidence of narcotics-induced damage. Apart from a minimal diopter of 0.5 in the right eye, no abnormal or diseased condition was found to be present in L.B.G. However, since on the one hand considerable social conflicts and demonstrably misguided behavior are present, while on the other hand virtually each of these conflicts should be evidenced in L.B.G.'s endocrine system, the E. explains this normality by precisely that permanent and extreme polarity which in this case creates a balance. If, however, this complex balance brought about by constant and extreme inner tensions were to cease to exist, L.B.G. would within a short space of time develop serious diabetes, severe hepatitis, probably renal colic. It is therefore not considered advisable to prerelease him from prison, since it is there that he experiences this polarization and, furthermore, can satisfy both his solidarity complex and his xenophilia. The possibility even exists—at least it cannot be discounted—that L.B.G. has sought the extreme situation of imprisonment in order to maintain a social tension that may have been declining. Since in the meantime, as the E. has been informed, a considerable environmental solidarization has taken place in the case of L.B.G.'s mother, in other words this opportunity for polarization must be regarded as reduced, it is only by serving his full sentence that L.B.G. can be helped at the moment, especially since this would prevent any interruption of the heroizing process among his fellow workers.

"The E. cannot bring himself to adopt and apply to L.B.G. a newly developed theory that has been posited by Professor Hunx. This refers to the formerly controversial concept of 'normality-simulation' which Professor Hunx believes to have found in test-subjects who, as a result of 'hysterically directed compensation' (Hunx), conceal a strong latent homosexual tendency beneath extreme heterosexual activity. In connection with the new, scientifically accurate analysis of old Inquisition reports, Hunx attributes the 'beauty' of witches, their 'physical charms and fascination,' their 'skill in the arts of love' (which were related to a knowledge of internal secretion that was undoubtedly in advance of their times) to that 'hysterically directed compensation' which concealed their 'true nature.'

"The E. cannot arrive at the conclusion that the case of L.B.G. is one of 'normality-simulation,' rather does it appear to be a case of normality-rejection where the natural bent is toward normality. The fact that garbage collection is his occupational desire and aim proves that he has instinctively sought the appropriate polarization: an occupation that serves the purposes of cleanliness but is regarded as dirty."

12 Letter from a male nurse (B.E.), aged approximately fifty-five, to Leni:

"Dear Mrs. Pfeiffer,

"Your letter to Professor Kernlich came into my hands accidentally when in the performance of my duties I was tidying his desk and sorting the notes needed by him in order to compose some reports, which he usually dictates to me.

"In answering your letter I am guilty of a breach of confidence that would cost me dearly if you did not (which I sincerely ask you to do) preserve the utmost discretion toward Professor Kernlich, my fellow workers, and the nuns who work here as nursing sisters and supervisors. I am therefore taking that discretion for granted. I am reluctant to commit this indiscretion, to break the professional secrecy that has become second nature to me after working for over twelve years at the dermatological clinic. It is not only your grief-stricken letter, not only the remembrance of your deep and intense sorrow as I observed it at the funeral of Mrs. Schlömer; no, in writing to you I am carrying out a kind of mission or trust placed upon me by the deceased, who suffered a great deal from the ban on visitors placed upon her during the last two weeks of her life and which—it must be stressed—was entirely justified by her condition.

"No doubt you will remember me; on two or perhaps three occasions I had the opportunity of conducting you to the deceased, at a time when visitors were still permitted. Since for more than a year I have been occupied almost exclusively in Professor Kernlich's study, helping him assemble material for written opinions, reports, etc., it is possible that you do not recall me as a male nurse, but possibly you do recall the elderly, stoutish, bald-headed gentleman, weeping immoderately and wearing a dark-brown Burberry, who stood to one side at Mrs. Schlömer's funeral and whom you probably assumed to be one of her lovers whom you did not know. That is not so, and if I add a not quite convincing, heartfelt 'unfortunately,' please do not infer from this any insult to the deceased who was so dear to you, or any intended familiarity. Indeed, it has not been vouchsafed to me to find a permanent life-companion, although on several occasions I have embarked on associations with, to me, honorable intentions, associations which—I wish to be sincere with you—failed to find fruition not only on account of the despicable behavior of the chosen ones but also on account of my occupation (necessitating as it does my being in constant contact with venereal-disease patients) and also of the many night shifts for which I volunteered.

"Professor Kernlich will not be answering your letter because you are not a relative of the deceased and, even if you were, he would not be obliged to supply you with the 'more detailed information' you desire on Mrs. Schlömer's death. That is proscribed by a doctor's duty to remain silent, it is also proscribed by a nurse's duty to remain silent which I do not wish to violate. There is, I admit, a certain if not total indiscretion in my reporting to you on the last week of your deceased friend's life, and this is why I enjoin you to make no use of my letter. Naturally the statement on the death certificate as to cause of death is accurate: heart failure, complete circulatory debilitation, but how this point was finally reached, Mrs. Schlömer having been on the road to recovery as far as her acute illness was concerned, is what I would like to tell you.

"To begin with: the severe infection that brought your friend to our ward was contracted by her, as you now know, from a foreign statesman. No doubt you know better than I that during the last two years she had abandoned the frivolous mode of life which she doubtless conducted for many years, and that, after inheriting from her parents, she moved to the country in order to end her days in dignified tranquillity and remorse. By nature she was not, as no doubt you know better than I, in any way a prostitute, or even promiscuous, rather was she a woman forever enmeshed in certain masculine desires. She found it so hard to say 'No' when she felt it was within her power to give pleasure. I feel justified in putting it this way since during the night before her death Mrs. Schlömer recounted almost her entire life to me, revealing all the details of her 'fall,' and if—after working for twelve years in a university dermatological clinic and especially after the events still to be recounted—if, I say, I am far from inclining to idealize, let alone romanticize, the profession of prostitute, I do know that most of these women die in misery, ill, dirty, the wildest blasphemies on their lips, most of them so riddled with disease that not one of today's lighthearted sex-magazines would portray them on their covers. It is the most miserable death imaginable: abandoned, riddled with disease, joyless, destitute—and this is why I have gone along to most of the funerals, since usually only a social worker and a routinely functioning priest accompany these women on their final journey.

"How then, without further ado, am I to approach the highly delicate subject that loses none of its embarrassing aspects even when I visualize you as a modern, broad-minded woman who has been married and is not entirely unfamiliar with certain details still to be mentioned? Well, I too was once a medical practitioner, although I never qualified as a doctor; for reasons associated with the war—although those were not the only ones, there was also my dread of examinations, particularly of pre-med—I got no farther than the rank of medical orderly, and I subsequently accumulated so much knowledge and experience in German and Russian field hospitals that, when I was discharged in 1950 from a Russian POW camp at the age of thirty-five, I was irresponsible enough to pretend to be a doctor, and as such I carried on a successful practice, but then, found guilty of fraud, etc., in 1955, I spent some years in prison until, at the intervention of Professor Kernlich, with whom I had worked in my student days in 1937, I was prereleased, whereupon Professor Kernlich took me in and gave me employment; this was in 1958. So I am somewhat acquainted with the life of a person with a stain on his character. Incidentally, during my five years of 'medical' practice, no error was ever laid at my door. Now you know with whom you are dealing—*that* at least is off my chest.

"Now how do I go about getting the rest of it off my chest? I will try and take the bull by the horns! Your friend Margret was so far advanced in her recovery that there was no reason her discharge could not have been contemplated within six or eight weeks. All visits agitated her greatly, including the visits of that unexplained but pleasant gentleman who visited her frequently toward the end" (!!! Au.) "whom we first assumed to be an erstwhile lover, then a procurer, later a foreign-office official, i.e., the one who had effected that disastrous contact between her and the foreign statesman whom, in her own words, she was to, and did, get into a 'treaty mood' after other ladies had failed to do so.

"Well, shortly before she was to be discharged, something very strange, paradoxical one might say, took place. Accustomed as I am, after studying medicine and years of 'medical' practice, by an association over nearly thirty-five years with the cynical jargon of VD treatment centers, I find it difficult to commit to paper, in writing to a lady such as yourself, something that would be even more difficult to do verbally. Well, my dear Mrs. Pfeiffer, I refer to the muscle that in physical, biochemical, and psychic terms, reacts and functions in such a complex manner and is commonly known as the male sex organ. You will not be surprised to learn (oh how relieved I am that the word is out!) that the women who usually fill our wards do not give this attribute names that one might call exactly delicate. Today as in the past, a variety of masculine first names have been very popular. While out-and-out coarse epithets sound bad enough, at least they correspond to the milieu and retain an almost matter-of-fact, a well-nigh clinical, character that renders them less offensive than the 'genteel' ones.

"Now during the very weeks in which your friend was beginning to recover, the use of masculine first names as nicknames for the aforesaid attribute became fashionable in our ward in a manner that I can only call childishly silly. You must realize, my dear Mrs. Pfeiffer, that in these wards silly fads do occur, the kind one might expect to find only in girls' boarding schools, and what is more: they carry over onto the nursing and supervisory staff as well. As I had an opportunity to observe during my three years in prison, these 'dialectic carry-overs' also occur between prison inmates and their guards. Nuns, and nursing nuns, inclined as they are toward silliness, especially enjoy participating in such foolishness in dermatological wards; this is not to be condemned, it is rather a form of self-defense. Now the sisters had always been extremely kind to your friend, when it was a matter of visitors and gifts, alcohol, and cigarettes, they very often turned a blind eye, but since some of them have been associating for thirty or forty years with venereal-disease patients they have in many cases—in self-defense!—adopted their jargon as their own, in fact they not infrequently contribute to its enlargement.

"I now have something very strange to tell you that will either surprise you or, more likely, confirm your own impression. Mrs. Schlömer was an extremely modest woman. At first they used to tease her by speaking in the above context of 'Gustav Adolf' or 'Egon,' 'Friedrich,' etc., and were highly amused that Mrs. Schlömer did not know what they were talking about. It was all great fun, and the sisters would carry on like that for days and nights on end. At first the cruel game was restricted to out-and-out Protestant names: 'Gustav Adolf's been paying you too many visits,' or 'The trouble, is, you've loved Egon too much,' etc., etc. Then, when the allusions designed to 'rid her of that damned innocence' (Patient K.G., a professional procuress of over sixty) became so obvious that Mrs. Schlömer understood what they meant, she began to blush violently every time a masculine name was mentioned. Her frequent and violent blushing was in turn interpreted as prudishness and hypocrisy, whereupon the cruel game was stepped up until it became the most arrant sadism. Until they reached the point where, in order to make the cruelty complete, they started adding feminine names in the appropriate context. They were especially fond of combining very Protestant names with very Catholic ones, which were then called 'mixed marriages,' such as Alois and Luise, etc. Finally Mrs. Schlömer was, in laymen's terms, in a perpetual state of blushing, she even blushed when the name of a visitor or a nun or nurse was called out in the corridor in some harmless context. Once on this cruel path, and inwardly indignant over a sensitivity with which they were reluctant to credit Mrs. Schlömer, they eventually intensified these torments to the point of blasphemy, and from then on referred only to Saint Alois, who was at one time, of course, the patron saint of the chaste, to Saint Agatha, etc., and the stage was soon reached when psychological sensitivity was no longer required for Mrs. Schlömer not only to blush but actually to cry out in spiritual anguish whenever 'Heinrich' or 'Saint Heinrich' was mentioned.

"Now blushing, as you probably know, also has its medical context. What we call blushing is usually caused by a suddenly increased circulation of the blood through the vessels and capillaries of the facial skin through the action of the sympathetic nervous system caused by pleasant agitation or embarrassment (as was the case with Mrs. Schlömer). Other causes of blushing —e.g., overexertion, etc.—need not be mentioned here. Now in Mrs. Schlömer's case capillary permeability had anyway been increased. Hematomata (popularly known as 'bruises' or blue marks) soon began to form, as well as purpura, which might be known *vulgo* as red or purple marks. This, my dear Mrs. Pfeiffer, is what your friend died of. Ultimately—more than justifying the autopsy which then took place—her entire body was covered with hematomata and purpura, her sympathetic nervous system had been overtaxed, her circulation became blocked, her heart gave out; and since Mrs. Schlömer's blushing had turned into a massive neurosis, on the evening of the night during which she died she even blushed when the sisters in the chapel were singing the All Saints' Litany. I know I would never be able to produce scientific proof of my theory, or my claim, yet I feel constrained to tell you: your friend Margret Schlömer died of blushing.

"After she became too weak to talk coherently she would just keep whispering: 'Heinrich, Heinrich, Leni, Rahel, Leni, Heinrich,' and although it might have seemed appropriate to administer the last sacraments to her I decided in the end to refrain from doing so; it would have caused her too much anguish since toward the end they had even started, in their mounting blasphemy, to include in the above context the 'dear Savior,' the 'sweet Child Jesus,' and the Madonna, Holy Mary, the Most Blessed Virgin, in all Her epithets, even going so far as to take them from the Litany of Loretto, such as Rosa Mystica, etc. A liturgical text recited at her deathbed would, I am convinced, have tormented Mrs. Schlömer more than it would have consoled her.

"I consider it my duty to add that Mrs. Schlömer, apart from the names Heinrich, Leni, Rahel, also spoke warmly, almost affectionately, of 'that man who comes here sometimes.' She was probably alluding to the visitor who was not so much mysterious as obscure.

"In signing this letter 'Yours respectfully' I would ask you not to interpret this as an evasion into a conventional salutation. Since I do not feel I can say 'Yours sincerely' lest it imply a certain familiarity, allow me to conclude:

"With kind regards,

"Yours respectfully,
"Bernhard Ehlwein."

13 After giving the matter much thought K., who was now taking an active hand in the investigations, decided it would be better after all to convert the police officer's report into indirect speech rather than quote it verbatim. This results, of course, in a considerable shift in style, and many a nice little detail goes out the window (like the lady in hair curlers, for example, who appeared in the company of a gentleman in his undershirt whose hairy chest was described as "furry"; also a "pitifully whimpering dog," an installment-bill collector—all these fall victim to an iconoclasm of which the Au. by no means approves, victims of his lack of resistance). Whether the Au. is displaying d.u.a. or d.l.r. (deliberate lack of resistance) must remain an open question. K. deleted everything that seemed to her superfluous, using without a qualm the blue pencil that has become so familiar to her, and what is left is the "gist of it" (K.).

(1) Police Officer Dieter Wülffen, while seated in his parked patrol car outside the South Cemetery, was addressed a few days ago by a Mrs. Käthe Zwiefäller and asked to break open the apartment of Mrs. Ilse Kremer at 5 Nurgheimer Strasse. On being asked why she considered this necessary Mrs. Z. stated that, after a prolonged search (to be precise: after twenty-five years!—during which, she must admit, she had not been *solely* occupied with this search), she had discovered Mrs. Kremer's address and had taken time off to visit her and acquaint her with some important information.

Mrs. Z. was accompanied by her son, Heinrich Zwiefäller, aged twenty-five, a farmer like his mother (when applied to

Mrs. Z. this term should actually be farmer*ess*. Au.). They had come, she said, to inform Mrs. K. that her son Erich, who had died in 1944, had made an attempt to go over to the Americans in a village between Kommerscheidt and Simmerath. In the process he had been shot at by Americans and Germans, had sought and found shelter in the Zwiefäller farmhouse, spent several days there, and an intimate love affair had developed between her, Käthe Z., and Erich K., he aged seventeen, she aged nineteen; they had become "engaged," "sworn eternal devotion," and decided not to abandon the house, even when the fighting became fierce, in fact extremely dangerous; the house had been situated "between the lines." As the Americans advanced, Erich K. had tried to fasten a kitchen towel which, although it had red stripes, was mostly white, to the top of the door frame as a sign of capitulation, and while doing so had been killed by a sniper of the German Army with "a bullet through the heart." She, Mrs. Z., had actually seen the sniper seated on a raised hunting stand "between the lines," his rifle aimed not at the Americans but at the village, where admittedly after this occurence no one ("There were still about five people living in the village") had dared to run up a white flag. Mrs. Z. stated that she had pulled the dead K. into the house and laid him out in the barn, had wept many tears over him, then later, when the Americans captured the village, had laid him in "consecrated ground" with her own hands. She soon realized she was pregnant, and "in the fullness of time," on September 20, 1945, gave birth to a son and had him baptized with the name of Heinrich; her parents—at the end of 1944 she had been living alone in the house—had never returned from the evacuation, she had never heard of them again, they were regarded as having simply disappeared, probably killed in an air raid "somewhere along the way."

As an unwed mother, alone on the little farm, which she put back on its feet again, things had not been easy for her, yet "time heals all wounds," she had brought up her son, he had done well in school and become a farmer. When all was said and done, he had something many boys did not have, his father's grave close by. She, Mrs. Z., had tried "as early as" (!!) 1948 to find Mrs. K., and then "soon after that" (!!), in 1952, had tried again, but she had finally given it up as a bad job, even her next attempt, in 1960 (!!), had come to nothing. True, she said, at the time she had not known Erich K. to be illegitimate too, nor had she known his mother's first name and occupation. At last, some six months ago, with the assistance of a fertilizer salesman who had been kind enough to intervene in the matter, she had discovered Mrs. K.'s address, but still she had hesitated, not knowing how "she would take it." Finally the boy had insisted, they had come into town, located Mrs. K.'s apartment, but, after long and repeated knocking, the door had not been opened. Inquiries of the neighbors (this is where the lady in the curlers plays a considerable role, also the whimpering dog, etc.—all this now a victim of that cavalier iconoclasm, reminiscent of the liturgy reform!!) had yielded the information that Mrs. K. could not possibly have gone away, that she never had gone away. In short: she, Mrs. Z., "feared the worst."

(2) Wülffen was in a dilemma. Was this a case of "imminent danger," the sole legal justification for having Mrs. K.'s apartment broken open? Having meanwhile reached 5 Nurgheimer Strasse accompanied by Mrs. Z. and her son, he was able to ascertain that Mrs. K. had not been seen for a week. A neighbor (not the hairy-chested one, but a pensioner of Rhenish descent, known to be a drunkard, who referred to Mrs. K. as "that Ils"—— all deleted!) thought he had "heard her bird cheeping pathetically" for three days. Wülffen decided, not because he considered the term "imminent danger" to apply but merely out of compassion, to have the apartment opened up. Fortunately there was, likewise among the neighbors, a youthful person (with such colorless words is an interesting personality dismissed, one who had been convicted four or five times of assault, procuring, breaking and entering, and is known to all the neighbors as "Kröcke's Heini," a person whom even Police Officer Dieter Wülffen describes as having "a thick mane of greasy, long brown hair and known to the police"), who with suspicious dexterity

and the telltale words "This time I'm doing it *for* the police," broke open the apartment.

(3) Mrs. K. was found dead, from an overdose of sleeping pills, lying fully dressed on the bench in her kitchen. Decomposition had not yet set in. She had merely (!!)—apparently with her finger and using the remains of some tomato ketchup—written the verb "to have" in a number of variations on an old mirror that hung over her kitchen sink. "I have had enough. I had enough. For a long time I had had en . . ." At this point she had evidently used up all the ketchup. The dead bird, a budgerigar, was found in the adjoining bedroom under a chest of drawers.

(4) Dieter Wülffen admitted that Mrs. K. had been known to the police. According to the records of K. 14, the political branch of the police, she had been a Communist but since 1932 no longer politically active, although—this was also known to the police—especially after the German Communist Party was banned, she had received numerous visits from a person who had enjoined her to resume her activity. (Here K. had written out "Fritz's" name in full, and this time it was the Au.'s blue pencil that claimed a victim.)

(5) Mrs. Z. and her son lodged inheritance claims. Dieter W. took into safekeeping a purse containing DM.15.80, also a savings book showing a balance of DM.67.50. The sole article of value that was taken into safekeeping was a nearly new black-and-white television set on which Mrs. K. had stuck a slip of paper saying "Final installment paid." From a photo that hung, framed, above the bench Mrs. Z. recognized the father of her child, Erich K. A second photo showed "*his* father probably. Because of the amazing likeness." In a flower-painted canister bearing the name of a well-known brand of coffee was found: "A man's wrist watch, of almost no value but intact. A worn gold ring set with an artificial ruby, likewise of almost no value. A 10-mark bill from the year 1944. A Red Front party badge, the value of which cannot be ascertained by the undersigned. A pawn ticket dated 1936 with which a gold ring had been pawned for 2.50 Reichsmarks, another pawn ticket dated 1937 for which a

beaver collar had been pawned for 2.00 Reichsmarks. A duly receipted rent-receipt book." No food supplies of any value were found; half a bottle of vinegar, a can of oil, almost full (small size), some dried-out graham bread (five slices), an opened can of milk, some cocoa in a can—two or three ounces. A jar, only half full, of instant coffee, some salt, sugar, rice, a modest quantity of potatoes, as well as a package of birdseed, unopened. In addition, two small packages of cigarette paper and an opened package of fine-cut, "Turkish Gem" brand. Six novels by someone called Emile Zola, pocket edition, much read, not soiled. Probably of little value. A book entitled: "Songs of the Workers' Movement." The entire contents were dubbed by the neighbors who, impelled by curiosity, came crowding in and were promptly told to keep their distance, "nothing but a lot of junk." Having waited for the arrival of the police doctor, Dieter W. sealed up the apartment as required by regulations. Mrs. Z. was directed to the Department of Justice in the matter of her inheritance claims.

(6) An offer was made to Mrs. Z. to put her in touch with Mr. ("Fritz") who, it was thought, might be able to provide her with some interesting details concerning the life of the deceased woman and the father of the deceased Erich K. She declined. She wanted nothing to do with Communists, she said.

14

When not actually at work with her blue pencil, K. is almost indispensable. Her undeniable sensibility in regard to German language and literature, which fails her only when she has compositional or editorial ambitions, her fairly lengthy familiarity with spiritual practices, when applied secularly are on no account to be considered wasted; precisely because she is in a sense emancipated, she plunges with zest (from which the Au. greatly benefits) into cooking and kitchen activities, is positively addicted to dishwashing, takes frowning note of rising meat prices and rents, yet likes taking taxis, blushes now and again at displays of porno-violence; as to the editorial side, she has made herself independent, as it were, meaning that her blue pencil no longer goes to work on other people's texts, merely her own. As she puts it, Ilse Kremer's death "upset her terribly," many tears were (still are) shed over it, and she wants to write a brief biography of this woman whose "entire estate after years as a working woman consists of a recently paid-up television set, half a bottle of vinegar, and a few cigarette papers—plus a rent-receipt book. I can't get over it, I simply can't get over it." Surely those are praiseworthy insights and intentions.

In other respects K. performed invaluable services, if not exactly as an informer, certainly as an observer. Whereas the Au. has still not achieved the ardently desired state of total d.u.a., she is approaching the goal of doing only those things she enjoys. She enjoys going to see Schirtenstein and Scholsdorff and noting that they seem relaxed; the causes of this relaxation are revealed to her later: Schirtenstein "cheek to cheek and hand in hand with

Leni on a bench in Blücher Park," and as for Scholsdorff: on two occasions she was an eyewitness to a laying-on-of-hands at the Café Spertz; on one occasion she met someone in Leni's apartment who, judging by her description, can only have been Kurt Hoyser. Since she is fairly sure that Leni, in her present condition, is refusing intimate relations even to Mehmet, she finds that Leni, having "kissed Pelzer in the dark while sitting in a car not far from her own apartment," has gone far enough. She is reluctant to visit Pelzer because she feels he is "a person basically devoid of tenderness, quite capable of demanding concrete substitute-eroticism from me."

As for Lev Gruyten, she has no worries at all about him. "He'll soon be coming out anyway." Active as she is, she even took part in a demonstration of garbage collectors outside the courthouse, designed placard texts such as "IS SOLIDARITY A CRIME?", "IS LOYALTY AN OFFENSE?" and, more menacingly, "IF OUR BUDDIES ARE PUNISHED THE CITY WILL CHOKE IN GARBAGE." This earned her her first headline in a local rag: "REDHEAD EX-NUN MOUNTS BARRICADES FOR GARBAGEMEN!" In other ways, too, she is usefully employed: she gives German lessons in Leni's apartment to the Portuguese children, discusses the present state of the Soviet Union with Bogakov, allows Grete Helzen to "pamper her face," assists a variety of Turks and Italians to fill out forms for tax-refund applications. She telephones district attorneys (in connection with the trial, still going on, of the garbage-truck drivers), describes (likewise over the telephone) to the appropriate department the chaos that would result if the garbage collectors were to go on strike. Etc. Etc. The fact that from time to time she sheds a tear over *The Marquise of O—* and several over *The Country Doctor* and *The Penal Colony* surely goes without saying, yet even she, in spite of all her tears, has still not grasped the potential meaning of the words "with earthly vehicle, unearthly horses." She has radically, perhaps all too radically, turned her back on all unearthly things. It was not she who insisted on going to Gerselen, it was Leni who insisted on taking her when she discovered that a spa was actually to be opened there. Must we mention who has been earmarked for the posts of "Spa Director" and "Publicity Manager"? No other than Scheukens, who is busily running around with blueprints, carrying on imperious telephone conversations with tradesmen and architects, and has found a sure-fire method of suppressing that "goddamn plague of roses, by force if we have to." At a distance of fifty yards around the "priceless spring" he has installed a kind of poison-drainage that carries a virulent herbicide, and this has actually stopped the roses. Needless to say, this is too much for the handful of dust that was once called Rahel Ginzburg. In any event, Bogakov has, to his delight, already felt the benefits of this "salubrious" spring for his "damned arthritis." Ever since his success in persuading Lotte to adopt d.u.a., the two of them take frequent walks in the spa park.

K., the only one among all the persons mentioned here (including Mehmet) to be endowed with a faculty shared by former and nonformer nuns alike, stubbornness and tenacity, K.—by spend-hours silently watching Leni paint and helping the artist by making coffee and washing out her brushes, unstinting with her flattery—has, of course, won the privilege of seeing the Madonna appear on television. Her comment is almost too prosaic to warrant printer's ink: "It is herself, Leni herself, appearing to herself because of some still unexplained reflections." Well, there remain the "still unexplained reflections," there also remain some dark thunderclouds of foreboding in the background: Mehmet's jealousy, and his recently announced aversion to ballroom dancing.

Translator's Acknowledgment

William Vennewitz, my husband, has given me the utmost in patient and knowledgeable help in this translation, and I am deeply grateful to him.

I wish also to express my gratitude to Professor Frank Jones, of the University of Washington, for his assistance with the quotations from Brecht and Hölderlin. Fragments from these poets appearing, among other quotations, on pages 42–43 are his translations; those on page 261 have been translated jointly by Professor Jones and myself.

Leila Vennewitz

ABOUT THE AUTHOR

Heinrich Böll, winner of the Nobel Prize for Literature in 1972, is one of the most prolific, and most popular, of postwar German writers. Since 1947 he has been widely acclaimed for his novels and short stories, which have focused principally on the Second World War, its aftermath, and the havoc it wreaked on the people of Germany; his fiction constitutes a "working-through," not merely a remembering, of this horrendous Nazi experience. A master storyteller, Mr. Böll is in the first rank of contemporary European writers. Included among his books previously published in this country are: *Billiards at Half-past Nine* (1962); *The Clown* (1965); *Absent Without Leave* (1965); *18 Stories* (1966); *Irish Journal* (1967); *End of a Mission* (1968); *Children Are Civilians Too* (1970); and *Adam and The Train* (1970).

Heinrich Böll is also President of the International P.E.N. and in that capacity is active on behalf of writers throughout the world. He and his wife live in Cologne but spend much of their time at their farmhouse in a tiny hamlet in the foothills of the Eifel range.